STONEBREAKER

Publisher Tom Kaczynski
Associate Publisher Jordan Shiveley

ODOD BOOKS is an imprint of Uncivilized Books
P.O. Box 6534
Minneapolis, MN 55406
USA
uncivilizedbooks.com/odod

ISBN: 978-1-941250-35-8

DISTRIBUTED TO THE TRADE BY:
Consortium Book Sales & Distribution, LLC.
34 Thirteenth Avenue NE, Suite 101
Minneapolis, MN 55413-1007
cbsd.com
Orders: (800) 283-3572

First Edition, April 2019

10 9 8 7 6 5 4 3 2 1

Printed in USA

PETER WARTMAN

STONEBREAKER

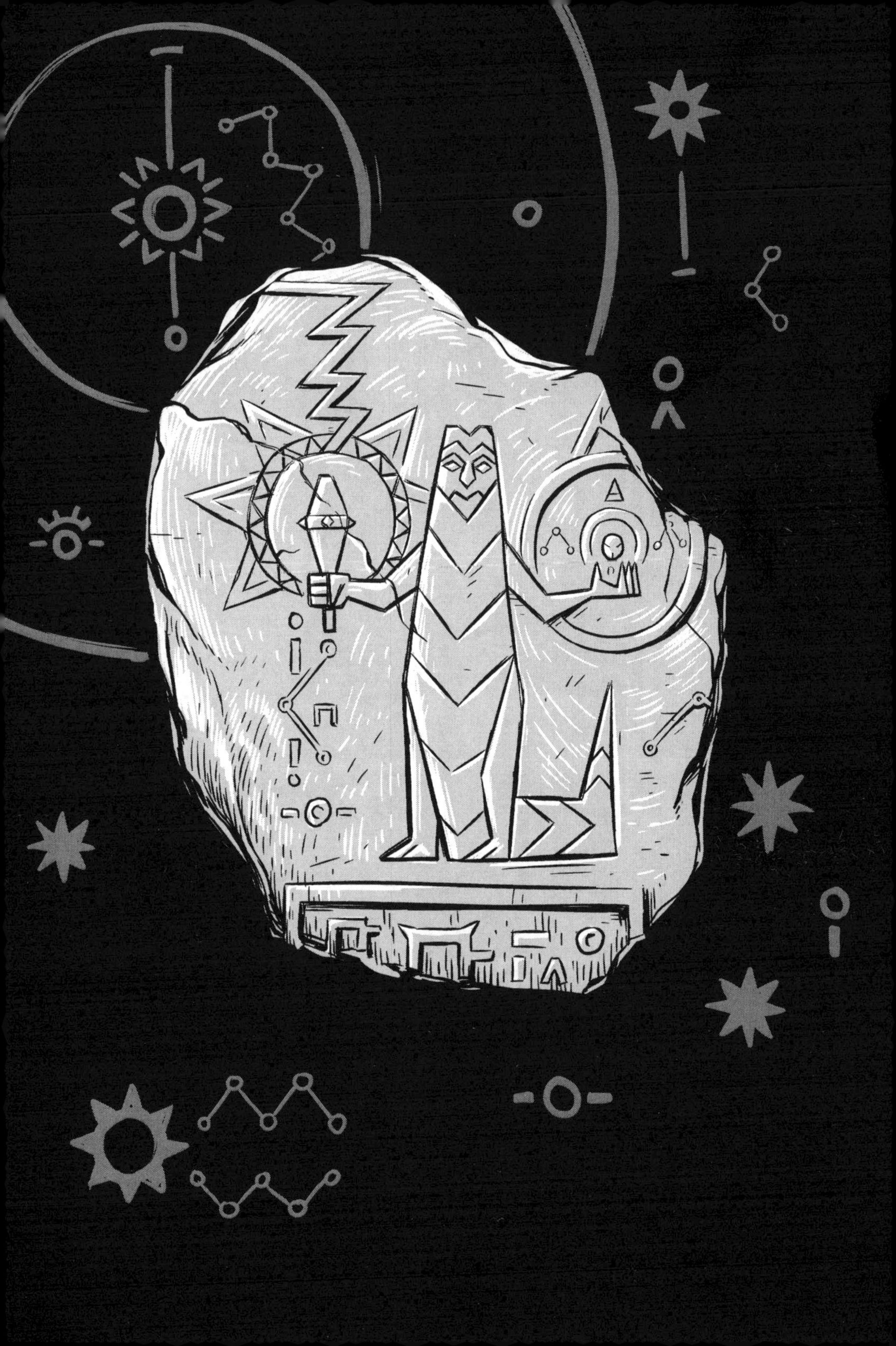

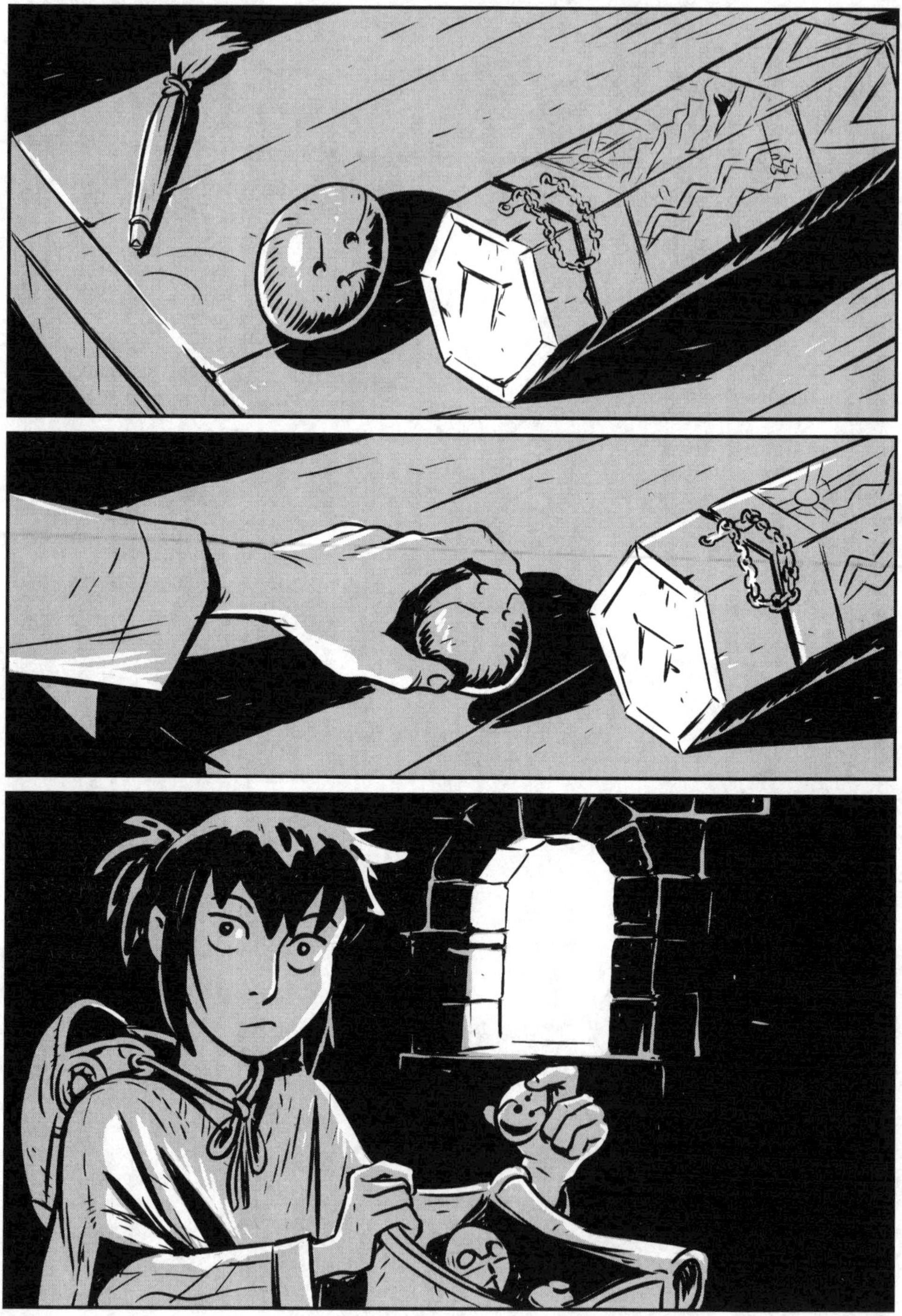

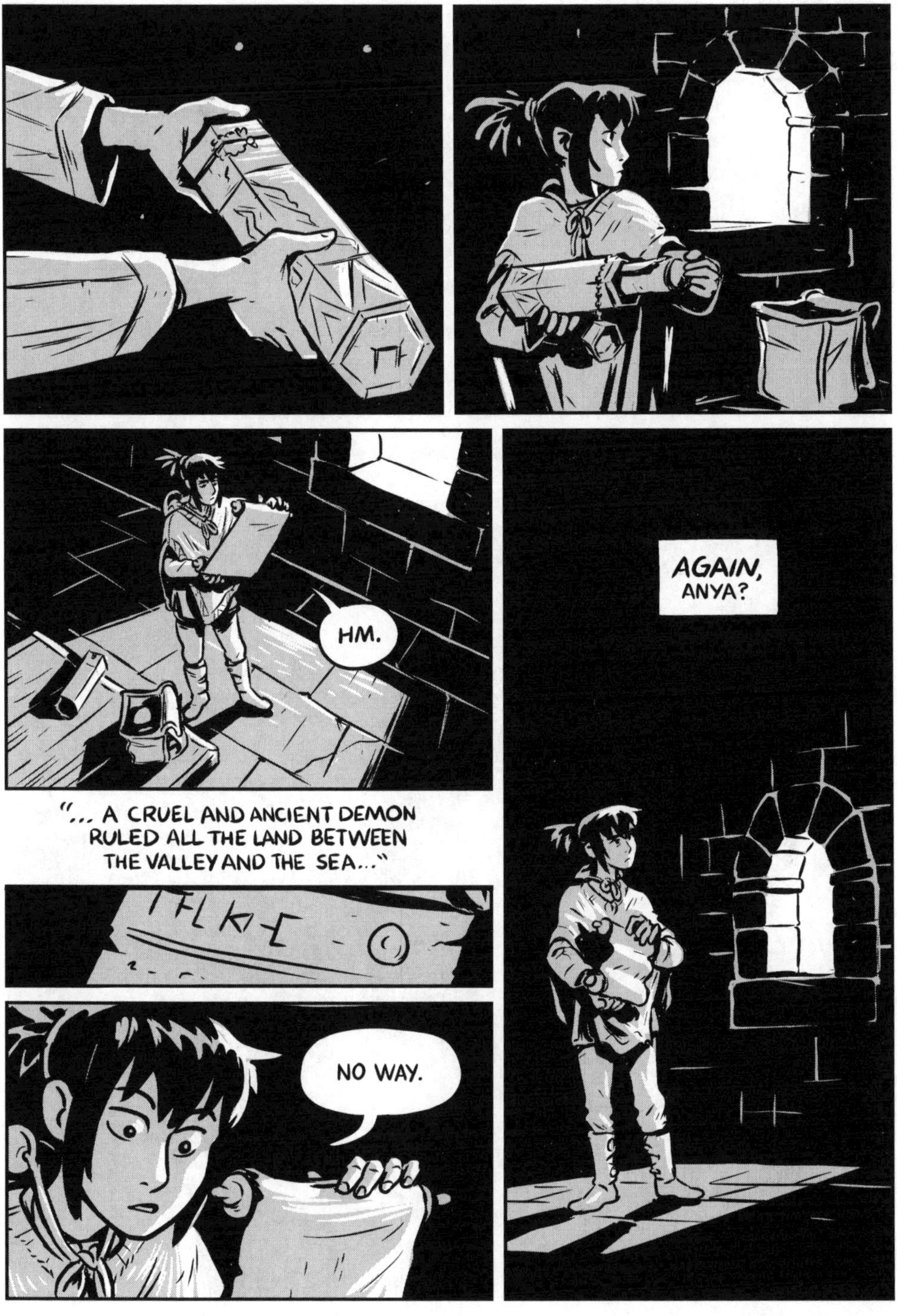
HM.
AGAIN, ANYA?
"... A CRUEL AND ANCIENT DEMON RULED ALL THE LAND BETWEEN THE VALLEY AND THE SEA..."
NO WAY.

DIDN'T I **JUST** TELL THAT ONE?

TELL IT AGAIN!

I HAVE **OTHER** STORIES YOU KNOW.

BUT I WANT **STONE-BAKER!**

FINE, FINE.

I KNOW BETTER THEN TO ARGUE WITH YOU.

YAY!

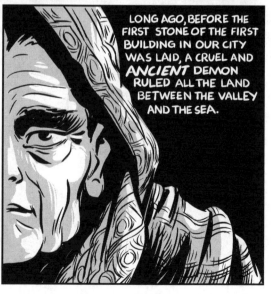

LONG AGO, BEFORE THE FIRST STONE OF THE FIRST BUILDING IN OUR CITY WAS LAID, A CRUEL AND **ANCIENT** DEMON RULED ALL THE LAND BETWEEN THE VALLEY AND THE SEA.

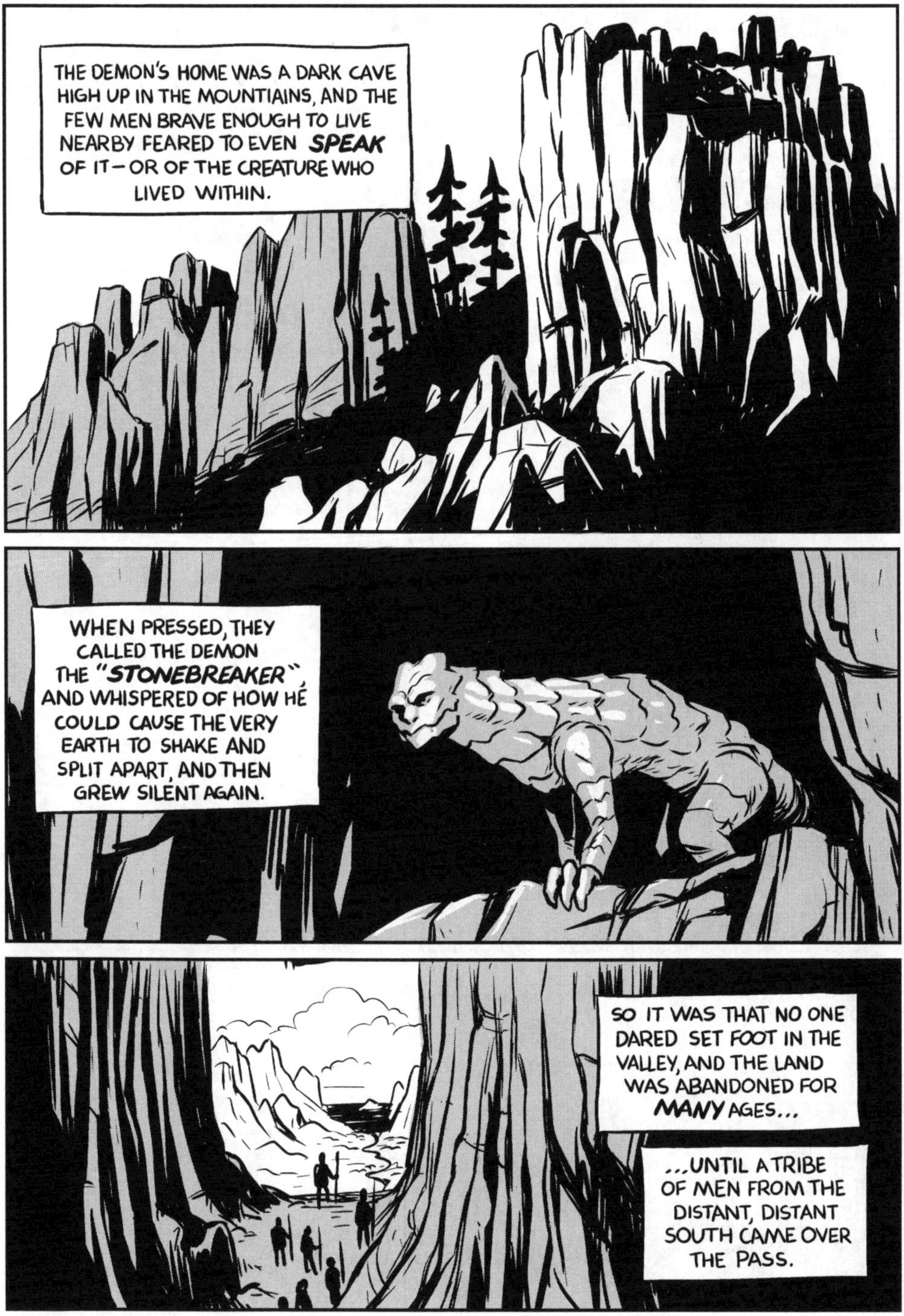
THE DEMON'S HOME WAS A DARK CAVE HIGH UP IN THE MOUNTIAINS, AND THE FEW MEN BRAVE ENOUGH TO LIVE NEARBY FEARED TO EVEN SPEAK OF IT—OR OF THE CREATURE WHO LIVED WITHIN.
WHEN PRESSED, THEY CALLED THE DEMON THE "STONEBREAKER", AND WHISPERED OF HOW HE COULD CAUSE THE VERY EARTH TO SHAKE AND SPLIT APART, AND THEN GREW SILENT AGAIN.
SO IT WAS THAT NO ONE DARED SET FOOT IN THE VALLEY, AND THE LAND WAS ABANDONED FOR MANY AGES...
...UNTIL A TRIBE OF MEN FROM THE DISTANT, DISTANT SOUTH CAME OVER THE PASS.

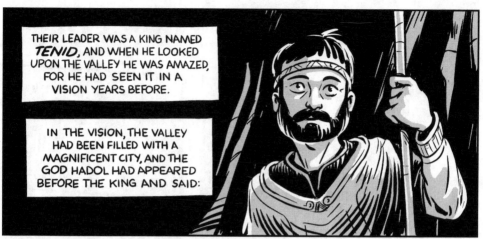

THEIR LEADER WAS A KING NAMED *TENID*, AND WHEN HE LOOKED UPON THE VALLEY HE WAS AMAZED, FOR HE HAD SEEN IT IN A VISION YEARS BEFORE.

IN THE VISION, THE VALLEY HAD BEEN FILLED WITH A MAGNIFICENT CITY, AND THE GOD HADOL HAD APPEARED BEFORE THE KING AND SAID:

"IN THIS PLACE, YOU WILL FOUND A CITY, ONE THAT WILL BECOME THE GREATEST THE WORLD HAS EVER SEEN—*IF* YOU PROVE YOURSELF *WORTHY*, AND TAKE YOUR PEOPLE NORTH."

AND SO TENID HAD TAKEN HIS PEOPLE ACROSS PLAINS AND MOUNTAINS AND SWAMPS, THROUGH LANDS FRIENDLY AND HOSTILE, GUIDED ALWAYS BY SIGNS LEFT BY THE GODS.

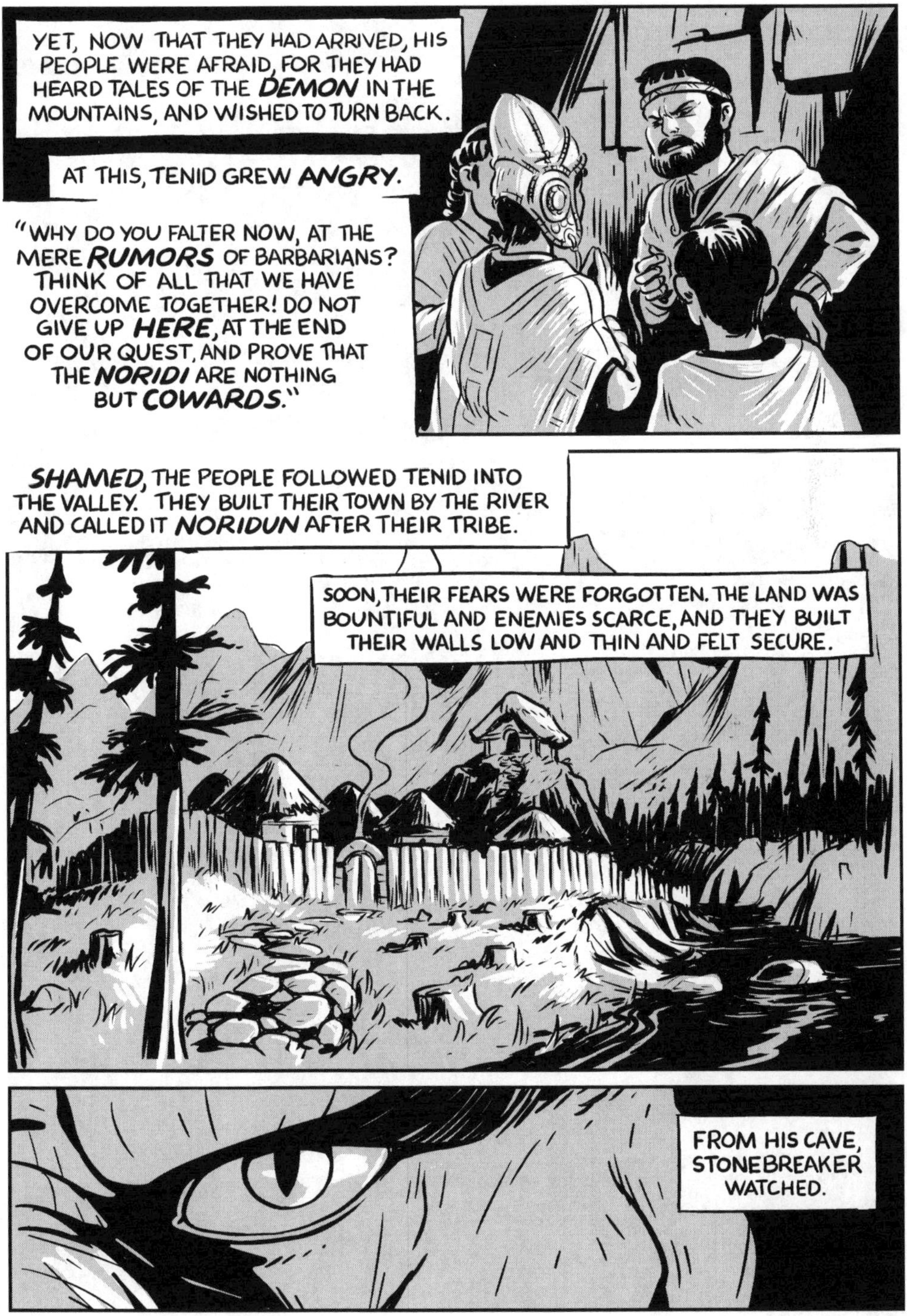
YET, NOW THAT THEY HAD ARRIVED, HIS PEOPLE WERE AFRAID, FOR THEY HAD HEARD TALES OF THE DEMON IN THE MOUNTAINS, AND WISHED TO TURN BACK.
AT THIS, TENID GREW ANGRY.
"WHY DO YOU FALTER NOW, AT THE MERE RUMORS OF BARBARIANS? THINK OF ALL THAT WE HAVE OVERCOME TOGETHER! DO NOT GIVE UP HERE, AT THE END OF OUR QUEST, AND PROVE THAT THE NORIDI ARE NOTHING BUT COWARDS."
SHAMED, THE PEOPLE FOLLOWED TENID INTO THE VALLEY. THEY BUILT THEIR TOWN BY THE RIVER AND CALLED IT NORIDUN AFTER THEIR TRIBE.
SOON, THEIR FEARS WERE FORGOTTEN. THE LAND WAS BOUNTIFUL AND ENEMIES SCARCE, AND THEY BUILT THEIR WALLS LOW AND THIN AND FELT SECURE.
FROM HIS CAVE, STONEBREAKER WATCHED.

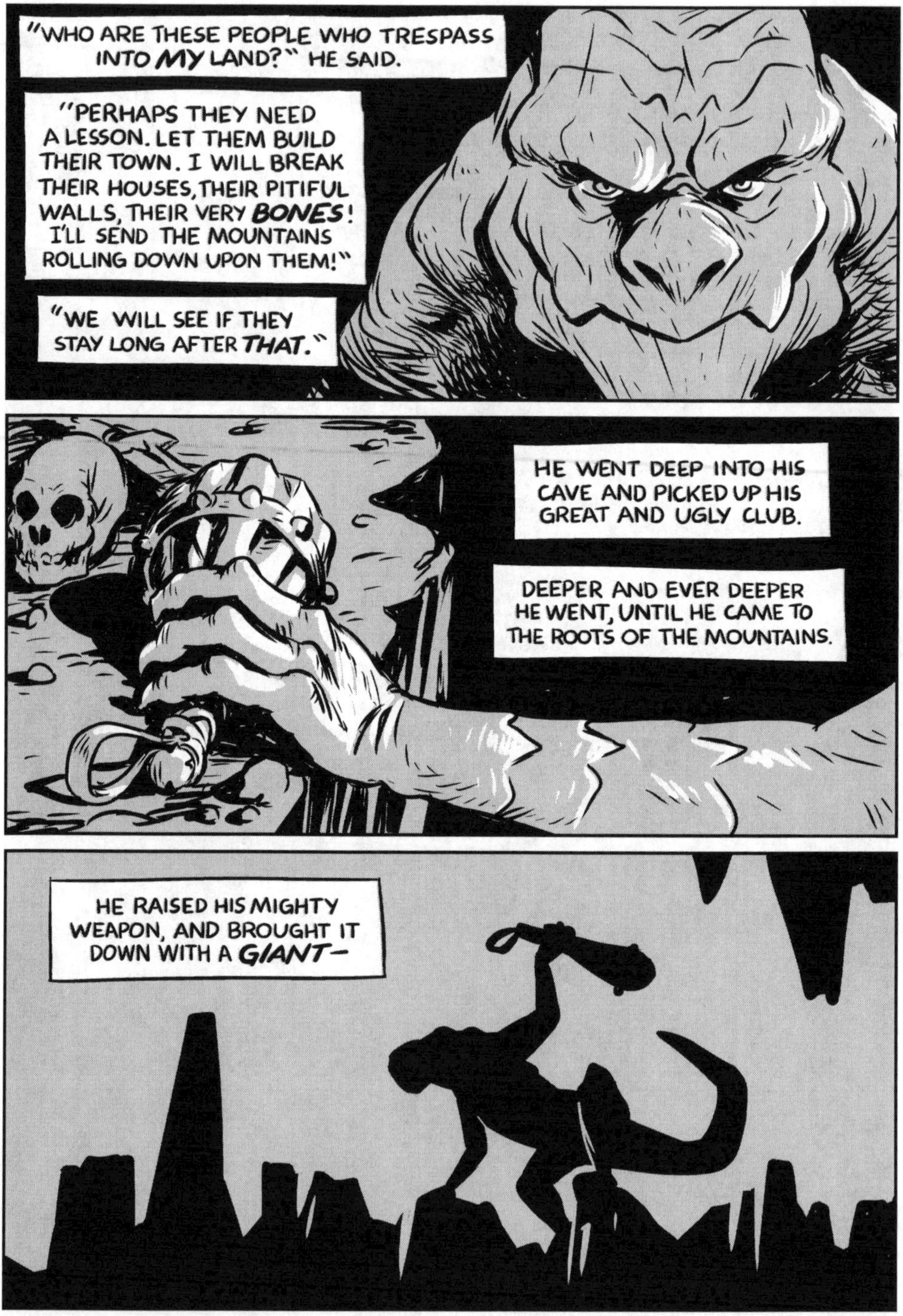
"WHO ARE THESE PEOPLE WHO TRESPASS INTO MY LAND?" HE SAID.
"PERHAPS THEY NEED A LESSON. LET THEM BUILD THEIR TOWN. I WILL BREAK THEIR HOUSES, THEIR PITIFUL WALLS, THEIR VERY BONES! I'LL SEND THE MOUNTAINS ROLLING DOWN UPON THEM!"
"WE WILL SEE IF THEY STAY LONG AFTER THAT."
HE WENT DEEP INTO HIS CAVE AND PICKED UP HIS GREAT AND UGLY CLUB.
DEEPER AND EVER DEEPER HE WENT, UNTIL HE CAME TO THE ROOTS OF THE MOUNTAINS.
HE RAISED HIS MIGHTY WEAPON, AND BROUGHT IT DOWN WITH A GIANT—

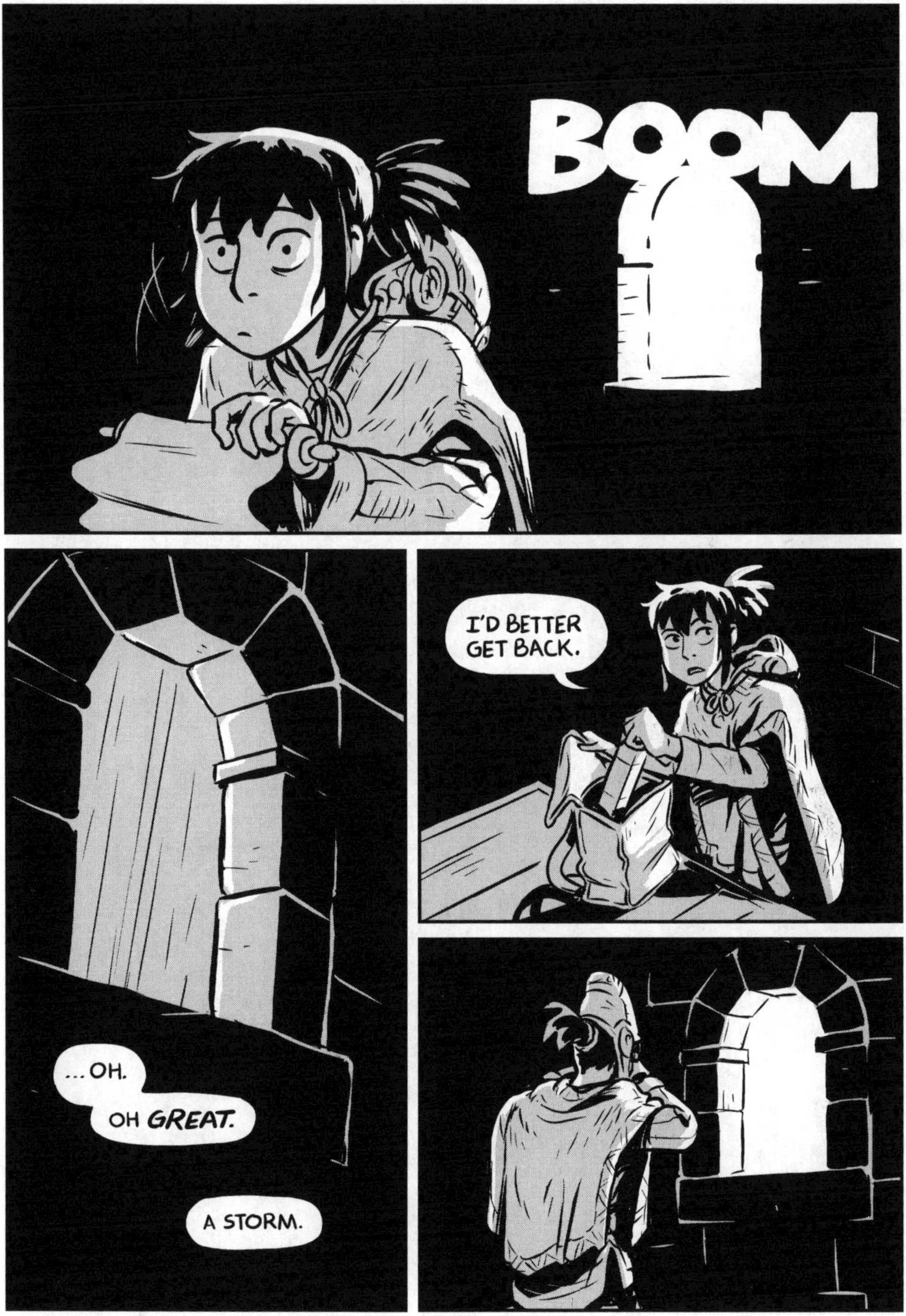
BOOM
I'D BETTER GET BACK.
...OH.
OH GREAT.
A STORM.

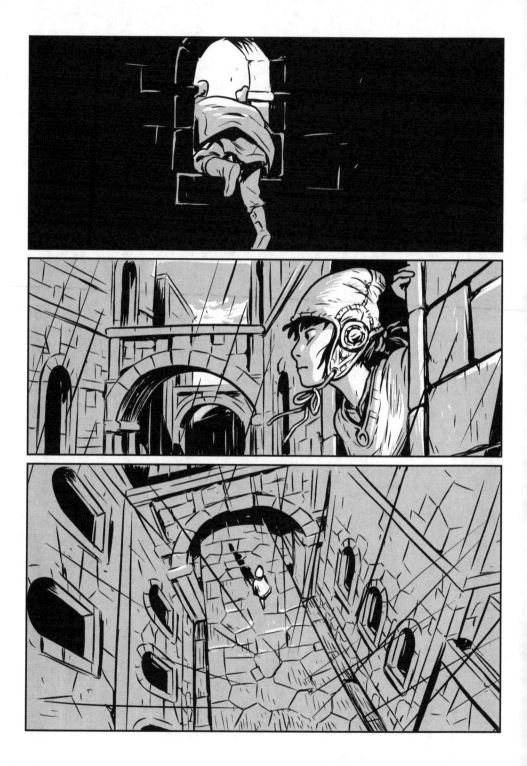

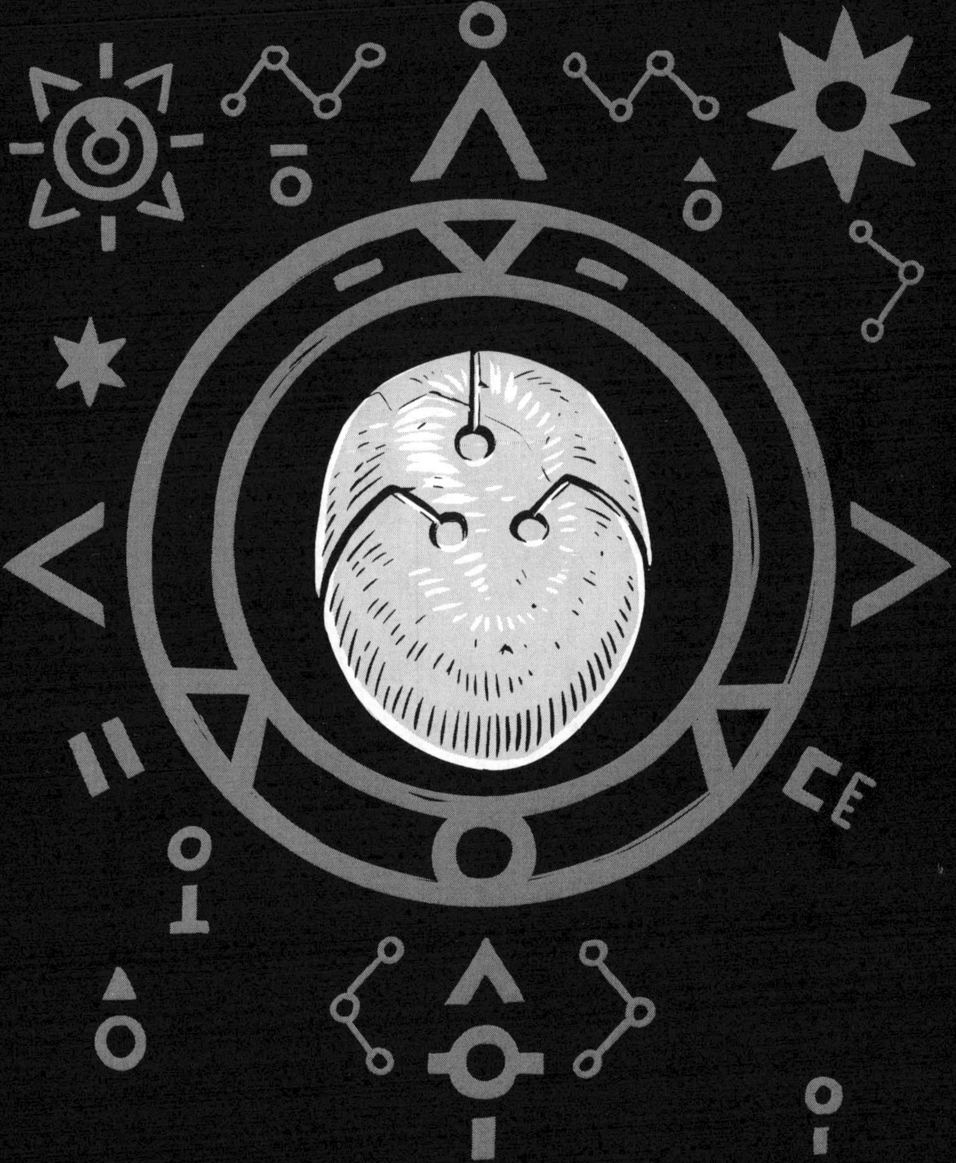

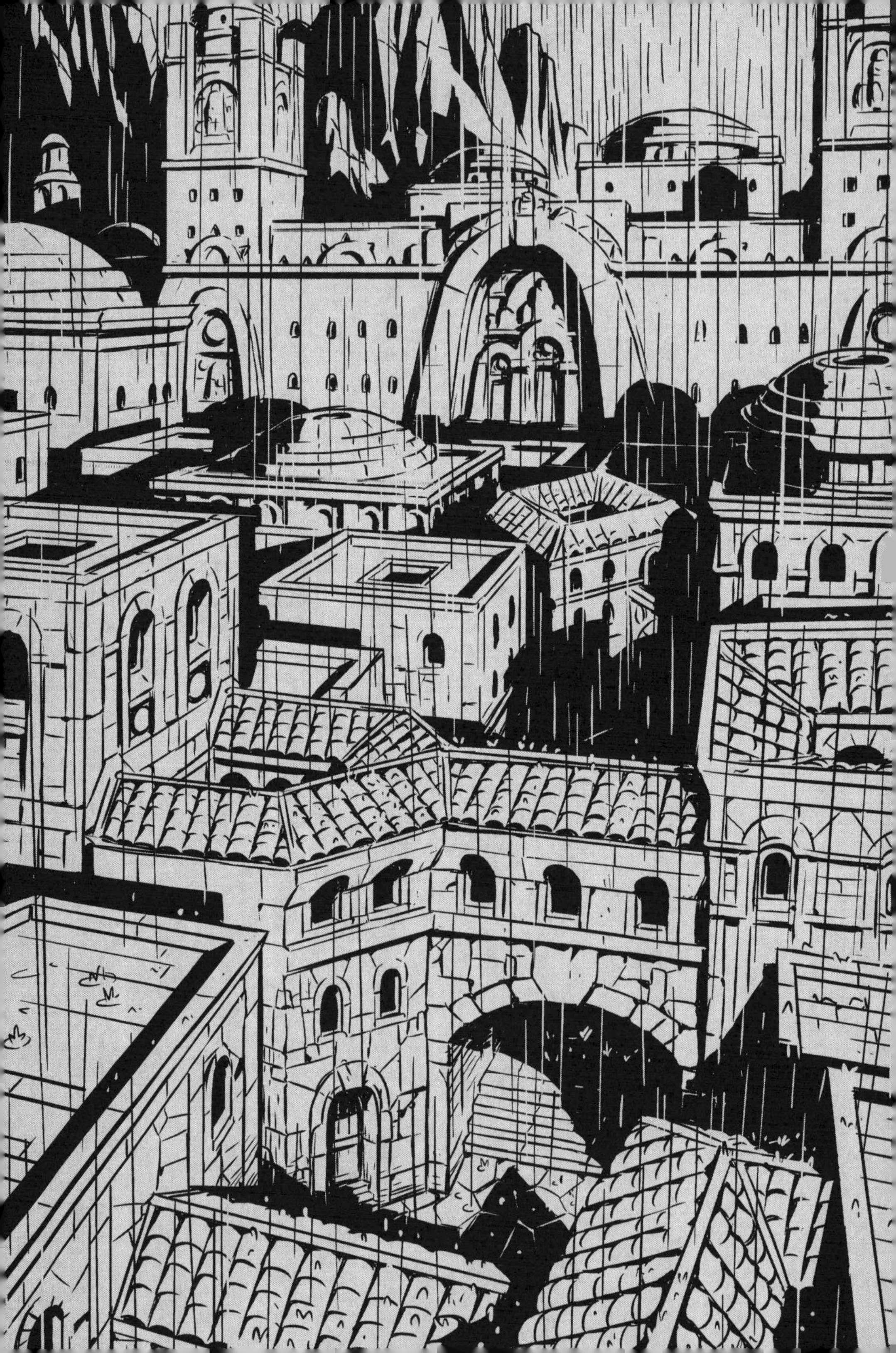

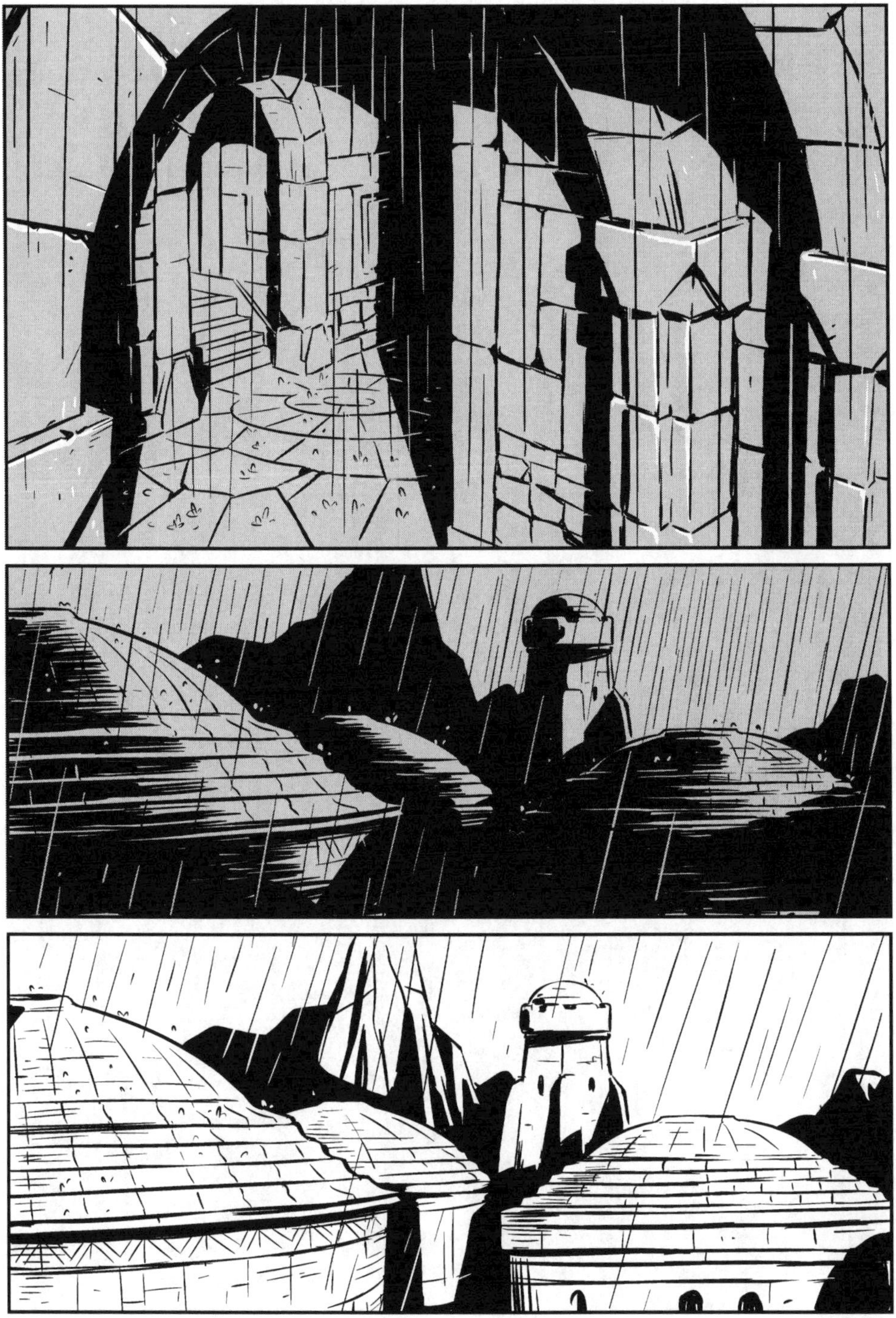

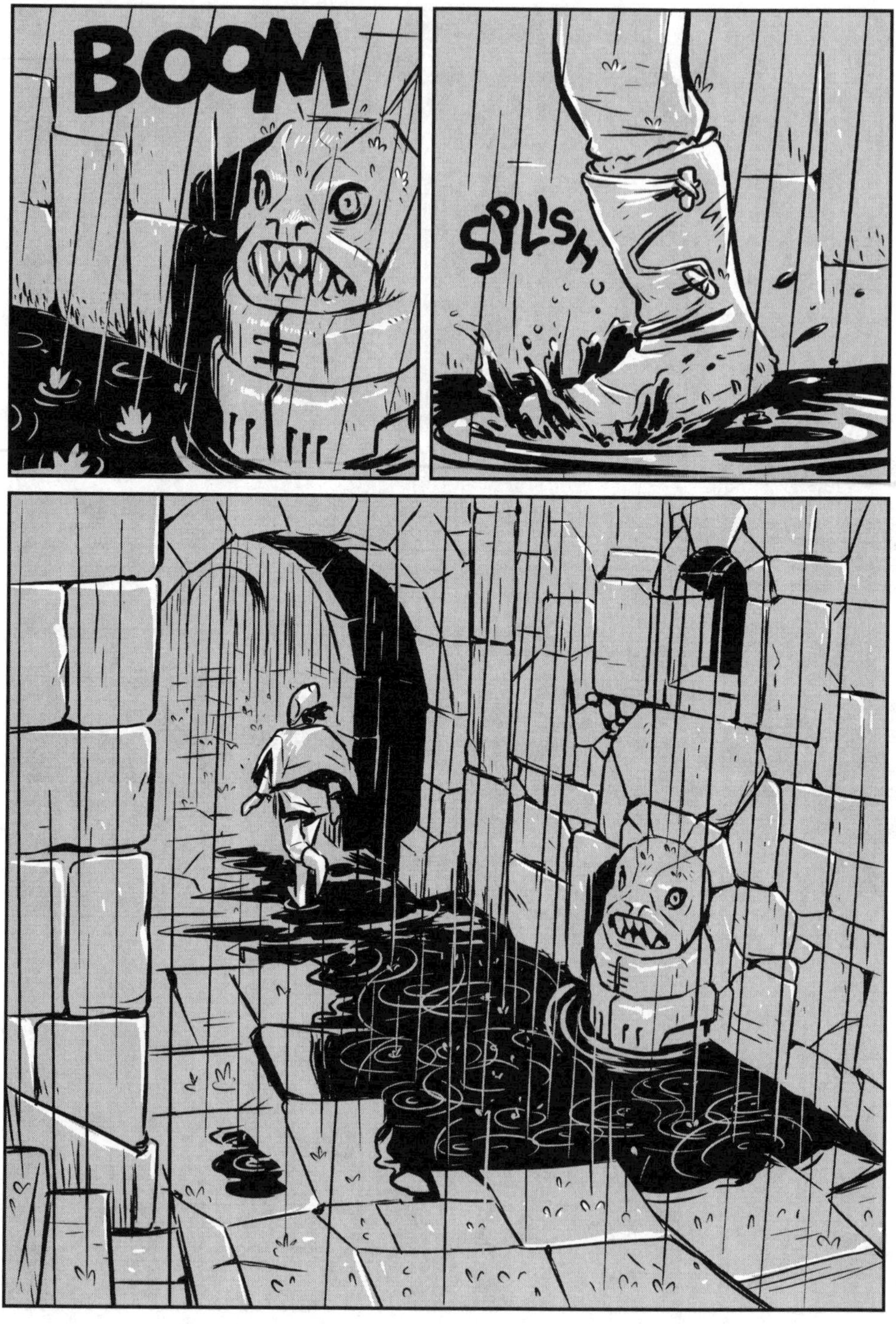
BOOM
SPLISH

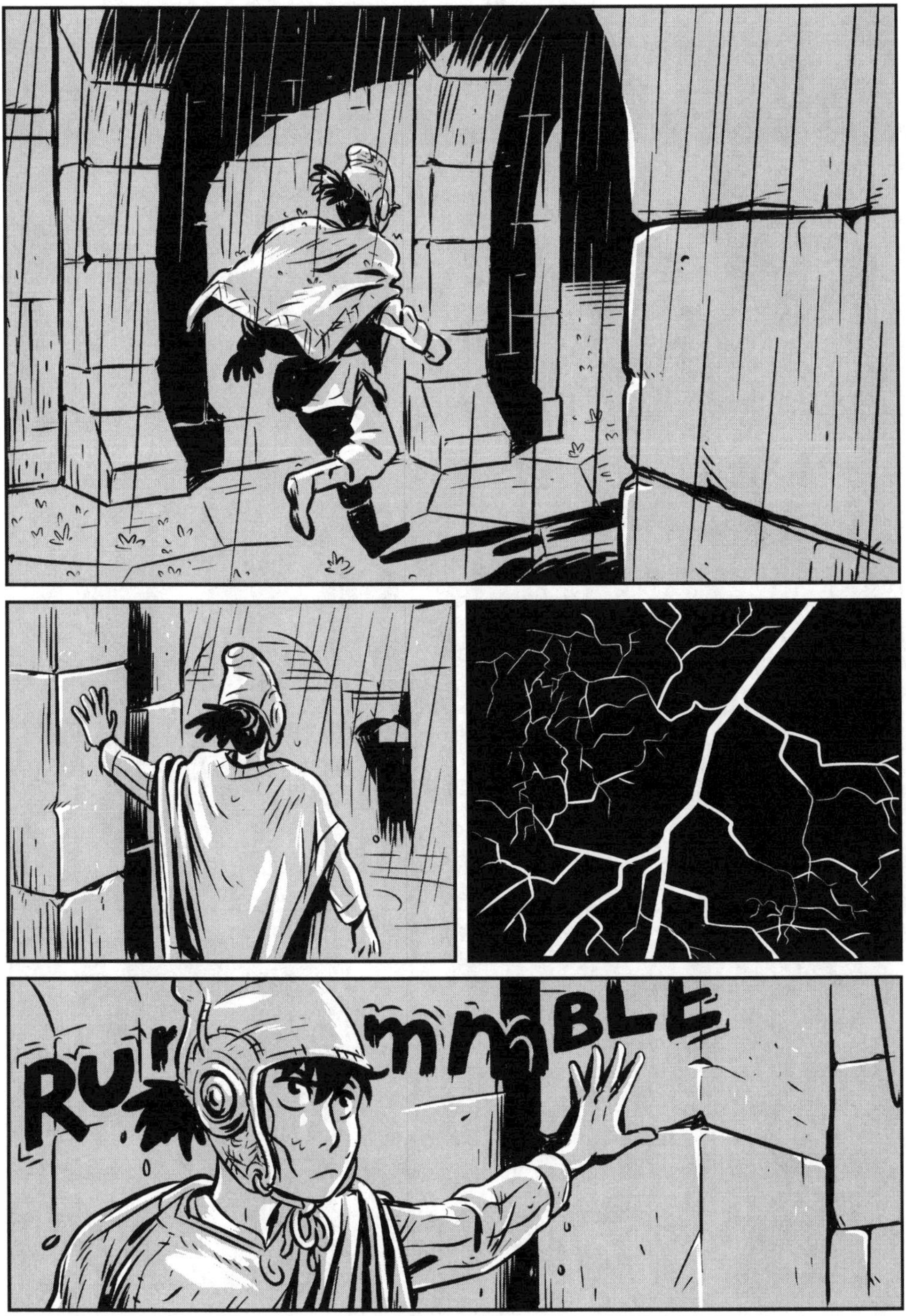
RUrmmmBLE

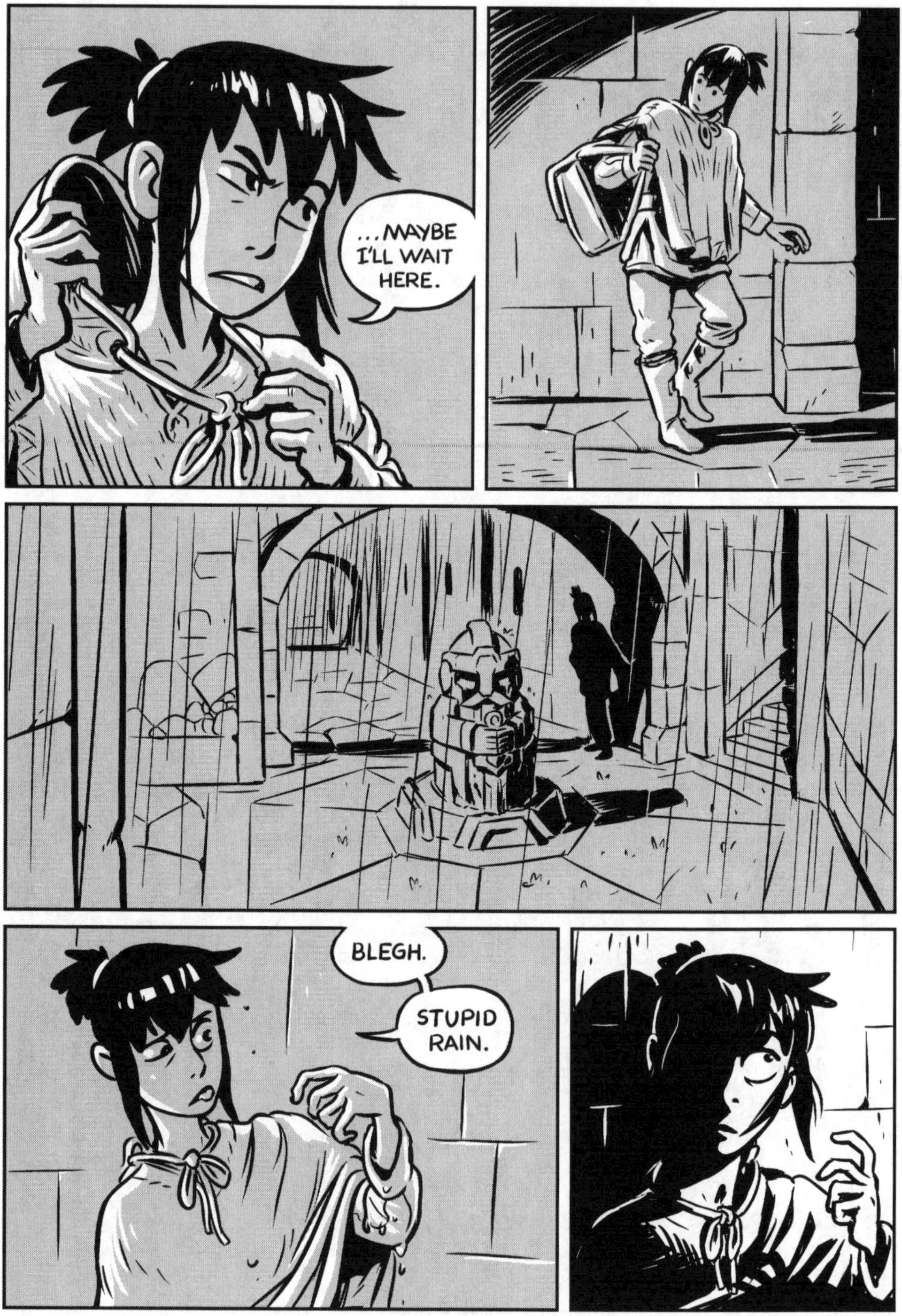
...MAYBE I'LL WAIT HERE.
BLEGH.
STUPID RAIN.

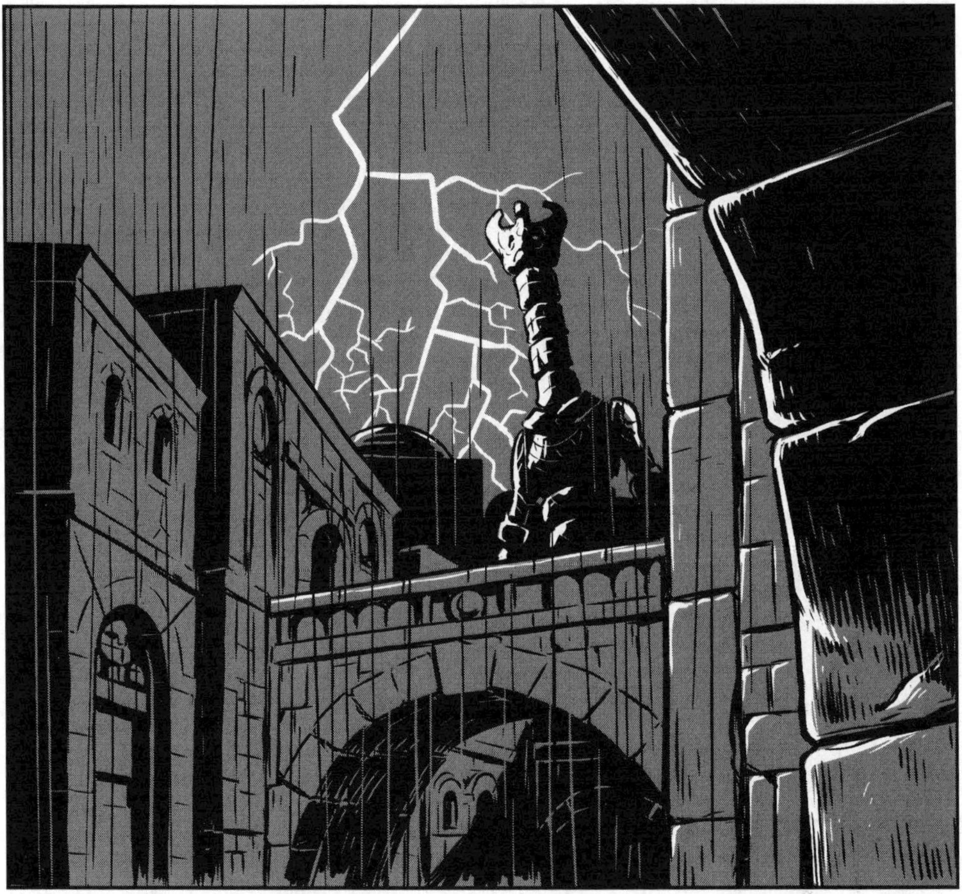
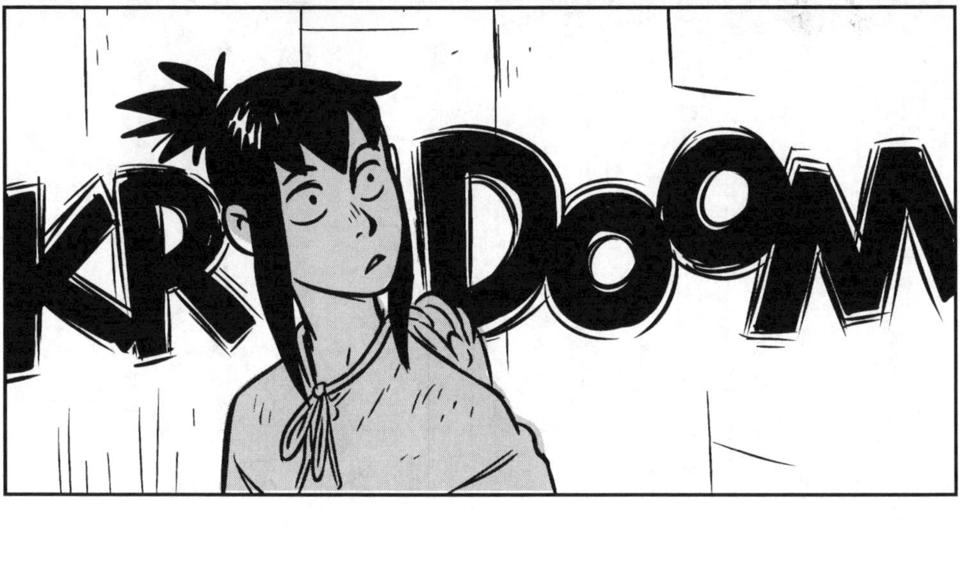
KRDOOM

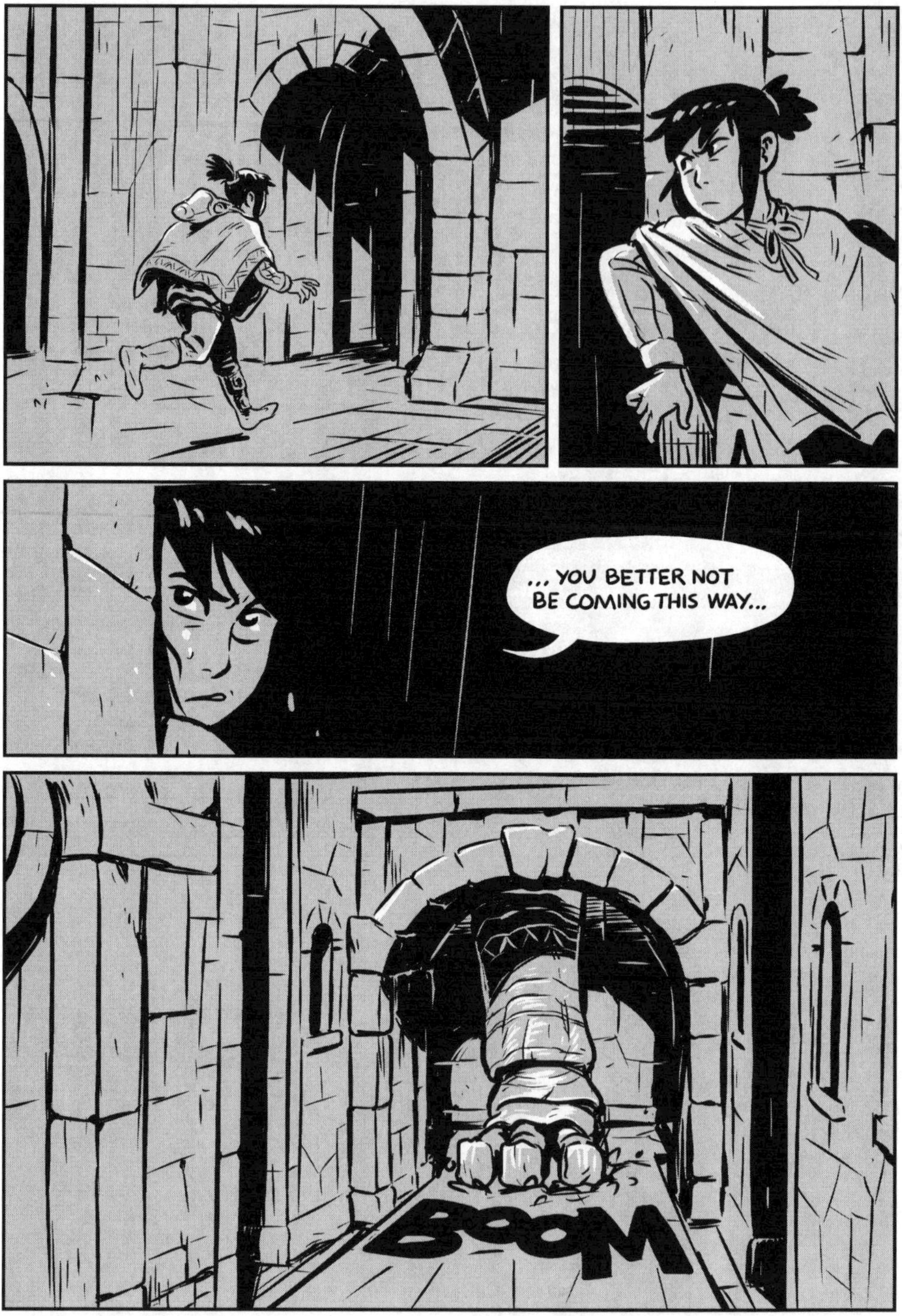
...YOU BETTER NOT BE COMING THIS WAY...
BOOM

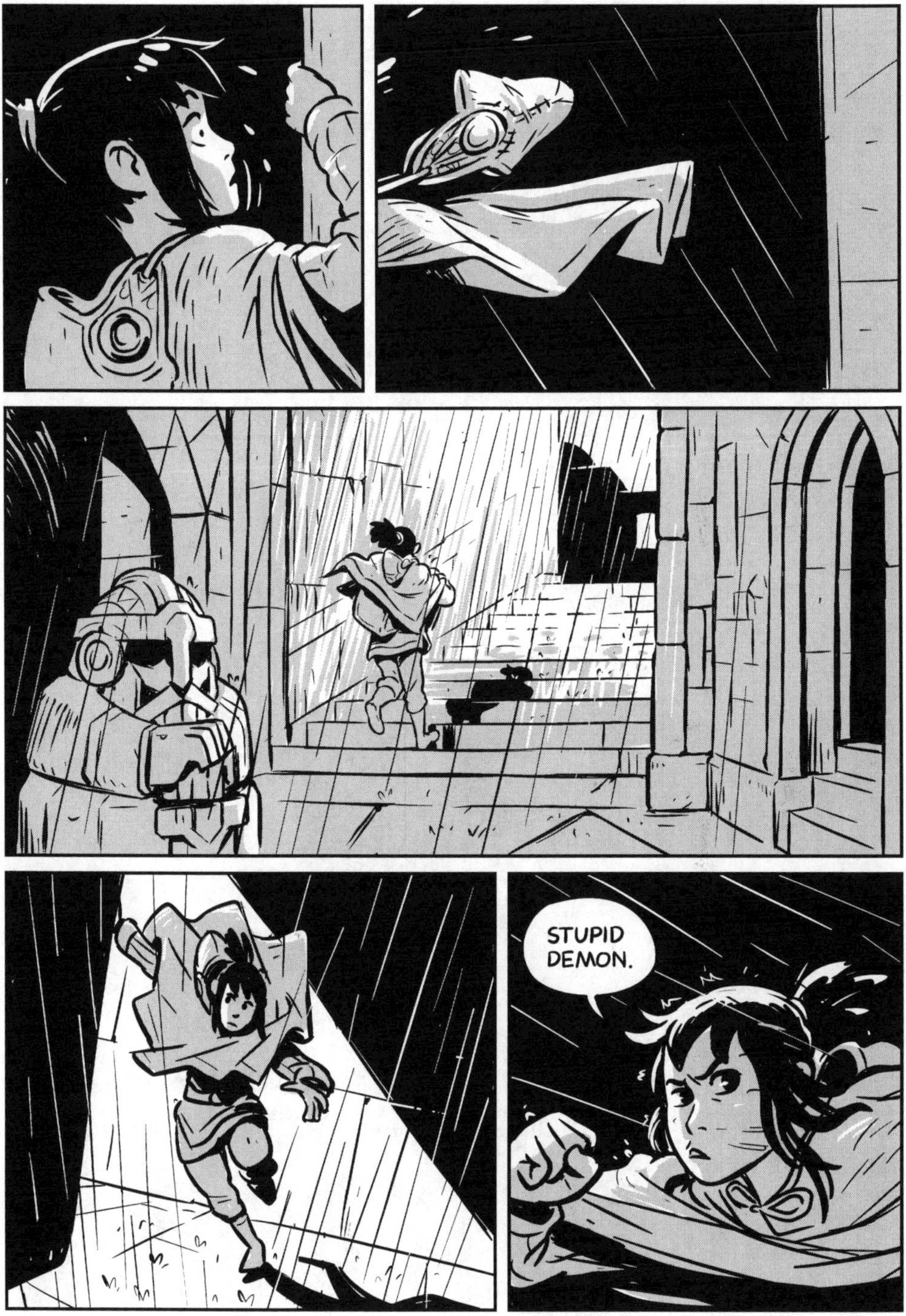
STUPID DEMON.

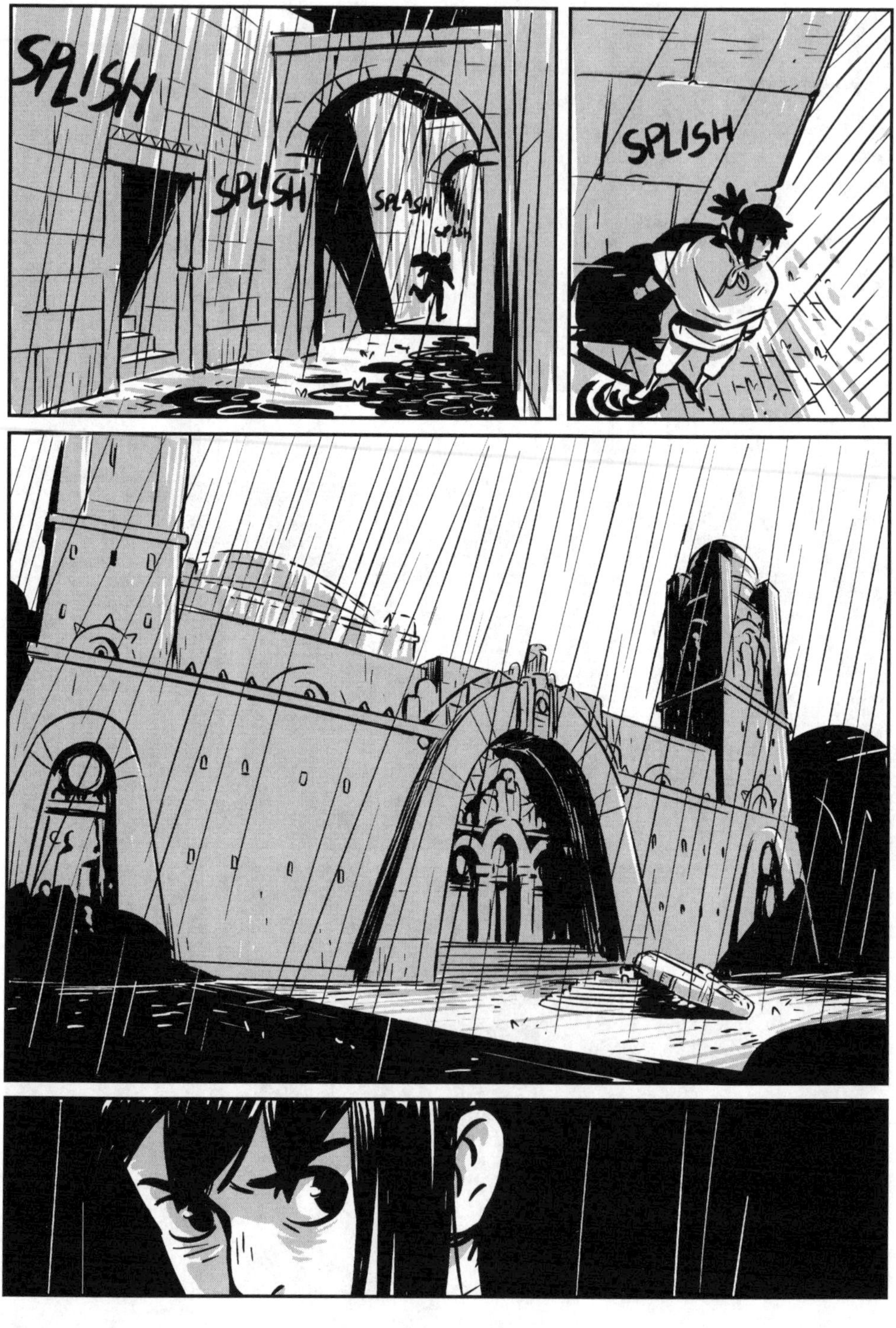
SPLISH
SPLISH
SPLASH
SPLISH
SPLISH

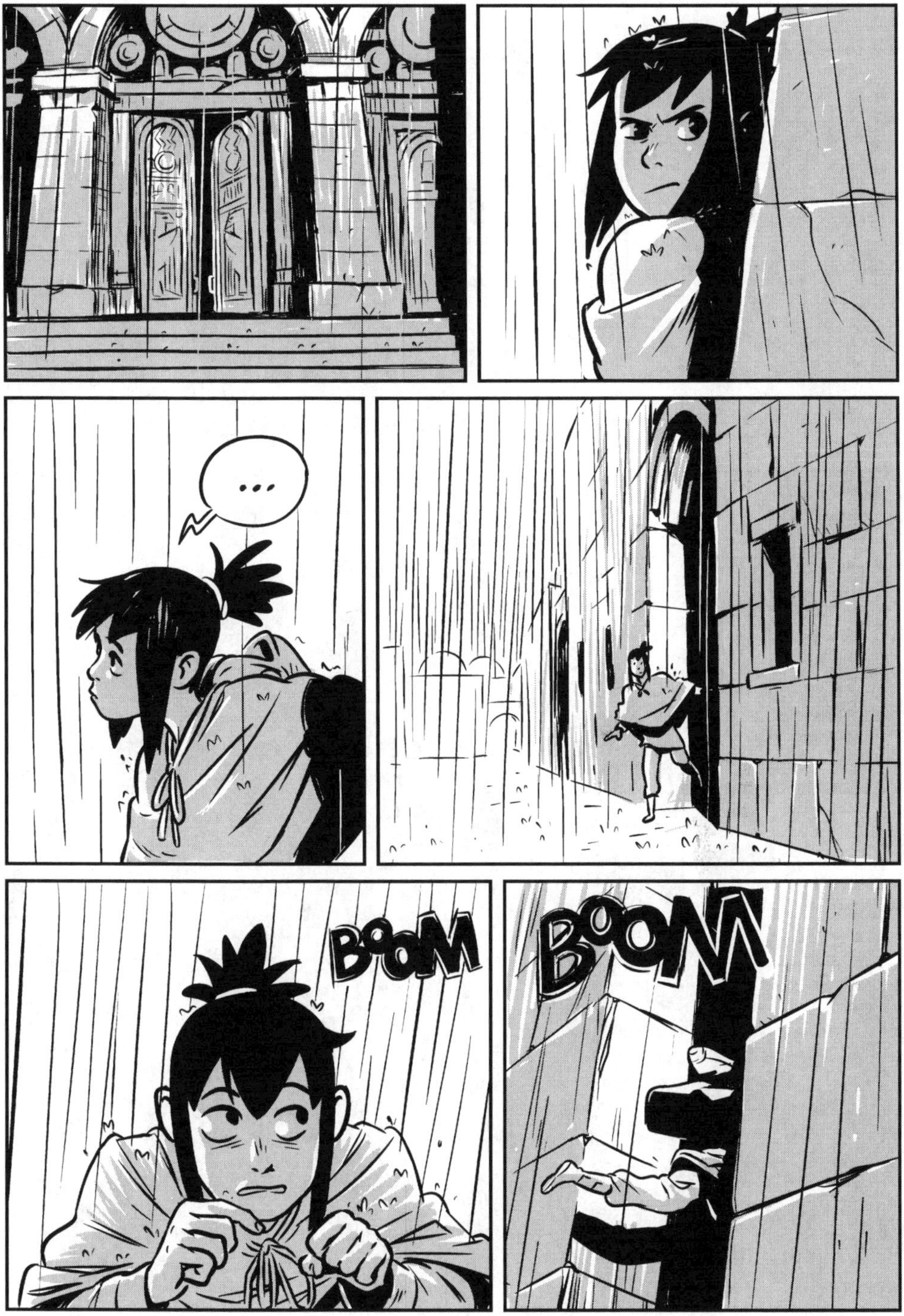
...
BOOM
BOOM

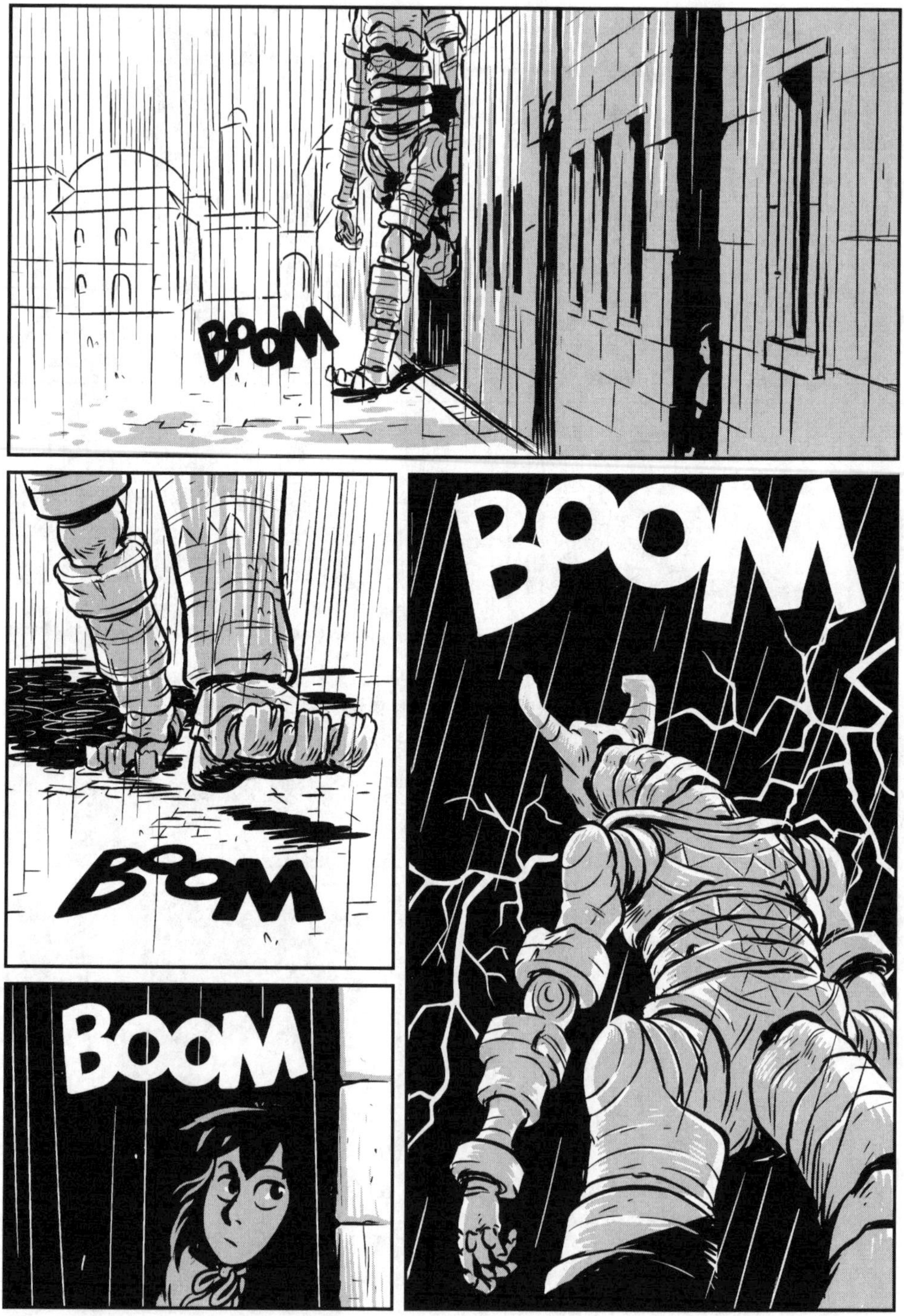
BOOM
BOOM
BOOM
BOOM

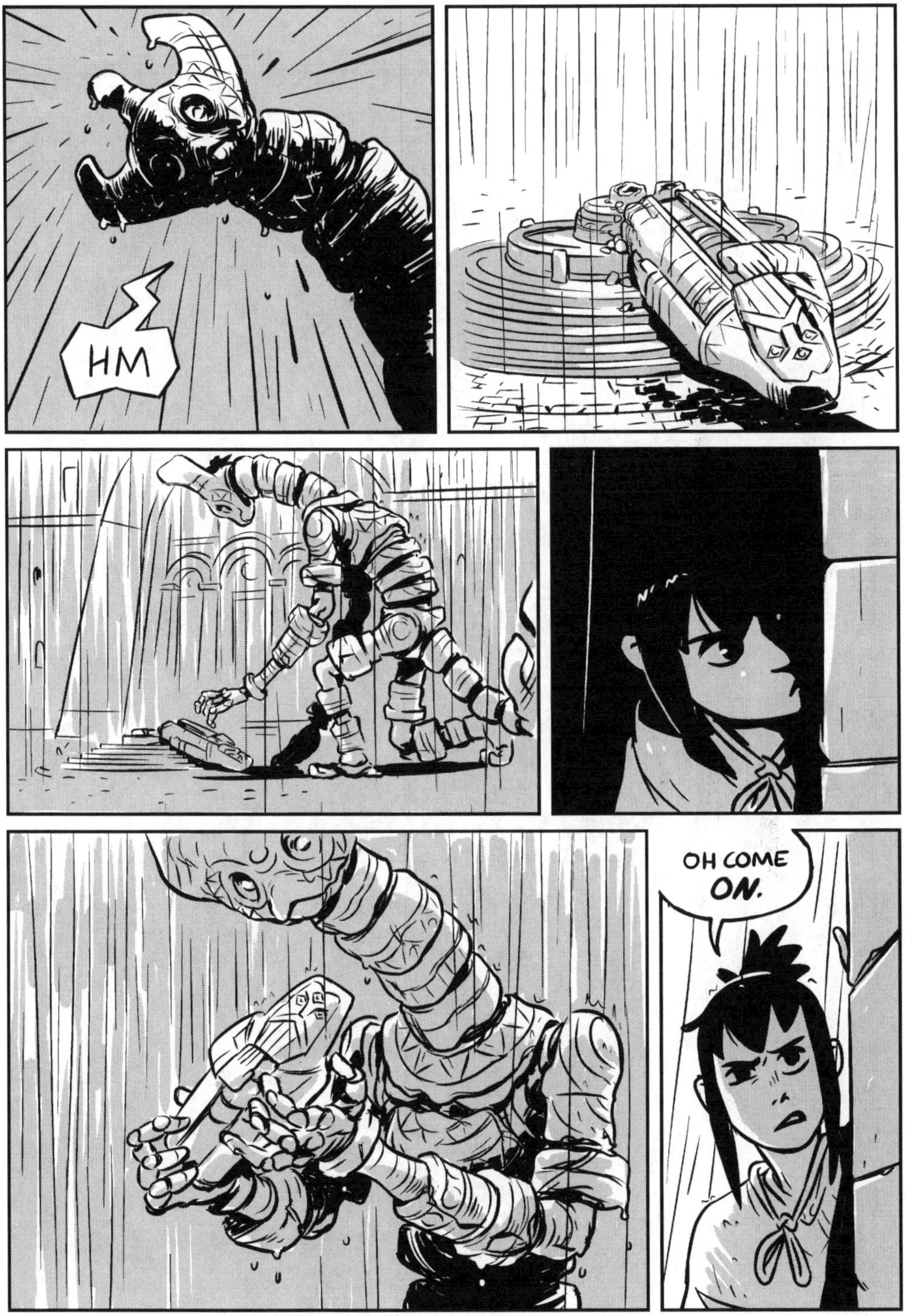
HM
OH COME ON.

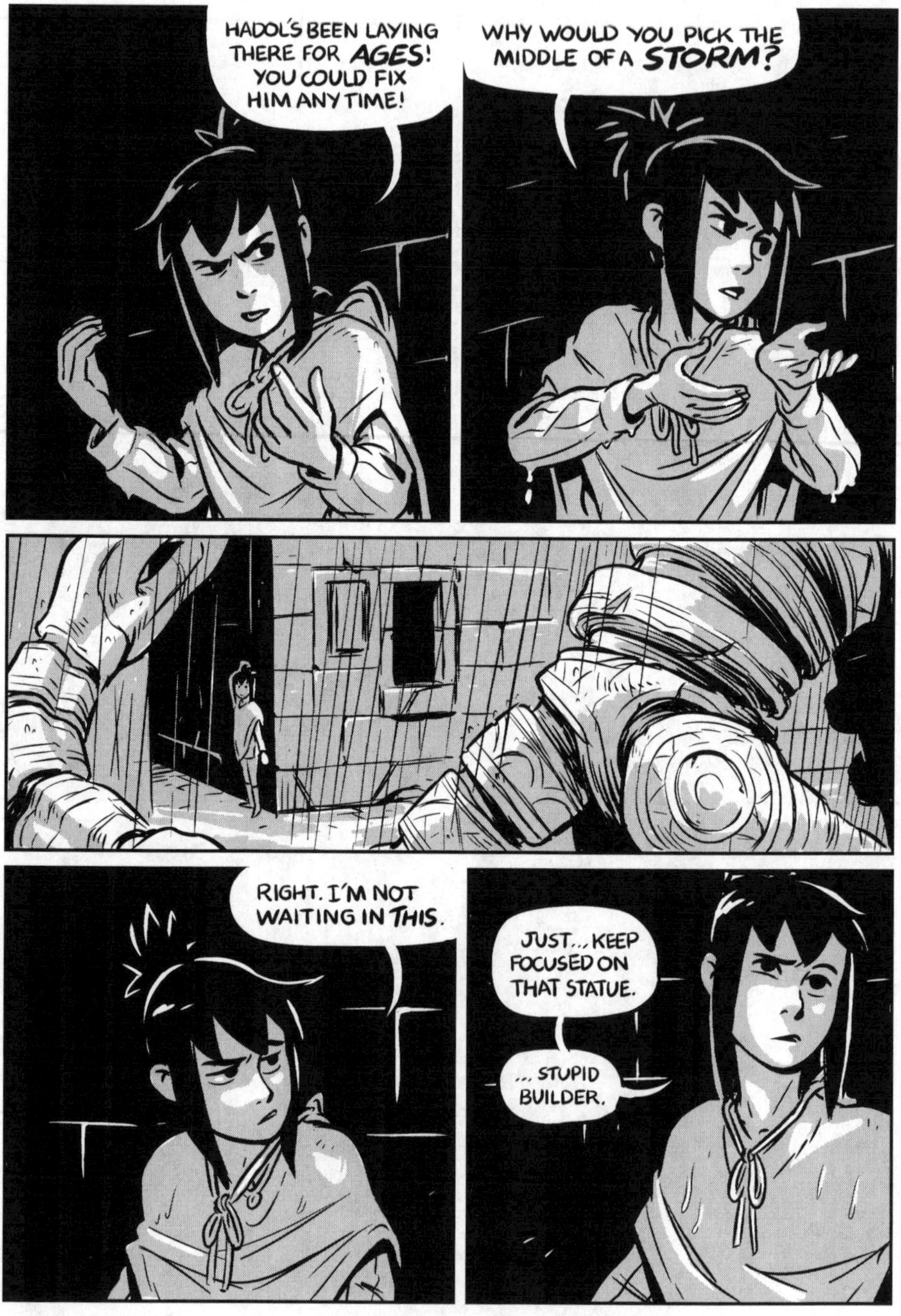
HADOL'S BEEN LAYING THERE FOR AGES! YOU COULD FIX HIM ANY TIME!
WHY WOULD YOU PICK THE MIDDLE OF A STORM?
RIGHT. I'M NOT WAITING IN THIS.
JUST... KEEP FOCUSED ON THAT STATUE.
... STUPID BUILDER.

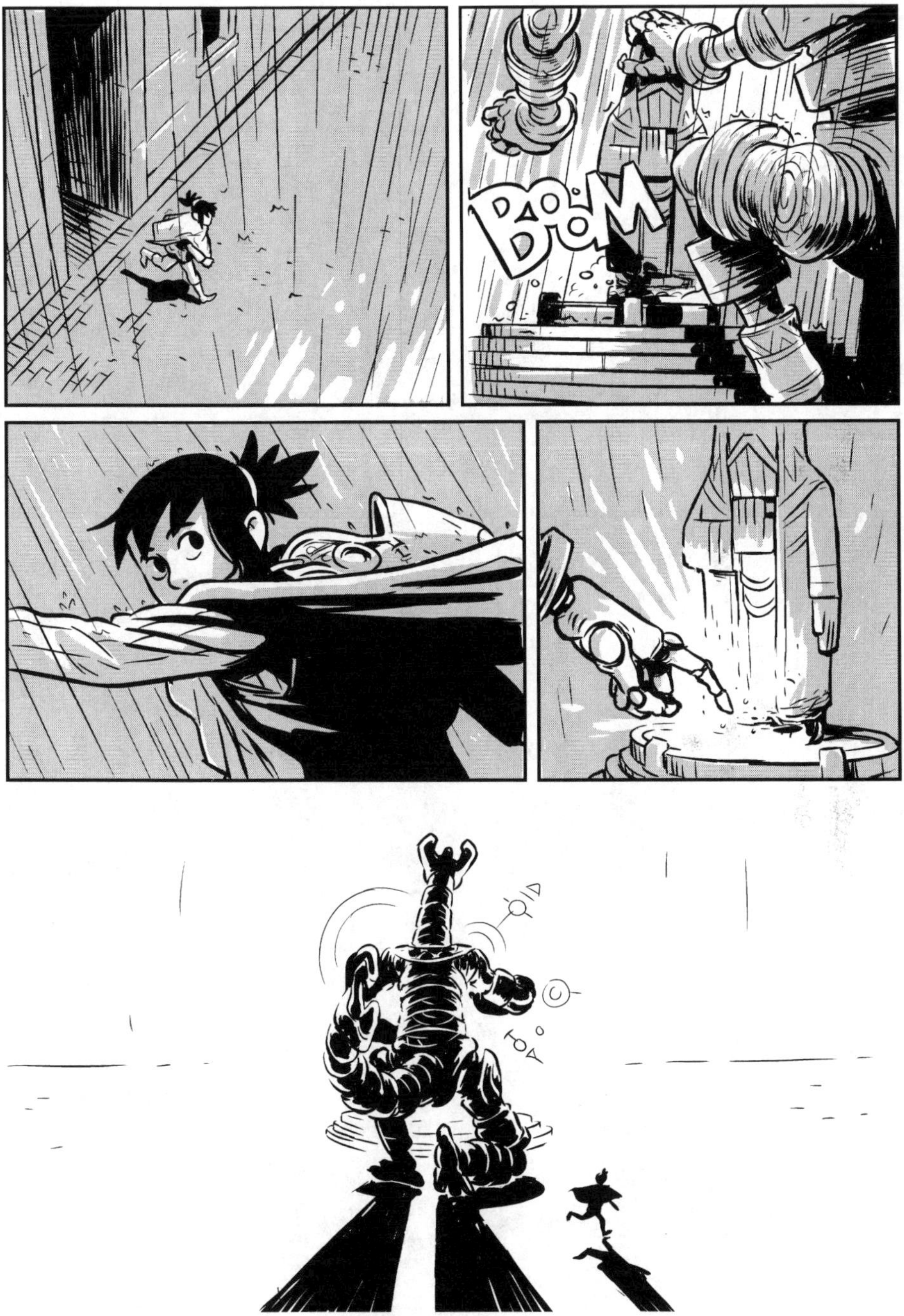
DOOM

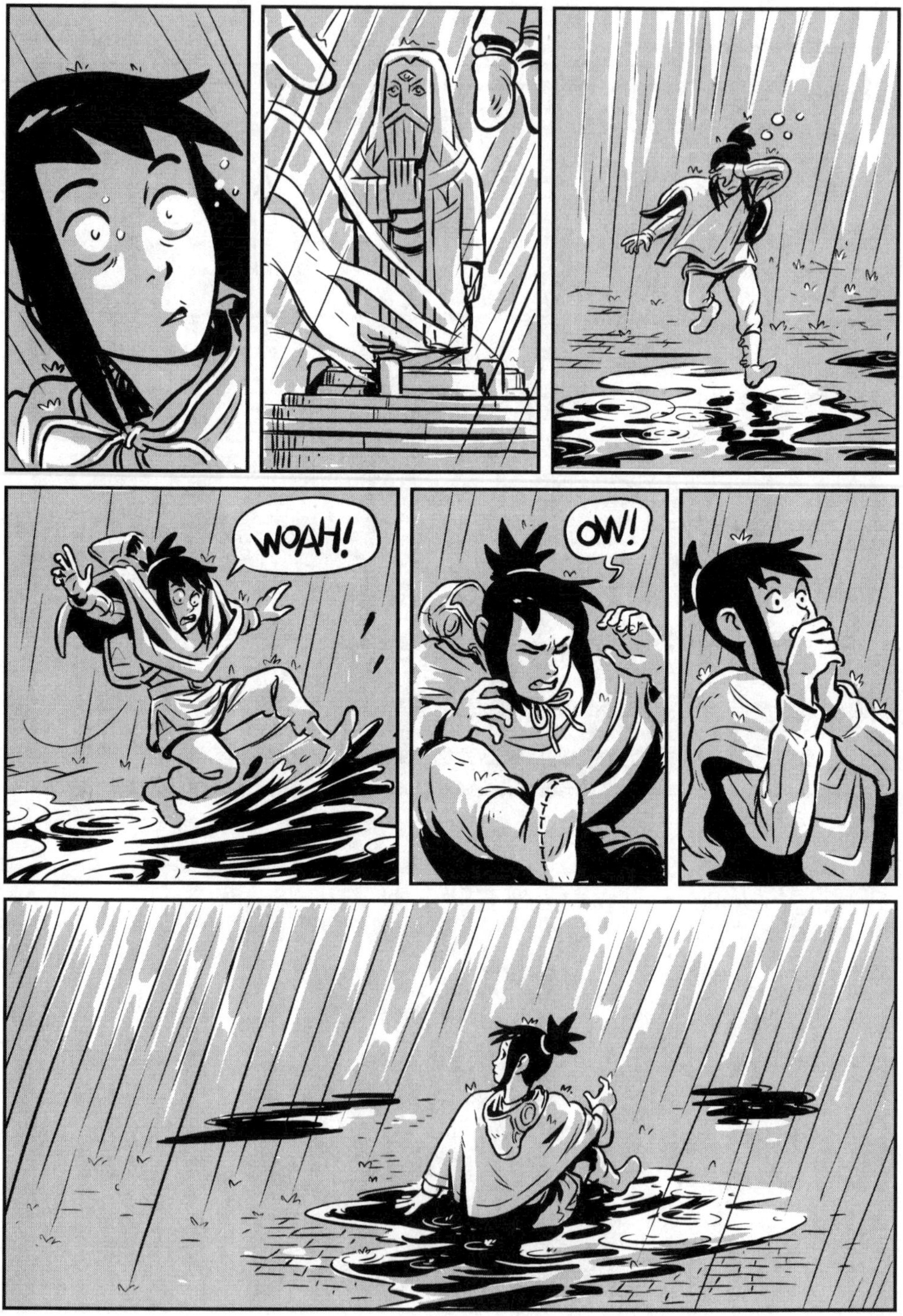
WOAH!
OW!

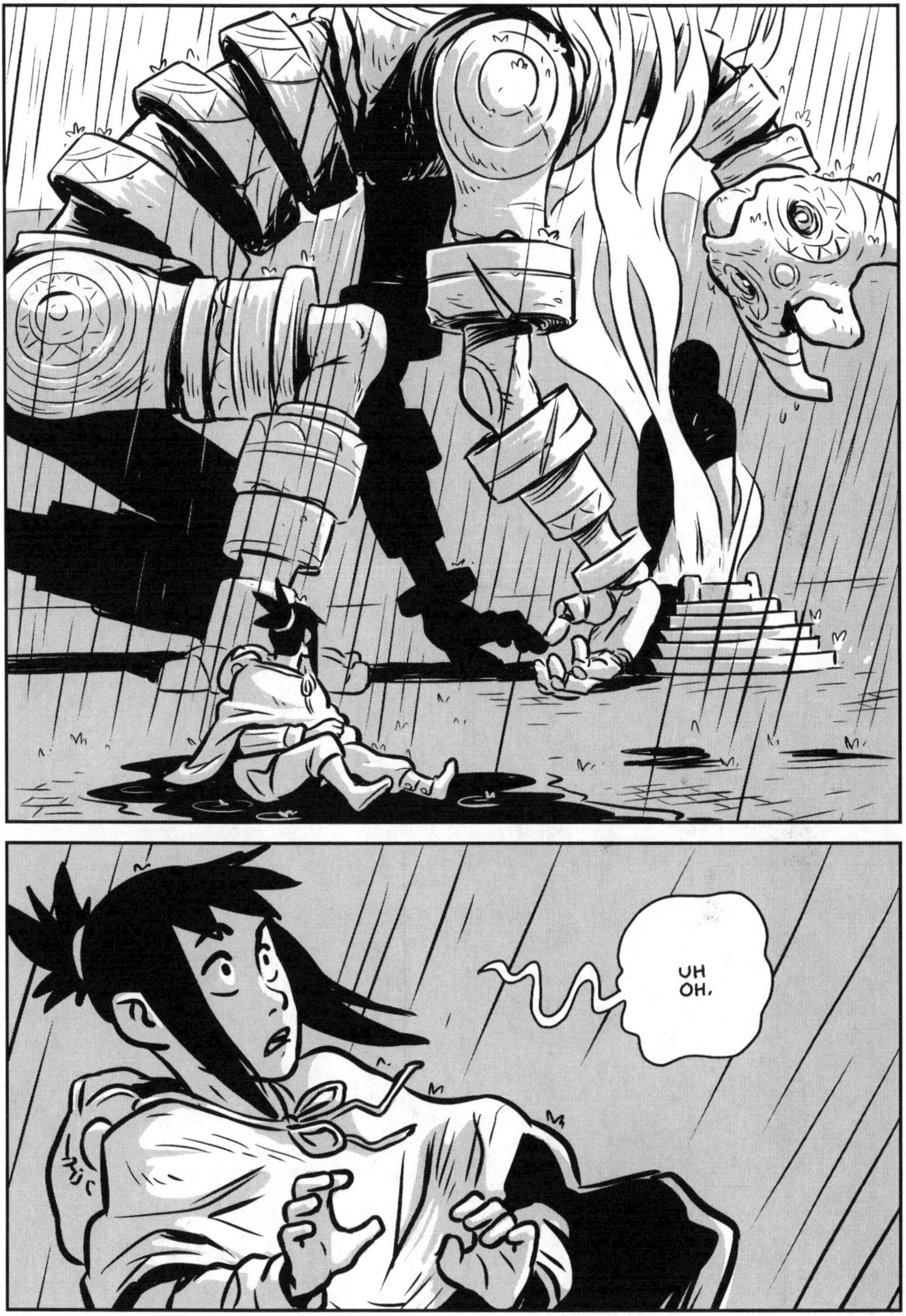
UH OH.

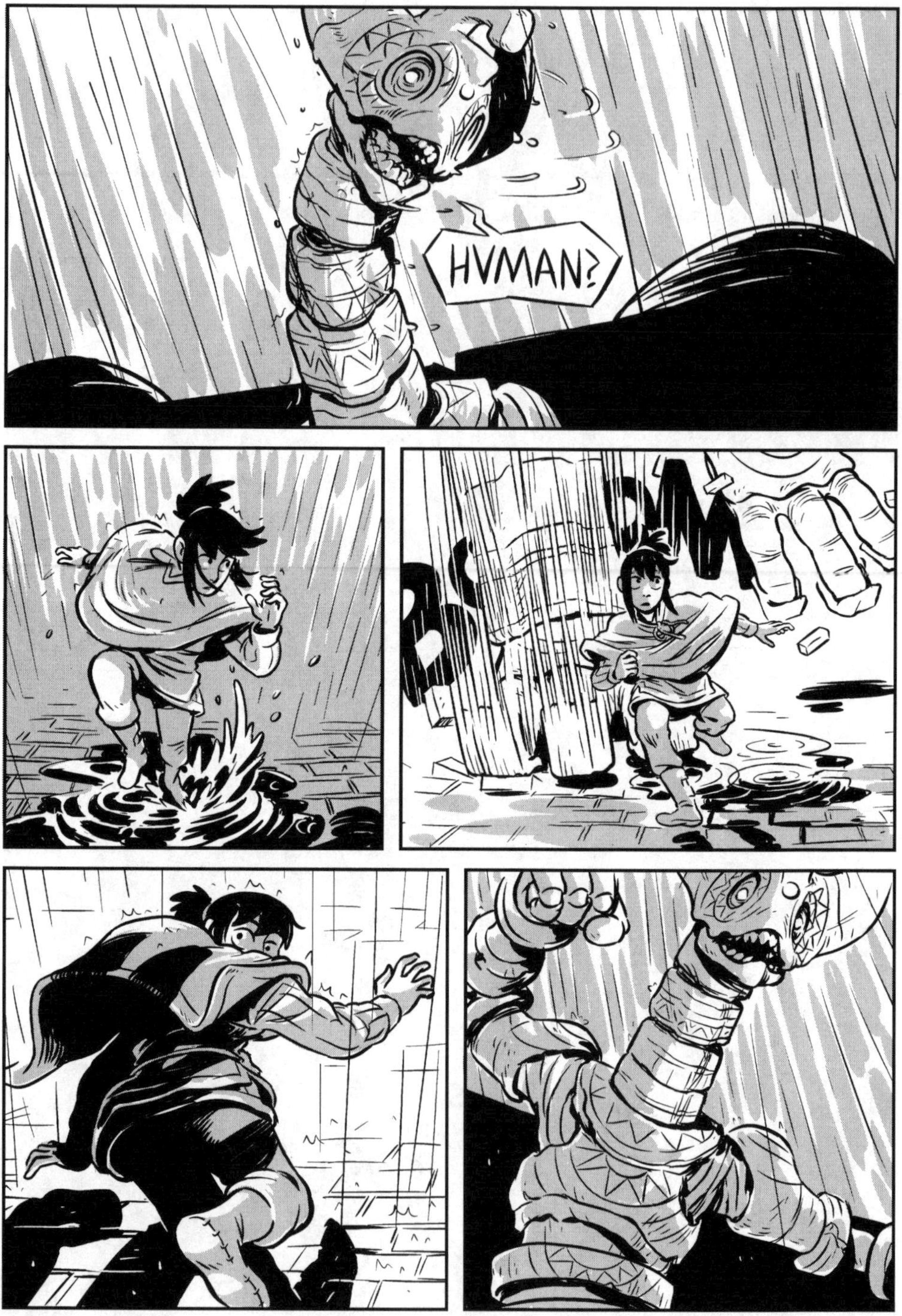
HVMAN?

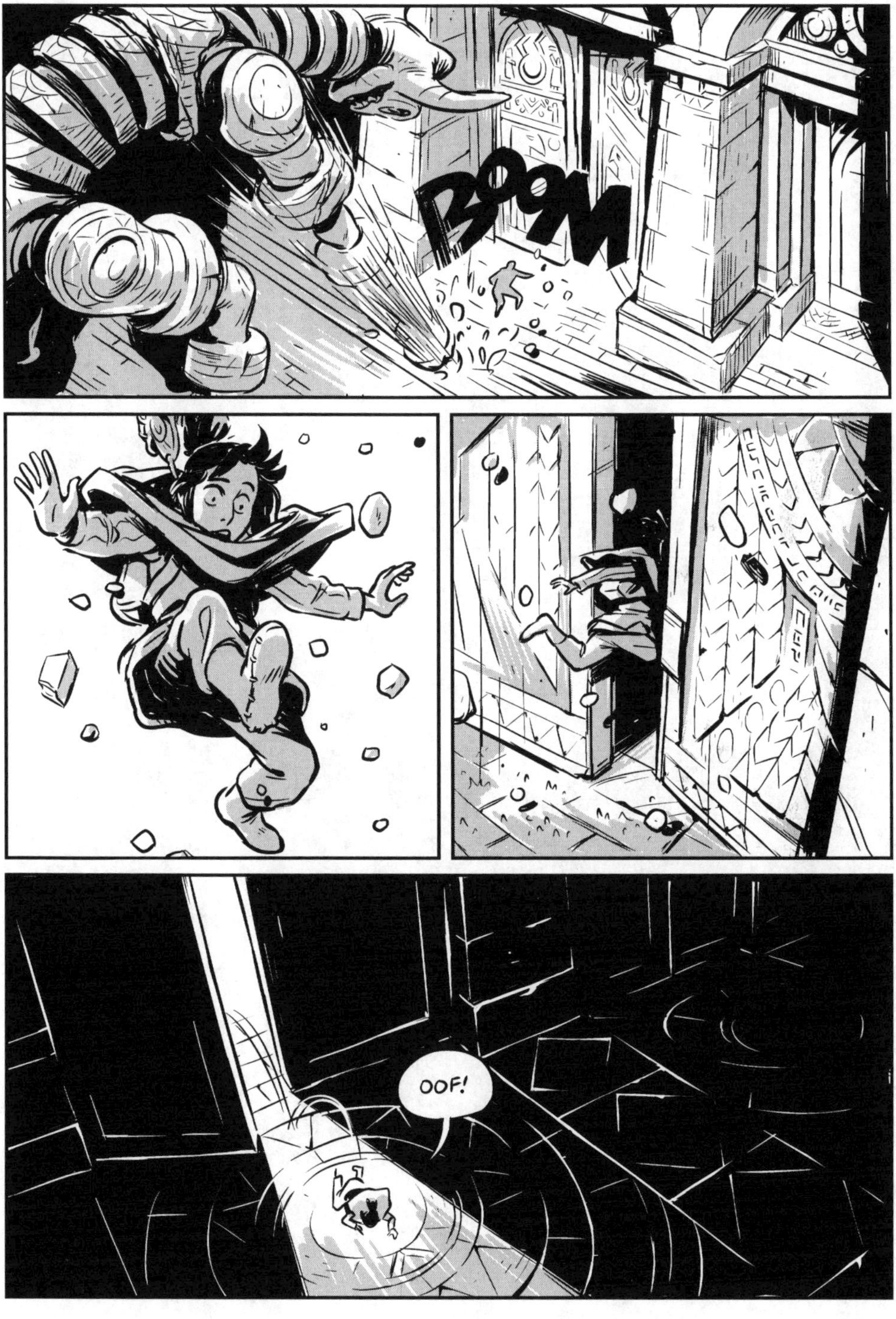
BOOM
OOF!

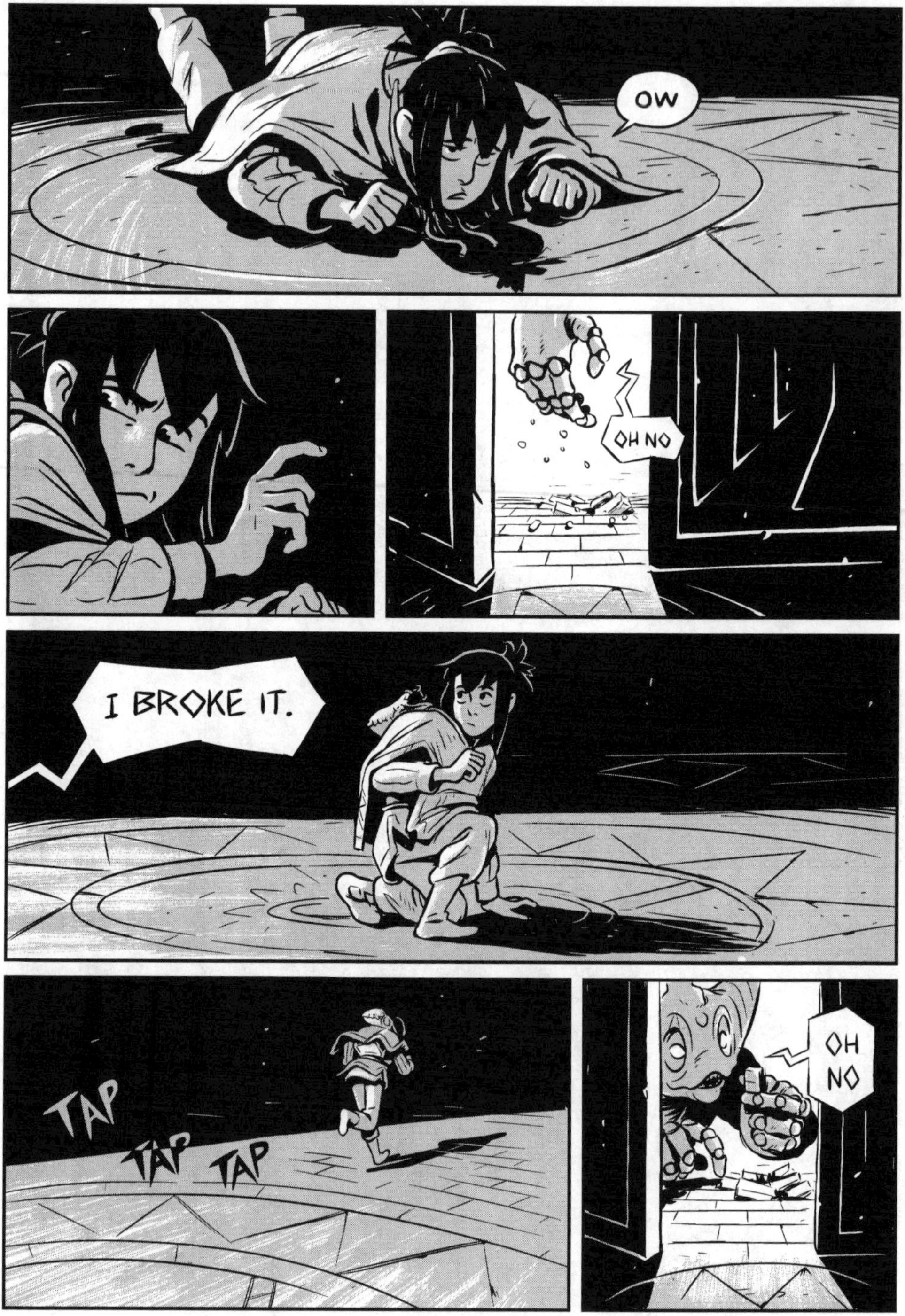
OW
OH NO
I BROKE IT.
TAP
TAP
TAP
OH
NO

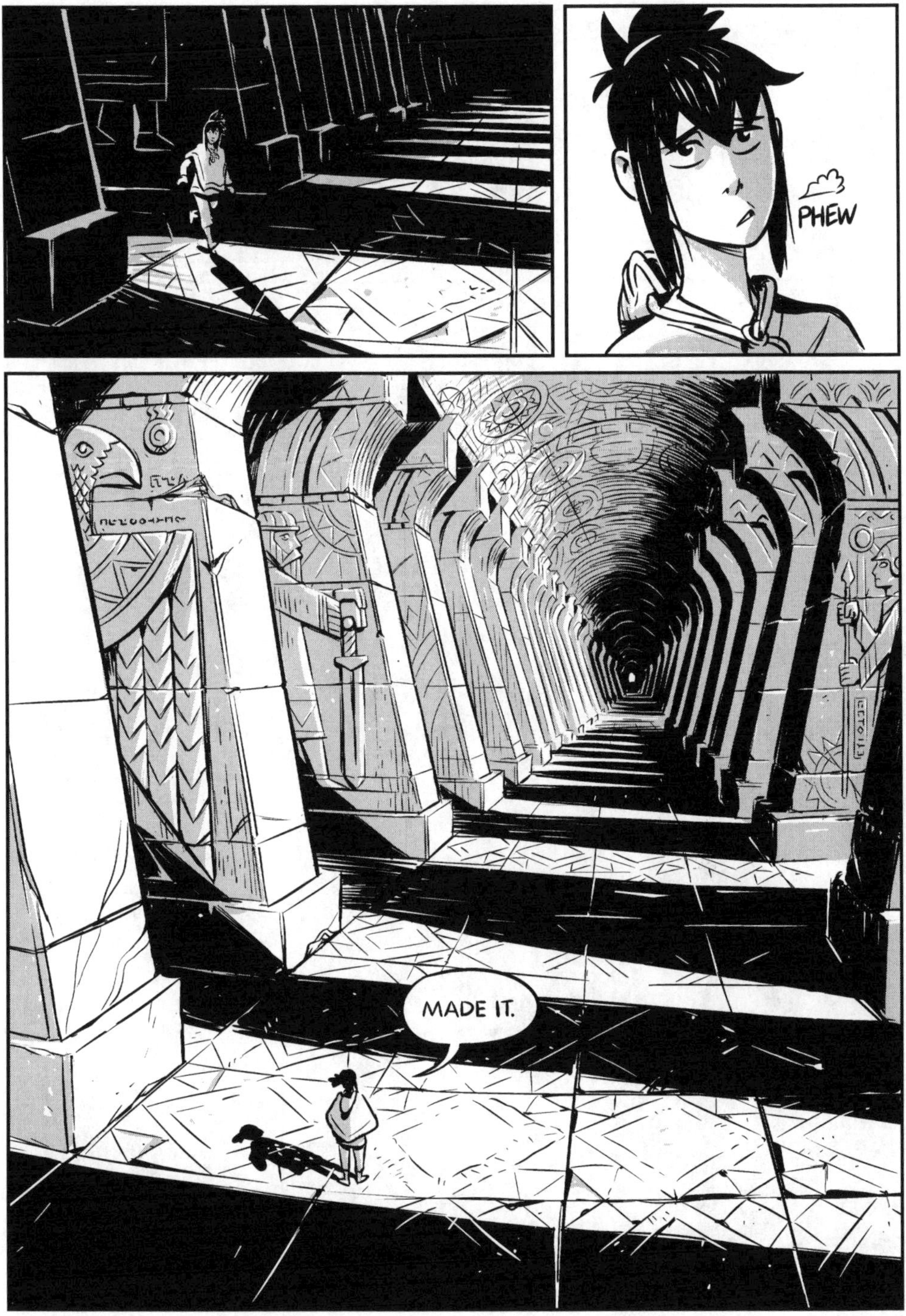
PHEW
MADE IT.

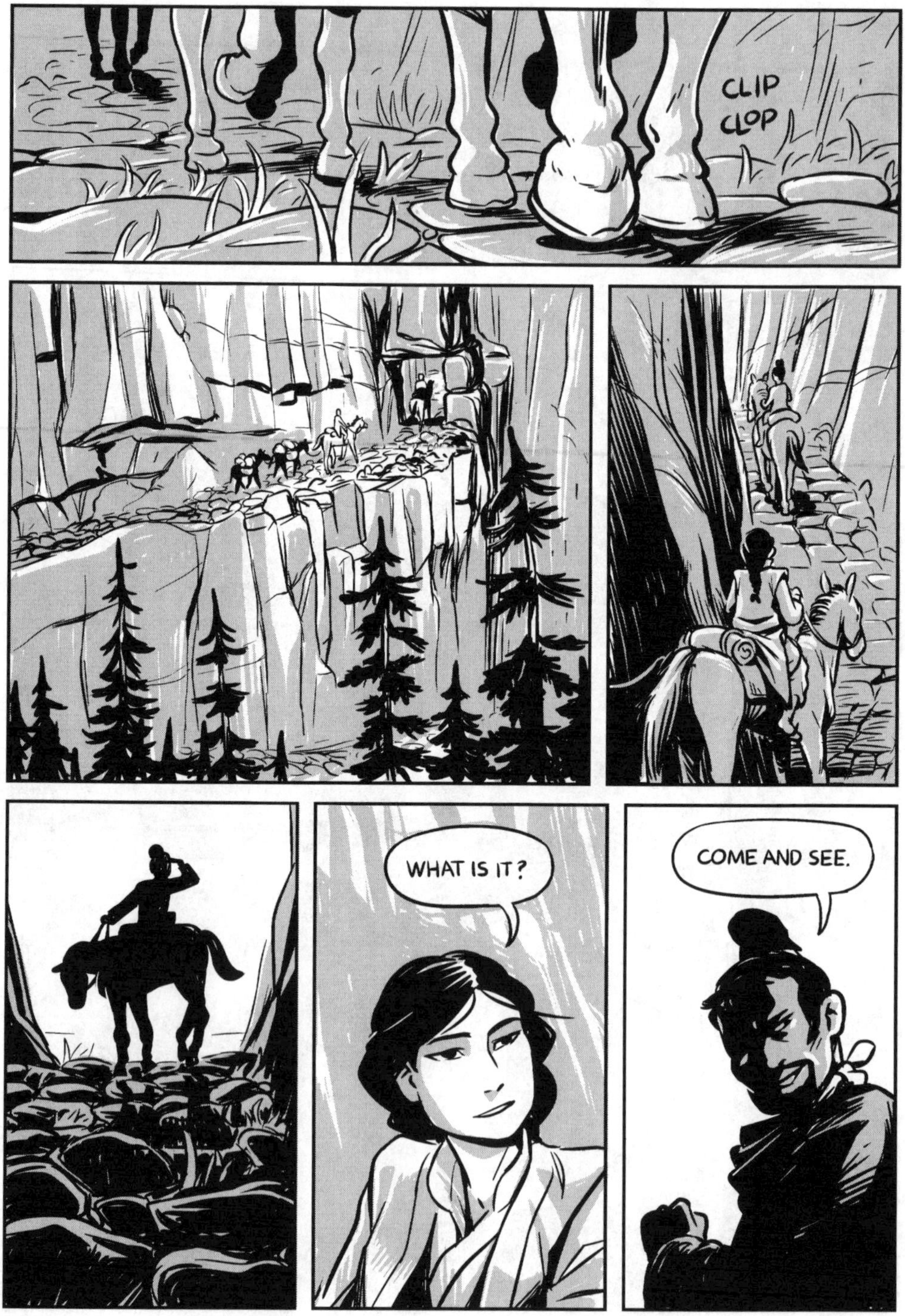
CLIP
CLOP
WHAT IS IT?
COME AND SEE.

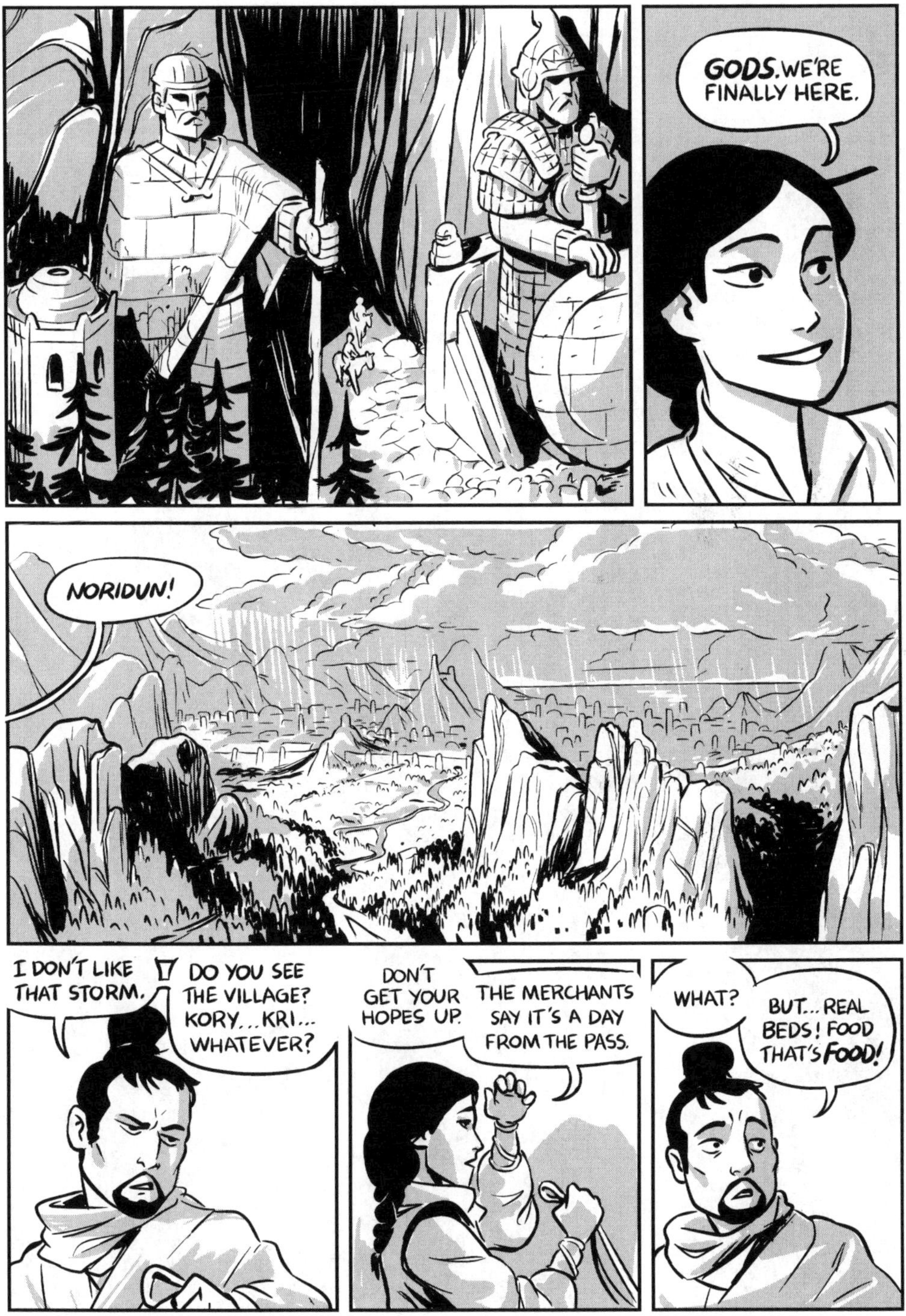
GODS. WE'RE FINALLY HERE.
NORIDUN!
I DON'T LIKE THAT STORM.
DO YOU SEE THE VILLAGE? KORY... KRI... WHATEVER?
DON'T GET YOUR HOPES UP.
THE MERCHANTS SAY IT'S A DAY FROM THE PASS.
WHAT?
BUT... REAL BEDS! FOOD THAT'S FOOD!

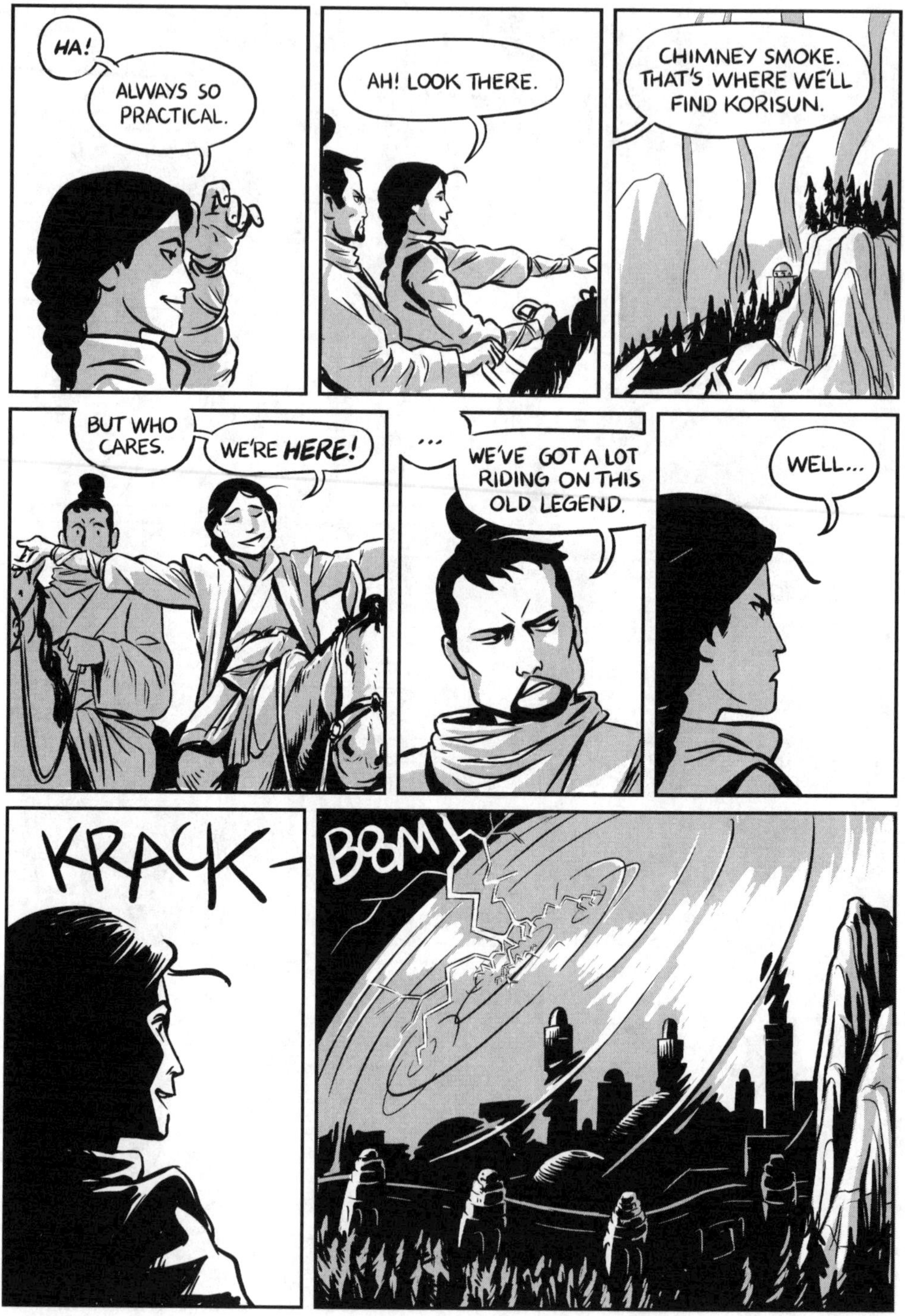
HA!
ALWAYS SO PRACTICAL.
AH! LOOK THERE.
CHIMNEY SMOKE. THAT'S WHERE WE'LL FIND KORISUN.
BUT WHO CARES.
WE'RE **HERE!**
...
WE'VE GOT A LOT RIDING ON THIS OLD LEGEND.
WELL...
KRACK-
BOOM

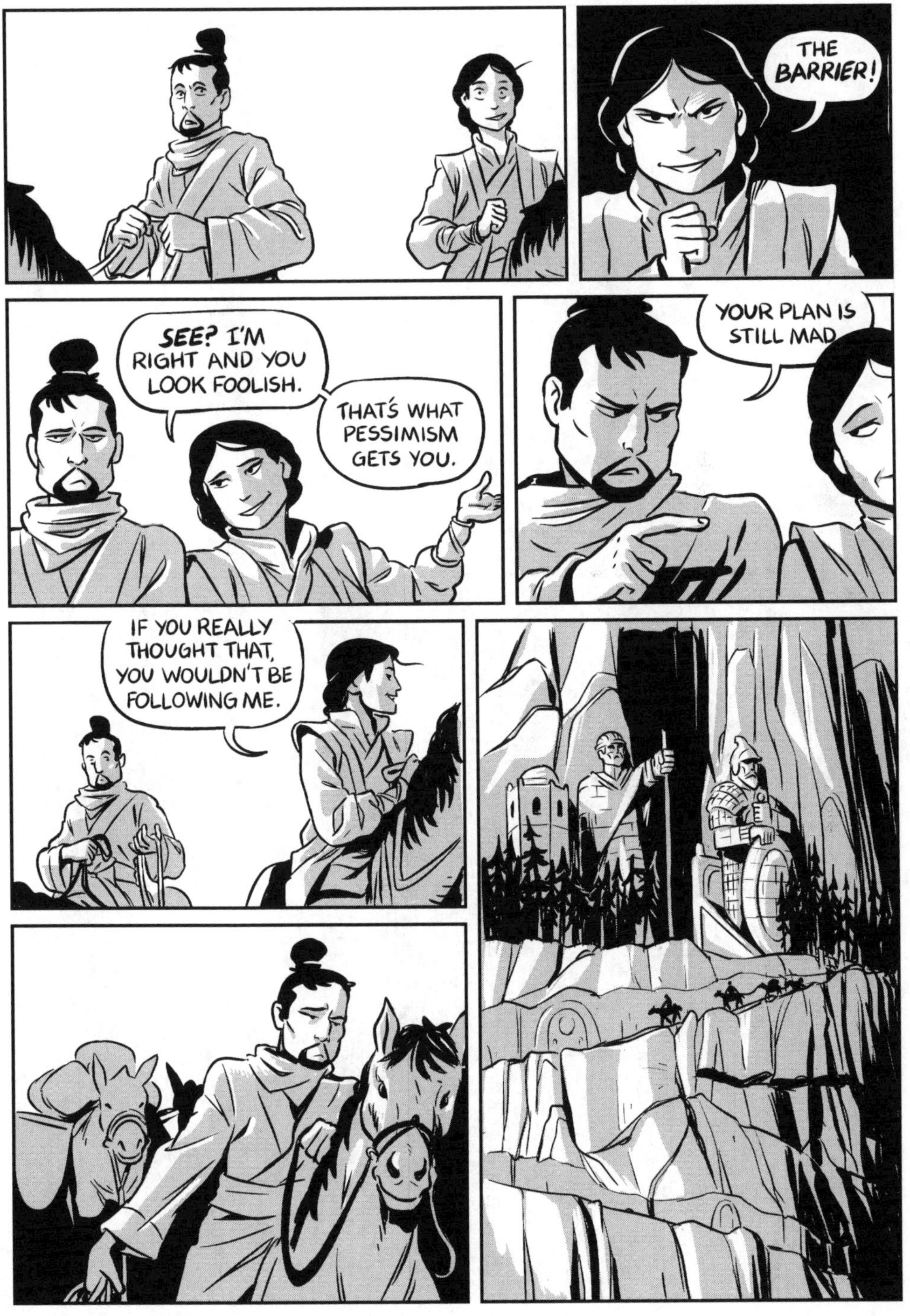
THE BARRIER!
SEE? I'M RIGHT AND YOU LOOK FOOLISH.
THAT'S WHAT PESSIMISM GETS YOU.
YOUR PLAN IS STILL MAD
IF YOU REALLY THOUGHT THAT, YOU WOULDN'T BE FOLLOWING ME.

TAP
TAP
TAP
TAP TAP
...WHAT'S SHE GOTTEN INTO NOW.

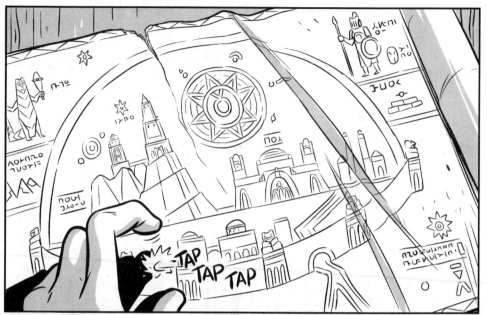

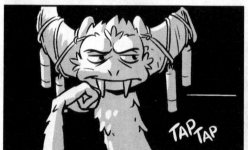

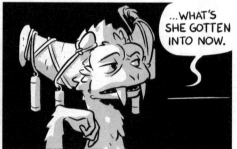

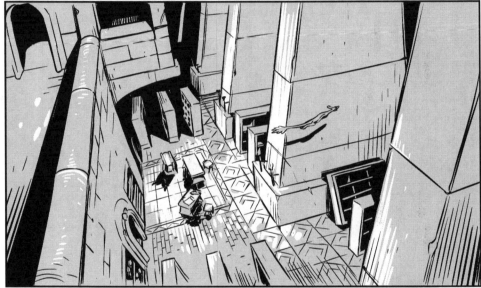

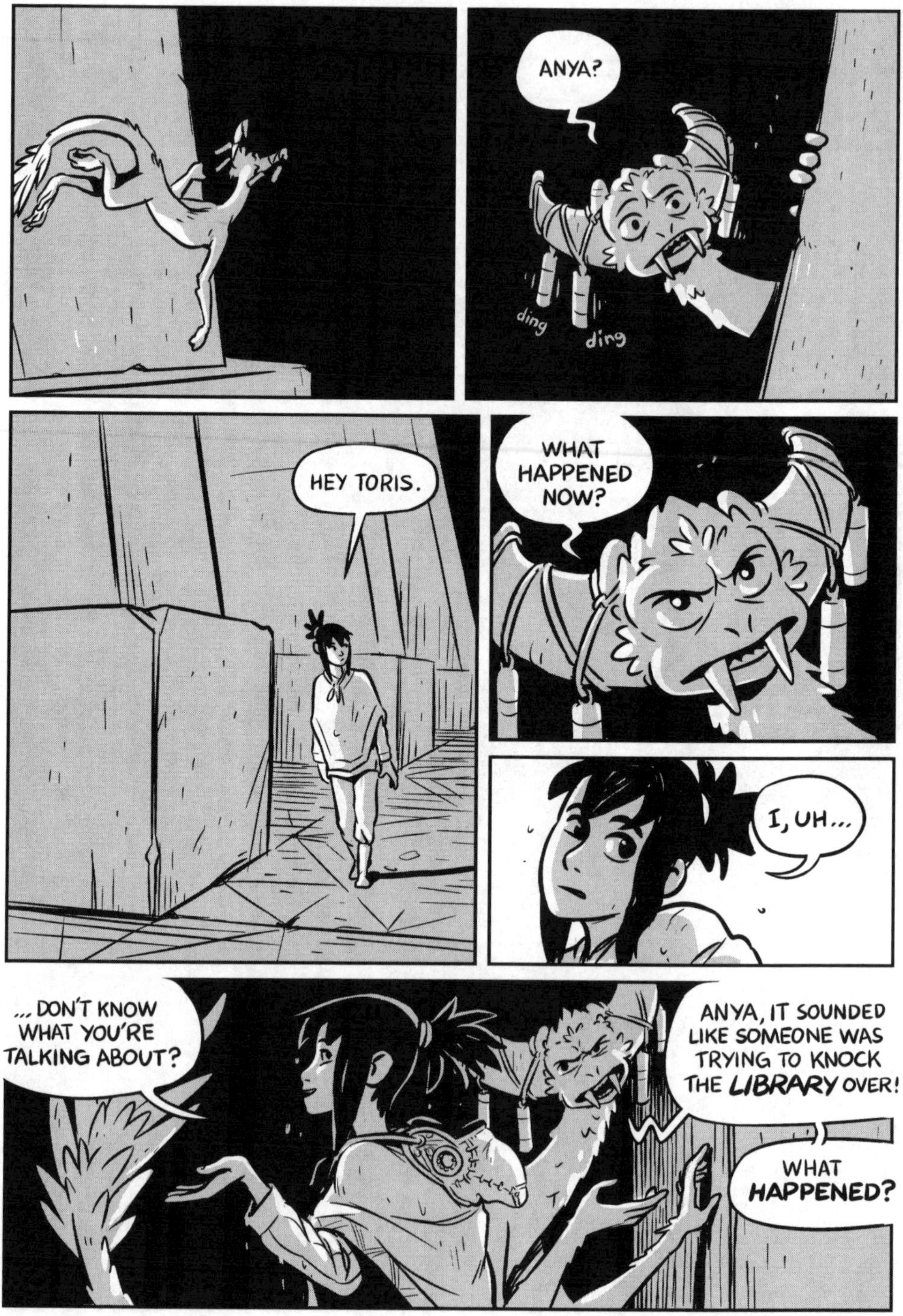
ANYA?
ding
ding
HEY TORIS.
WHAT HAPPENED NOW?
I, UH...
...DON'T KNOW WHAT YOU'RE TALKING ABOUT?
ANYA, IT SOUNDED LIKE SOMEONE WAS TRYING TO KNOCK THE LIBRARY OVER!
WHAT HAPPENED?

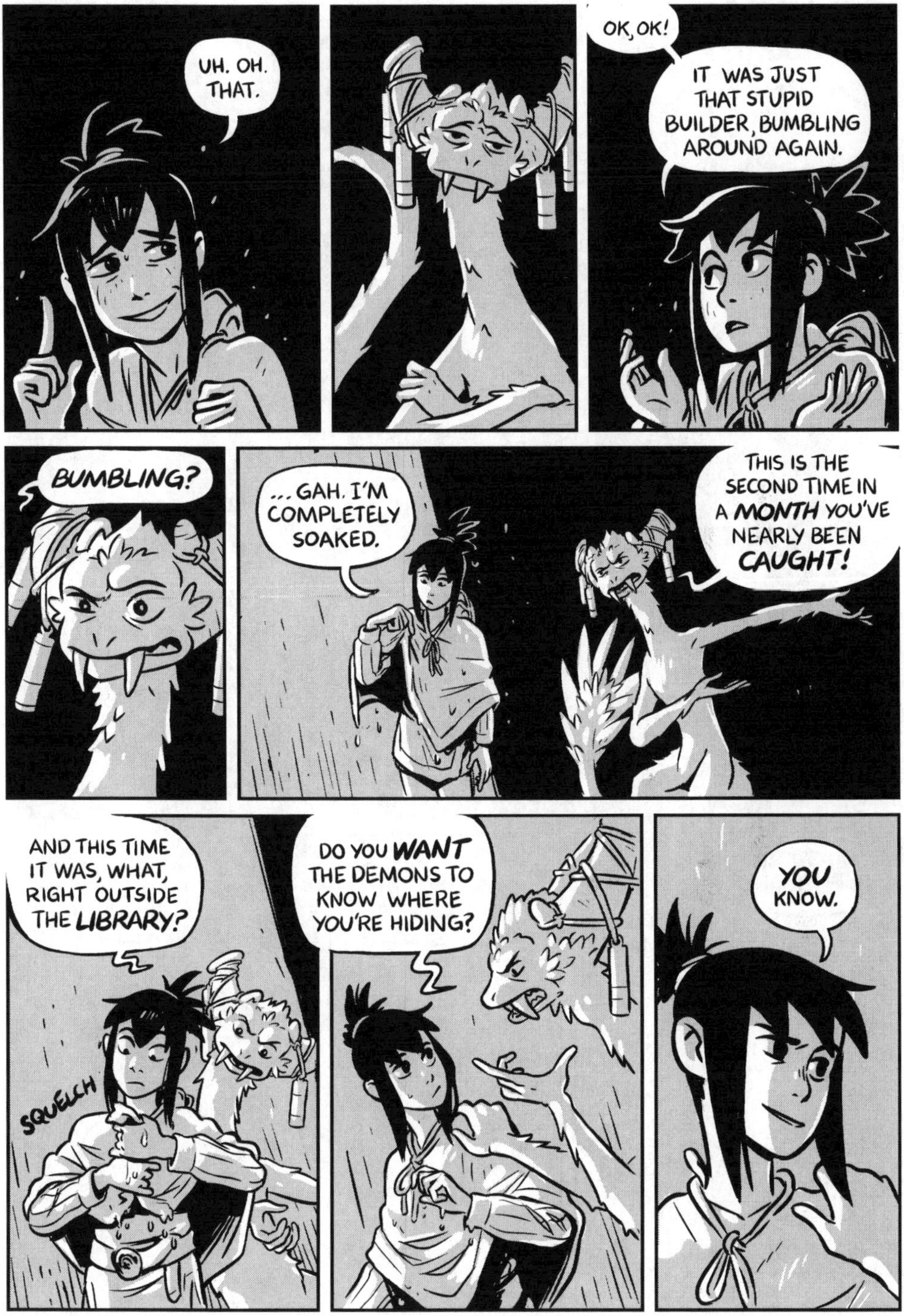
UH. OH. THAT.
OK, OK!
IT WAS JUST THAT STUPID BUILDER, BUMBLING AROUND AGAIN.
BUMBLING?
...GAH. I'M COMPLETELY SOAKED.
THIS IS THE SECOND TIME IN A MONTH YOU'VE NEARLY BEEN CAUGHT!
AND THIS TIME IT WAS, WHAT, RIGHT OUTSIDE THE LIBRARY?
SQUELCH
DO YOU WANT THE DEMONS TO KNOW WHERE YOU'RE HIDING?
YOU KNOW.

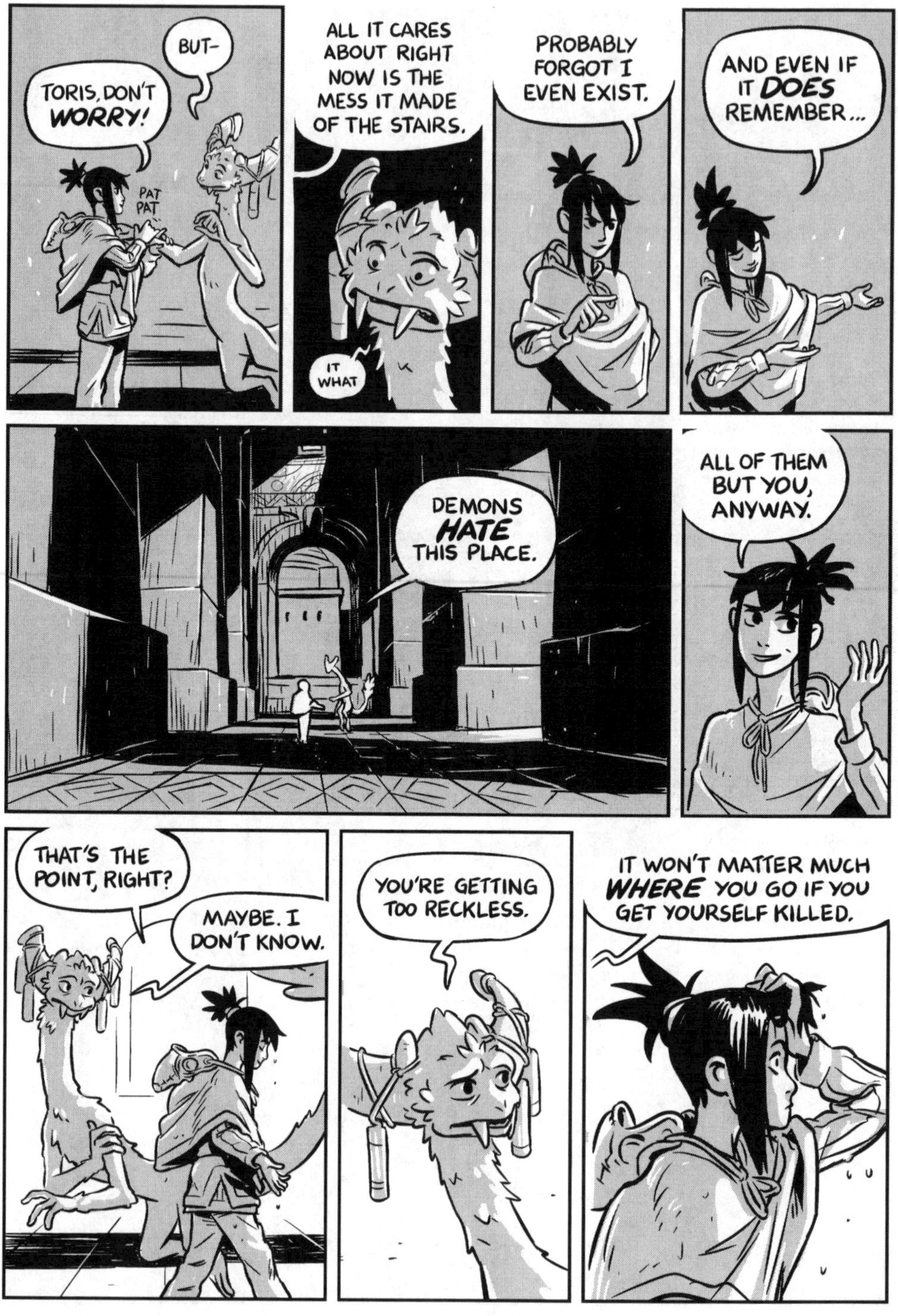
TORIS, DON'T WORRY!
BUT-
PAT PAT
ALL IT CARES ABOUT RIGHT NOW IS THE MESS IT MADE OF THE STAIRS.
IT WHAT
PROBABLY FORGOT I EVEN EXIST.
AND EVEN IF IT DOES REMEMBER...
DEMONS HATE THIS PLACE.
ALL OF THEM BUT YOU, ANYWAY.
THAT'S THE POINT, RIGHT?
MAYBE. I DON'T KNOW.
YOU'RE GETTING TOO RECKLESS.
IT WON'T MATTER MUCH WHERE YOU GO IF YOU GET YOURSELF KILLED.

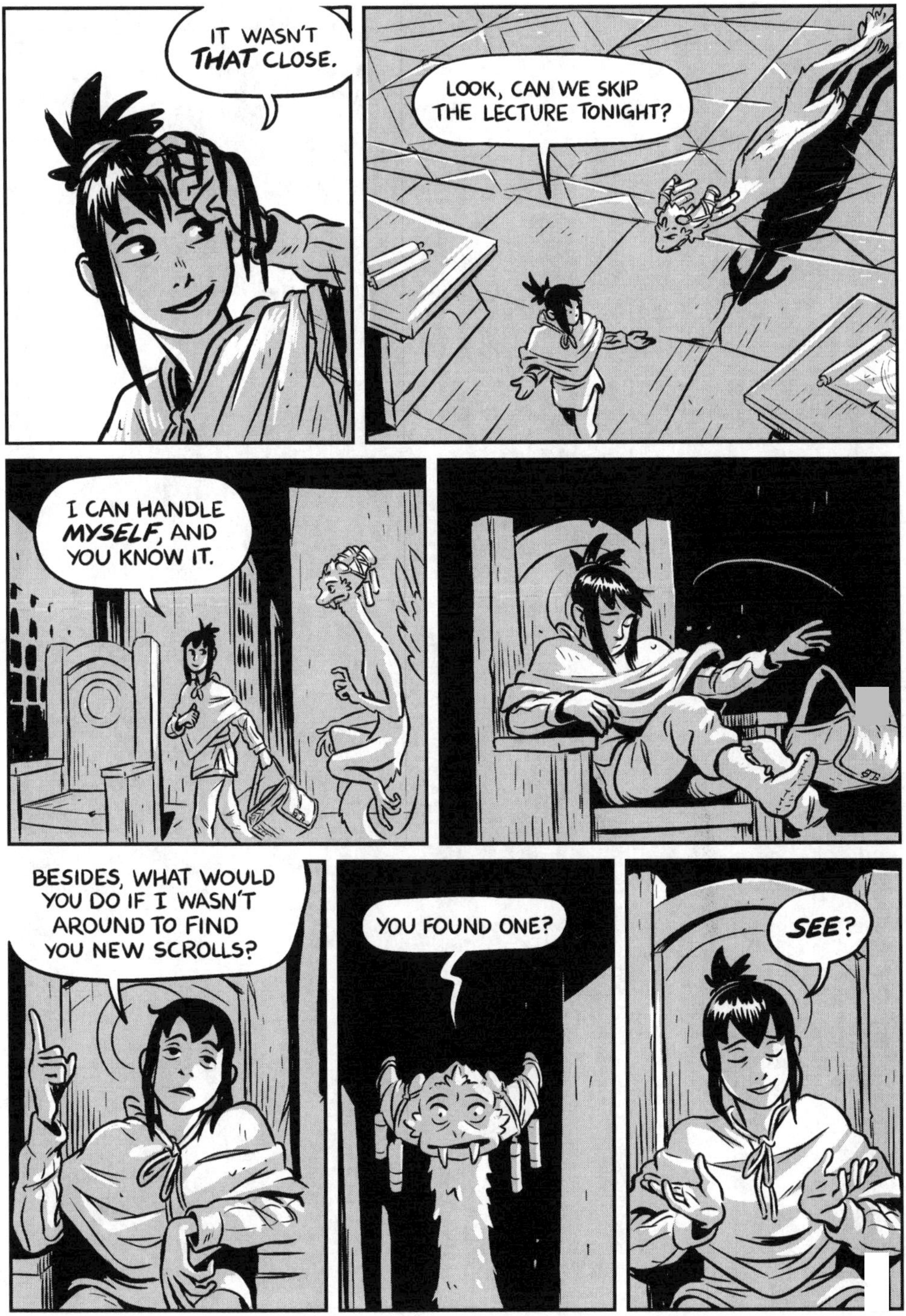
IT WASN'T THAT CLOSE.
LOOK, CAN WE SKIP THE LECTURE TONIGHT?
I CAN HANDLE MYSELF, AND YOU KNOW IT.
BESIDES, WHAT WOULD YOU DO IF I WASN'T AROUND TO FIND YOU NEW SCROLLS?
YOU FOUND ONE?
SEE?

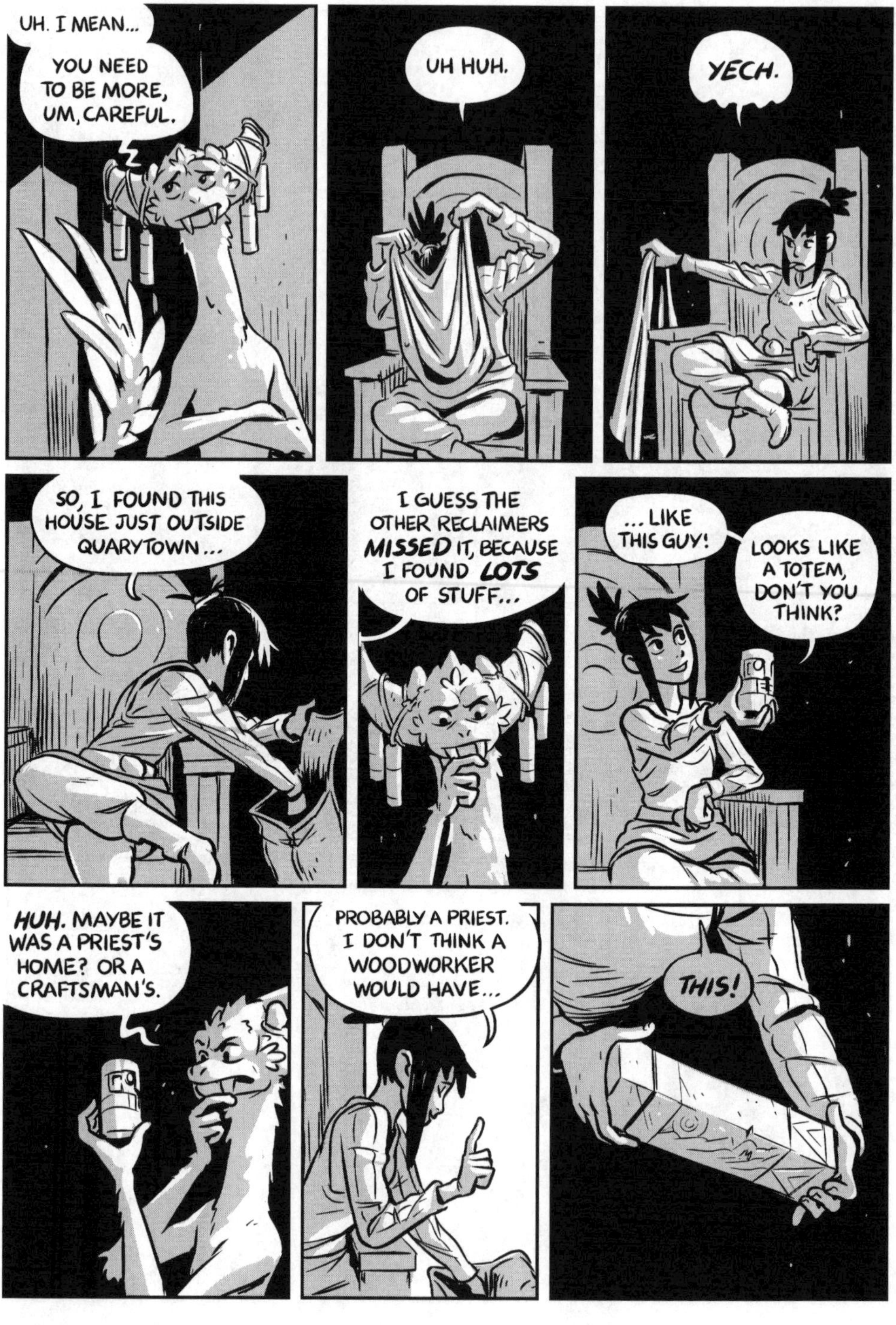
UH. I MEAN...
YOU NEED TO BE MORE, UM, CAREFUL.
UH HUH.
YECH.
SO, I FOUND THIS HOUSE JUST OUTSIDE QUARYTOWN...
I GUESS THE OTHER RECLAIMERS MISSED IT, BECAUSE I FOUND LOTS OF STUFF...
...LIKE THIS GUY!
LOOKS LIKE A TOTEM, DON'T YOU THINK?
HUH. MAYBE IT WAS A PRIEST'S HOME? OR A CRAFTSMAN'S.
PROBABLY A PRIEST. I DON'T THINK A WOODWORKER WOULD HAVE...
THIS!

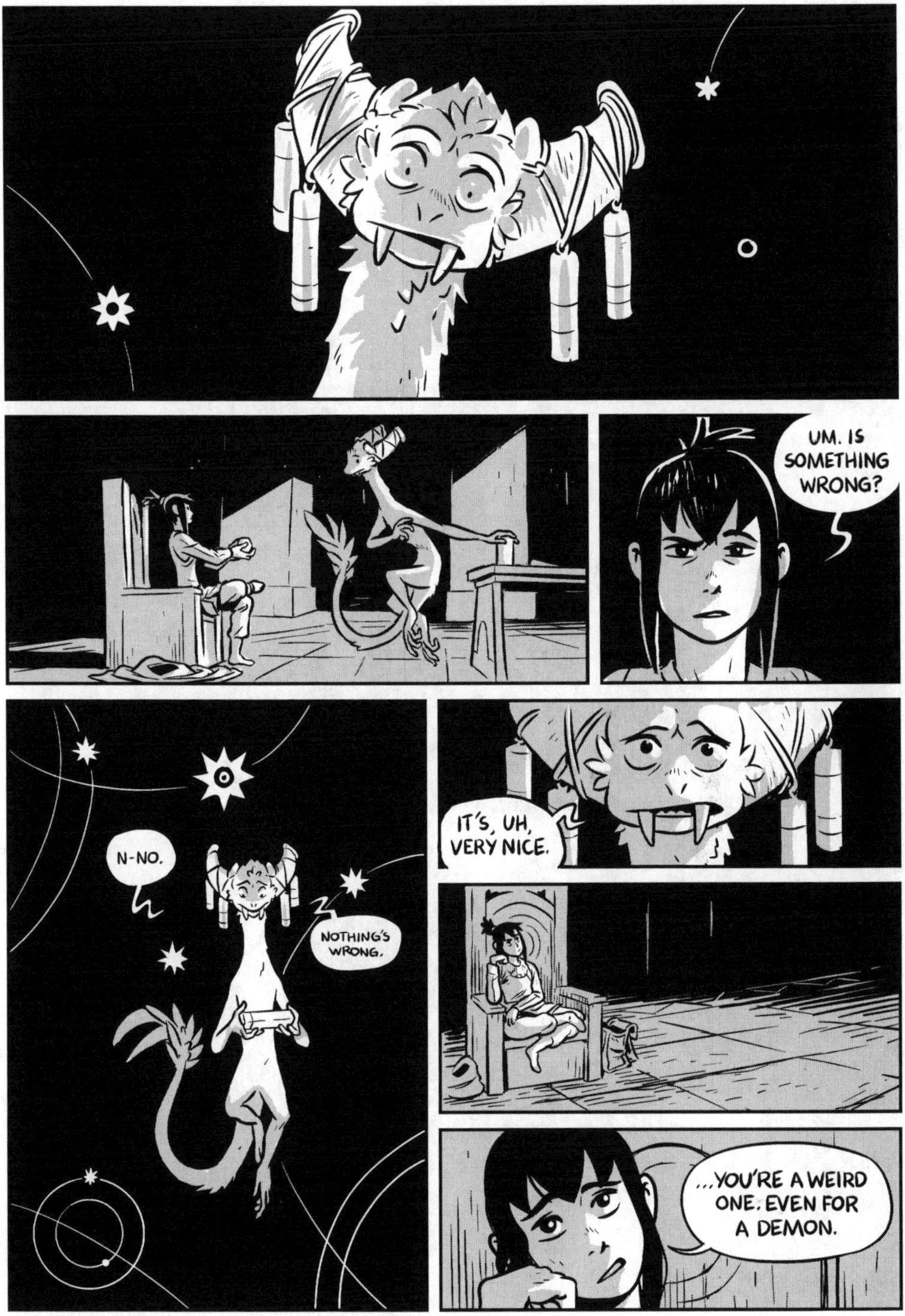
UM. IS SOMETHING WRONG?
N-NO.
NOTHING'S WRONG.
IT'S, UH, VERY NICE.
...YOU'RE A WEIRD ONE. EVEN FOR A DEMON.

ANY... ANYTHING ELSE?

JUST ONE.

I FOUND THIS BY THE SCROLL.

I THINK IT'S A *FOCUS STONE*.

YOU SEE ANYTHING? ANY SIGNS?

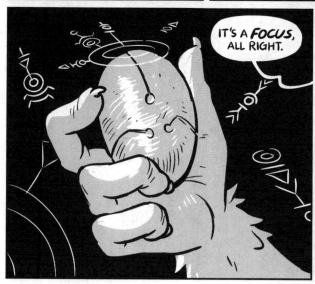

IT'S A *FOCUS*, ALL RIGHT.

THE SIGNS ARE HARD TO READ, BUT I THINK IT MAKES...ILLUSIONS OF SOMETHING. *BIRDS*, MAYBE.

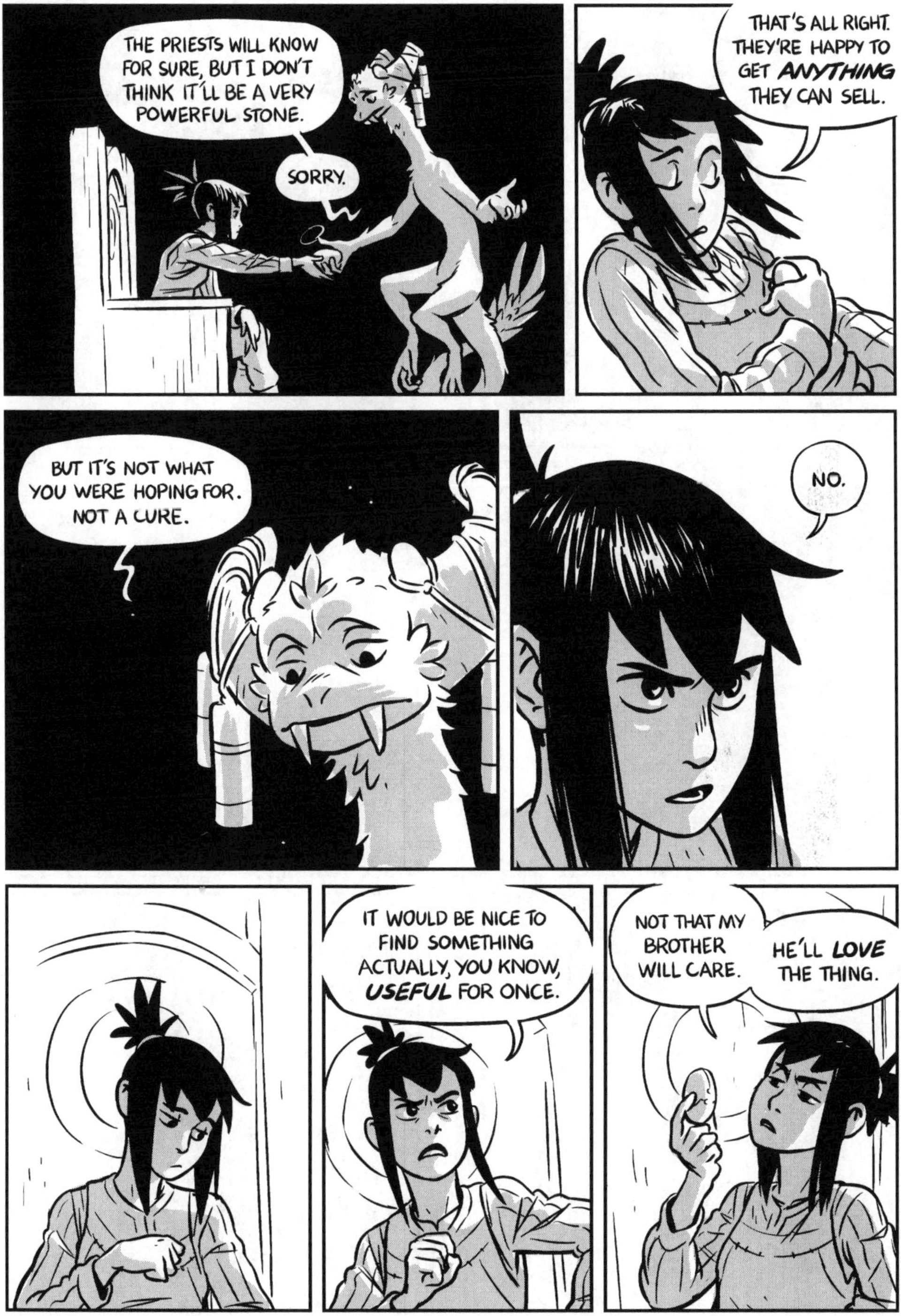
THE PRIESTS WILL KNOW FOR SURE, BUT I DON'T THINK IT'LL BE A VERY POWERFUL STONE.
SORRY.
THAT'S ALL RIGHT. THEY'RE HAPPY TO GET *ANYTHING* THEY CAN SELL.
BUT IT'S NOT WHAT YOU WERE HOPING FOR. NOT A CURE.
NO.
IT WOULD BE NICE TO FIND SOMETHING ACTUALLY, YOU KNOW, *USEFUL* FOR ONCE.
NOT THAT MY BROTHER WILL CARE.
HE'LL *LOVE* THE THING.

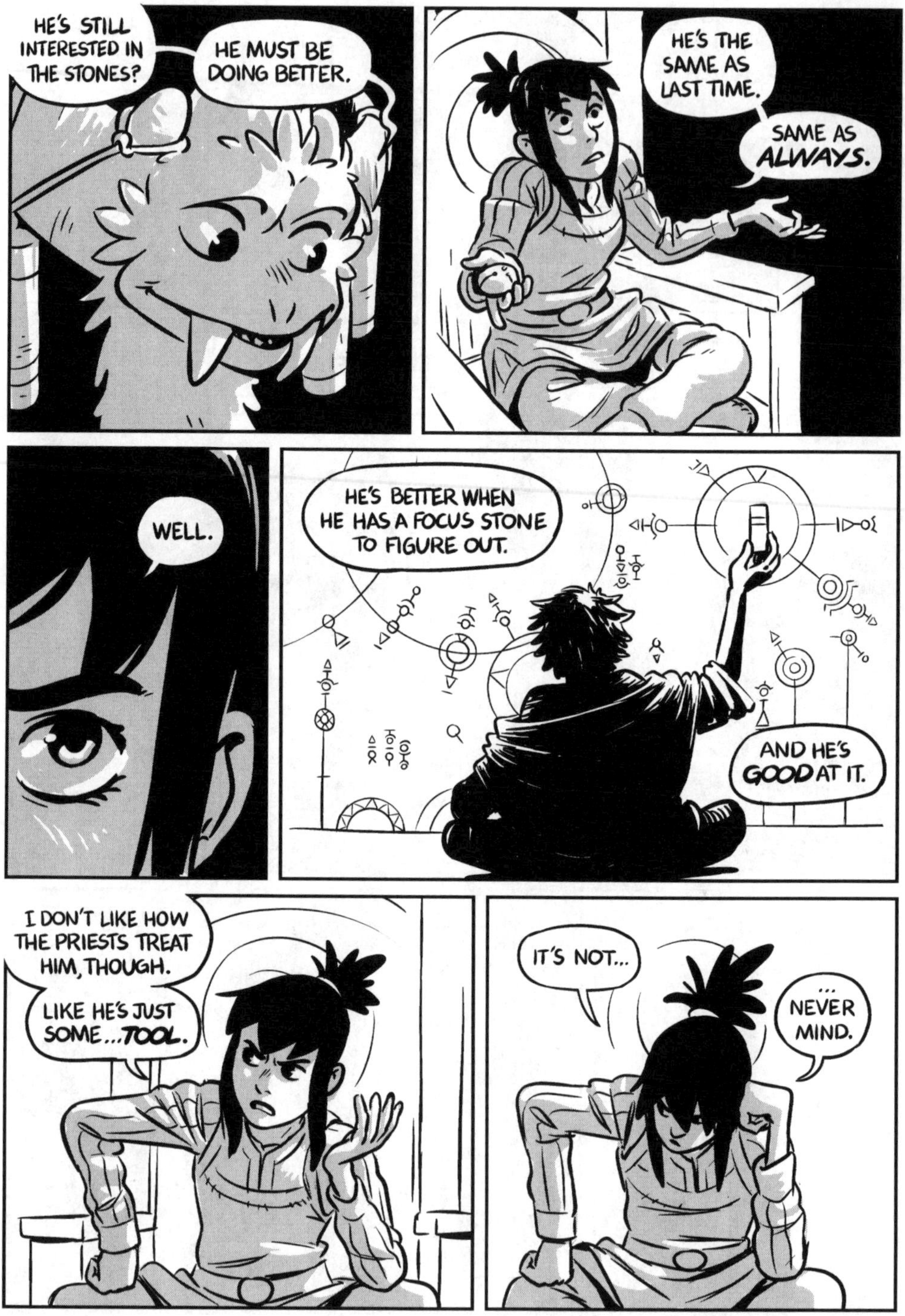
HE'S STILL INTERESTED IN THE STONES?
HE MUST BE DOING BETTER.
HE'S THE SAME AS LAST TIME.
SAME AS ALWAYS.
WELL.
HE'S BETTER WHEN HE HAS A FOCUS STONE TO FIGURE OUT.
AND HE'S GOOD AT IT.
I DON'T LIKE HOW THE PRIESTS TREAT HIM, THOUGH.
LIKE HE'S JUST SOME...TOOL.
IT'S NOT...
... NEVER MIND.

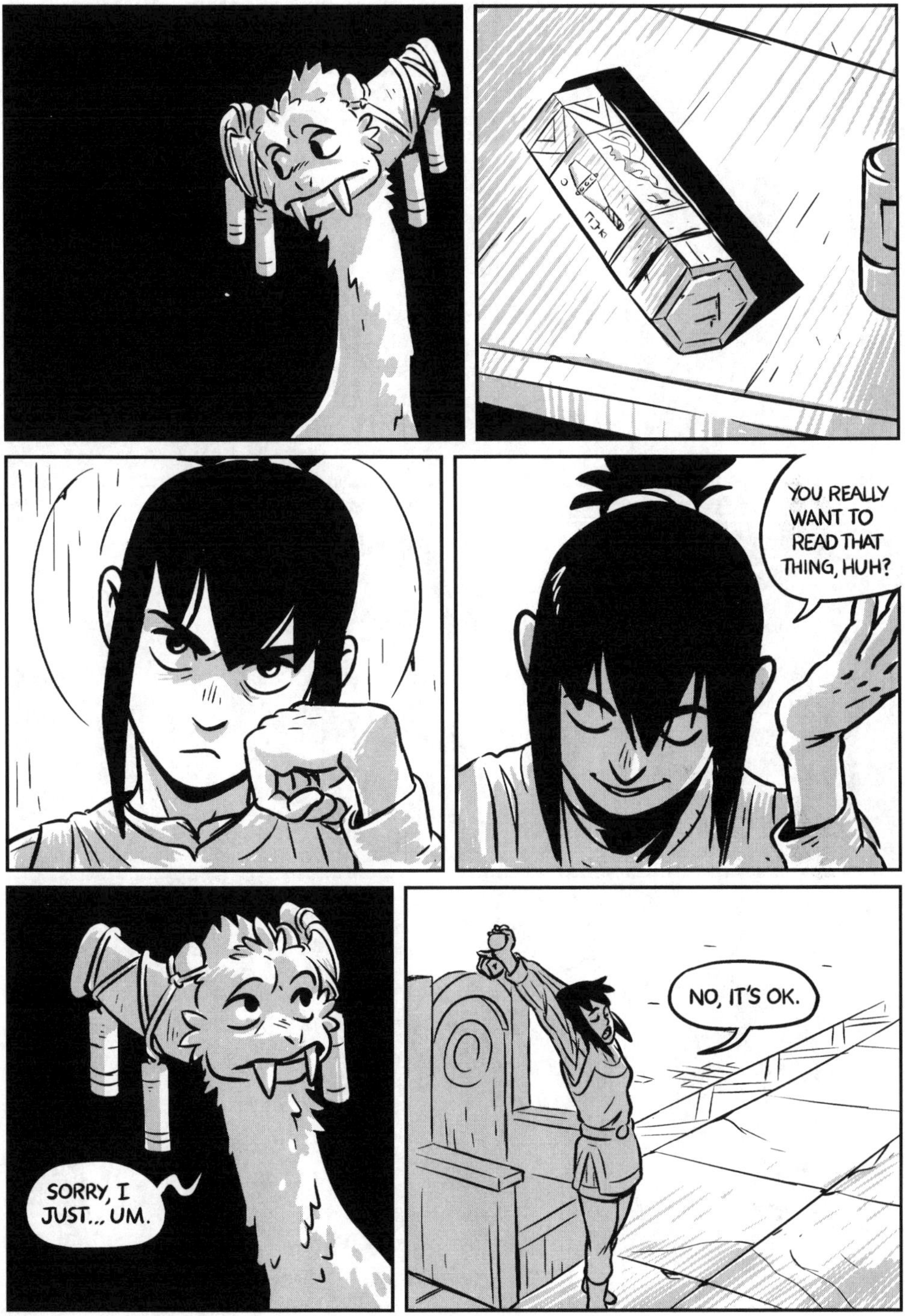
YOU REALLY WANT TO READ THAT THING, HUH?
SORRY, I JUST... UM.
NO, IT'S OK.

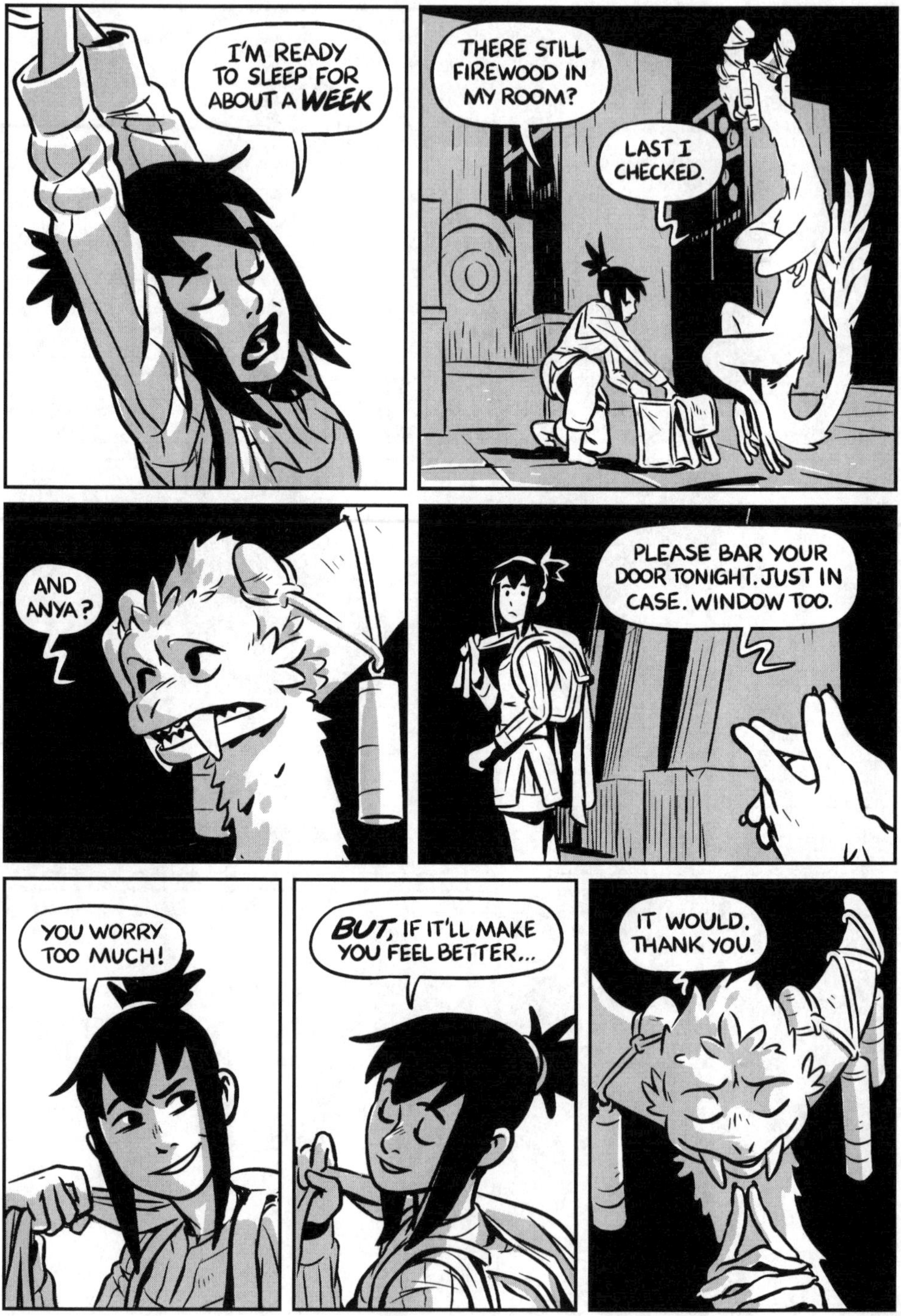
I'M READY TO SLEEP FOR ABOUT A WEEK
THERE STILL FIREWOOD IN MY ROOM?
LAST I CHECKED.
AND ANYA?
PLEASE BAR YOUR DOOR TONIGHT. JUST IN CASE. WINDOW TOO.
YOU WORRY TOO MUCH!
BUT, IF IT'LL MAKE YOU FEEL BETTER...
IT WOULD. THANK YOU.

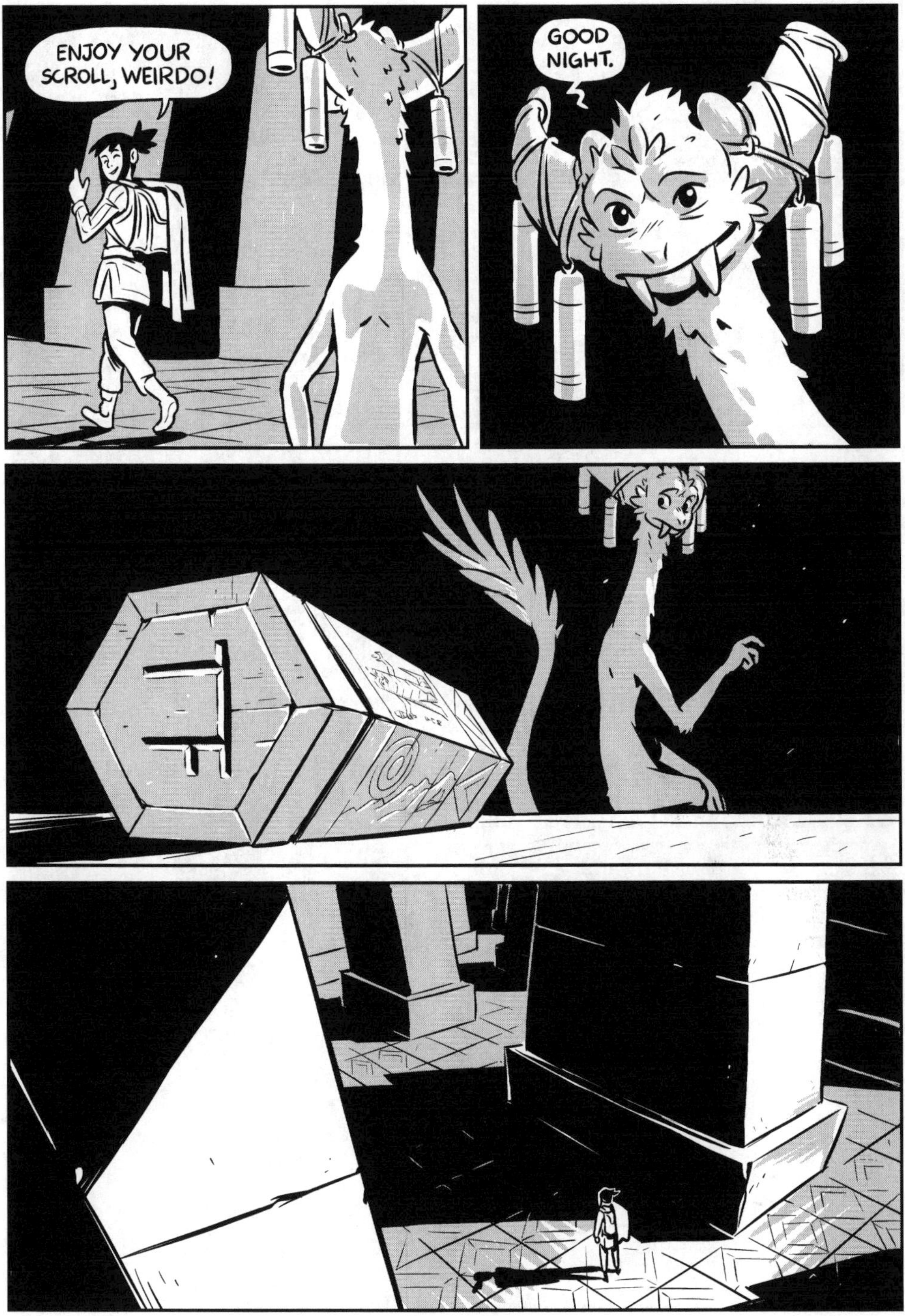
ENJOY YOUR SCROLL, WEIRDO!
GOOD NIGHT.

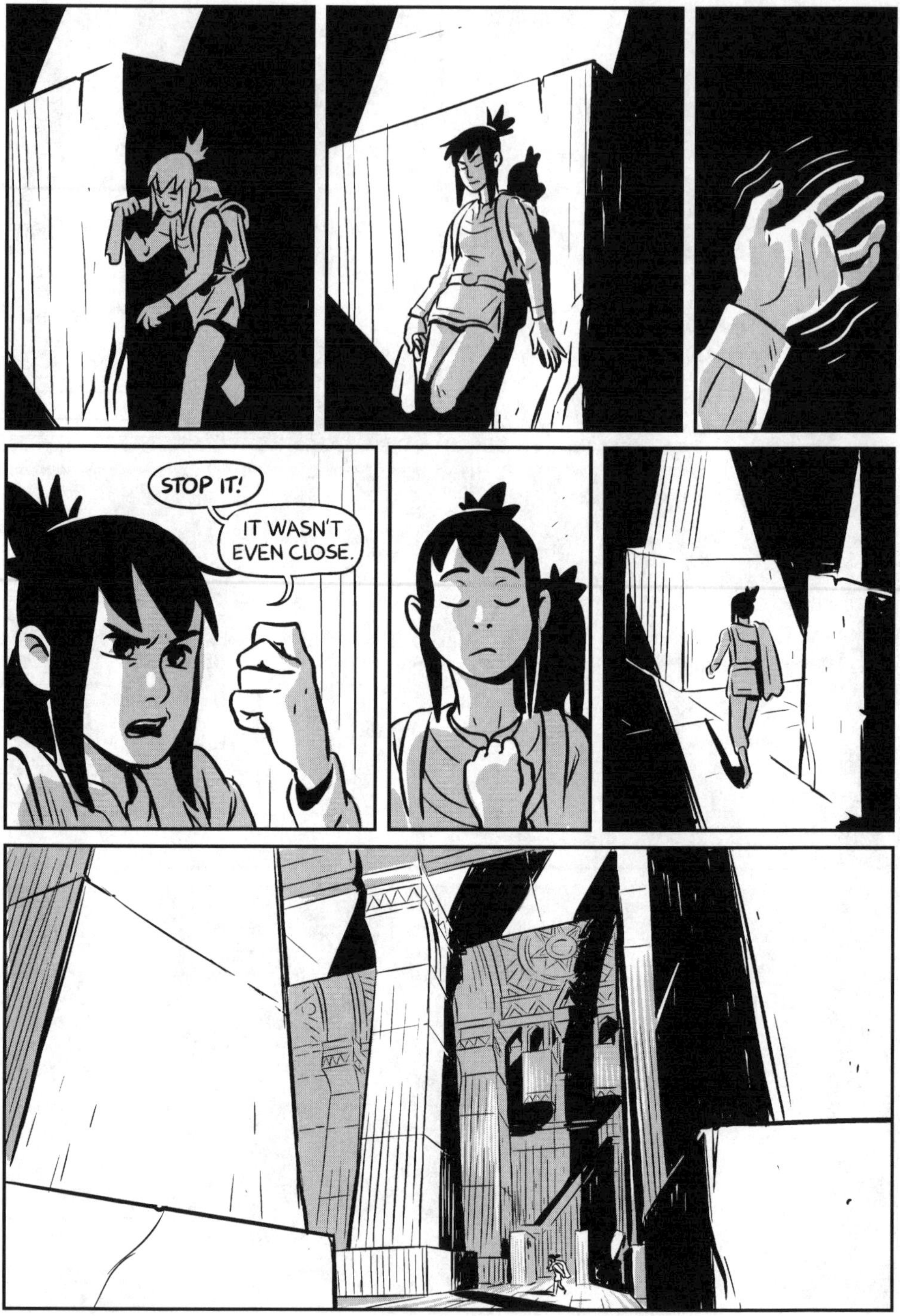
STOP IT!
IT WASN'T EVEN CLOSE.

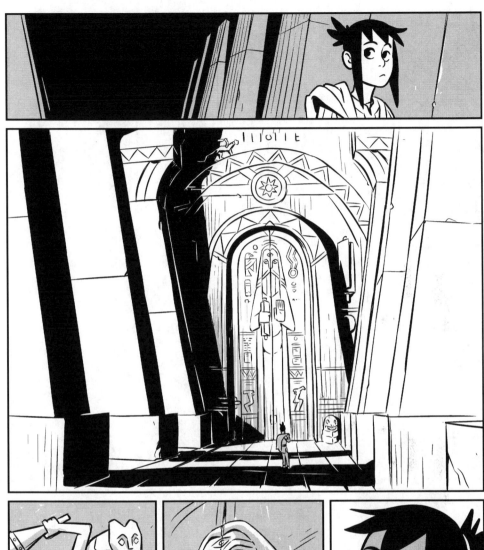

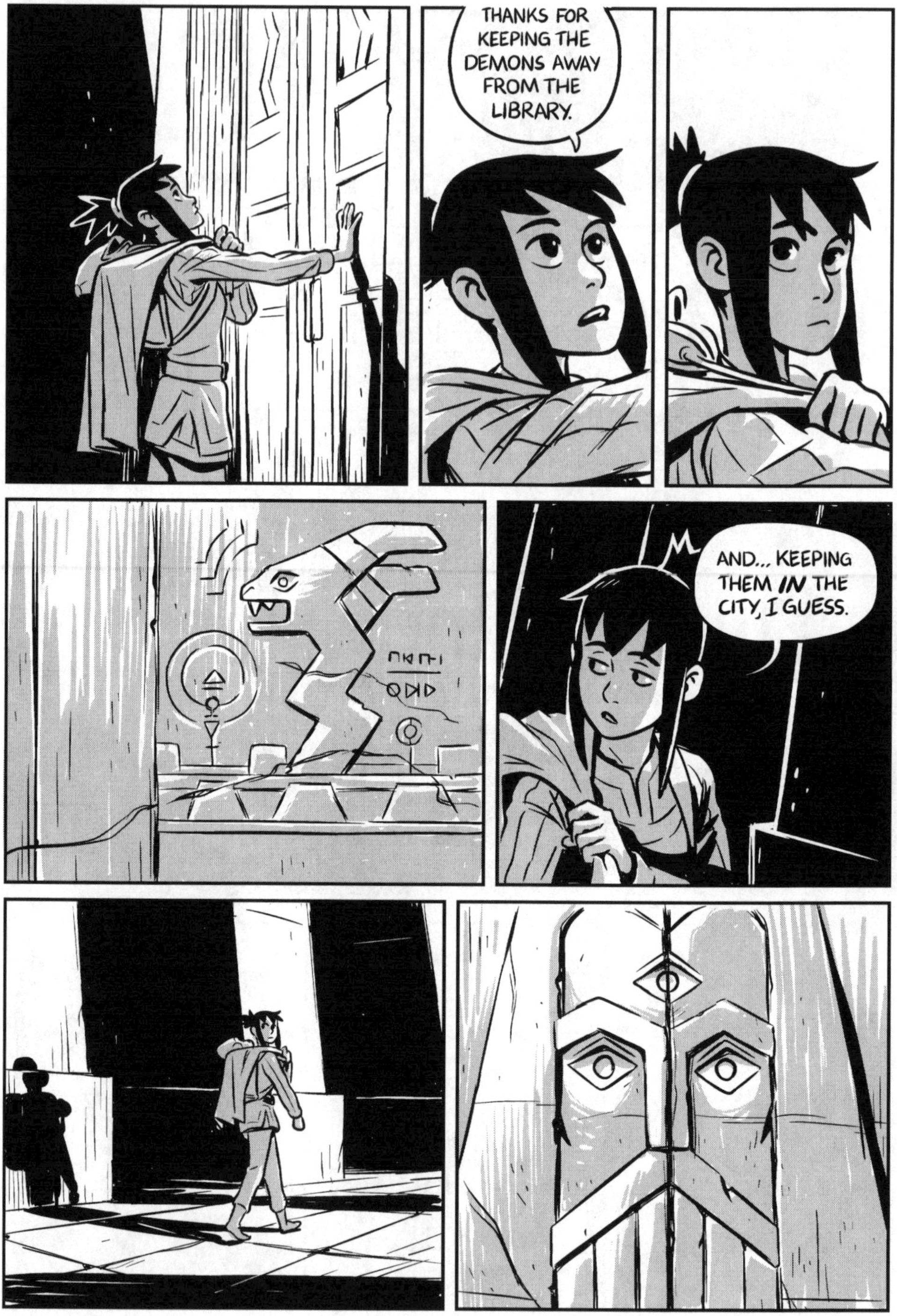
THANKS FOR KEEPING THE DEMONS AWAY FROM THE LIBRARY.
AND... KEEPING THEM IN THE CITY, I GUESS.

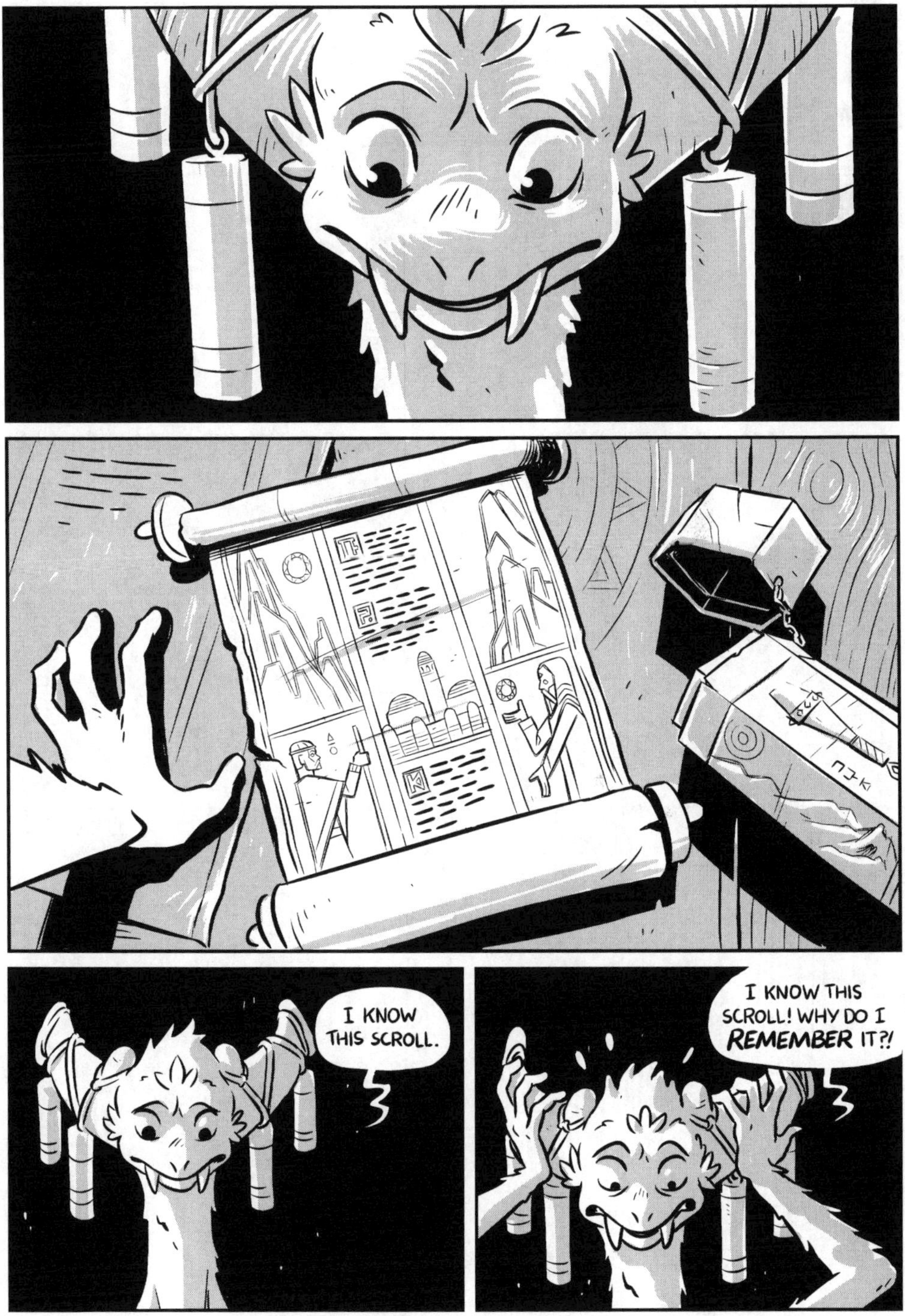
I KNOW THIS SCROLL.
I KNOW THIS SCROLL! WHY DO I *REMEMBER* IT?!

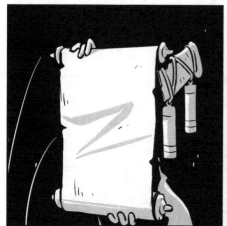

...NOTHING SPECIAL, JUST THE **STONEBREAKER** STORY. READ IT...

...READ IT A MILLION...

TONEBREAKER BROVGHT DOWN HIS MIGHTY CLVB, AND SHOOK THE EARTH ASVNDER·

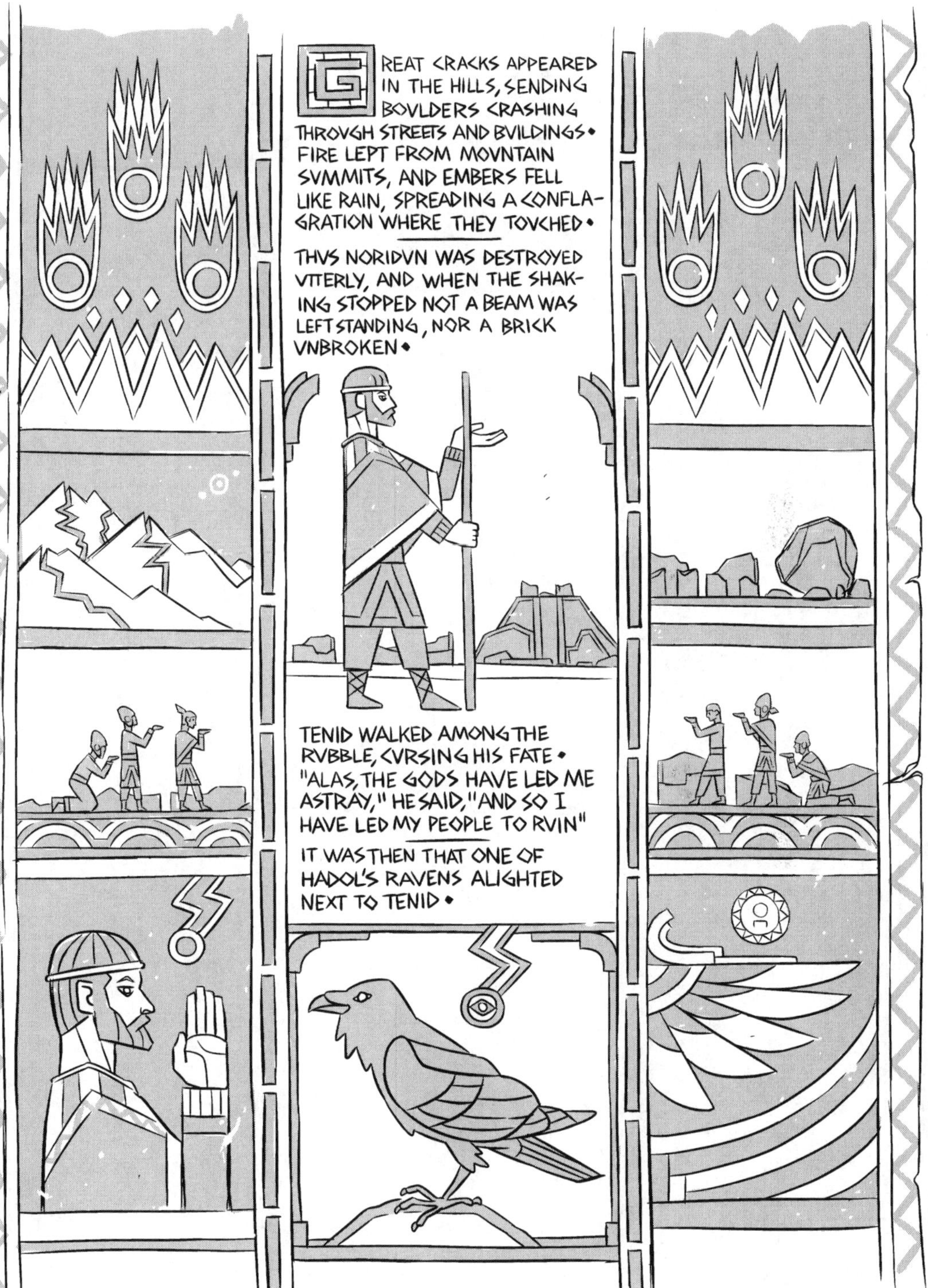
GREAT CRACKS APPEARED IN THE HILLS, SENDING BOVLDERS CRASHING THROVGH STREETS AND BVILDINGS• FIRE LEPT FROM MOVNTAIN SVMMITS, AND EMBERS FELL LIKE RAIN, SPREADING A CONFLAGRATION WHERE THEY TOVCHED•
THVS NORIDVN WAS DESTROYED VTTERLY, AND WHEN THE SHAKING STOPPED NOT A BEAM WAS LEFT STANDING, NOR A BRICK VNBROKEN•
TENID WALKED AMONG THE RVBBLE, CVRSING HIS FATE• "ALAS, THE GODS HAVE LED ME ASTRAY," HE SAID, "AND SO I HAVE LED MY PEOPLE TO RVIN"
IT WAS THEN THAT ONE OF HADOL'S RAVENS ALIGHTED NEXT TO TENID•

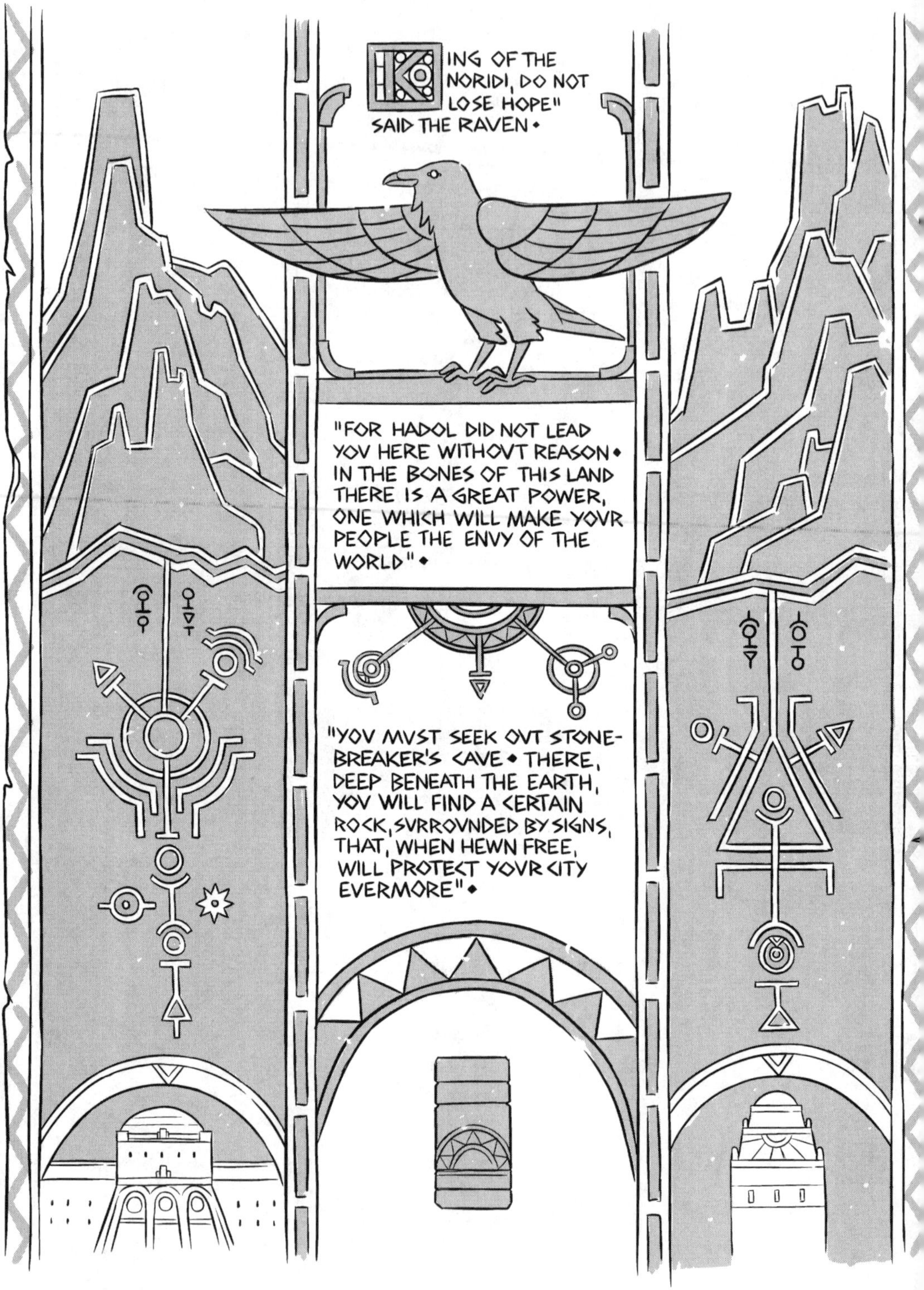
"KING OF THE NORIDI, DO NOT LOSE HOPE" SAID THE RAVEN •
"FOR HADOL DID NOT LEAD YOU HERE WITHOUT REASON • IN THE BONES OF THIS LAND THERE IS A GREAT POWER, ONE WHICH WILL MAKE YOUR PEOPLE THE ENVY OF THE WORLD" •
"YOU MUST SEEK OUT STONE-BREAKER'S CAVE • THERE, DEEP BENEATH THE EARTH, YOU WILL FIND A CERTAIN ROCK, SURROUNDED BY SIGNS, THAT, WHEN HEWN FREE, WILL PROTECT YOUR CITY EVERMORE" •

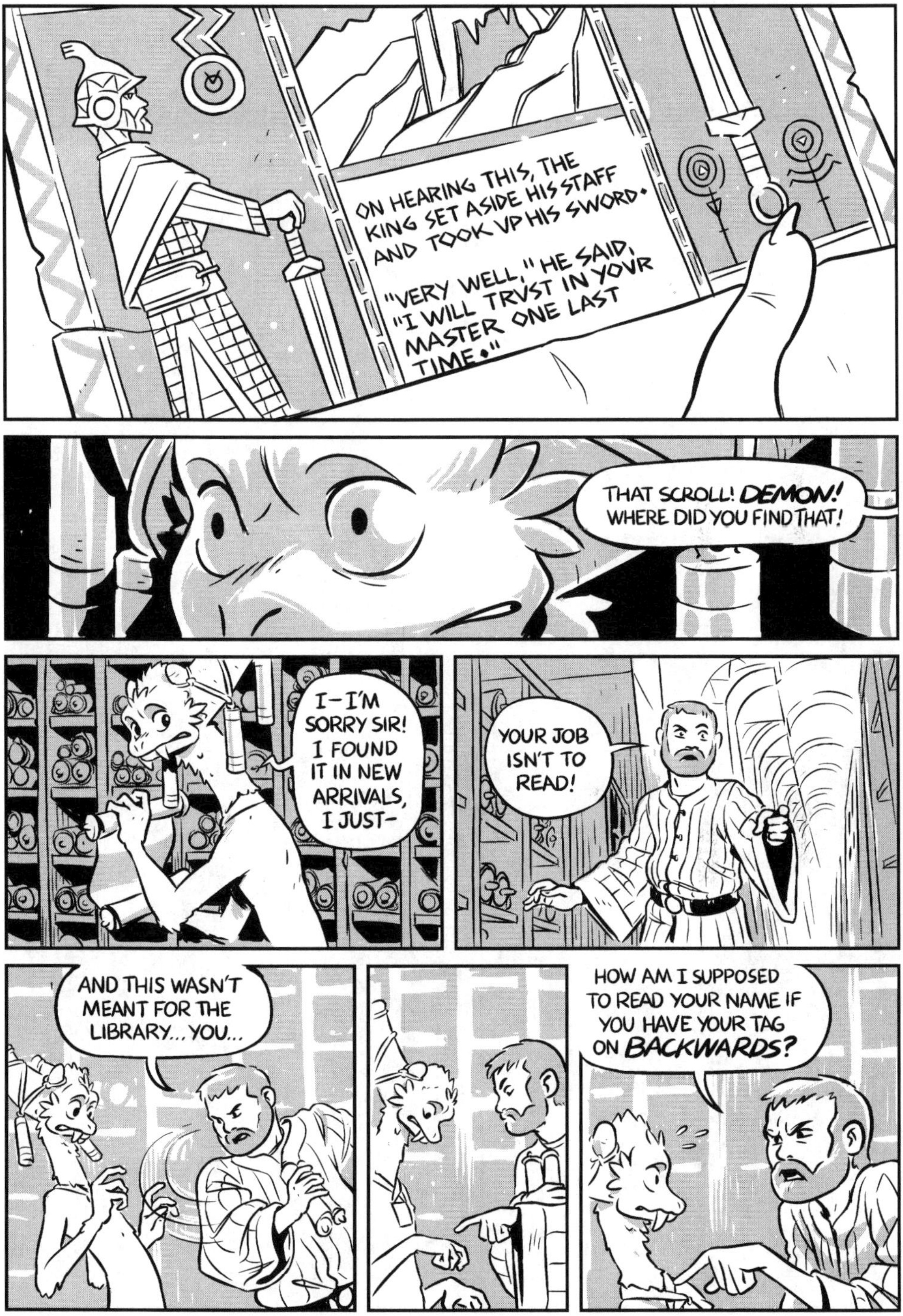
ON HEARING THIS, THE KING SET ASIDE HIS STAFF AND TOOK UP HIS SWORD.
"VERY WELL," HE SAID, "I WILL TRUST IN YOUR MASTER ONE LAST TIME."
THAT SCROLL! DEMON! WHERE DID YOU FIND THAT!
I-I'M SORRY SIR! I FOUND IT IN NEW ARRIVALS, I JUST-
YOUR JOB ISN'T TO READ!
AND THIS WASN'T MEANT FOR THE LIBRARY... YOU...
HOW AM I SUPPOSED TO READ YOUR NAME IF YOU HAVE YOUR TAG ON BACKWARDS?

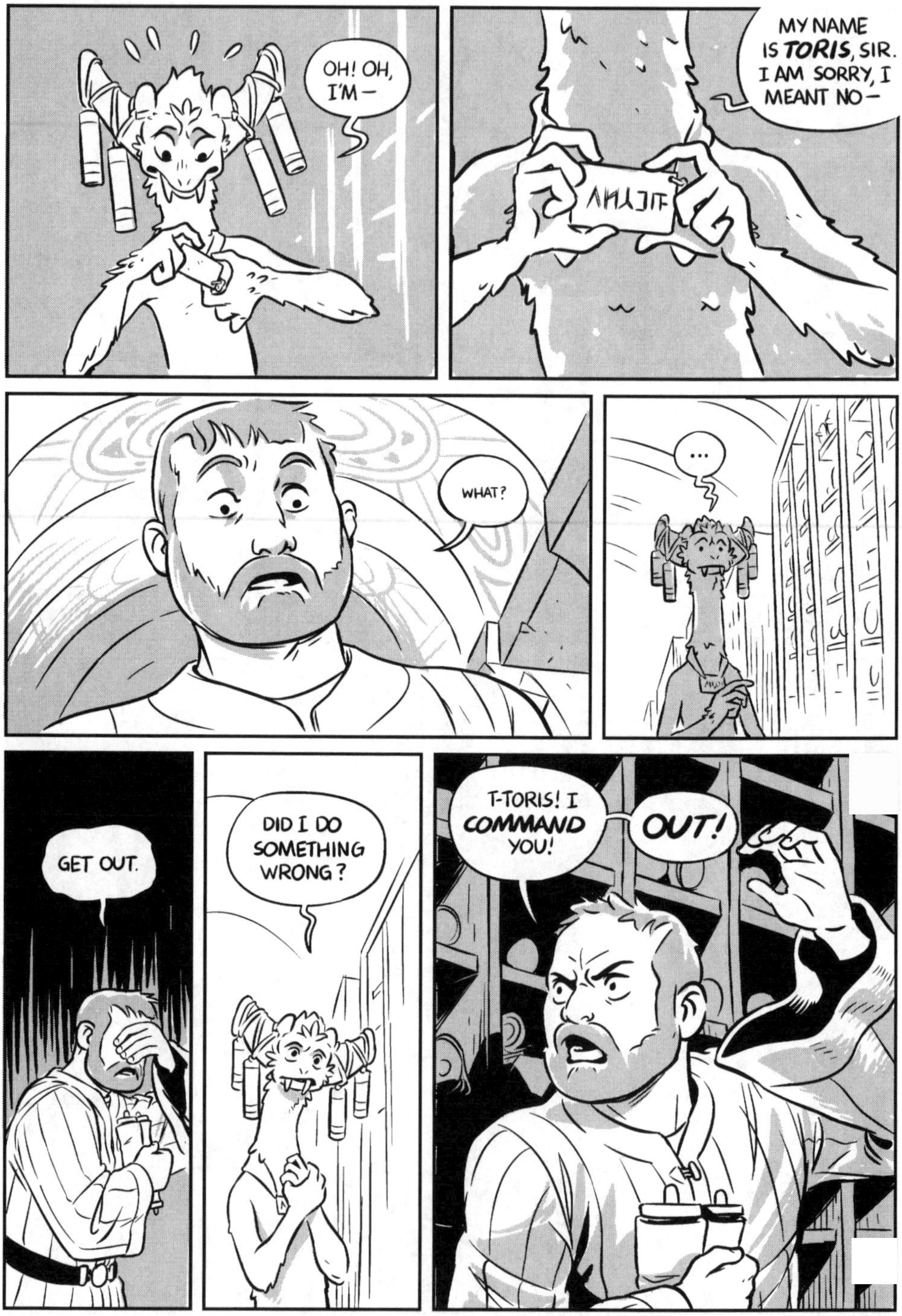
OH! OH, I'M—
MY NAME IS **TORIS**, SIR. I AM SORRY, I MEANT NO—
WHAT?
...
GET OUT.
DID I DO SOMETHING WRONG?
T-TORIS! I **COMMAND** YOU!
OUT!

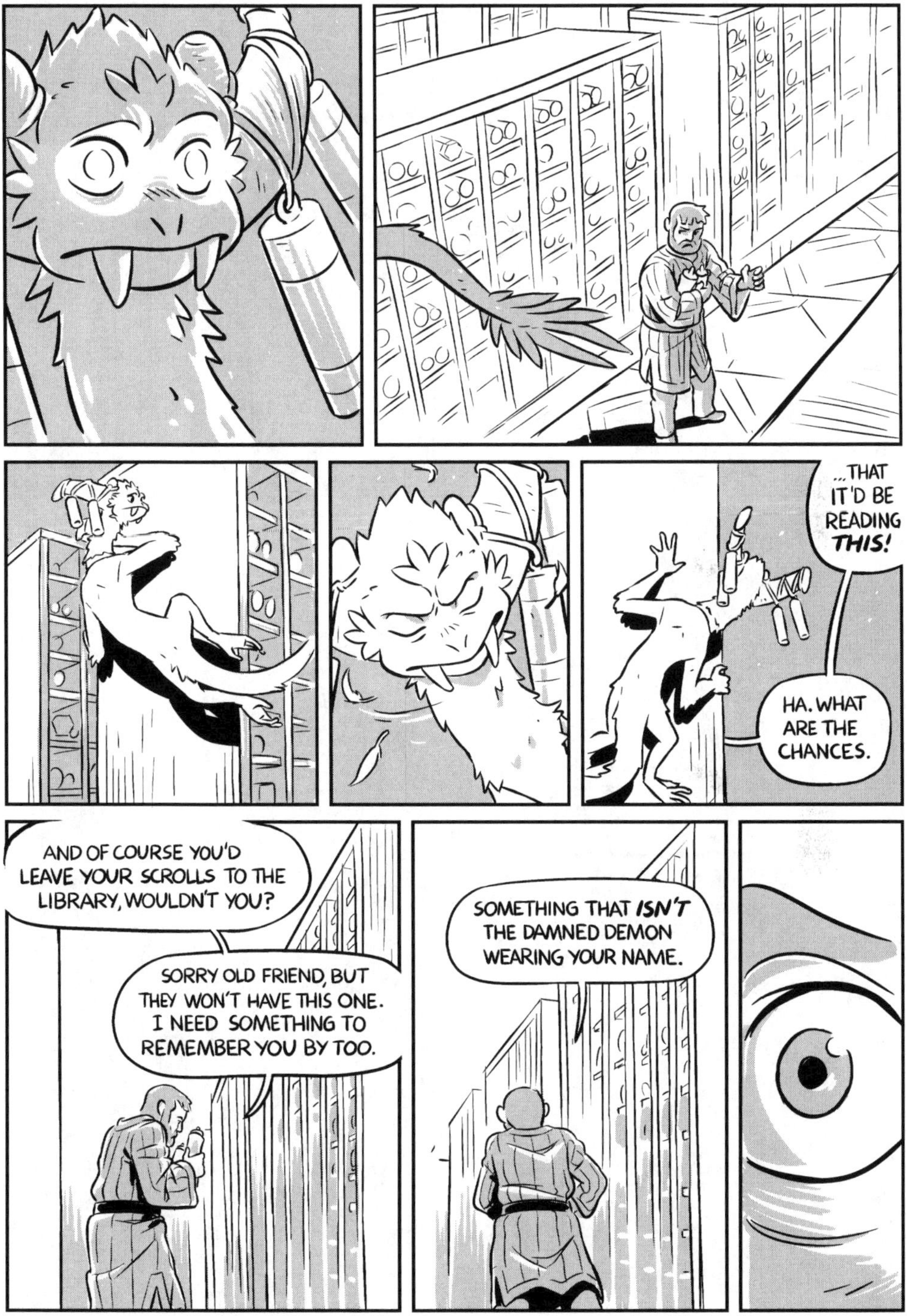
...THAT IT'D BE READING **THIS!**
HA. WHAT ARE THE CHANCES.
AND OF COURSE YOU'D LEAVE YOUR SCROLLS TO THE LIBRARY, WOULDN'T YOU?
SORRY OLD FRIEND, BUT THEY WON'T HAVE THIS ONE. I NEED SOMETHING TO REMEMBER YOU BY TOO.
SOMETHING THAT ***ISN'T*** THE DAMNED DEMON WEARING YOUR NAME.

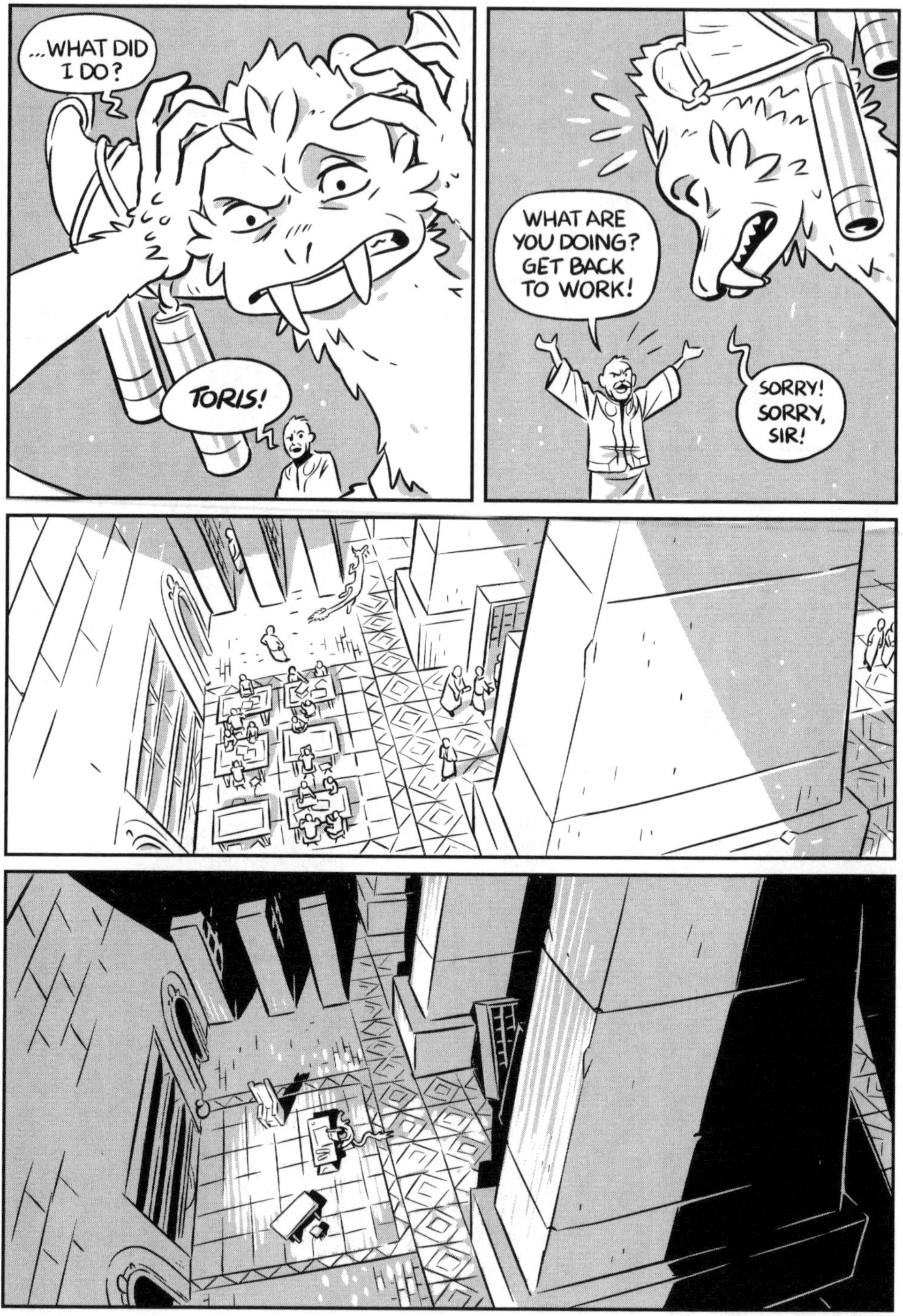
...WHAT DID I DO?
TORIS!
WHAT ARE YOU DOING? GET BACK TO WORK!
SORRY! SORRY, SIR!

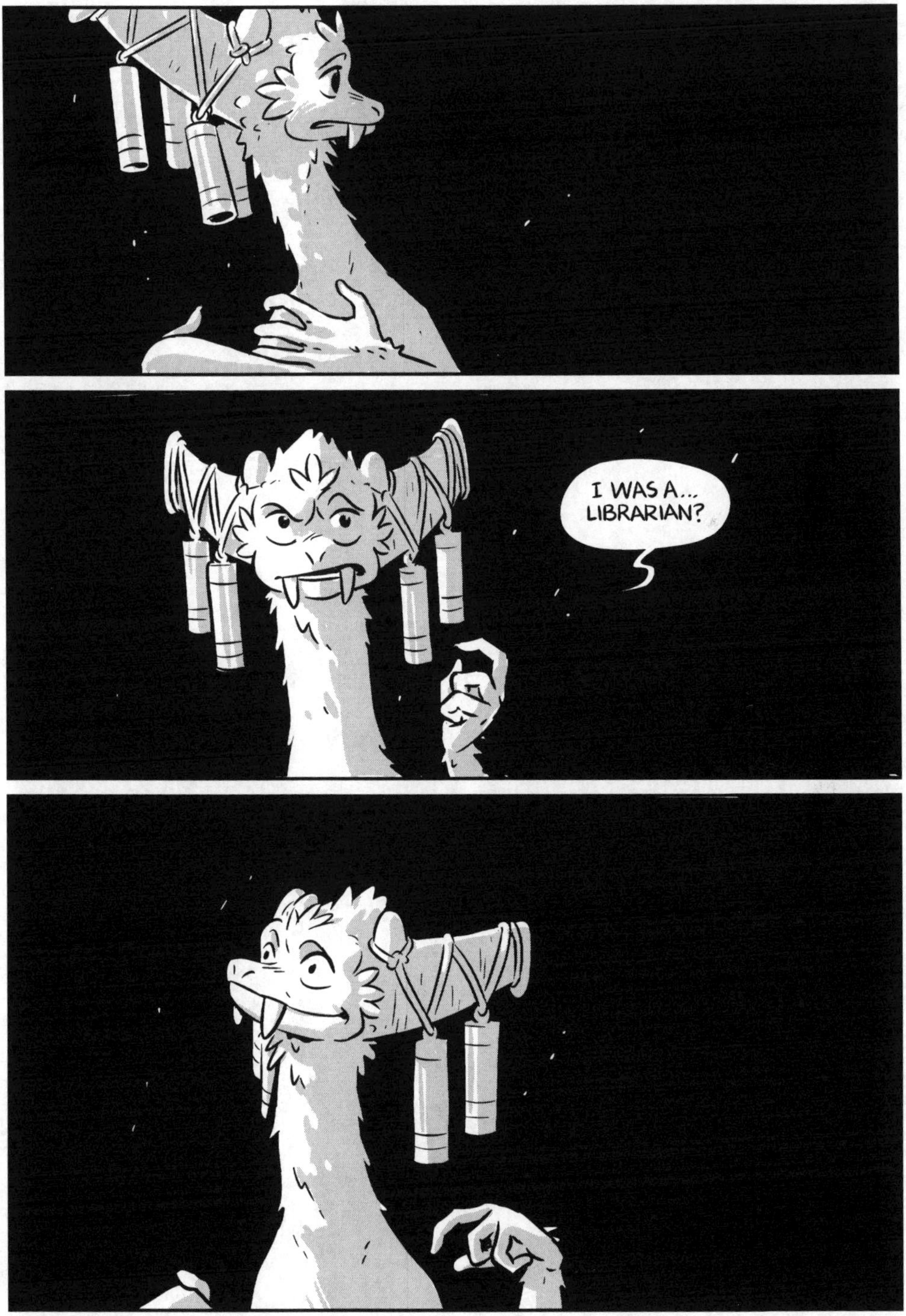
I WAS A... LIBRARIAN?

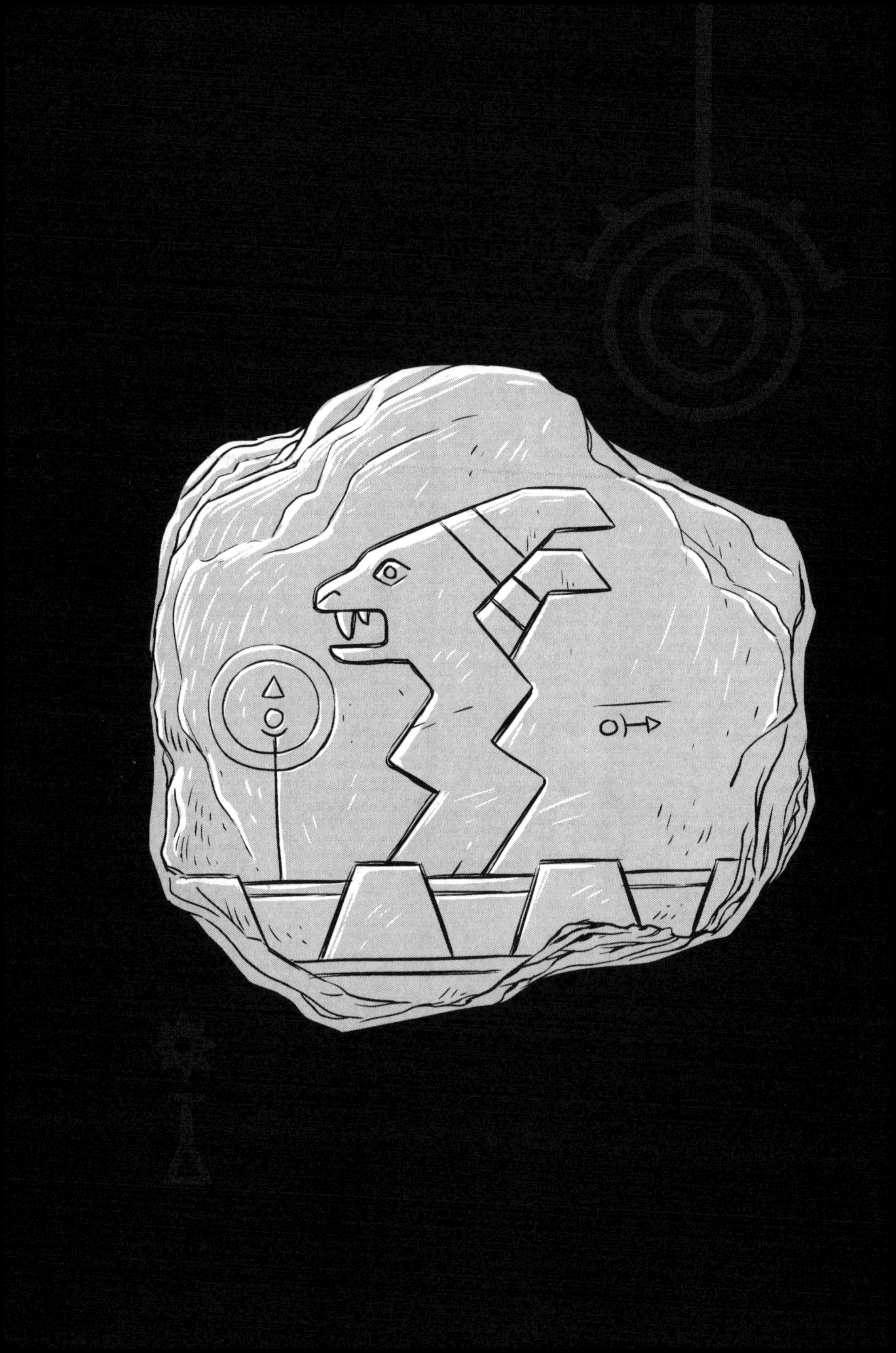

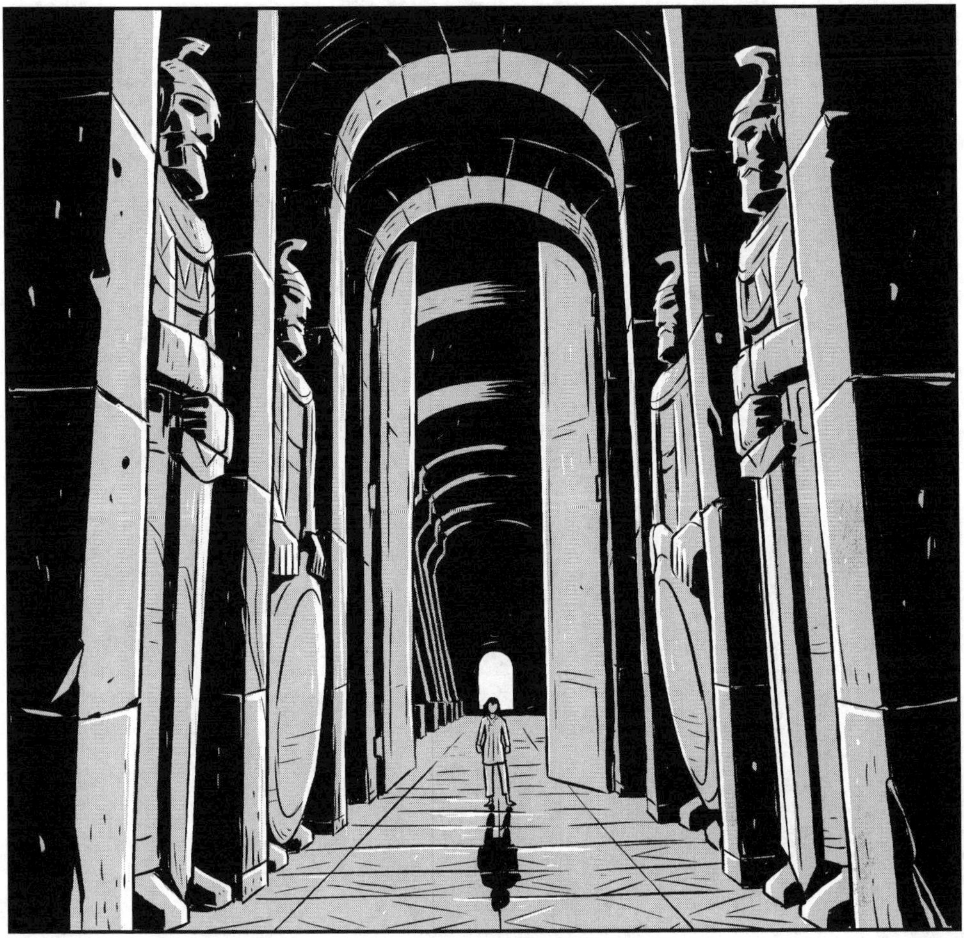

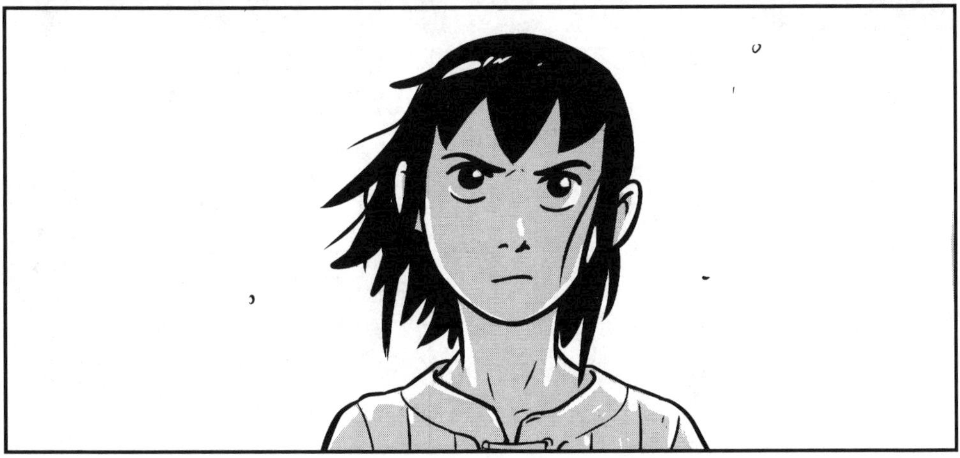

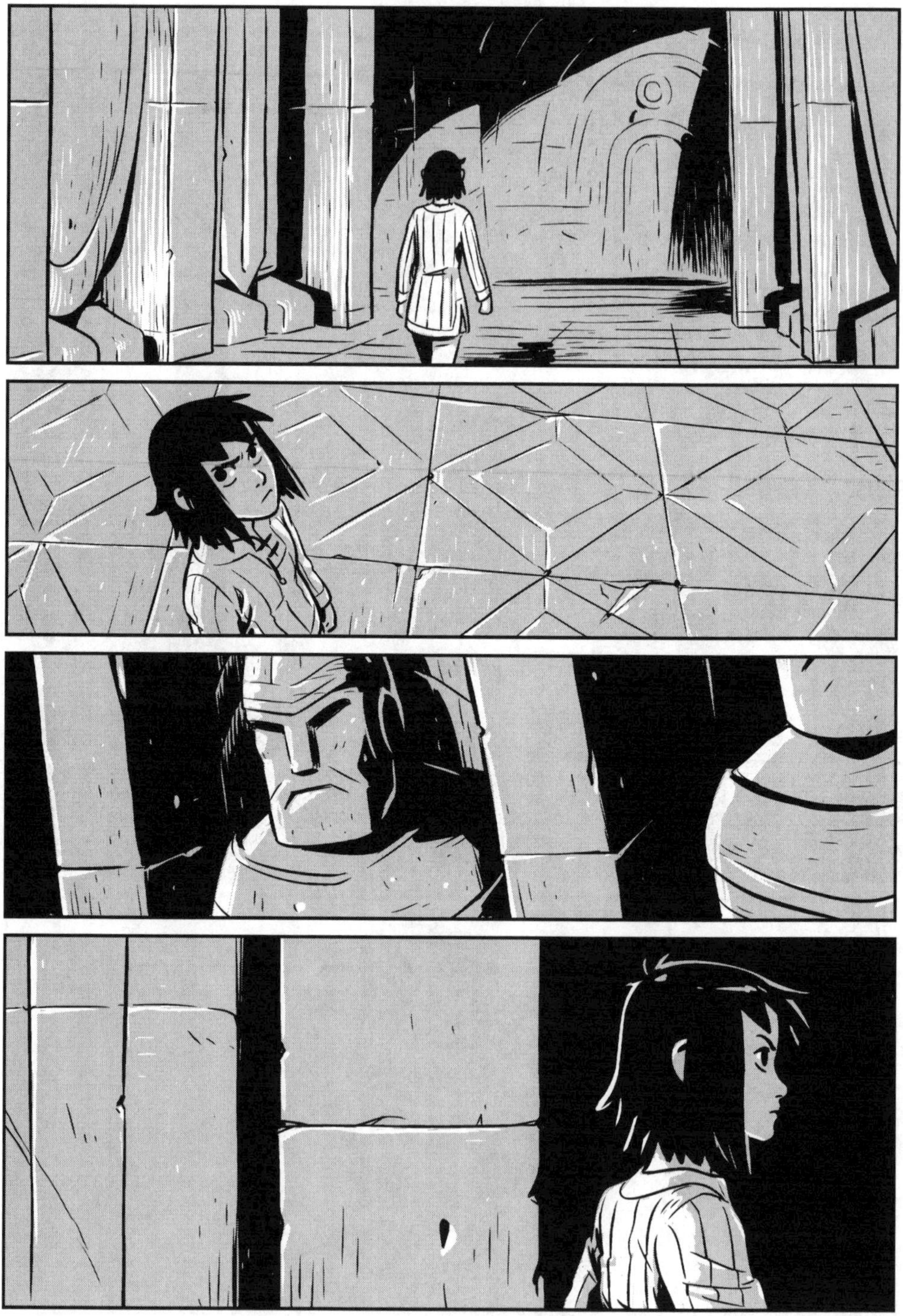

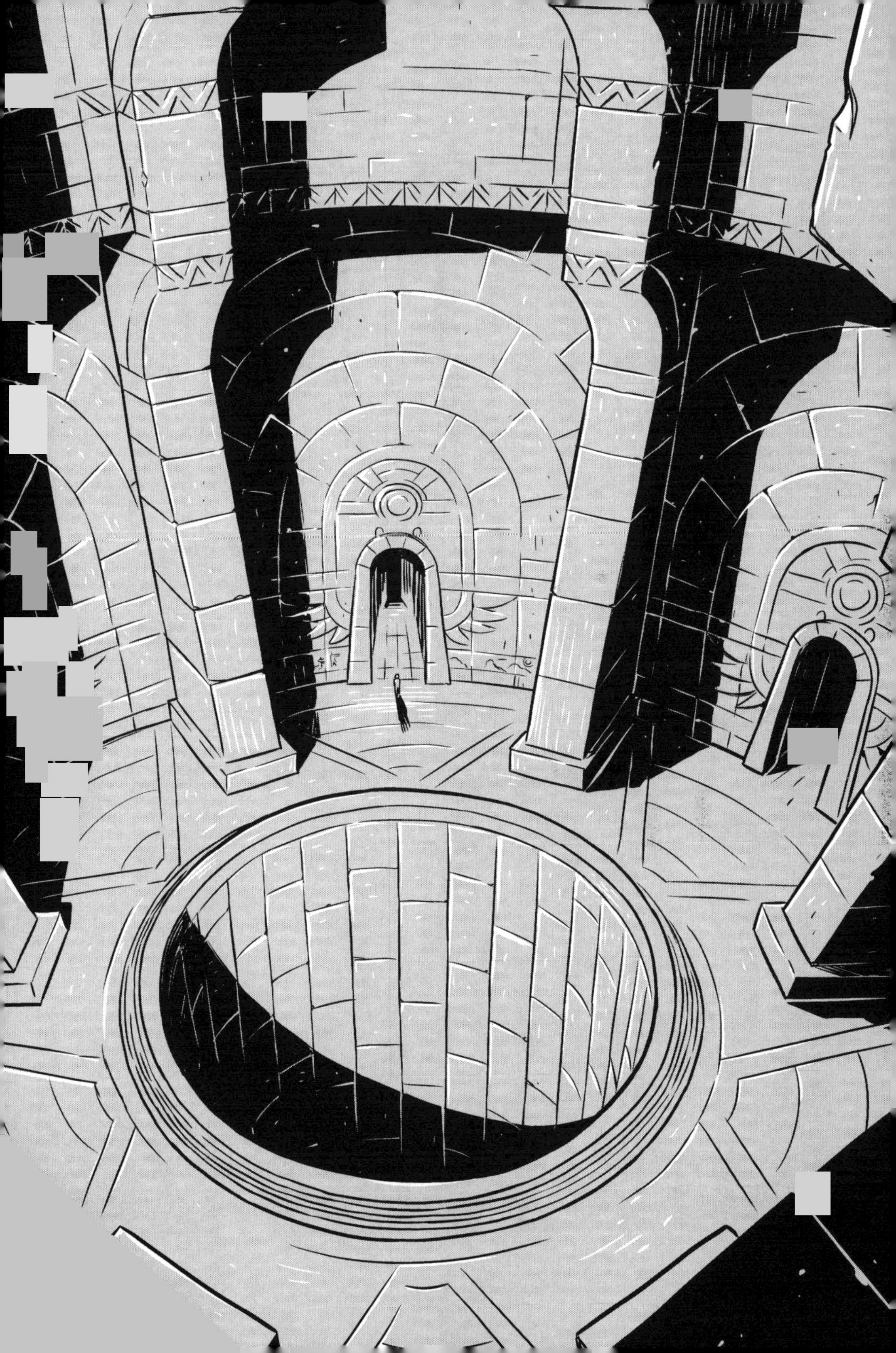

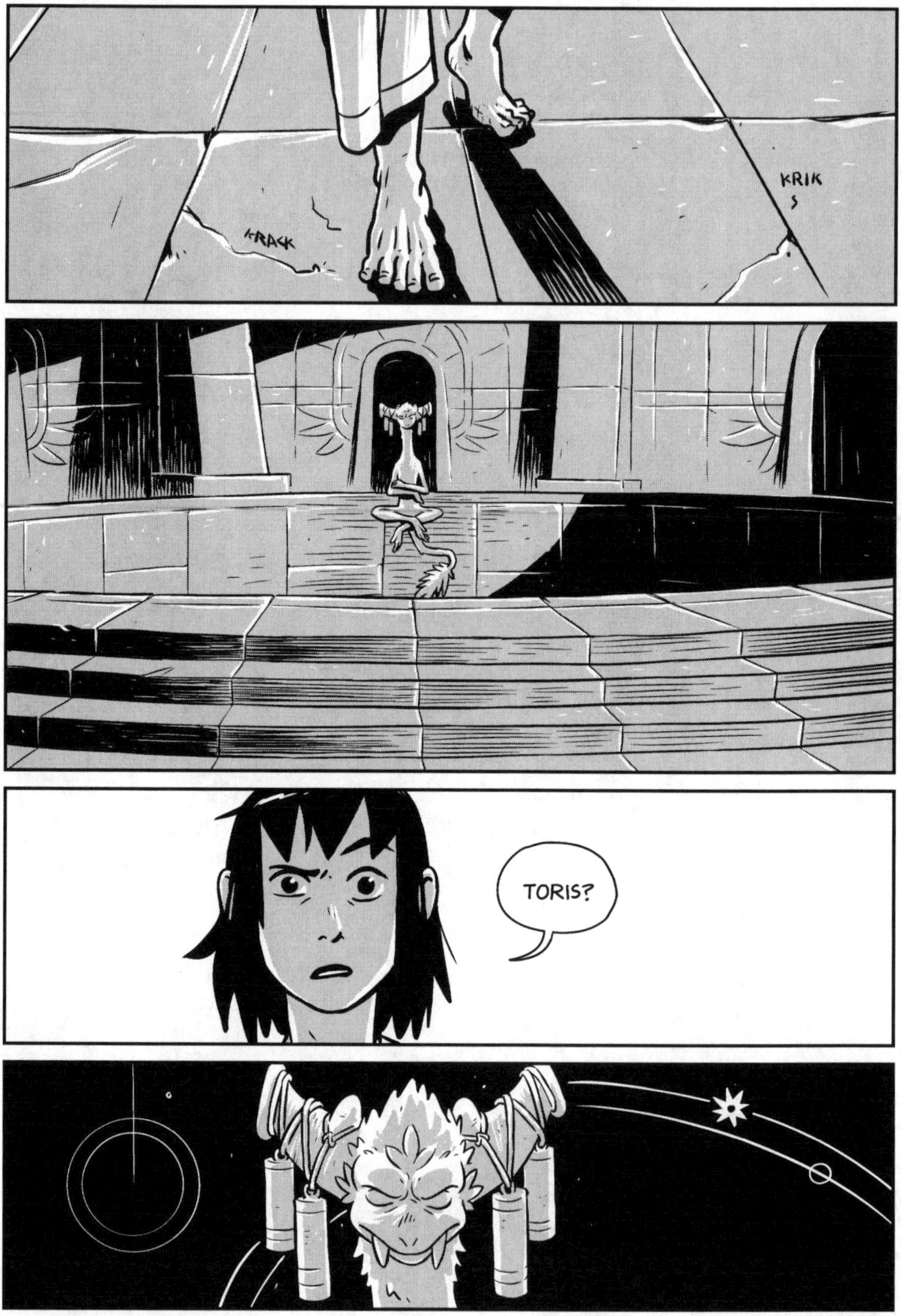
KRACK
KRIK
S
TORIS?

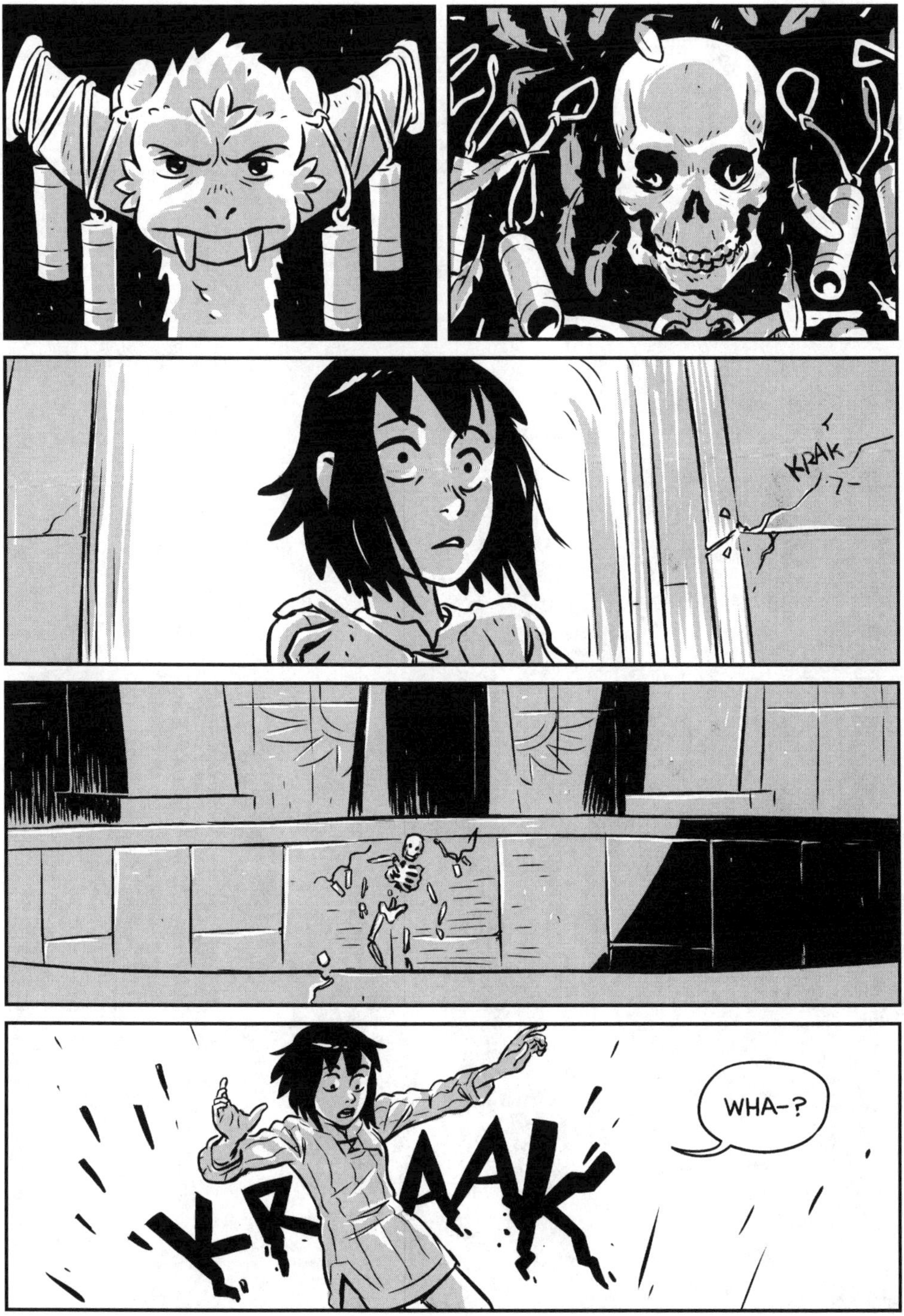
KRAK
KRAAK
WHA-?

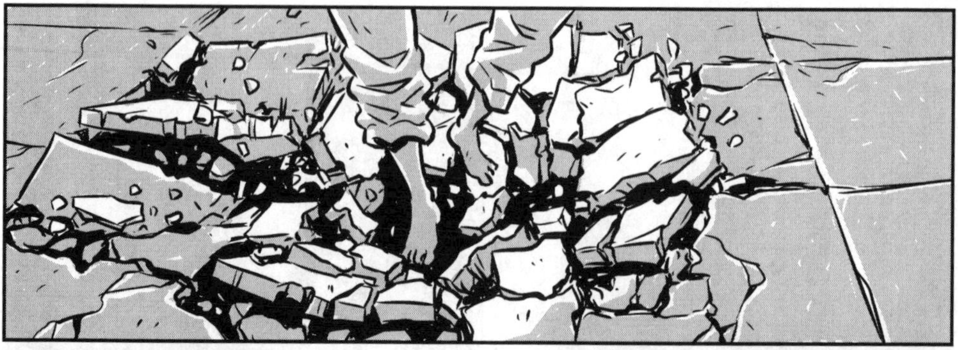
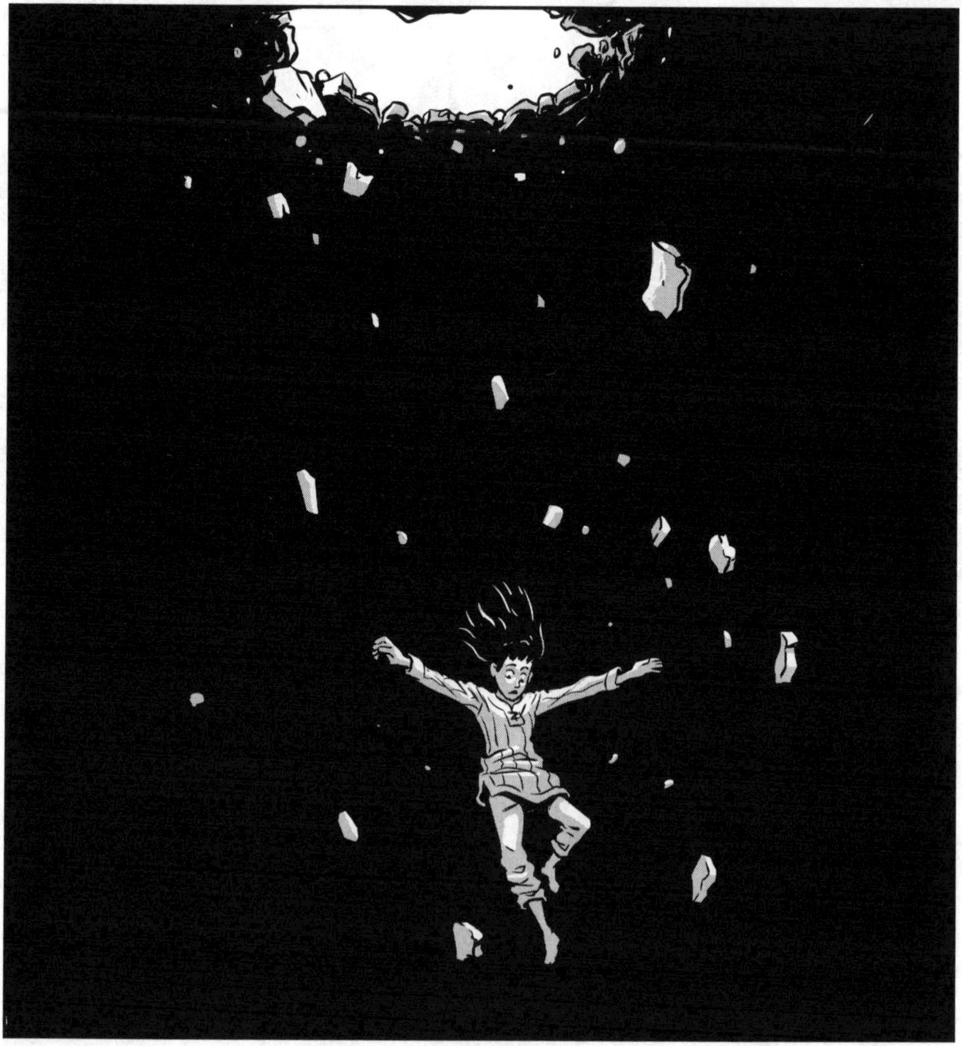

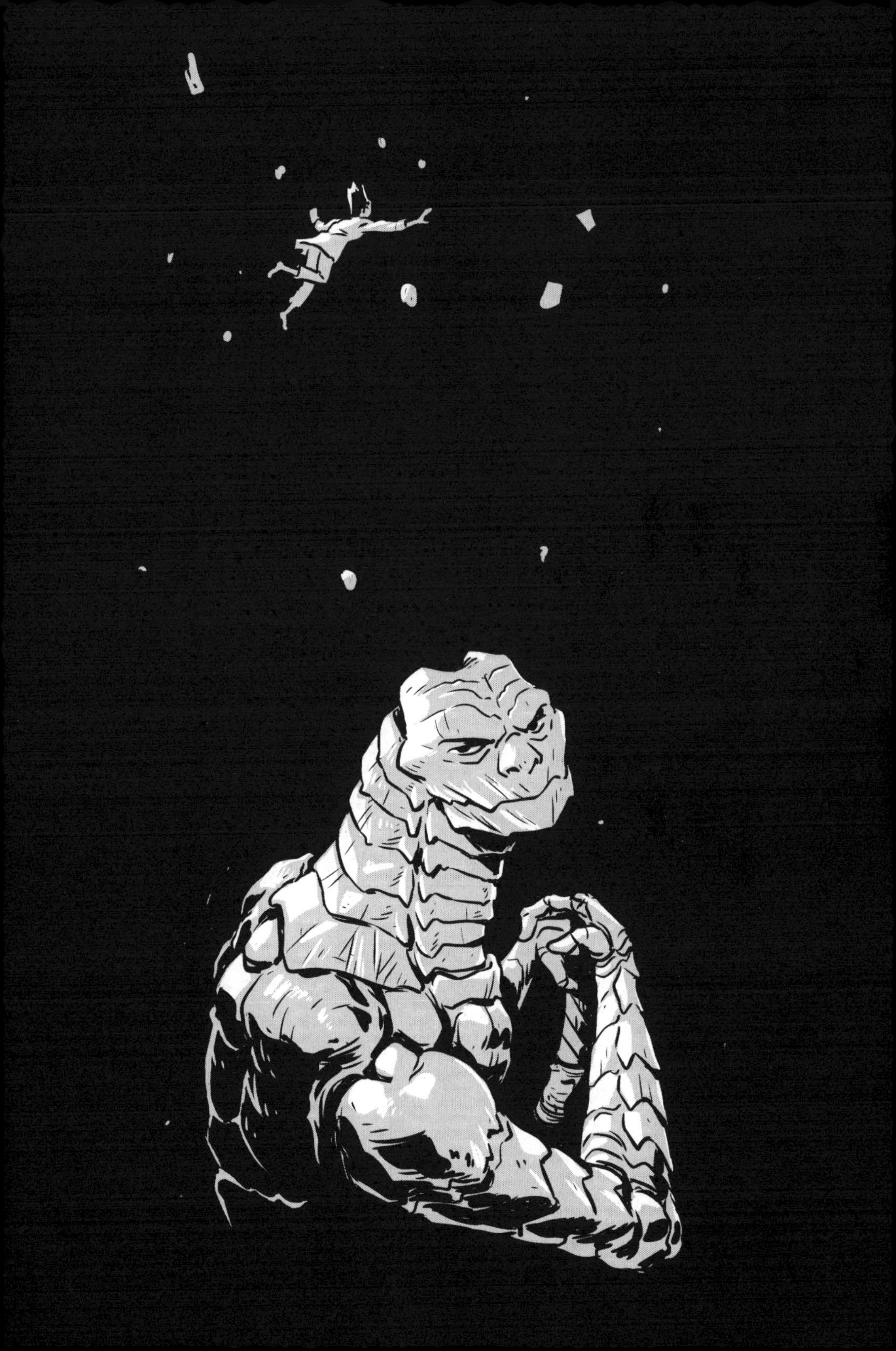

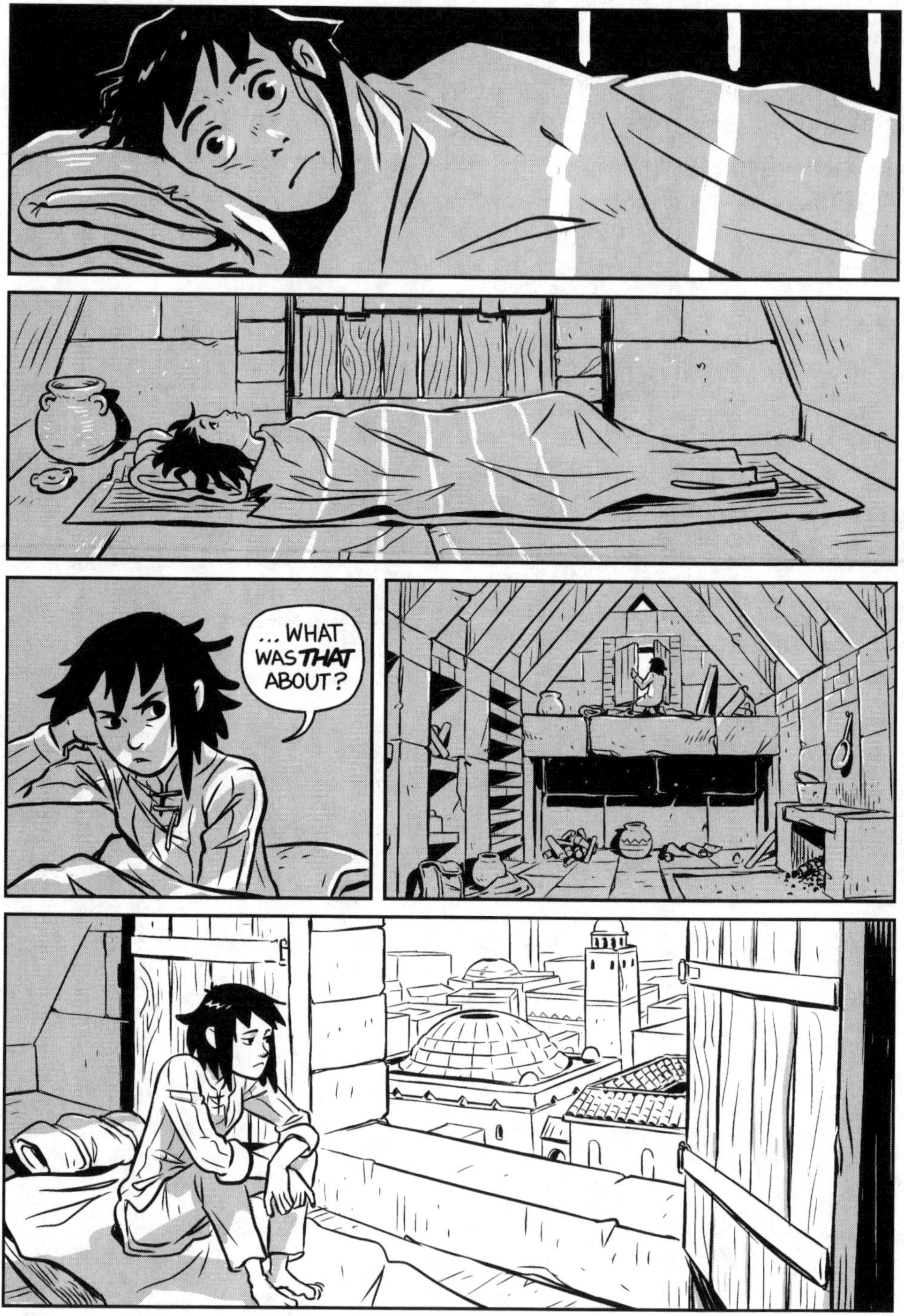

...WHAT WAS THAT ABOUT?

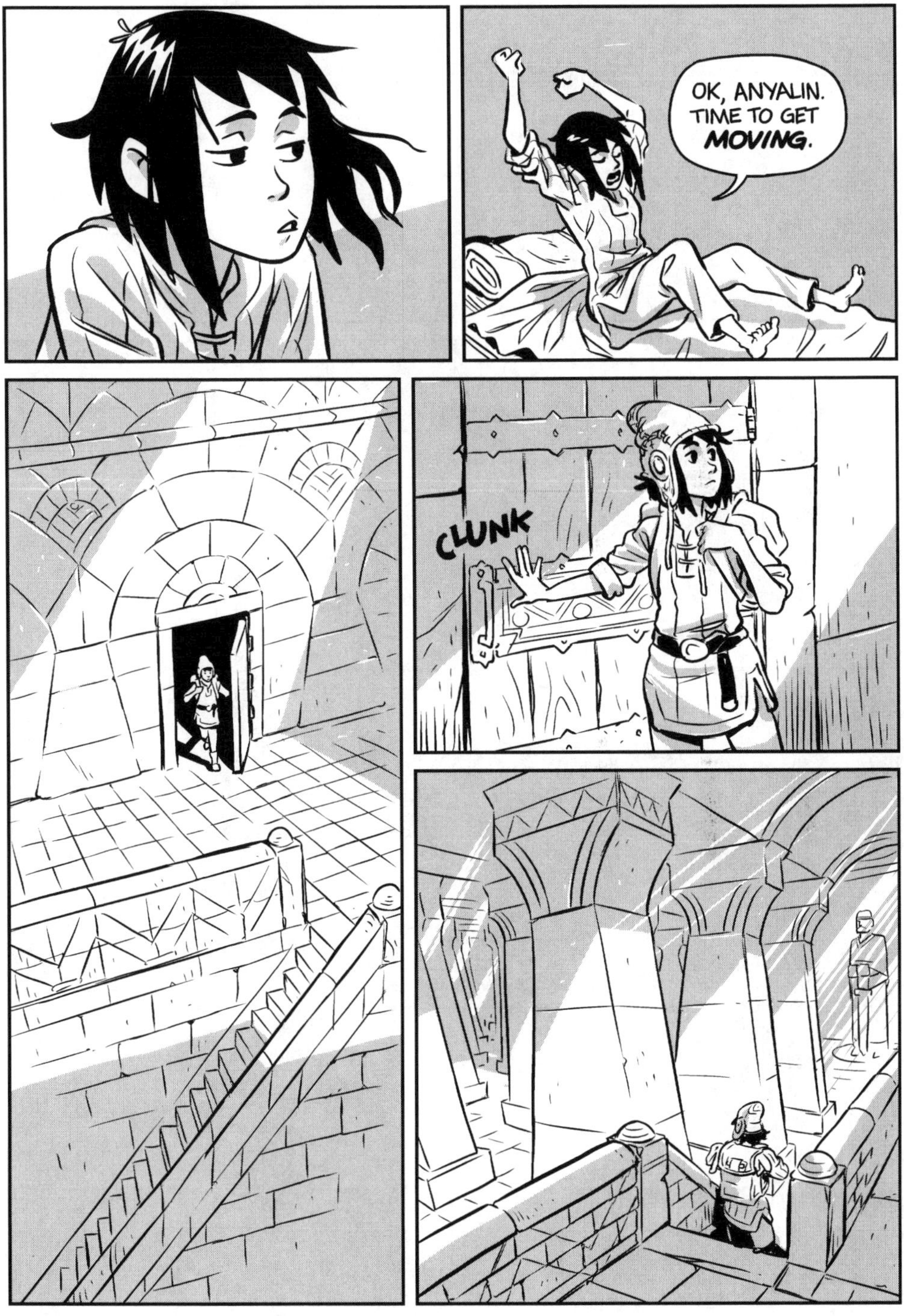

OK, ANYALIN. TIME TO GET MOVING.
CLUNK

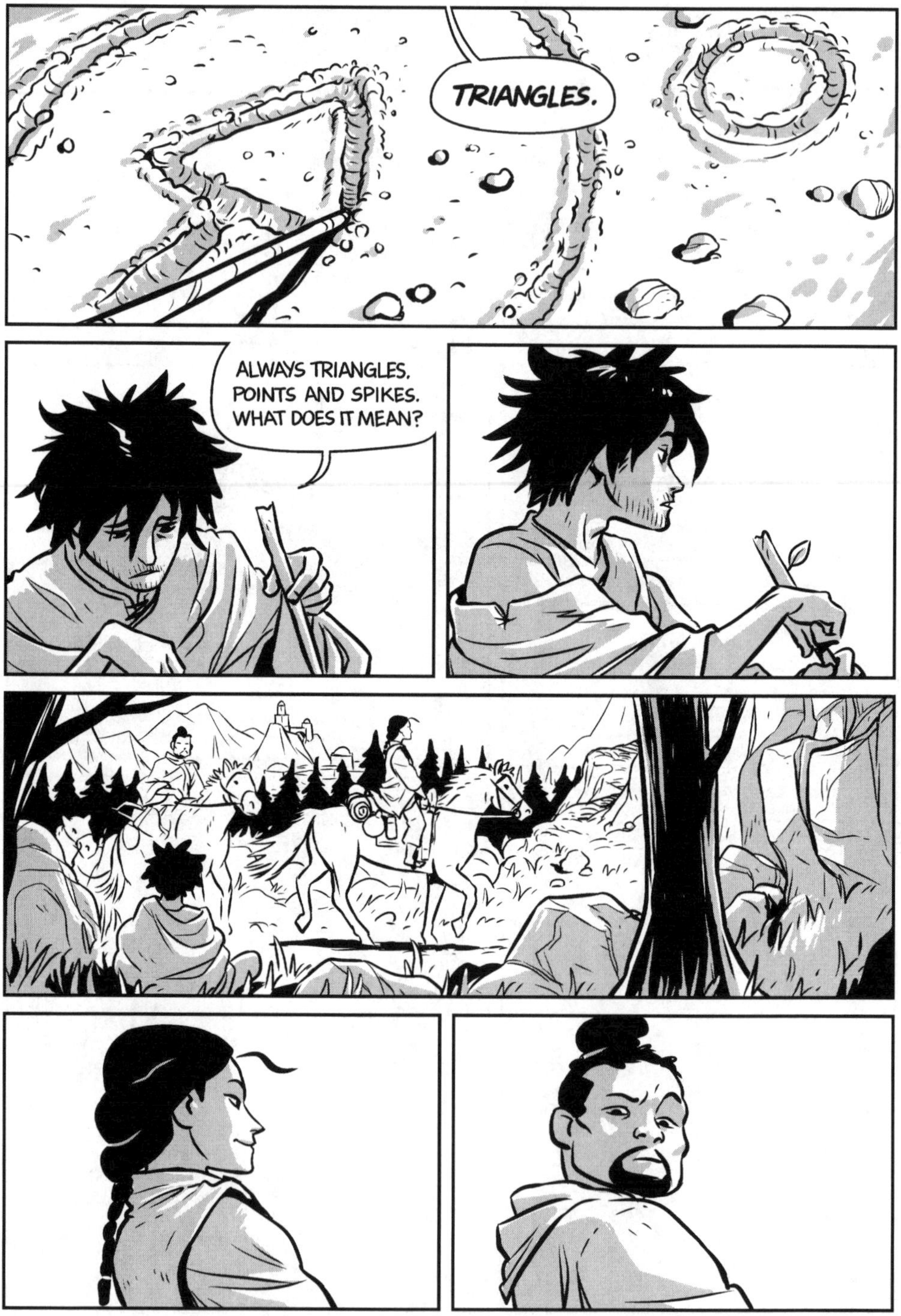
TRIANGLES.
ALWAYS TRIANGLES. POINTS AND SPIKES. WHAT DOES IT MEAN?

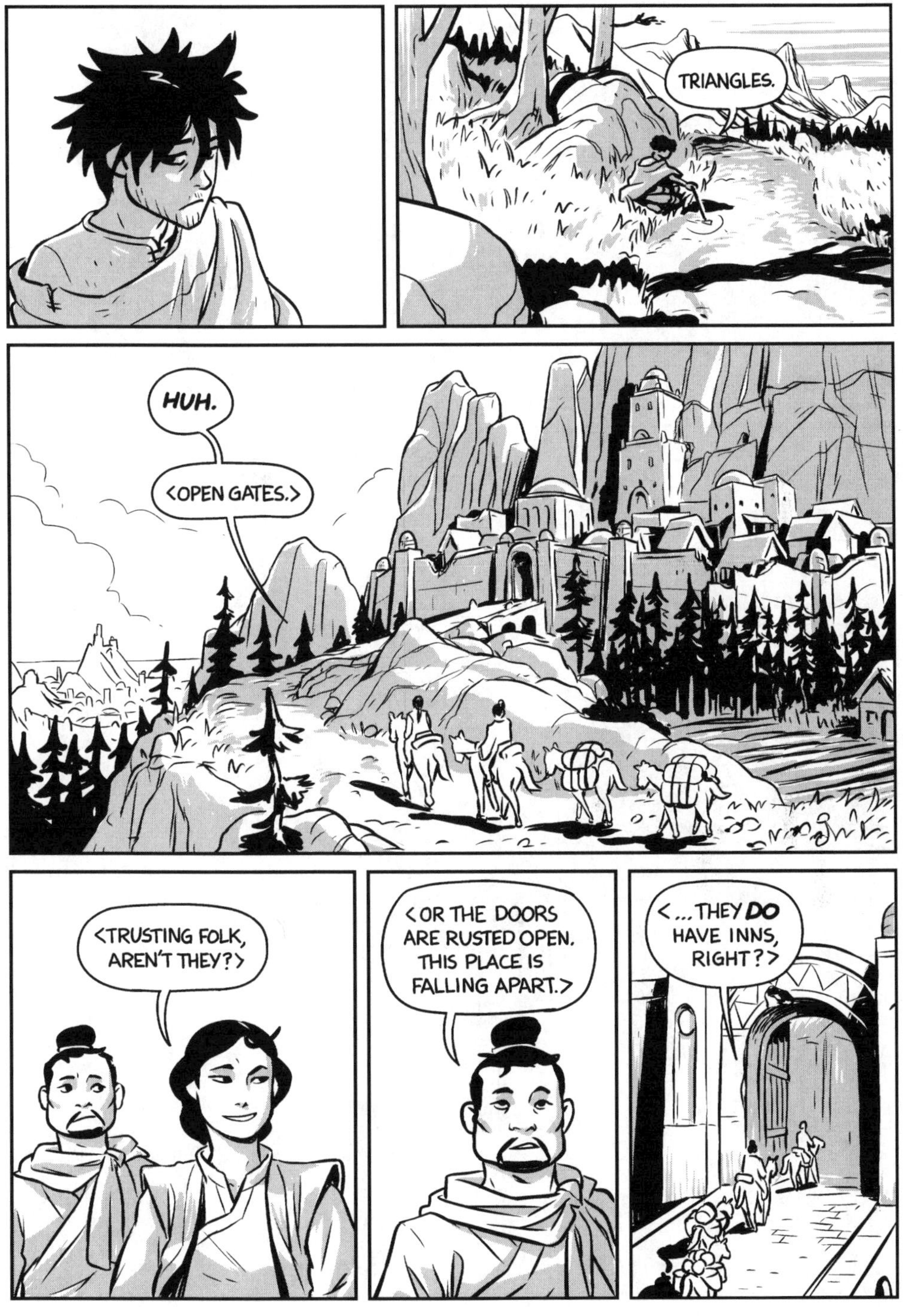
TRIANGLES.
HUH.
<OPEN GATES.>
<TRUSTING FOLK, AREN'T THEY?>
<OR THE DOORS ARE RUSTED OPEN. THIS PLACE IS FALLING APART.>
<...THEY **DO** HAVE INNS, RIGHT?>

<MERCHANTS HAVE TO STAY **SOMEWHERE**.>
<...I HOPE>
AH! NEW ARRIVALS.
NOT A COMMON OCCURRENCE, I TAKE IT.

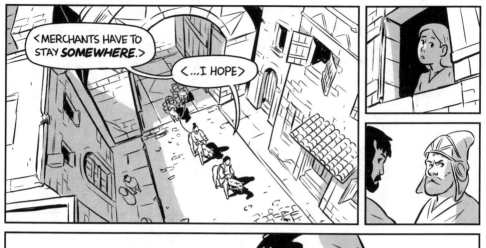

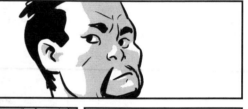

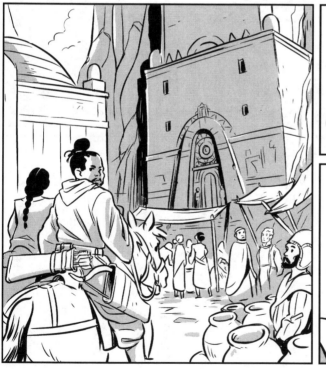

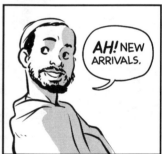

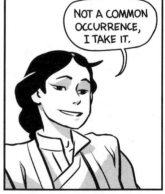

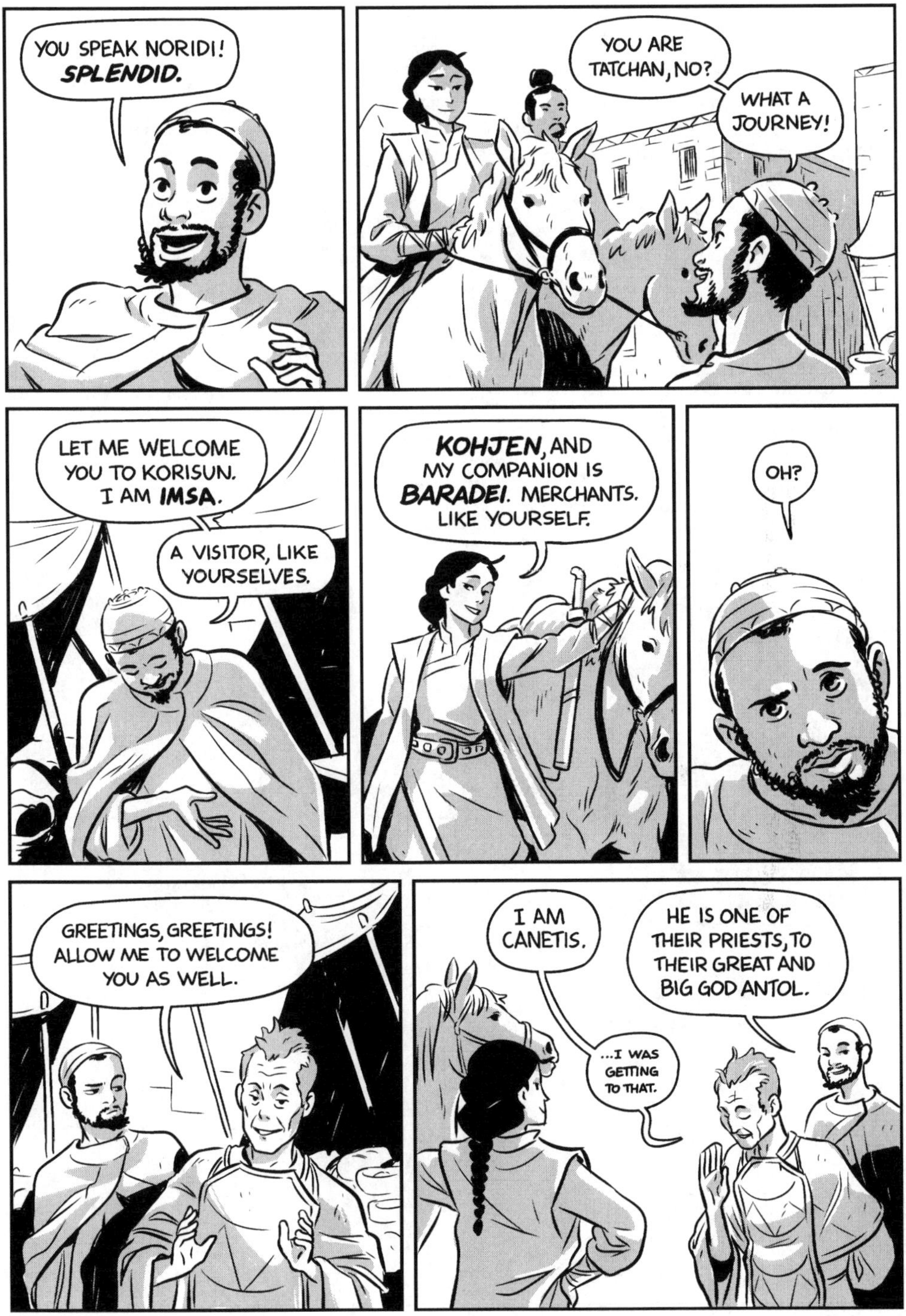
YOU SPEAK NORIDI! SPLENDID.
YOU ARE TATCHAN, NO?
WHAT A JOURNEY!
LET ME WELCOME YOU TO KORISUN. I AM IMSA.
A VISITOR, LIKE YOURSELVES.
KOHJEN, AND MY COMPANION IS BARADEI. MERCHANTS. LIKE YOURSELF.
OH?
GREETINGS, GREETINGS! ALLOW ME TO WELCOME YOU AS WELL.
I AM CANETIS.
HE IS ONE OF THEIR PRIESTS, TO THEIR GREAT AND BIG GOD ANTOL.
...I WAS GETTING TO THAT.

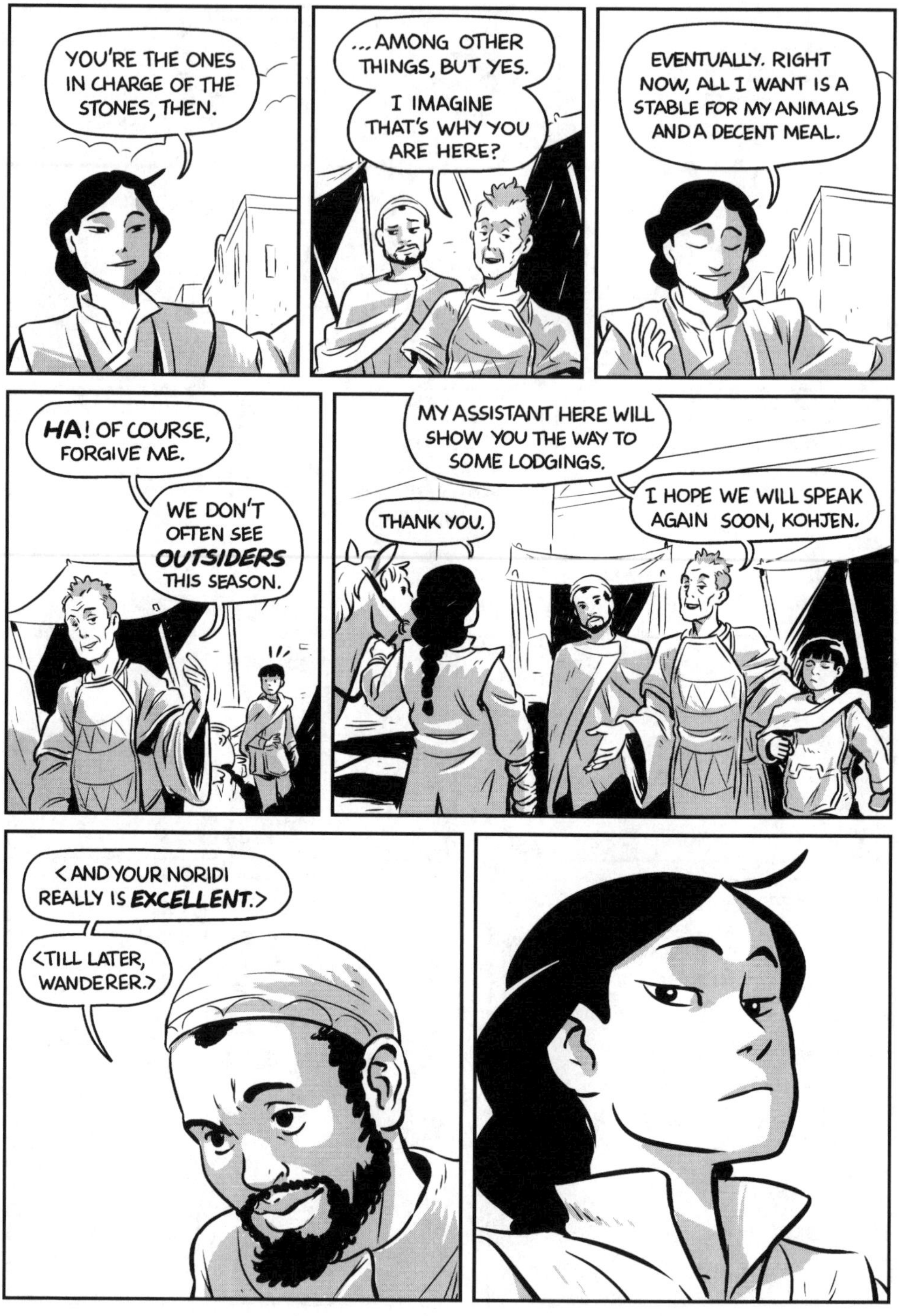
YOU'RE THE ONES IN CHARGE OF THE STONES, THEN.
...AMONG OTHER THINGS, BUT YES.
I IMAGINE THAT'S WHY YOU ARE HERE?
EVENTUALLY. RIGHT NOW, ALL I WANT IS A STABLE FOR MY ANIMALS AND A DECENT MEAL.
HA! OF COURSE, FORGIVE ME.
WE DON'T OFTEN SEE OUTSIDERS THIS SEASON.
MY ASSISTANT HERE WILL SHOW YOU THE WAY TO SOME LODGINGS.
THANK YOU.
I HOPE WE WILL SPEAK AGAIN SOON, KOHJEN.
<AND YOUR NORIDI REALLY IS EXCELLENT.>
<TILL LATER, WANDERER.>

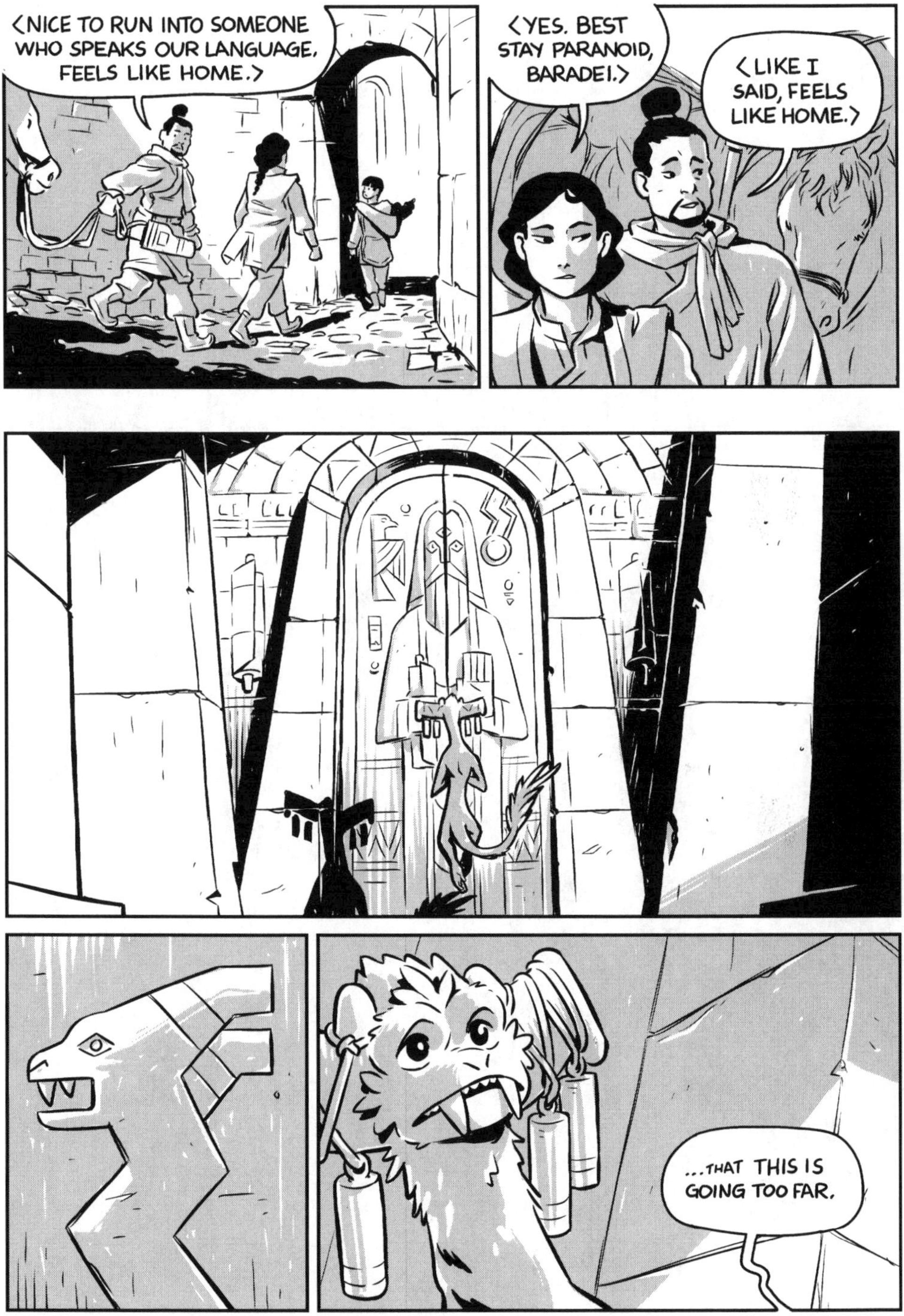
<NICE TO RUN INTO SOMEONE WHO SPEAKS OUR LANGUAGE, FEELS LIKE HOME.>
<YES. BEST STAY PARANOID, BARADEI.>
<LIKE I SAID, FEELS LIKE HOME.>
...THAT THIS IS GOING TOO FAR.

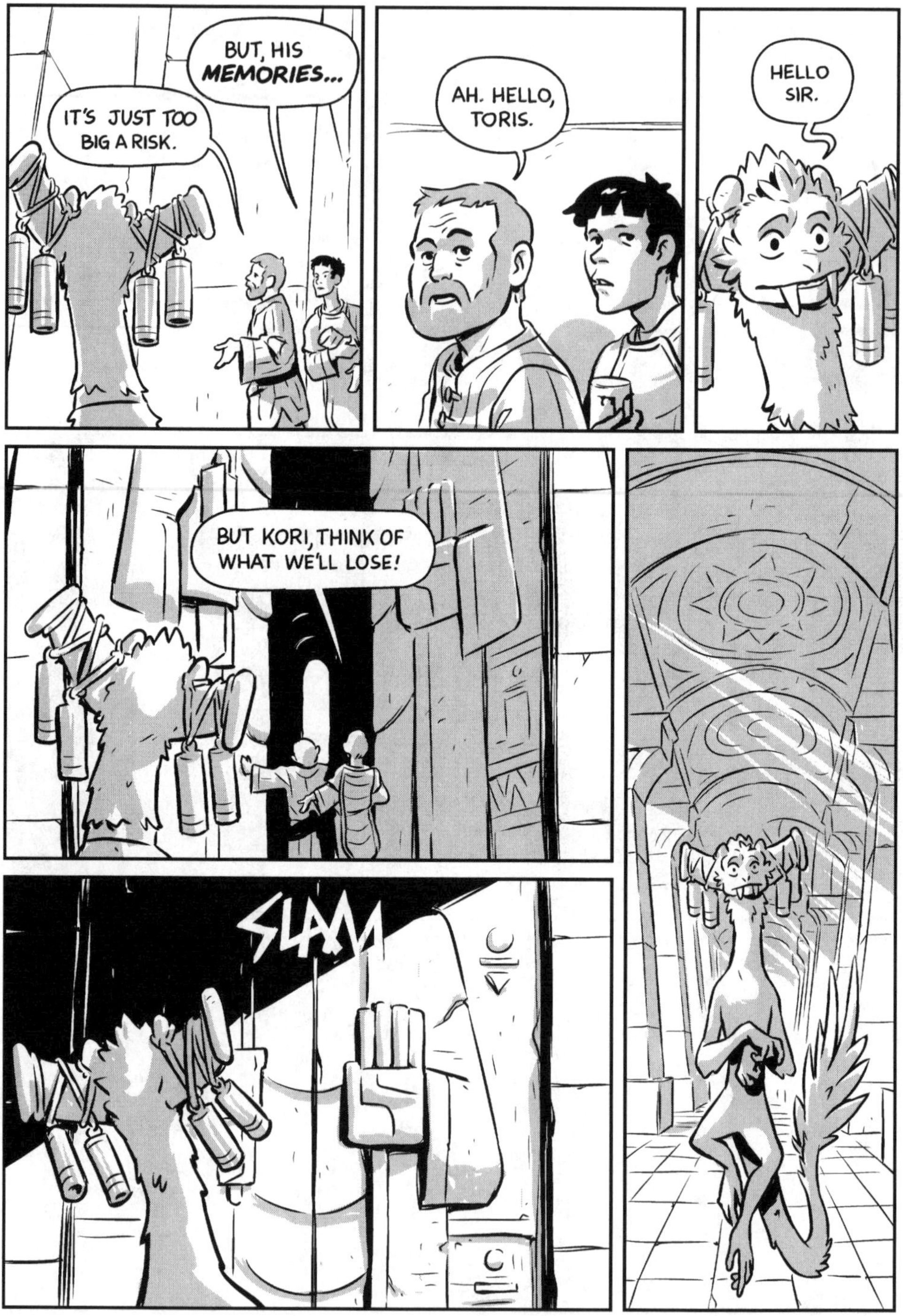
IT'S JUST TOO BIG A RISK.
BUT, HIS MEMORIES...
AH. HELLO, TORIS.
HELLO SIR.
BUT KORI, THINK OF WHAT WE'LL LOSE!
SLAM

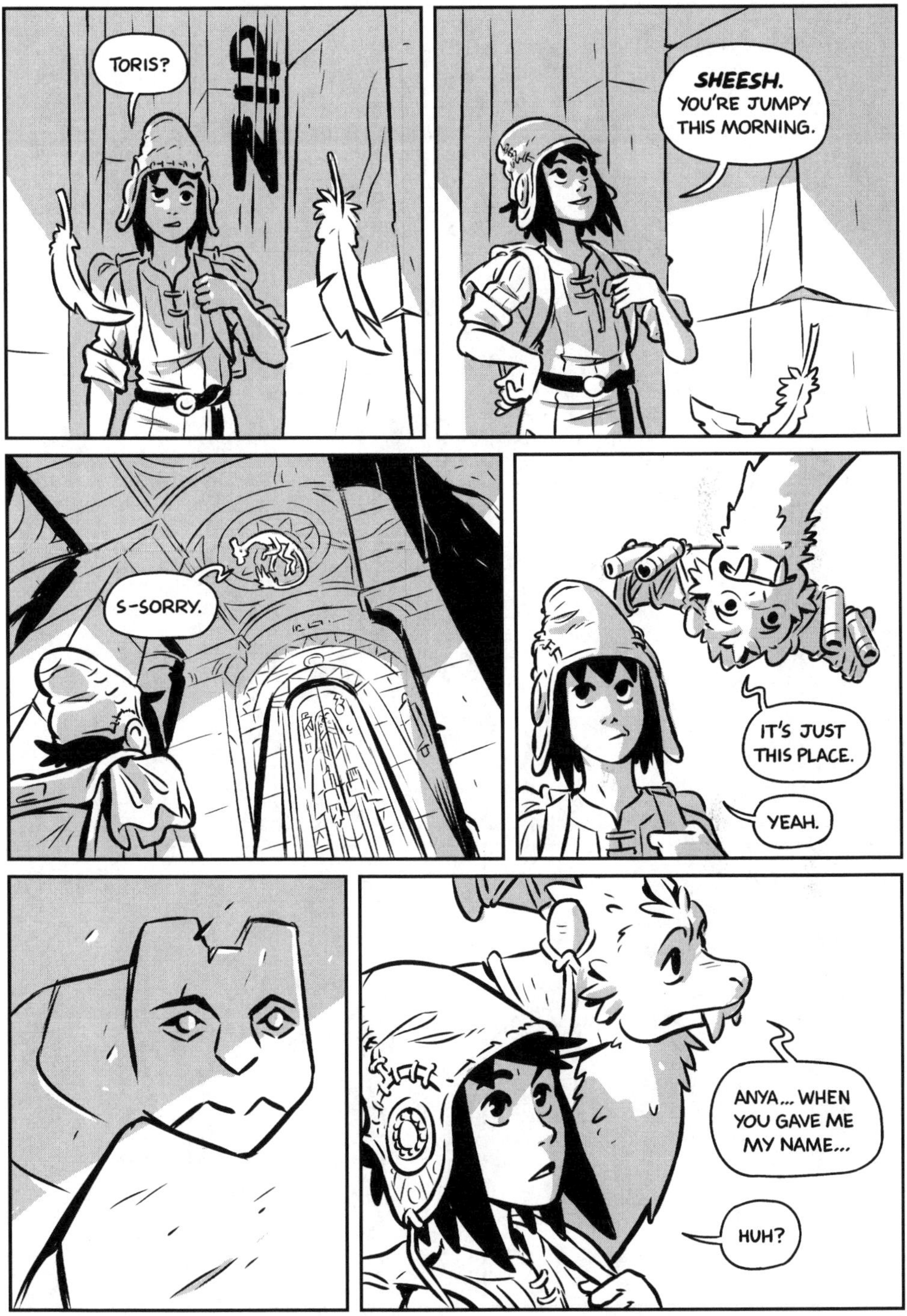
TORIS?
SHEESH. YOU'RE JUMPY THIS MORNING.
S-SORRY.
IT'S JUST THIS PLACE.
YEAH.
ANYA... WHEN YOU GAVE ME MY NAME...
HUH?

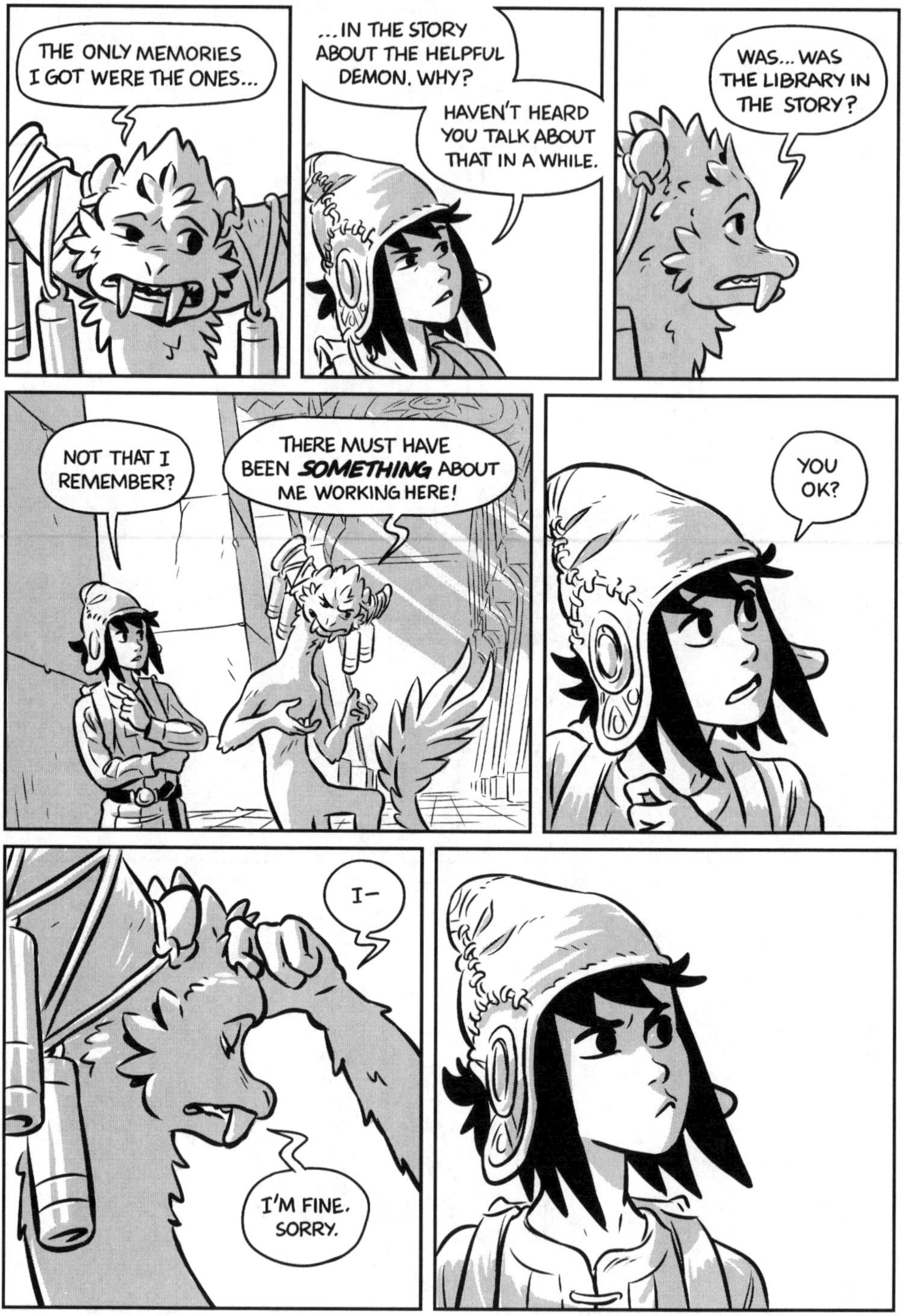
THE ONLY MEMORIES I GOT WERE THE ONES...
...IN THE STORY ABOUT THE HELPFUL DEMON. WHY?
HAVEN'T HEARD YOU TALK ABOUT THAT IN A WHILE.
WAS... WAS THE LIBRARY IN THE STORY?
NOT THAT I REMEMBER?
THERE MUST HAVE BEEN SOMETHING ABOUT ME WORKING HERE!
YOU OK?
I-
I'M FINE. SORRY.

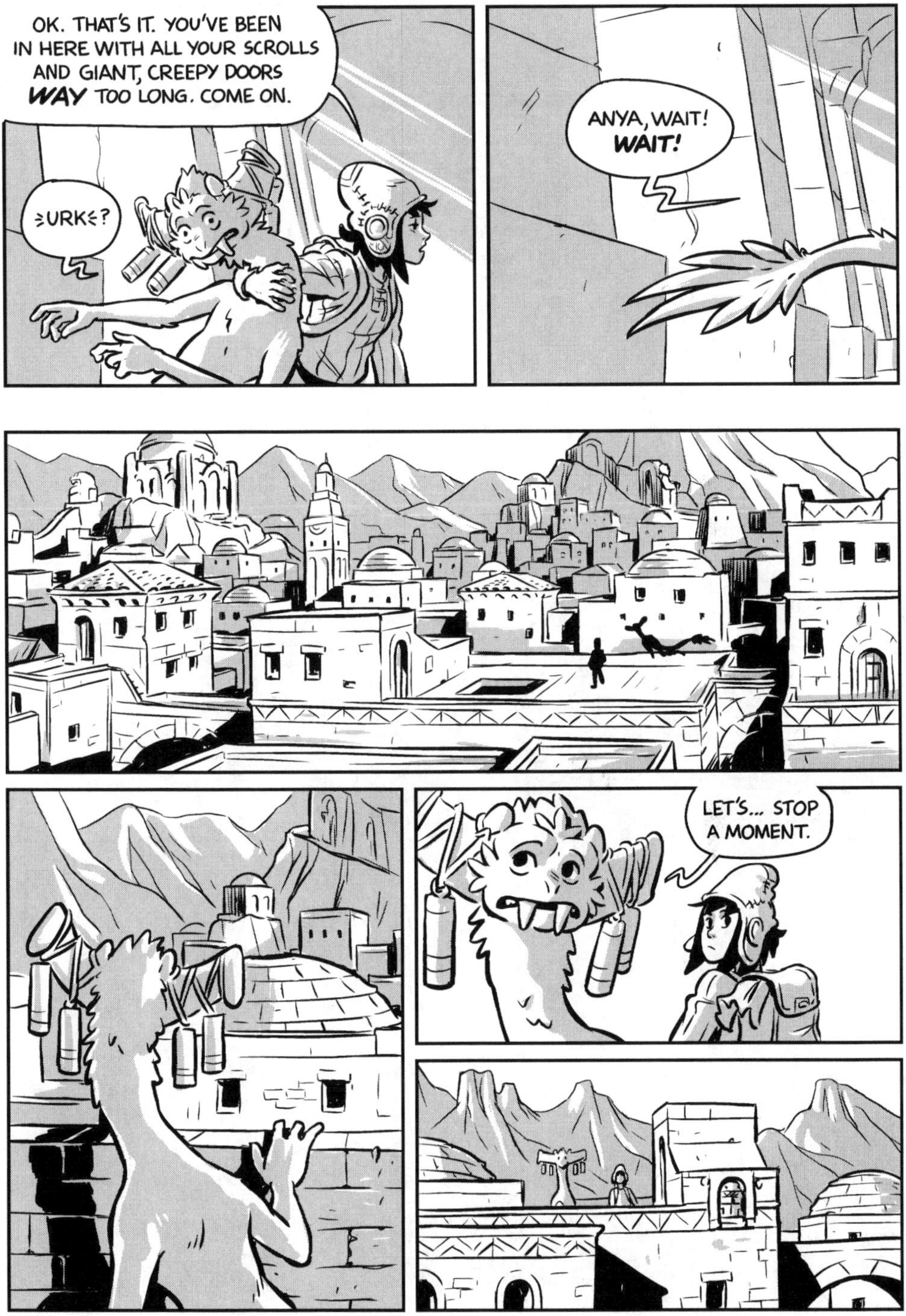
OK. THAT'S IT. YOU'VE BEEN IN HERE WITH ALL YOUR SCROLLS AND GIANT, CREEPY DOORS WAY TOO LONG. COME ON.
URK?
ANYA, WAIT! WAIT!
LET'S... STOP A MOMENT.

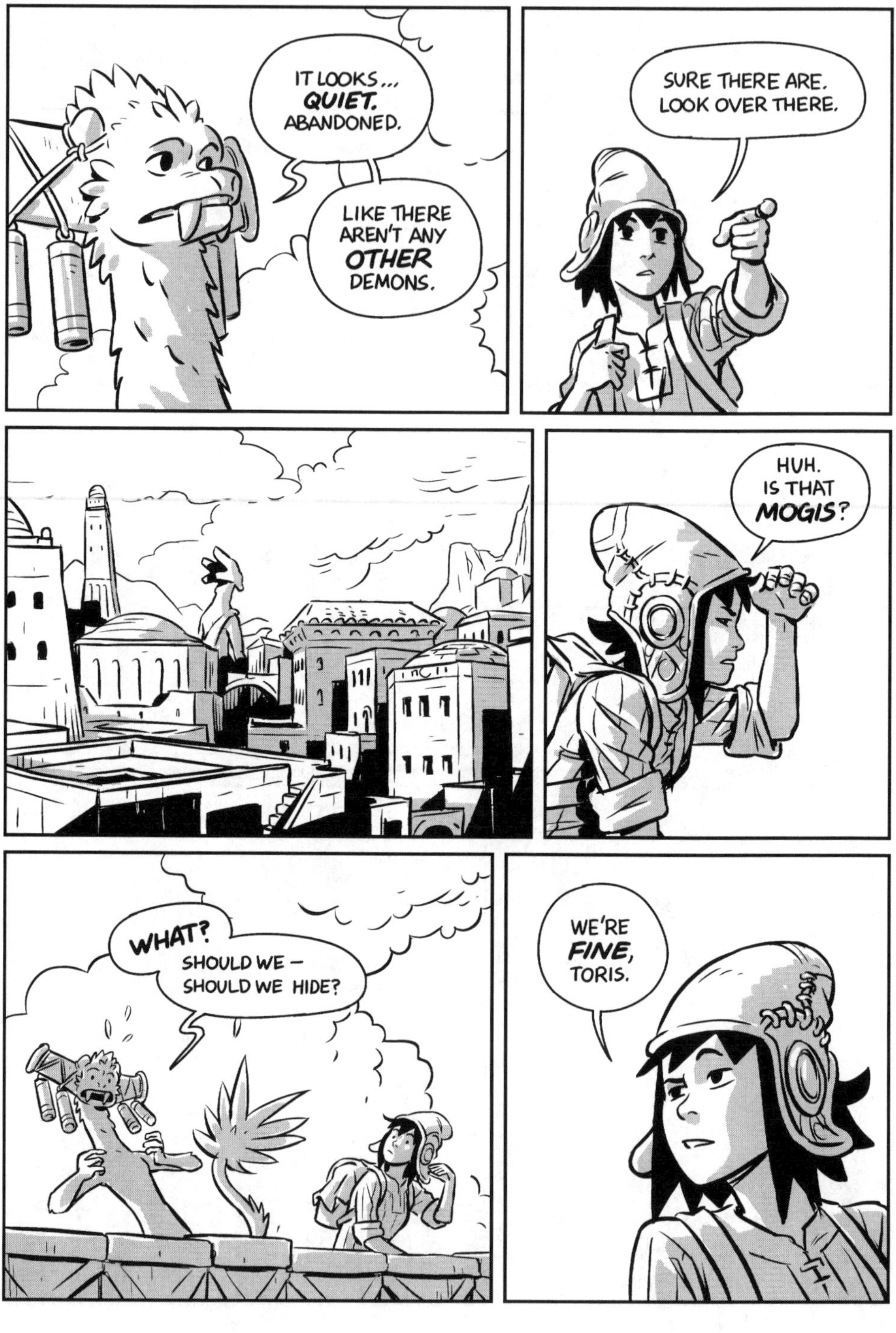
IT LOOKS... QUIET. ABANDONED.
LIKE THERE AREN'T ANY OTHER DEMONS.
SURE THERE ARE. LOOK OVER THERE.
HUH. IS THAT MOGIS?
WHAT? SHOULD WE — SHOULD WE HIDE?
WE'RE FINE, TORIS.

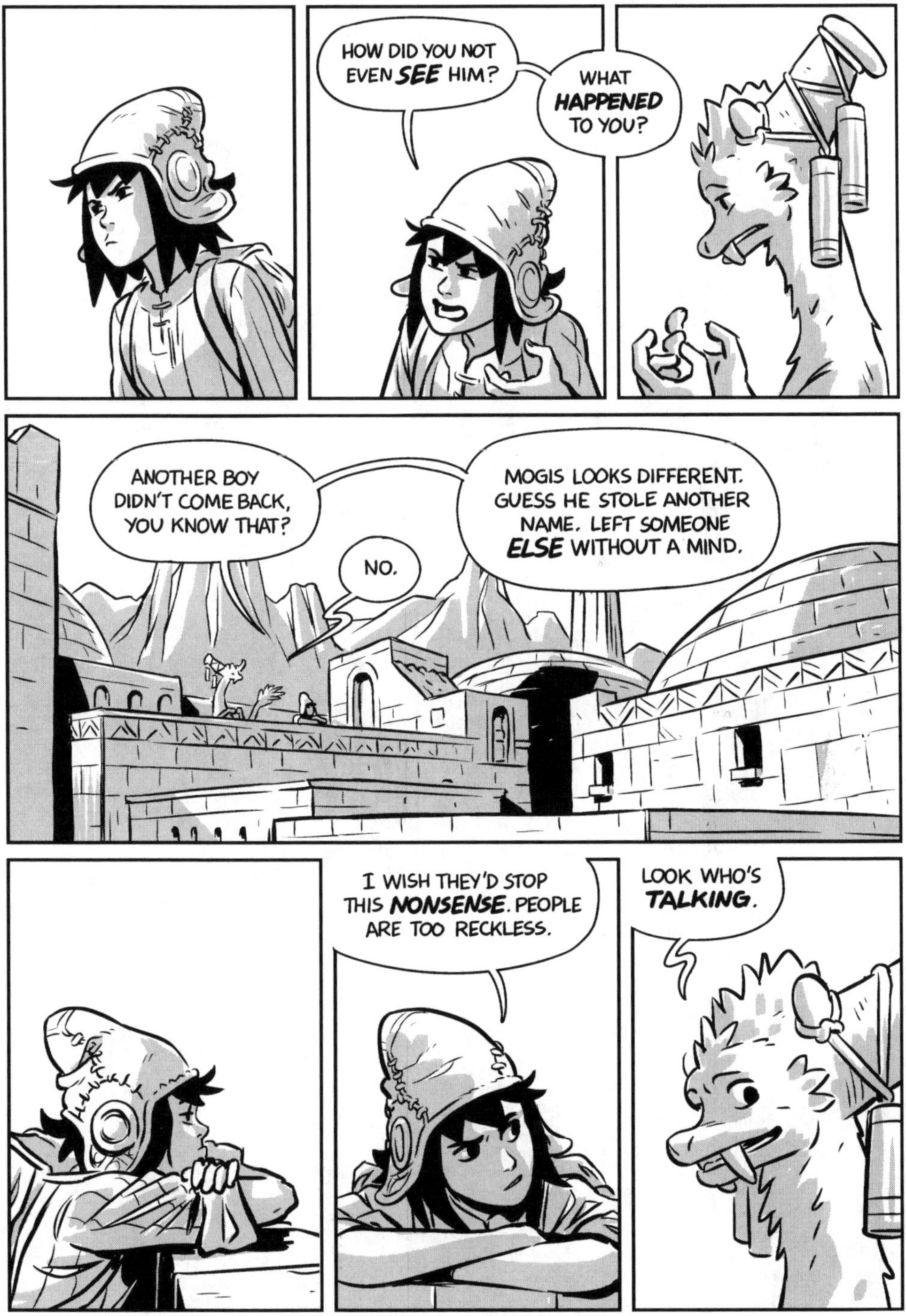
HOW DID YOU NOT EVEN **SEE** HIM?
WHAT **HAPPENED** TO YOU?
ANOTHER BOY DIDN'T COME BACK, YOU KNOW THAT?
NO.
MOGIS LOOKS DIFFERENT. GUESS HE STOLE ANOTHER NAME. LEFT SOMEONE **ELSE** WITHOUT A MIND.
I WISH THEY'D STOP THIS **NONSENSE**. PEOPLE ARE TOO RECKLESS.
LOOK WHO'S **TALKING**.

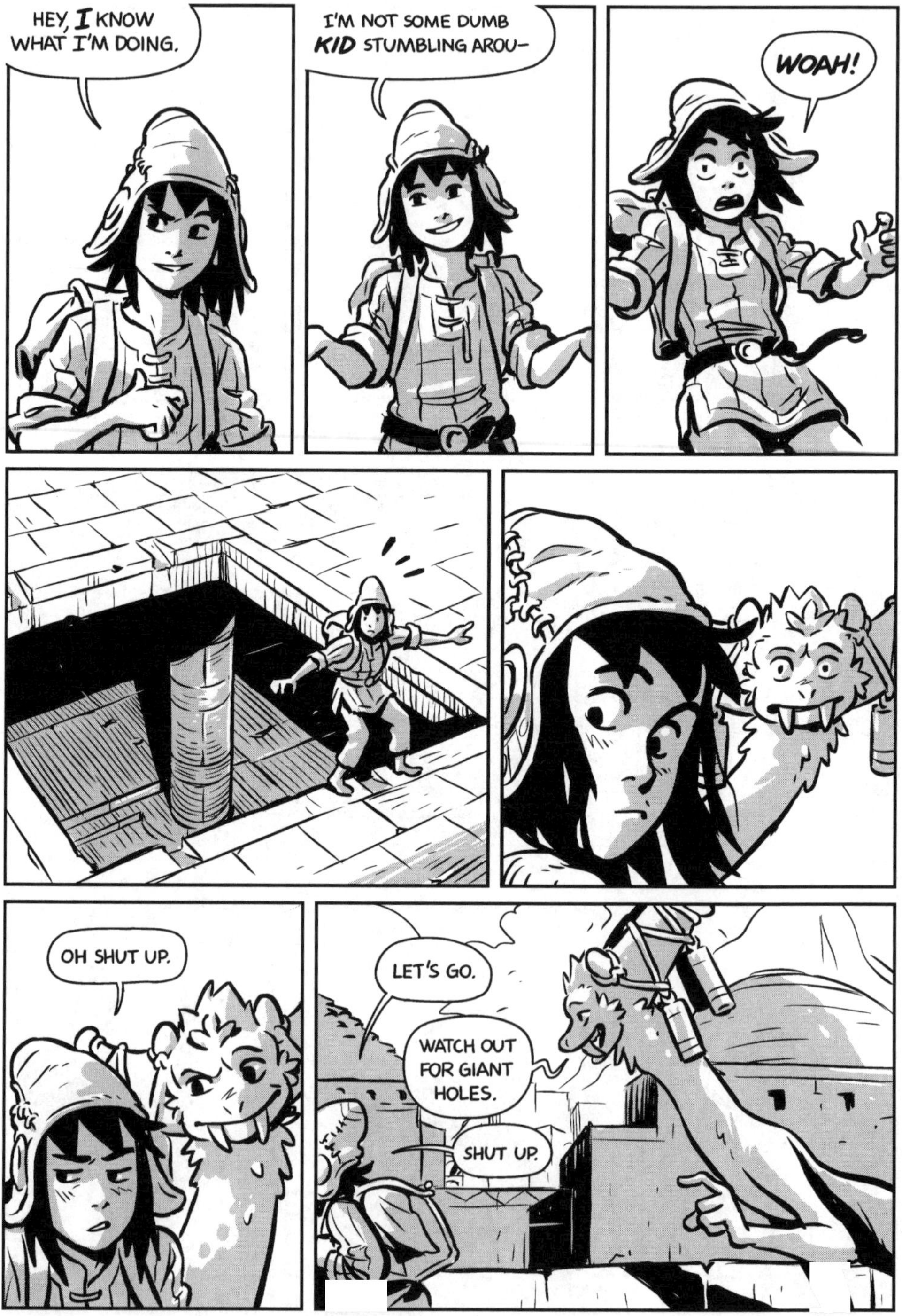
HEY, I KNOW WHAT I'M DOING.
I'M NOT SOME DUMB KID STUMBLING AROU-
WOAH!
OH SHUT UP.
LET'S GO.
WATCH OUT FOR GIANT HOLES.
SHUT UP.

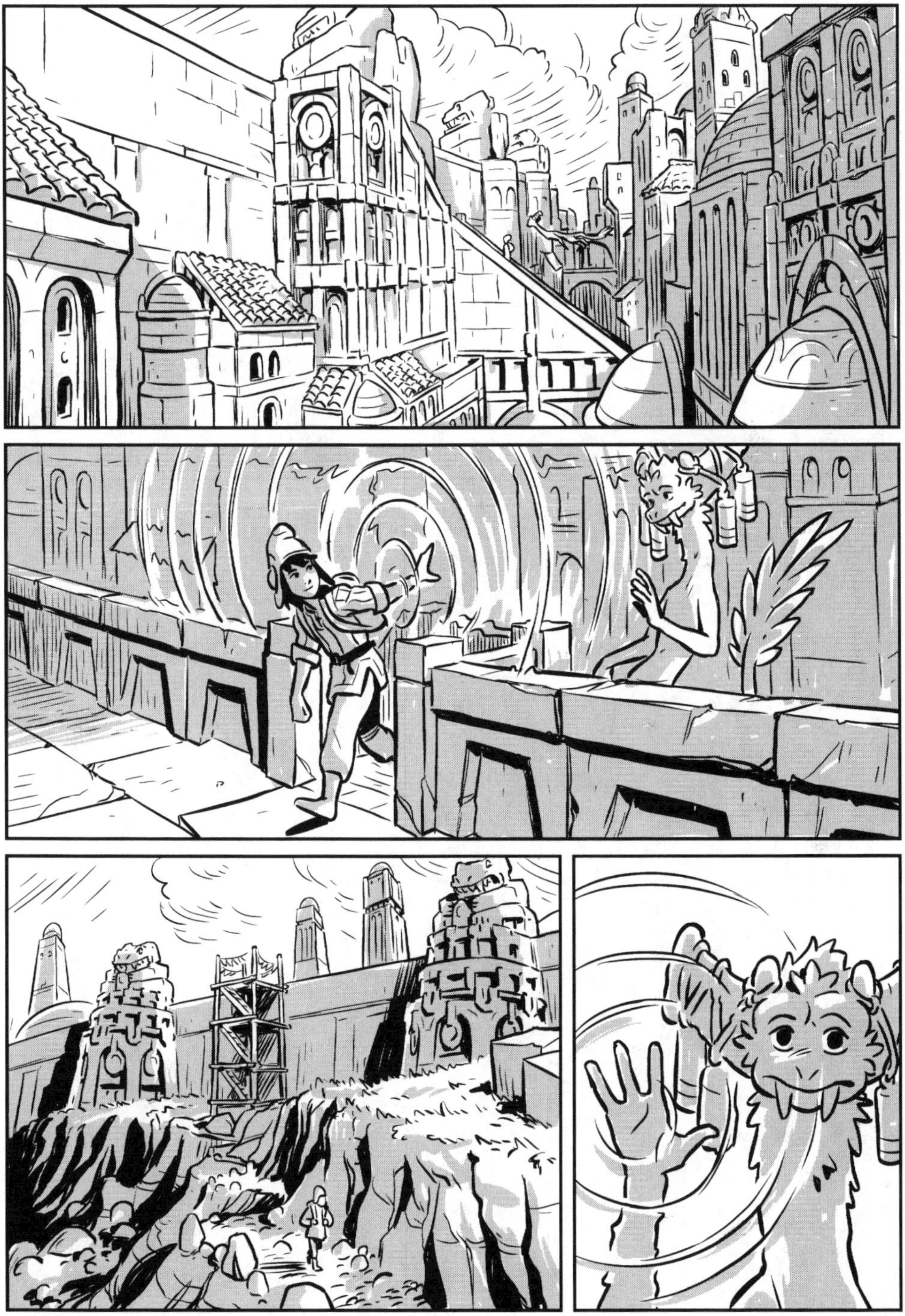

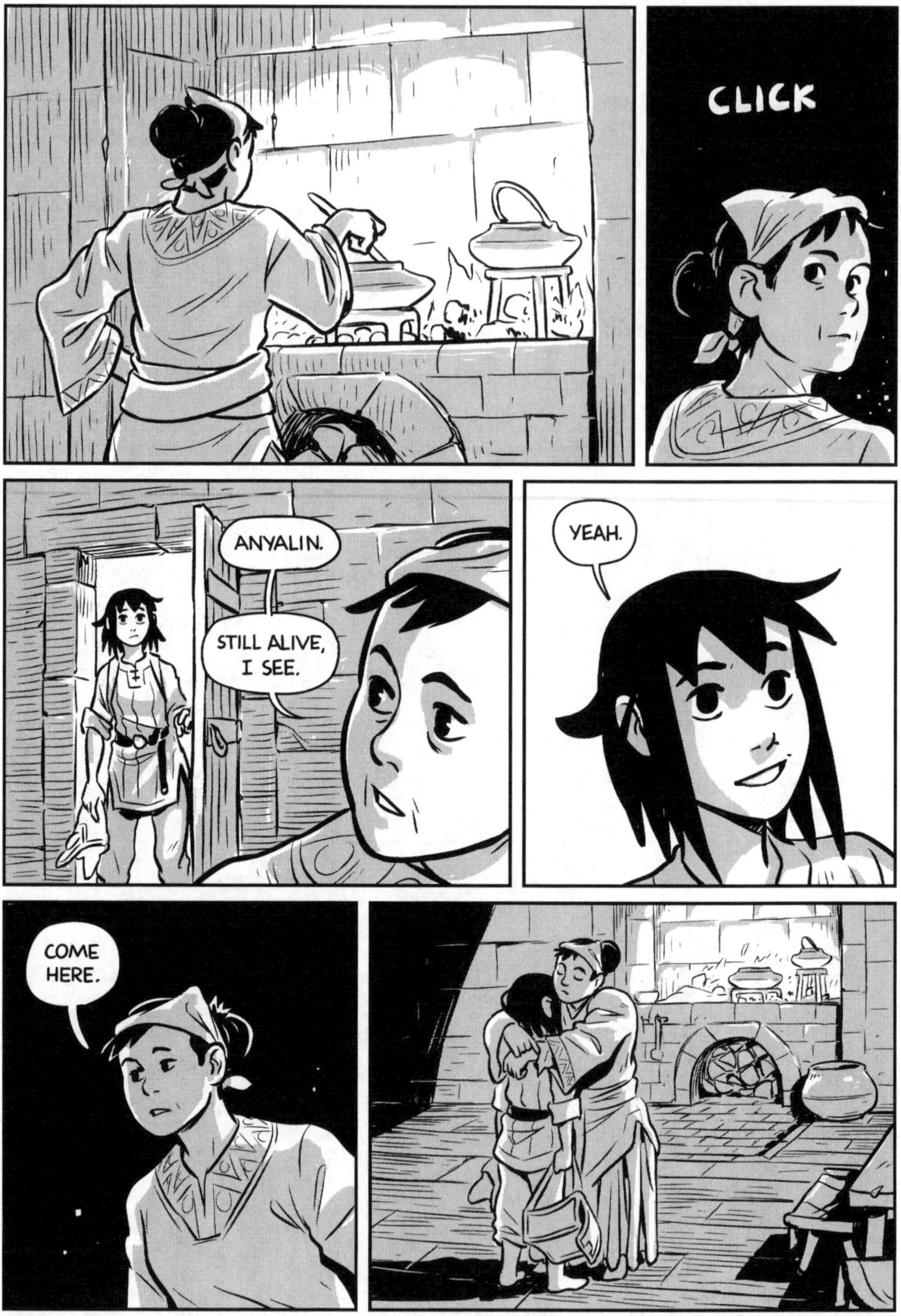
CLICK
ANYALIN.
STILL ALIVE, I SEE.
YEAH.
COME HERE.

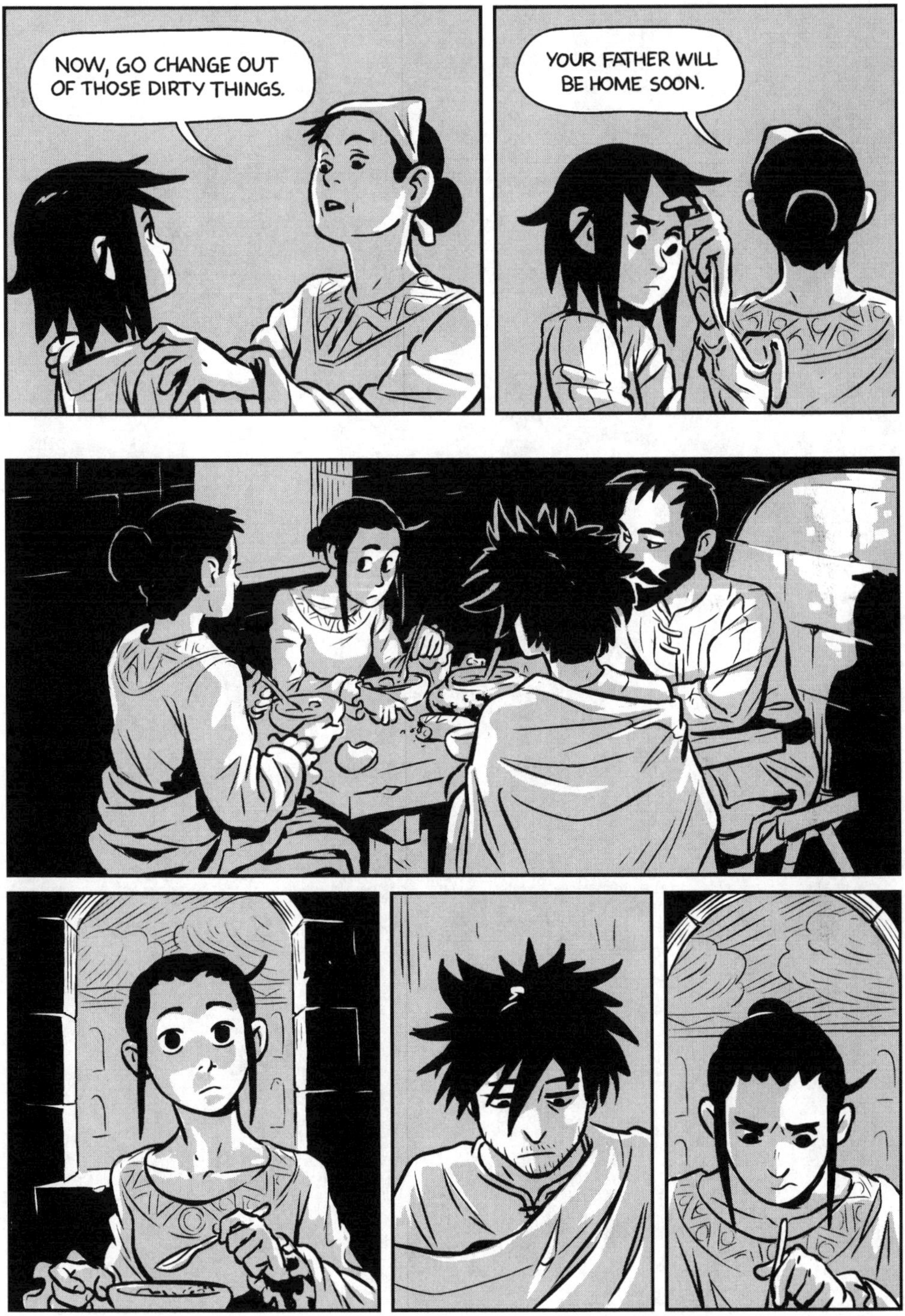
NOW, GO CHANGE OUT OF THOSE DIRTY THINGS.
YOUR FATHER WILL BE HOME SOON.

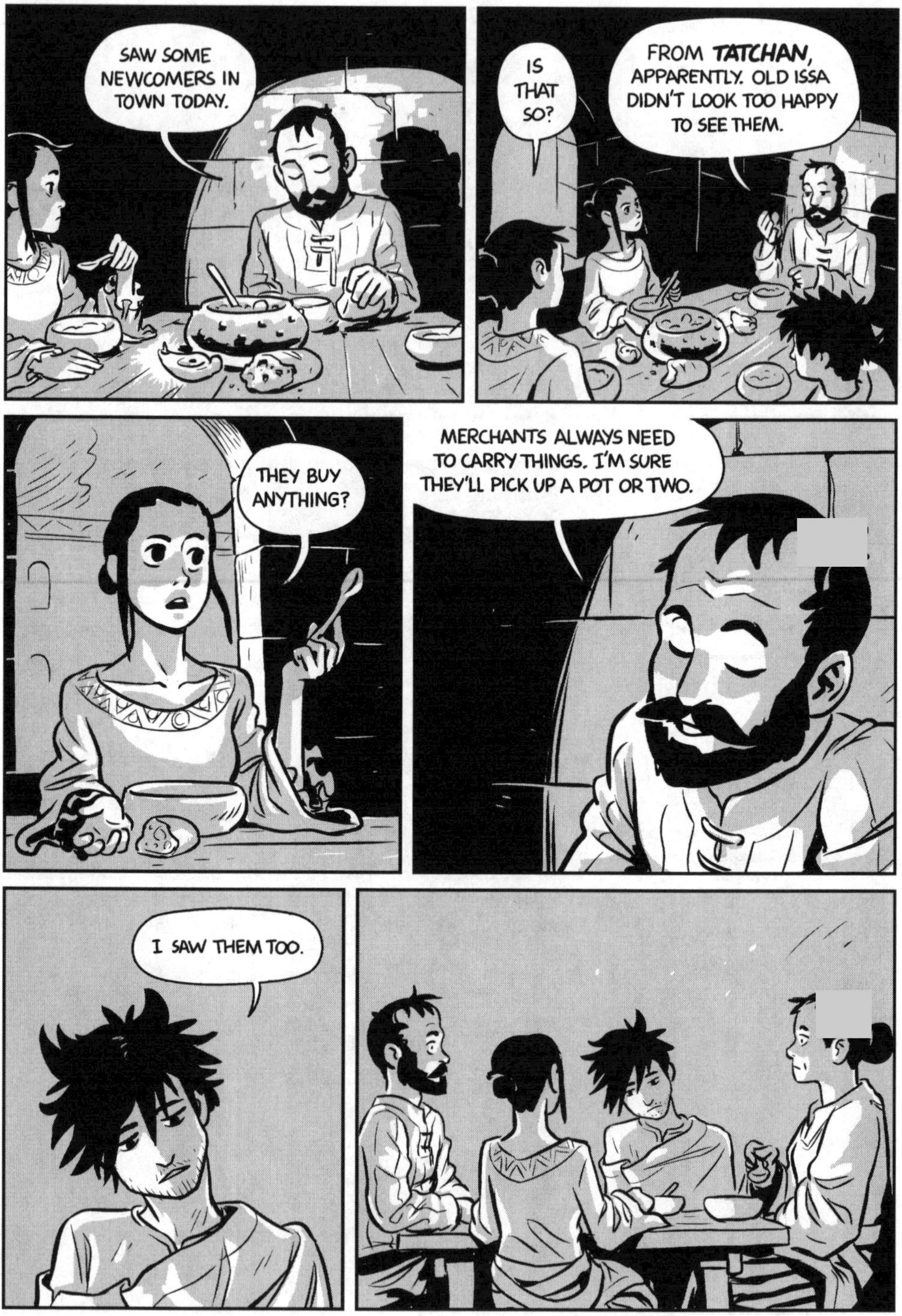
SAW SOME NEWCOMERS IN TOWN TODAY.
IS THAT SO?
FROM TATCHAN, APPARENTLY. OLD ISSA DIDN'T LOOK TOO HAPPY TO SEE THEM.
THEY BUY ANYTHING?
MERCHANTS ALWAYS NEED TO CARRY THINGS. I'M SURE THEY'LL PICK UP A POT OR TWO.
I SAW THEM TOO.

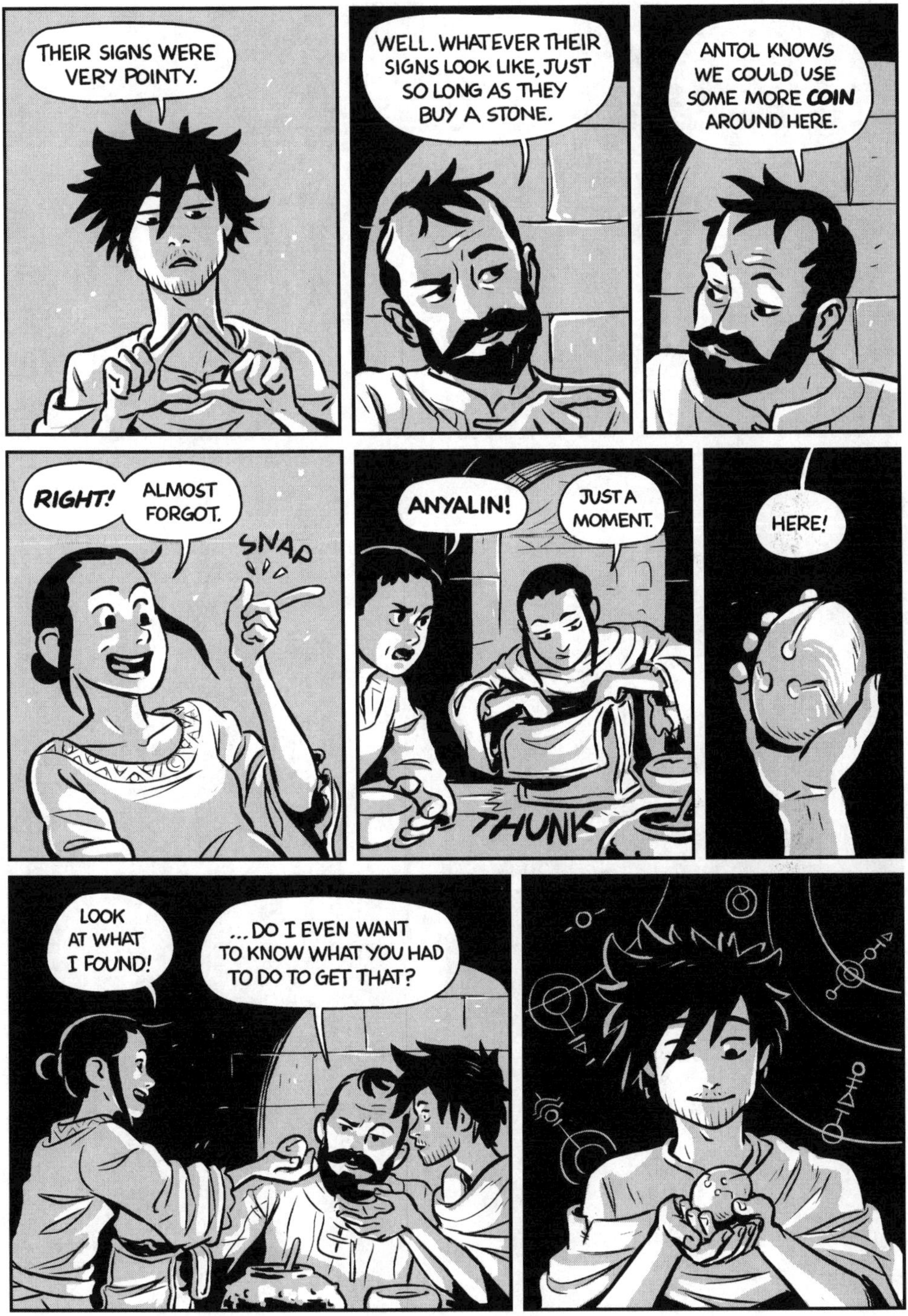
THEIR SIGNS WERE VERY POINTY.
WELL. WHATEVER THEIR SIGNS LOOK LIKE, JUST SO LONG AS THEY BUY A STONE.
ANTOL KNOWS WE COULD USE SOME MORE **COIN** AROUND HERE.
RIGHT!
ALMOST FORGOT.
SNAP
ANYALIN!
JUST A MOMENT.
THUNK
HERE!
LOOK AT WHAT I FOUND!
...DO I EVEN WANT TO KNOW WHAT YOU HAD TO DO TO GET THAT?

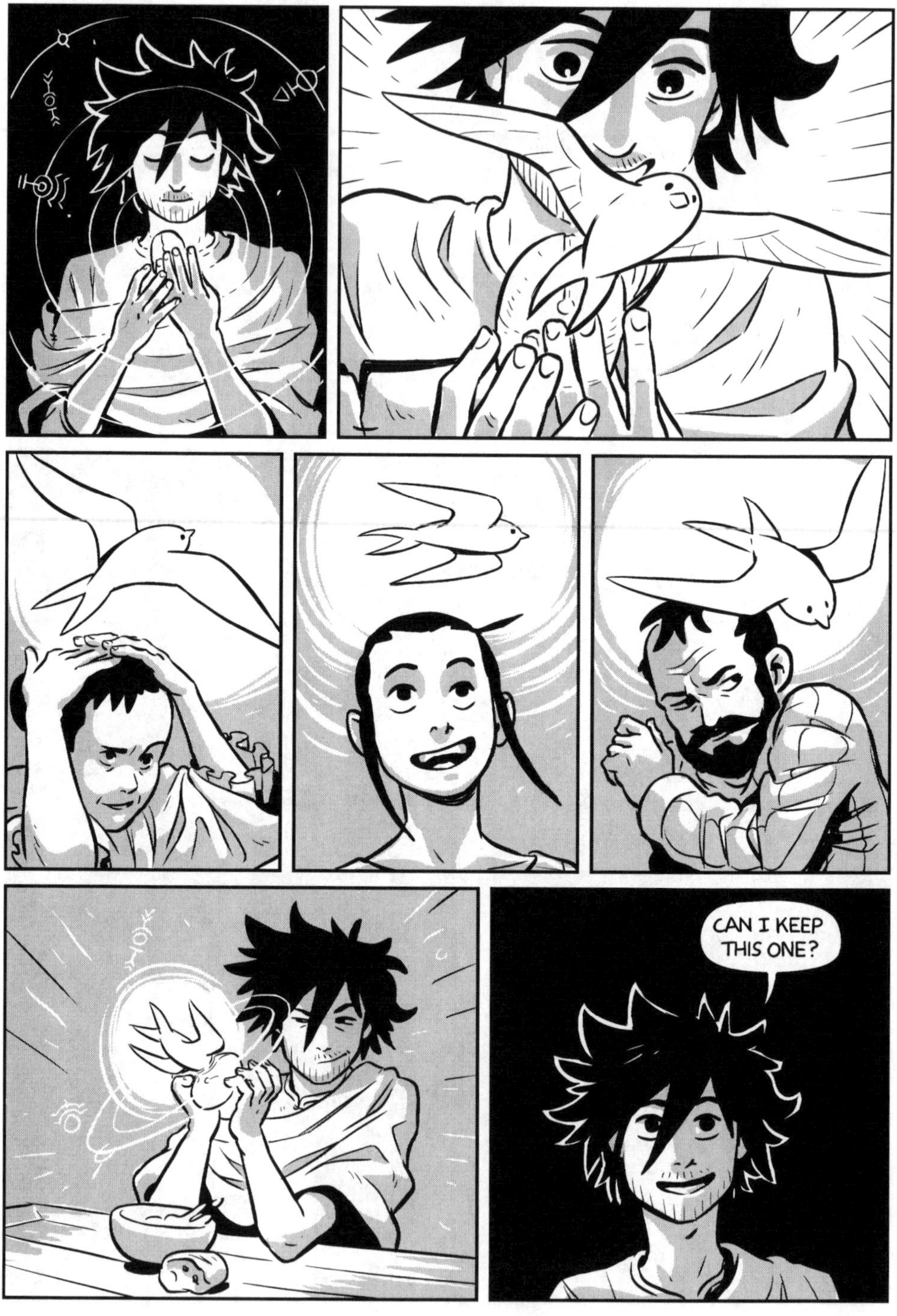
CAN I KEEP THIS ONE?

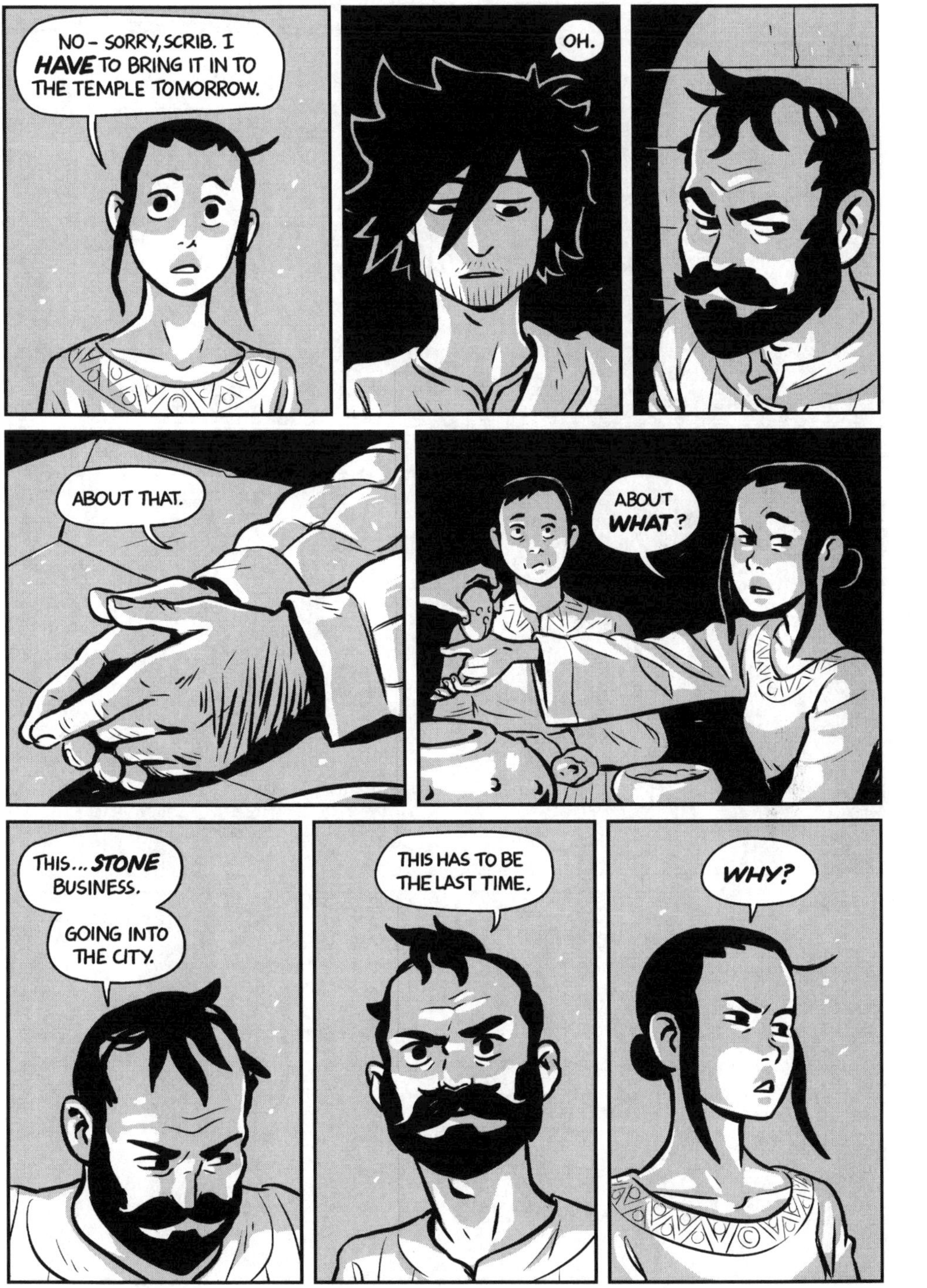
NO – SORRY, SCRIB. I **HAVE** TO BRING IT IN TO THE TEMPLE TOMORROW.
OH.
ABOUT THAT.
ABOUT **WHAT**?
THIS... **STONE** BUSINESS.
GOING INTO THE CITY.
THIS HAS TO BE THE LAST TIME.
WHY?

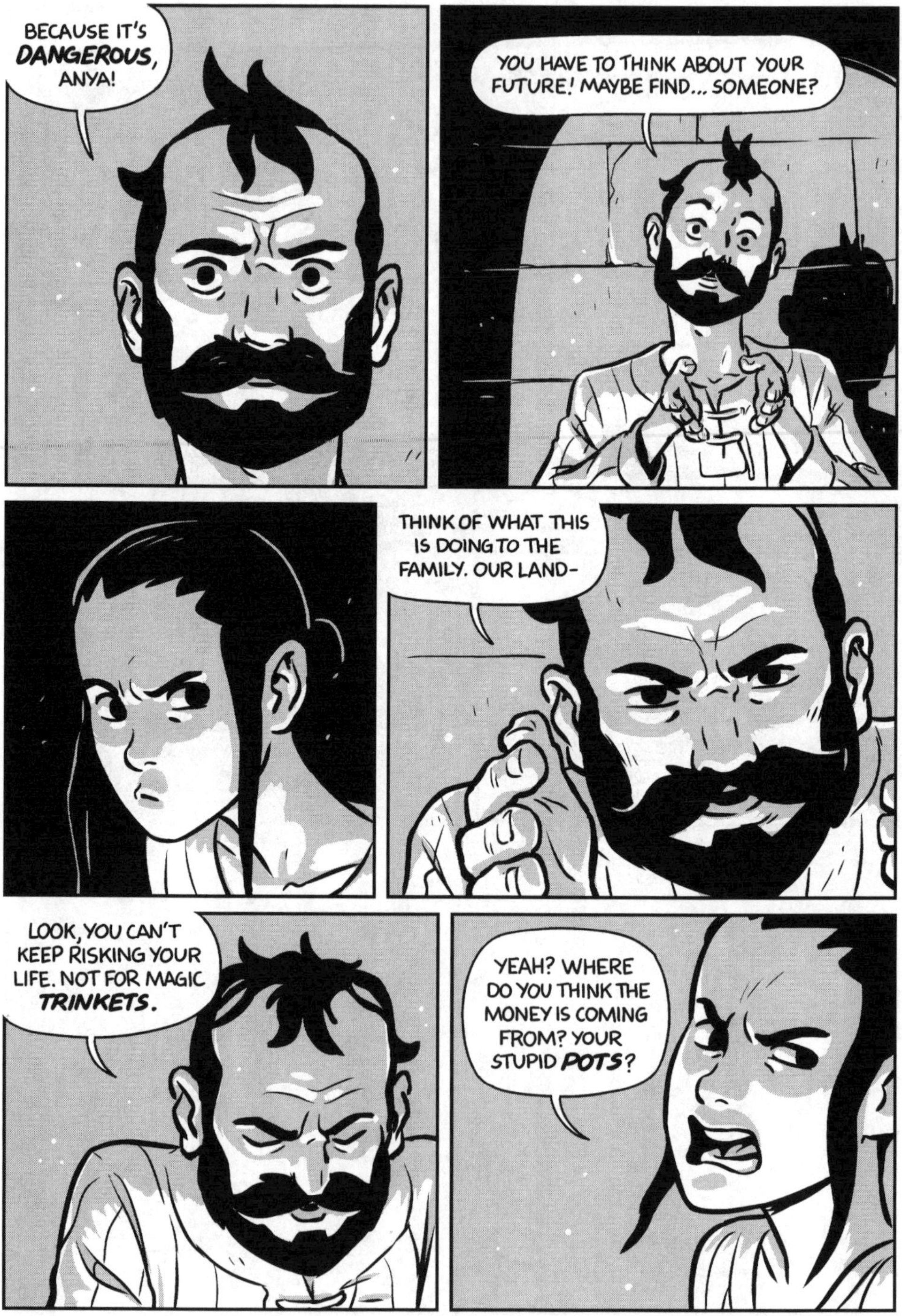
BECAUSE IT'S **DANGEROUS**, ANYA!
YOU HAVE TO THINK ABOUT YOUR FUTURE! MAYBE FIND... SOMEONE?
THINK OF WHAT THIS IS DOING TO THE FAMILY. OUR LAND-
LOOK, YOU CAN'T KEEP RISKING YOUR LIFE. NOT FOR MAGIC **TRINKETS**.
YEAH? WHERE DO YOU THINK THE MONEY IS COMING FROM? YOUR STUPID **POTS**?

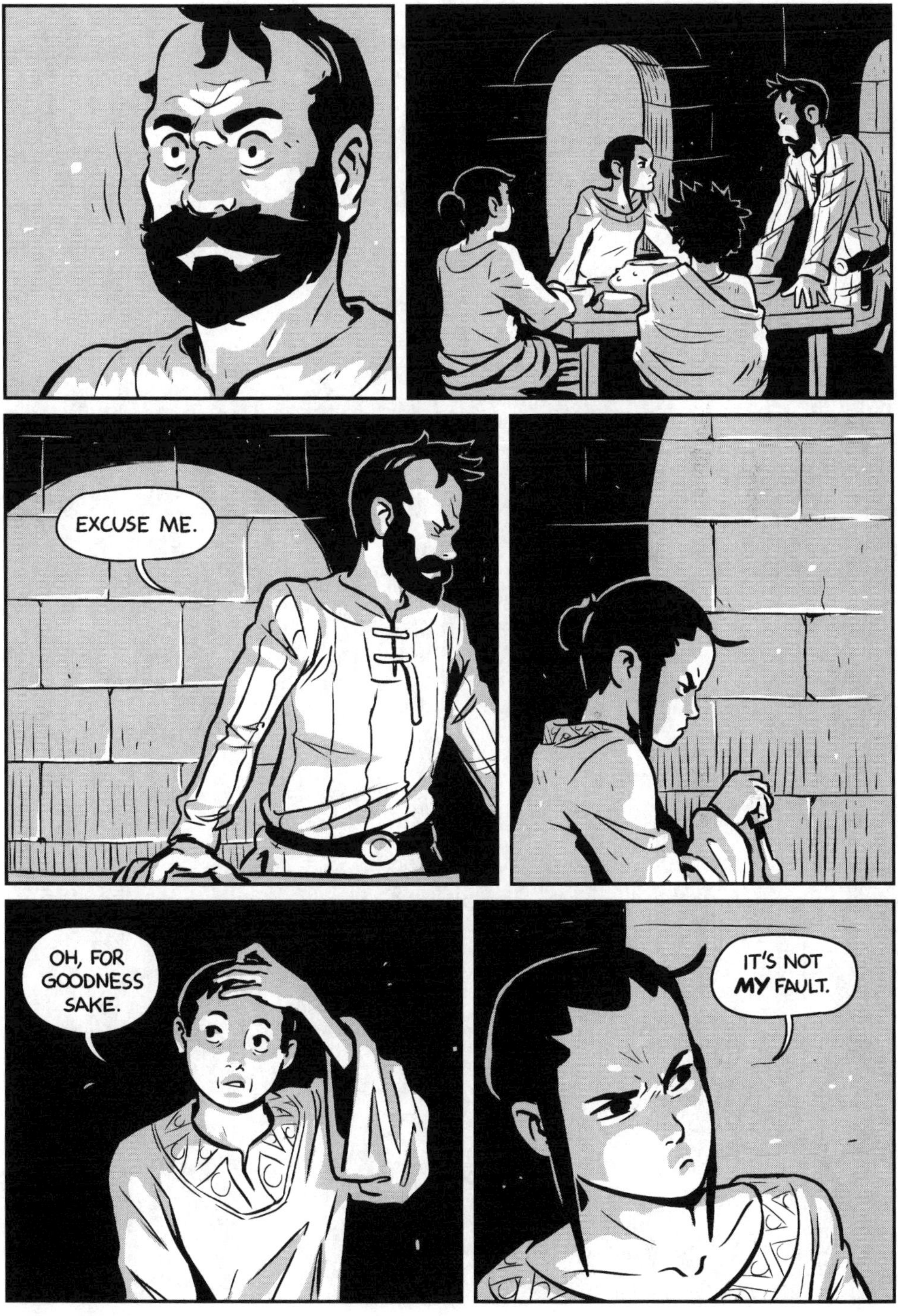
EXCUSE ME.
OH, FOR GOODNESS SAKE.
IT'S NOT MY FAULT.

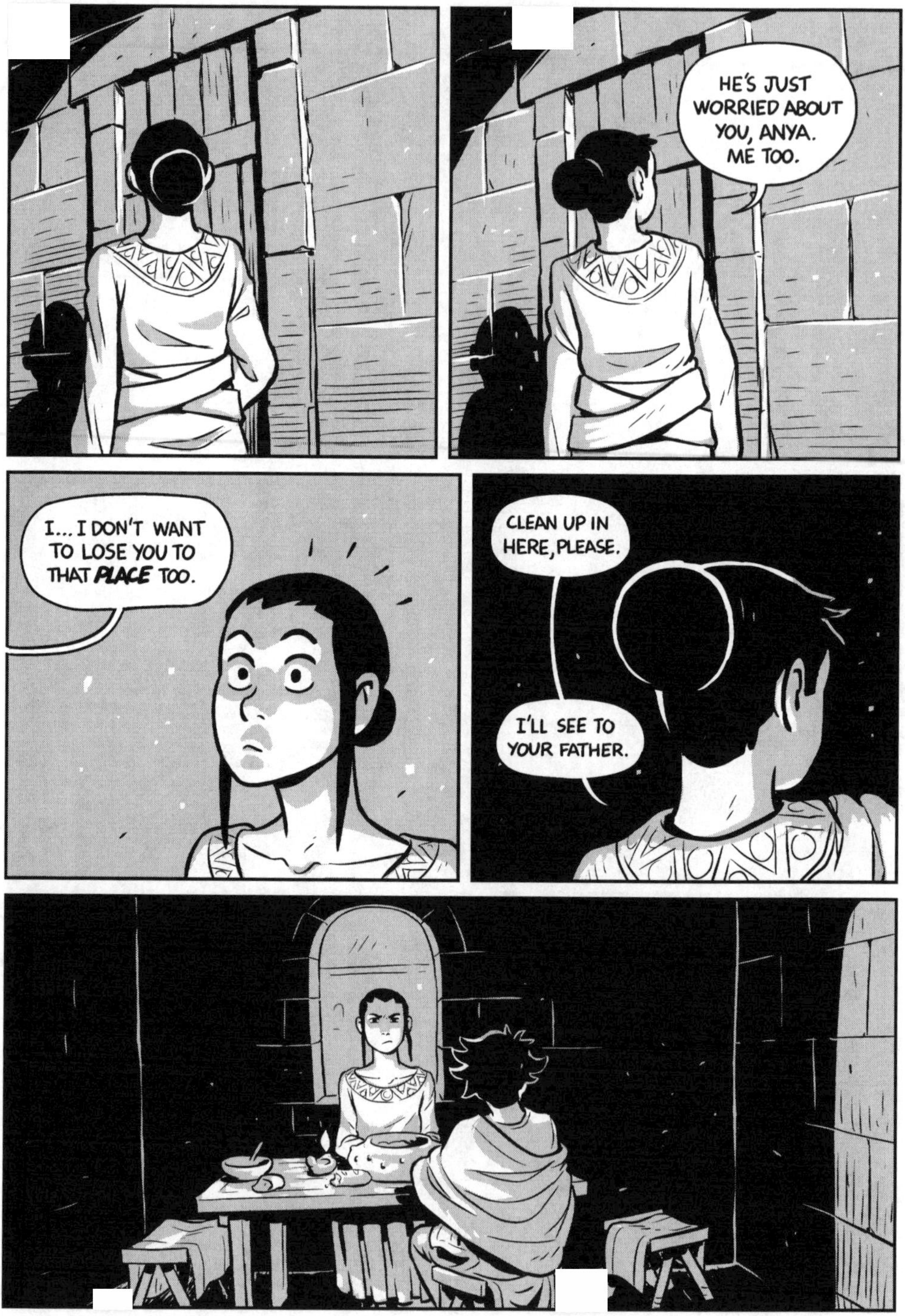
HE'S JUST WORRIED ABOUT YOU, ANYA. ME TOO.
I... I DON'T WANT TO LOSE YOU TO THAT PLACE TOO.
CLEAN UP IN HERE, PLEASE.
I'LL SEE TO YOUR FATHER.

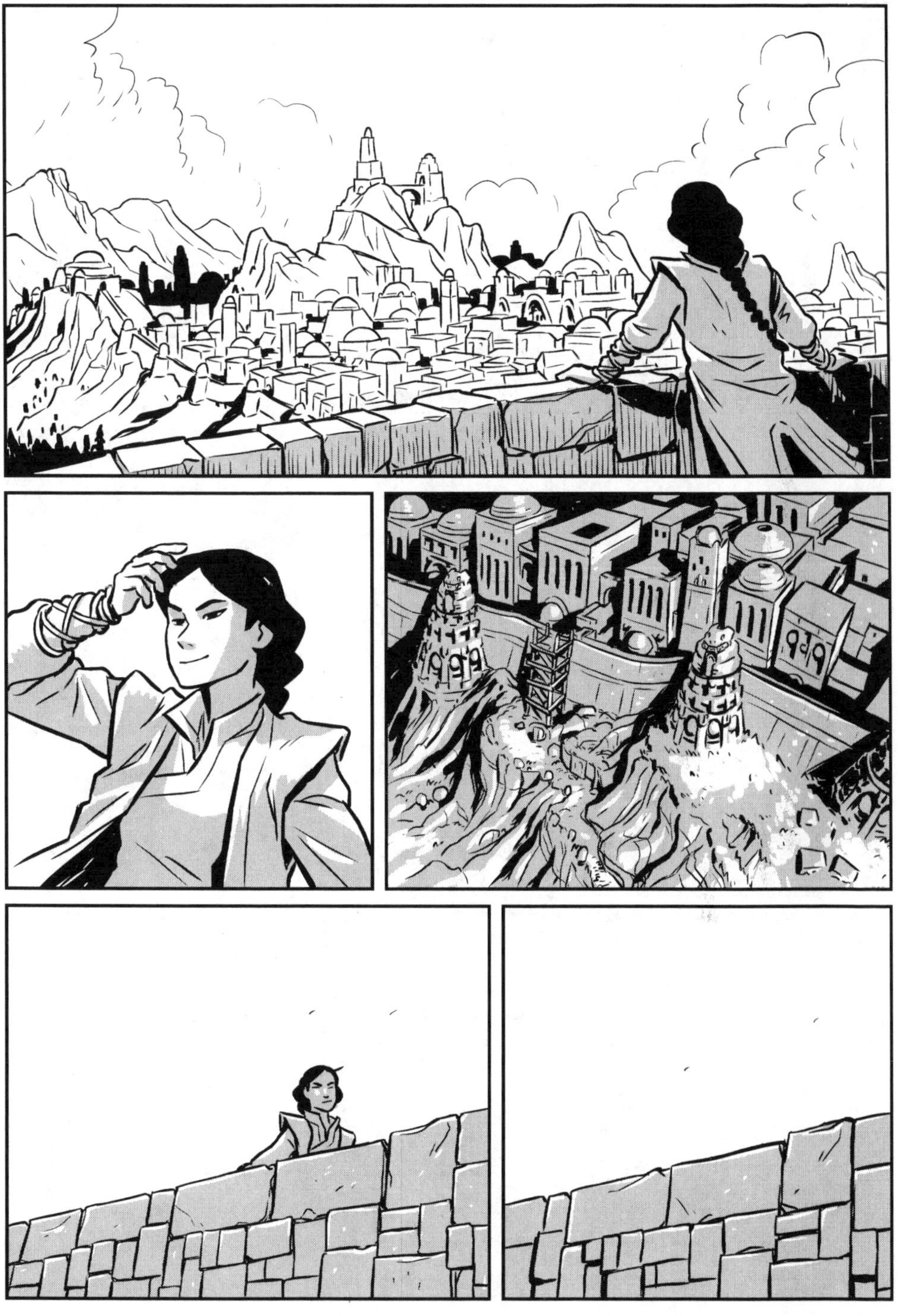

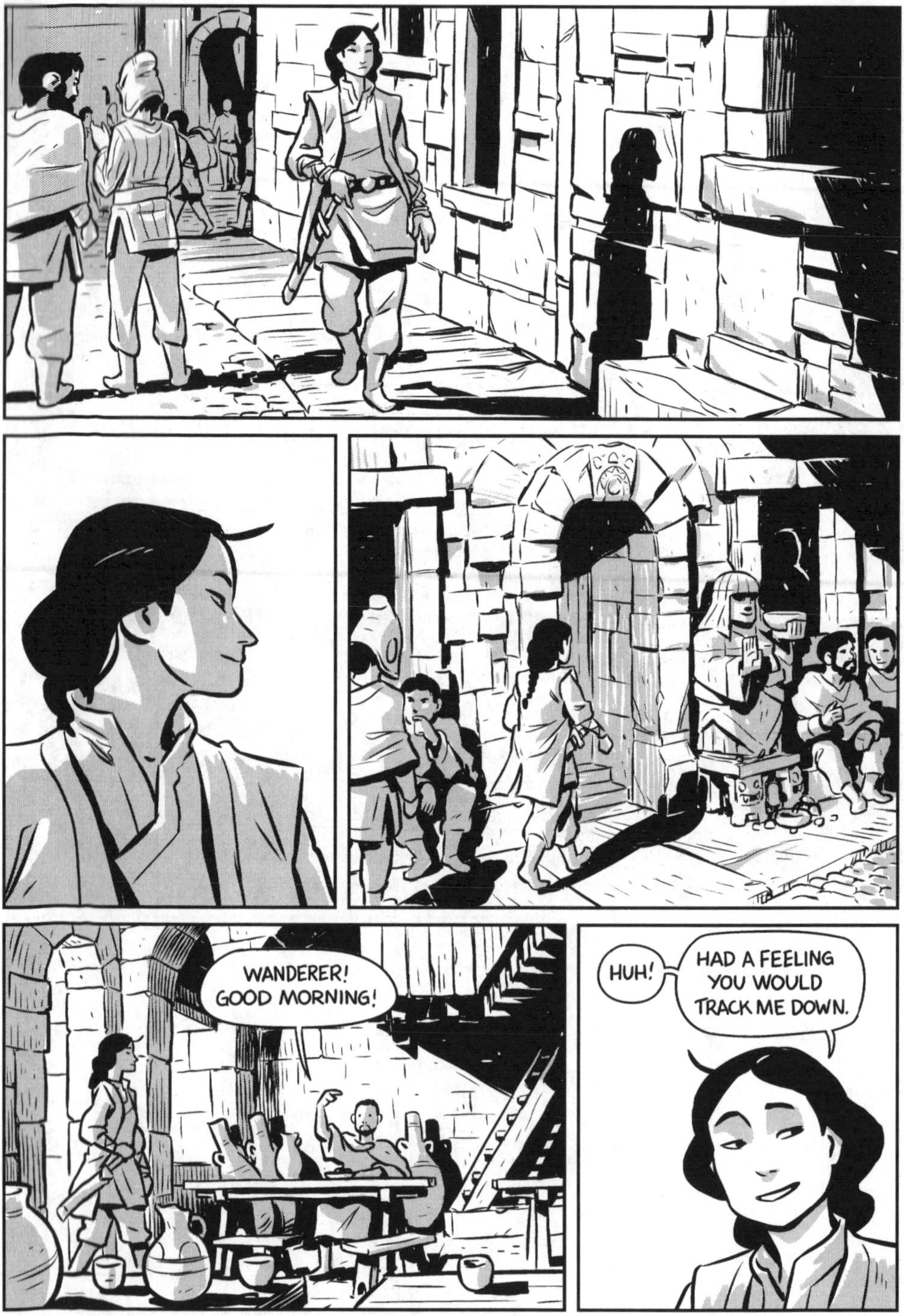
WANDERER! GOOD MORNING!
HUH!
HAD A FEELING YOU WOULD TRACK ME DOWN.

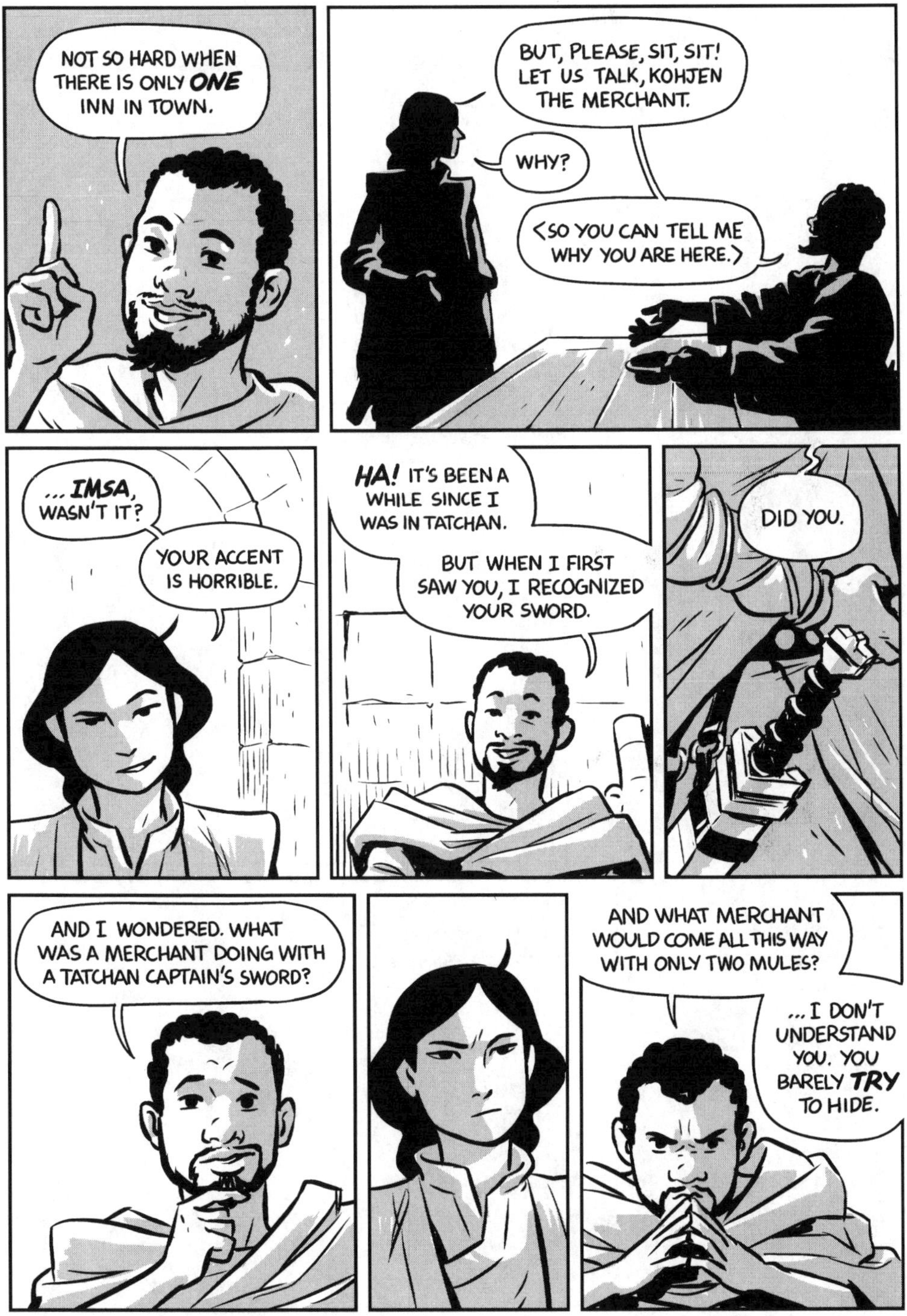

NOT SO HARD WHEN THERE IS ONLY ONE INN IN TOWN.
BUT, PLEASE, SIT, SIT! LET US TALK, KOHJEN THE MERCHANT.
WHY?
<SO YOU CAN TELL ME WHY YOU ARE HERE.>
...IMSA, WASN'T IT?
YOUR ACCENT IS HORRIBLE.
HA! IT'S BEEN A WHILE SINCE I WAS IN TATCHAN.
BUT WHEN I FIRST SAW YOU, I RECOGNIZED YOUR SWORD.
DID YOU.
AND I WONDERED. WHAT WAS A MERCHANT DOING WITH A TATCHAN CAPTAIN'S SWORD?
AND WHAT MERCHANT WOULD COME ALL THIS WAY WITH ONLY TWO MULES?
...I DON'T UNDERSTAND YOU. YOU BARELY TRY TO HIDE.

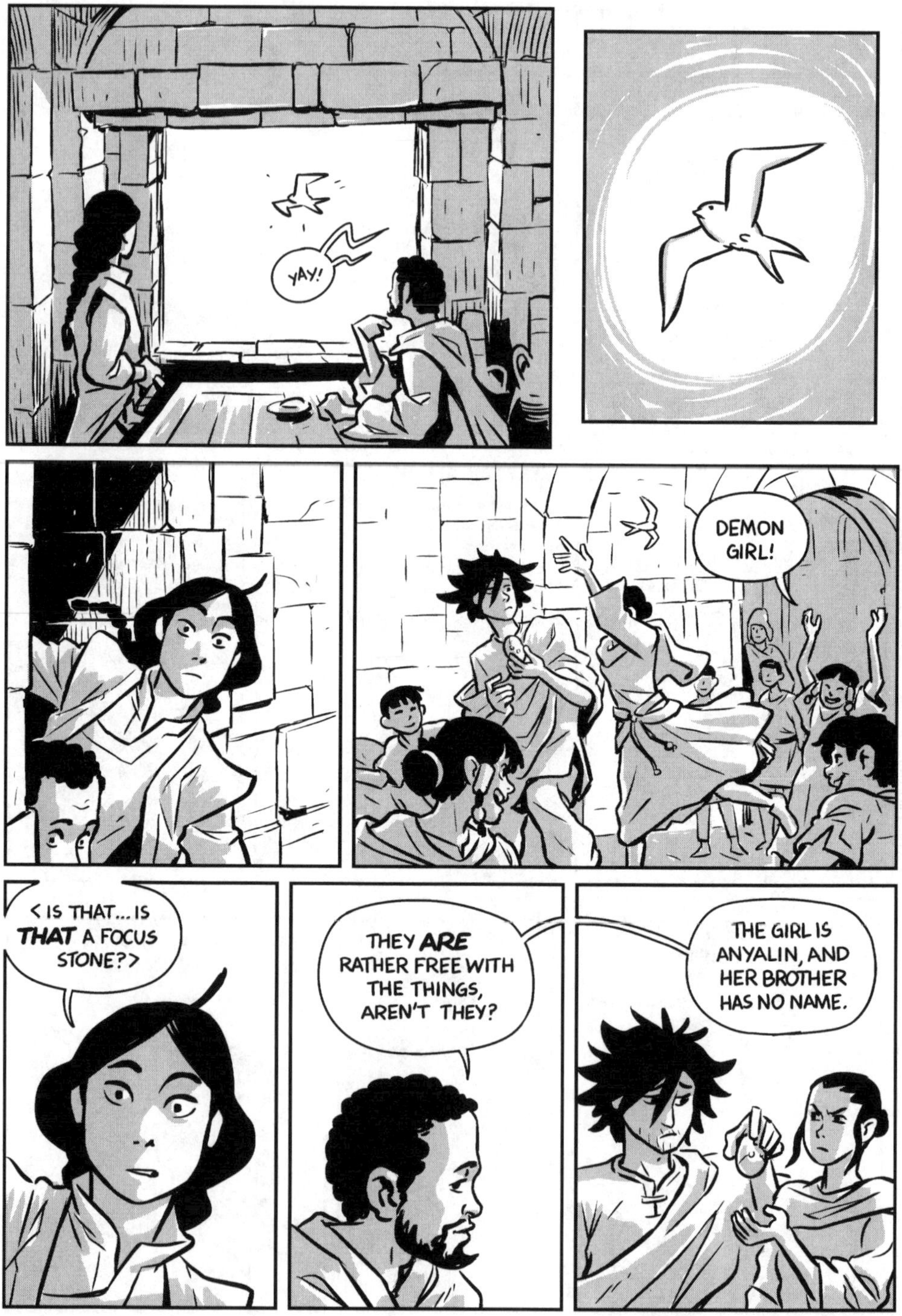
YAY!
DEMON GIRL!
< IS THAT... IS **THAT** A FOCUS STONE?>
THEY **ARE** RATHER FREE WITH THE THINGS, AREN'T THEY?
THE GIRL IS ANYALIN, AND HER BROTHER HAS NO NAME.

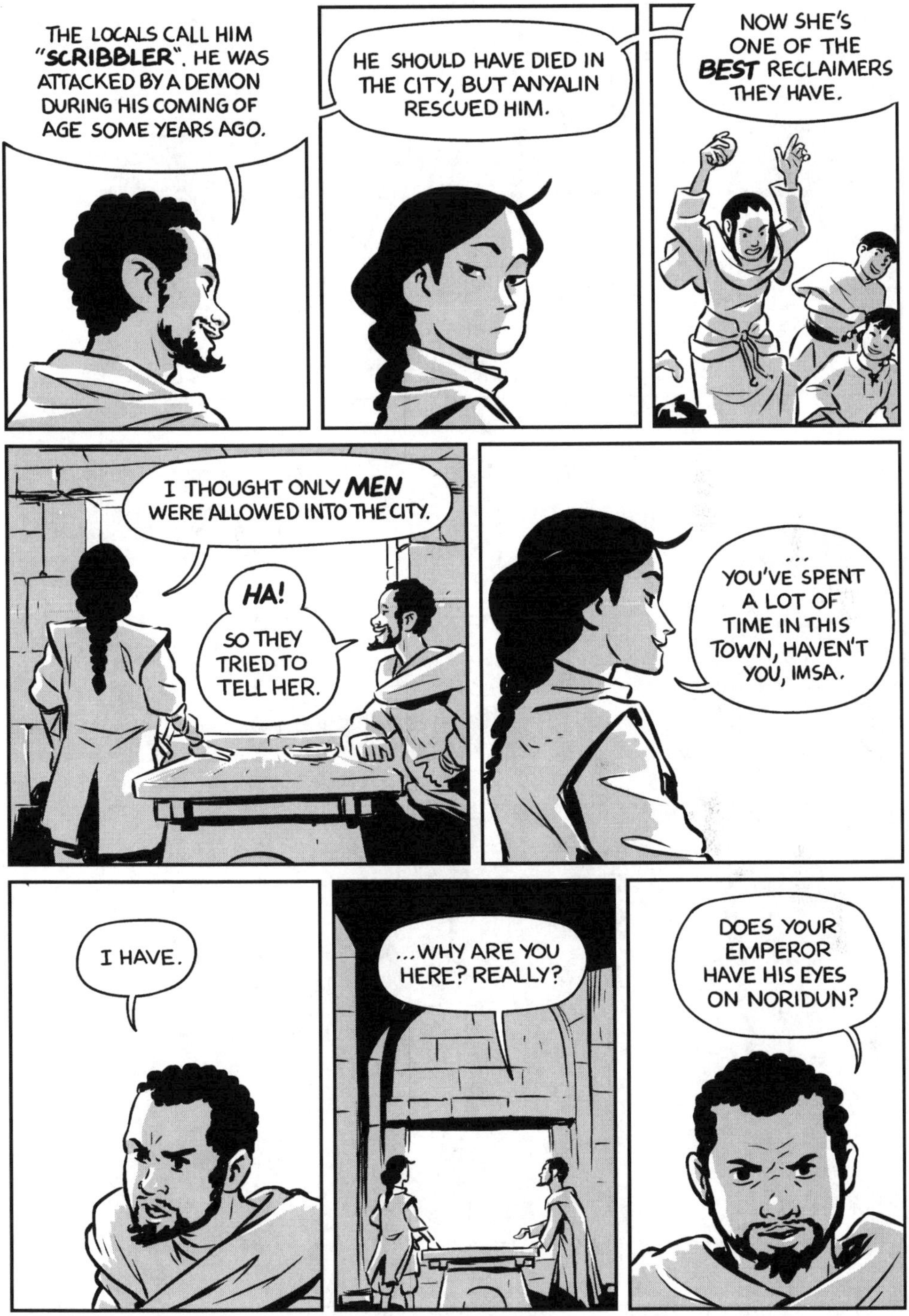
THE LOCALS CALL HIM "SCRIBBLER". HE WAS ATTACKED BY A DEMON DURING HIS COMING OF AGE SOME YEARS AGO.
HE SHOULD HAVE DIED IN THE CITY, BUT ANYALIN RESCUED HIM.
NOW SHE'S ONE OF THE BEST RECLAIMERS THEY HAVE.
I THOUGHT ONLY MEN WERE ALLOWED INTO THE CITY.
HA!
SO THEY TRIED TO TELL HER.
... YOU'VE SPENT A LOT OF TIME IN THIS TOWN, HAVEN'T YOU, IMSA.
I HAVE.
...WHY ARE YOU HERE? REALLY?
DOES YOUR EMPEROR HAVE HIS EYES ON NORIDUN?

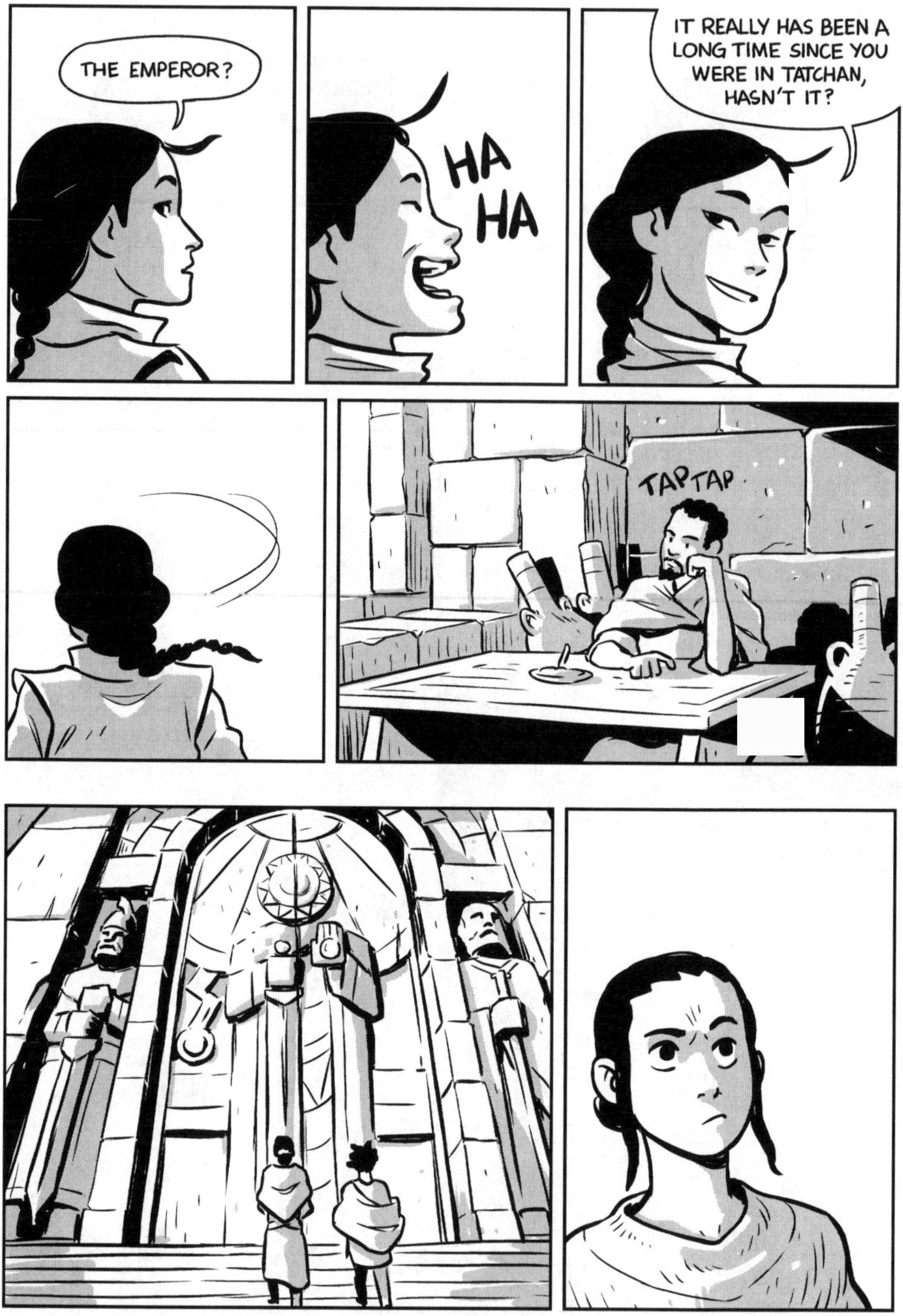
THE EMPEROR?
HA HA
IT REALLY HAS BEEN A LONG TIME SINCE YOU WERE IN TATCHAN, HASN'T IT?
TAP TAP

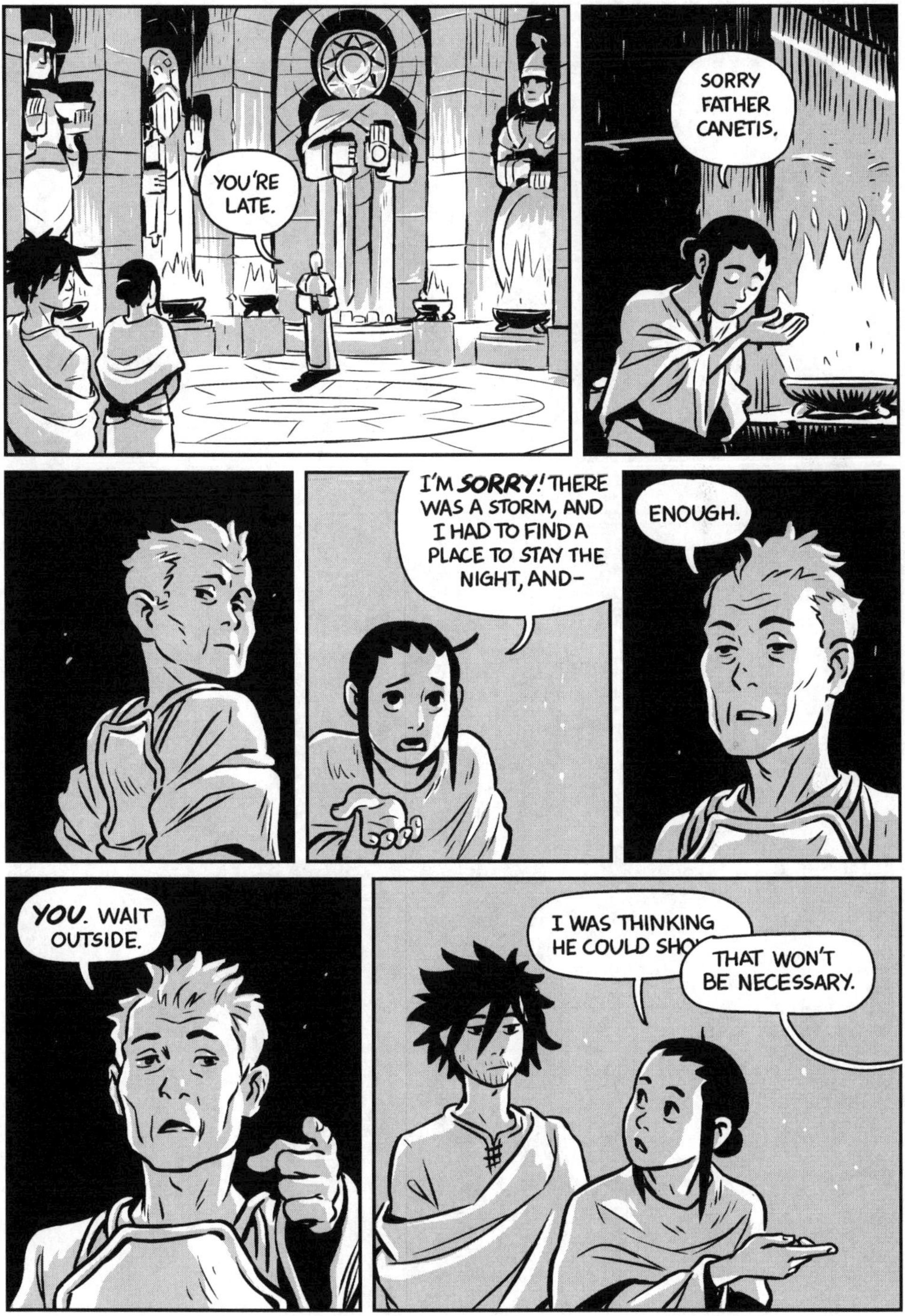
YOU'RE LATE.
SORRY FATHER CANETIS.
I'M **SORRY**! THERE WAS A STORM, AND I HAD TO FIND A PLACE TO STAY THE NIGHT, AND-
ENOUGH.
YOU. WAIT OUTSIDE.
I WAS THINKING HE COULD SHO
THAT WON'T BE NECESSARY.

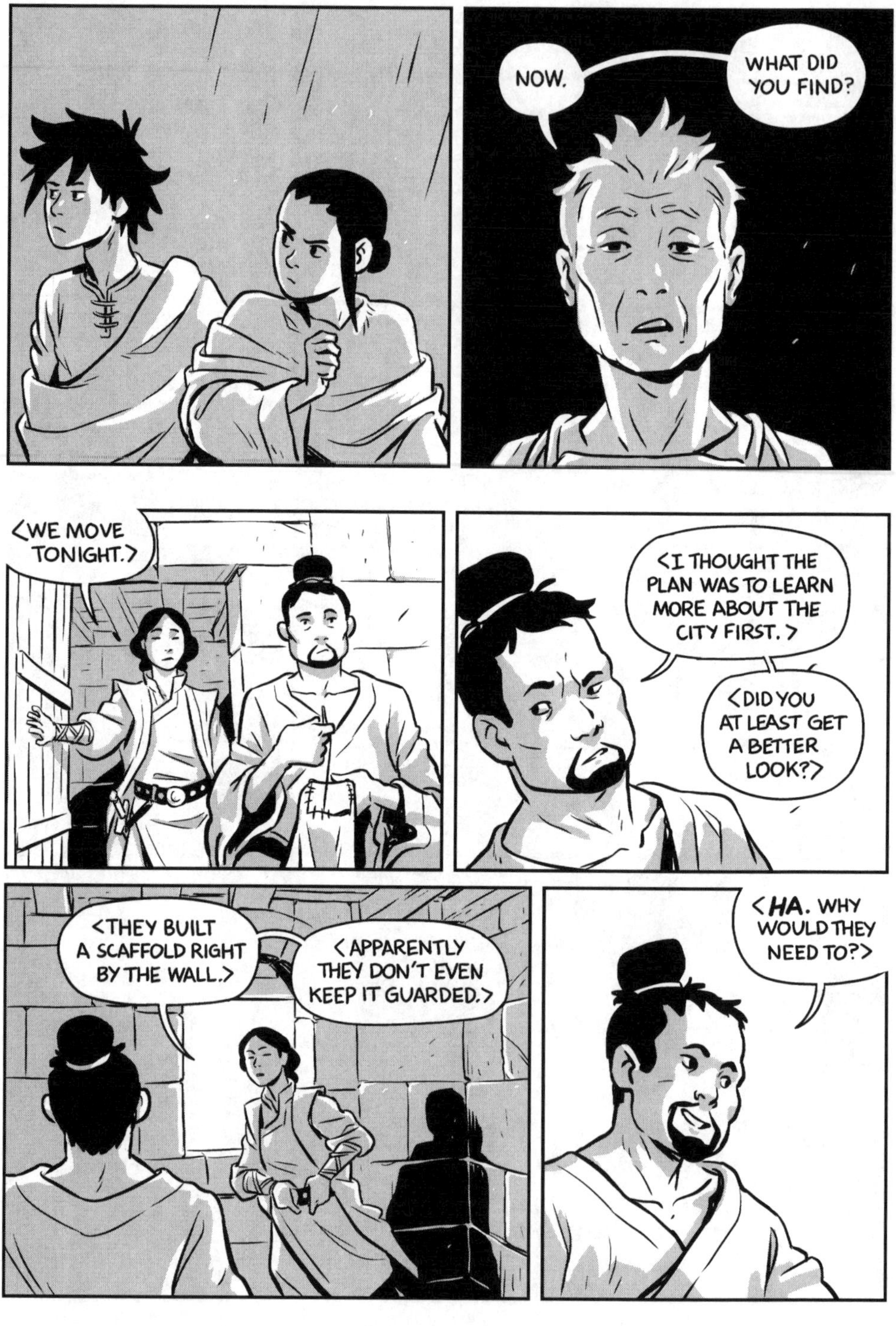
NOW.
WHAT DID YOU FIND?
<WE MOVE TONIGHT.>
<I THOUGHT THE PLAN WAS TO LEARN MORE ABOUT THE CITY FIRST.>
<DID YOU AT LEAST GET A BETTER LOOK?>
<THEY BUILT A SCAFFOLD RIGHT BY THE WALL.>
<APPARENTLY THEY DON'T EVEN KEEP IT GUARDED.>
<HA. WHY WOULD THEY NEED TO?>

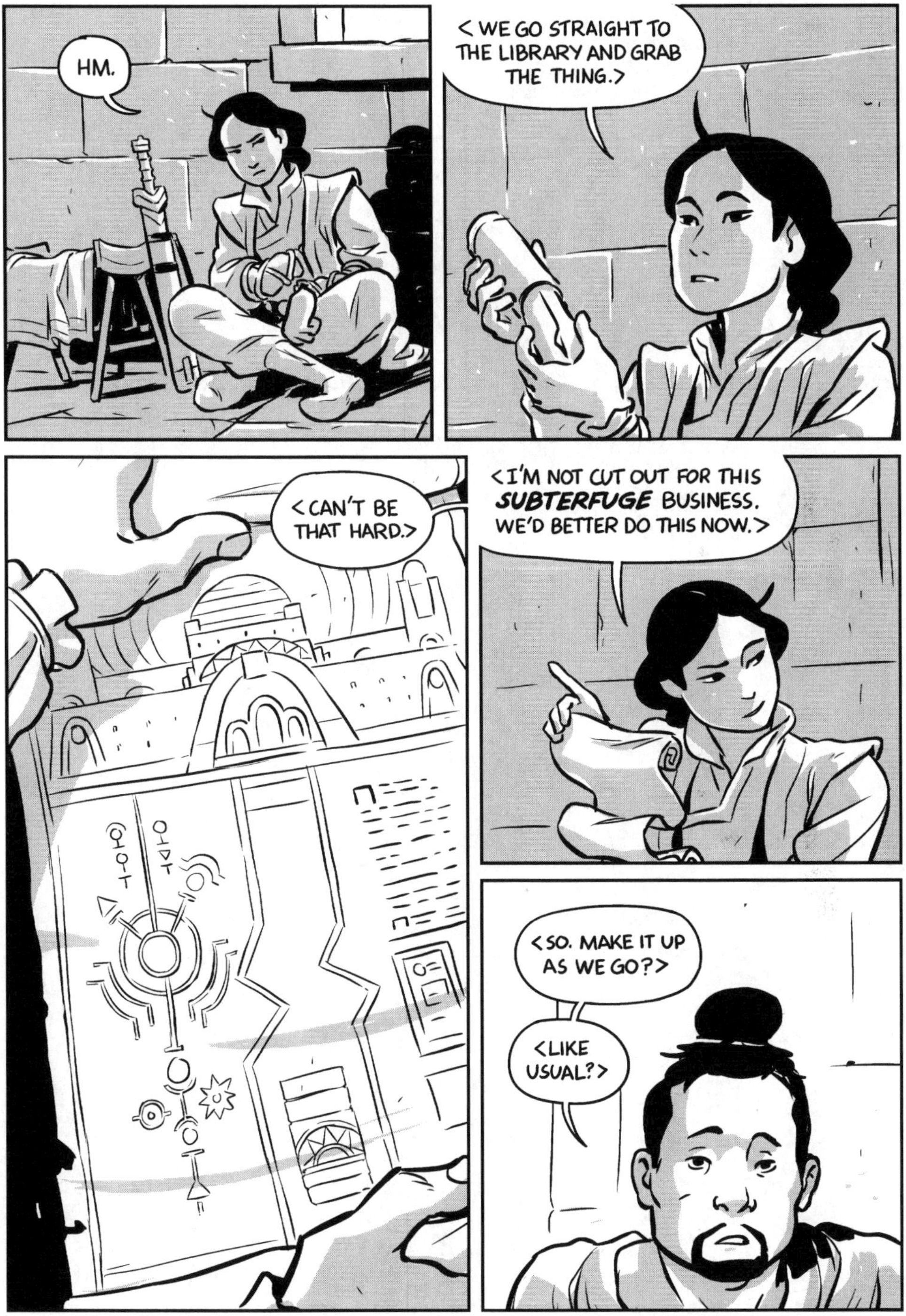
HM.
< WE GO STRAIGHT TO THE LIBRARY AND GRAB THE THING.>
<CAN'T BE THAT HARD.>
<I'M NOT CUT OUT FOR THIS SUBTERFUGE BUSINESS. WE'D BETTER DO THIS NOW.>
<SO. MAKE IT UP AS WE GO?>
<LIKE USUAL?>

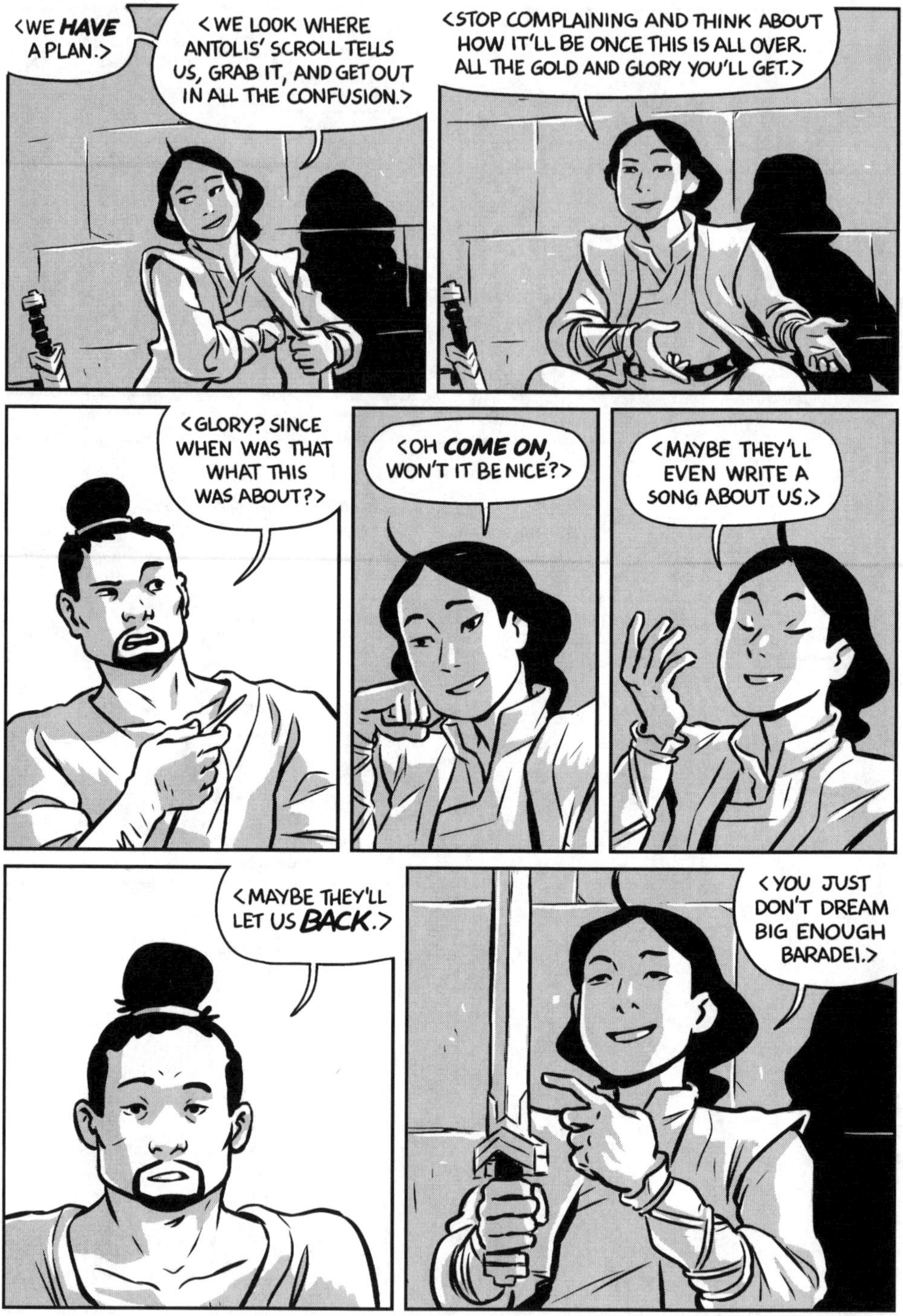

<WE HAVE A PLAN.>
<WE LOOK WHERE ANTOLIS' SCROLL TELLS US, GRAB IT, AND GET OUT IN ALL THE CONFUSION.>
<STOP COMPLAINING AND THINK ABOUT HOW IT'LL BE ONCE THIS IS ALL OVER. ALL THE GOLD AND GLORY YOU'LL GET.>
<GLORY? SINCE WHEN WAS THAT WHAT THIS WAS ABOUT?>
<OH COME ON, WON'T IT BE NICE?>
<MAYBE THEY'LL EVEN WRITE A SONG ABOUT US.>
<MAYBE THEY'LL LET US BACK.>
<YOU JUST DON'T DREAM BIG ENOUGH BARADEI.>

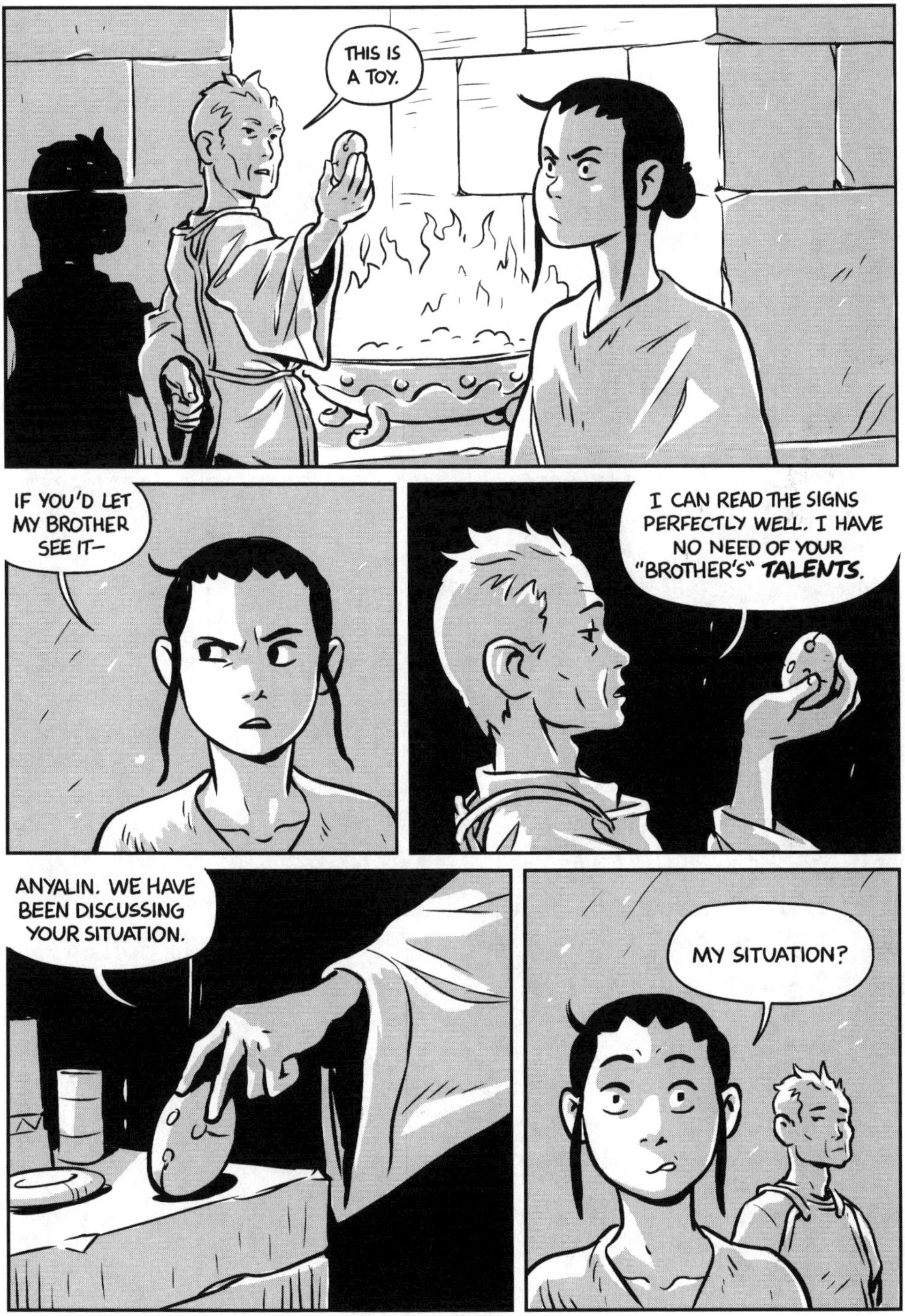
THIS IS A TOY.
IF YOU'D LET MY BROTHER SEE IT–
I CAN READ THE SIGNS PERFECTLY WELL. I HAVE NO NEED OF YOUR "BROTHER'S" TALENTS.
ANYALIN. WE HAVE BEEN DISCUSSING YOUR SITUATION.
MY SITUATION?

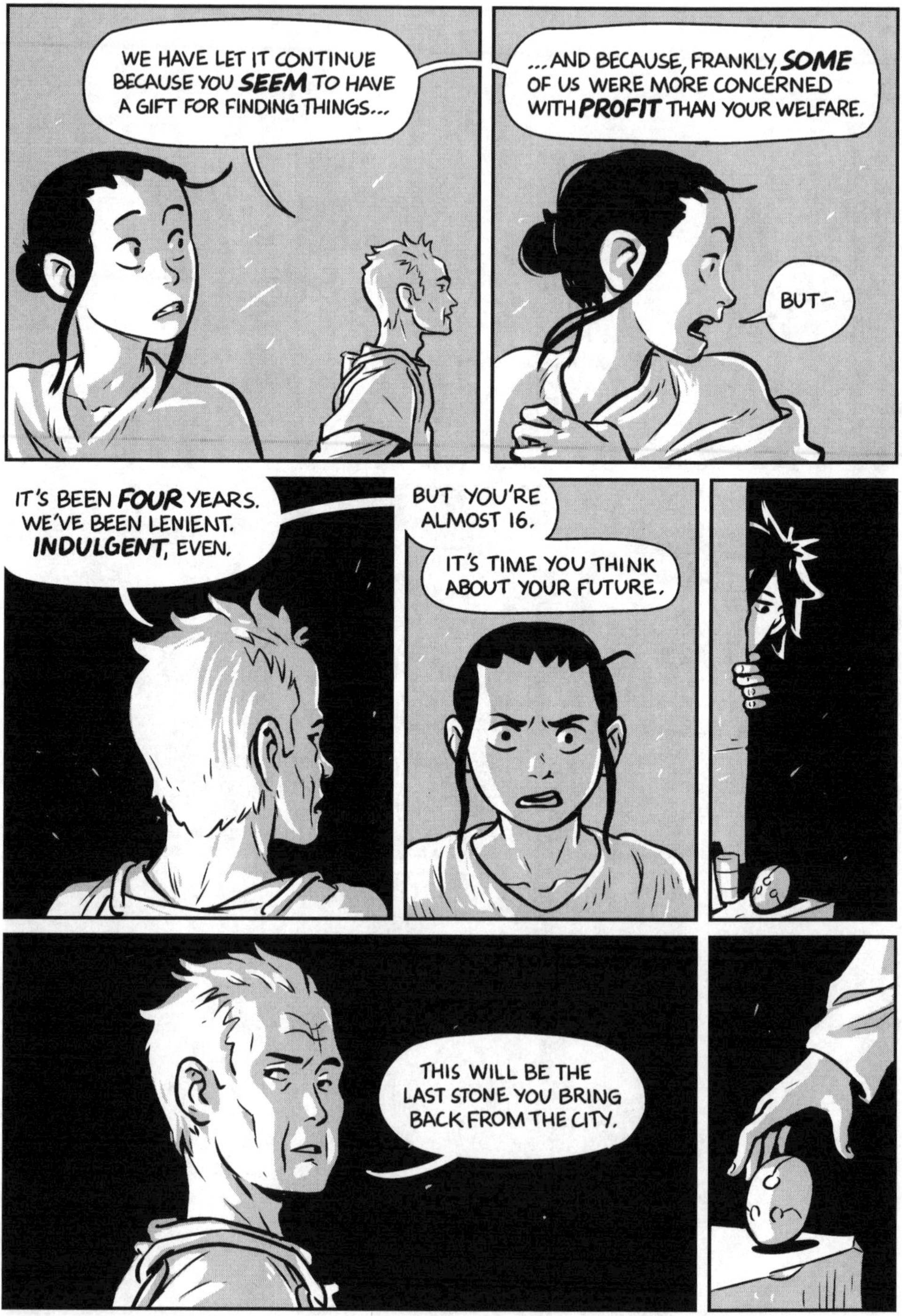
WE HAVE LET IT CONTINUE BECAUSE YOU SEEM TO HAVE A GIFT FOR FINDING THINGS...
...AND BECAUSE, FRANKLY, SOME OF US WERE MORE CONCERNED WITH PROFIT THAN YOUR WELFARE.
BUT-
IT'S BEEN FOUR YEARS. WE'VE BEEN LENIENT. INDULGENT, EVEN.
BUT YOU'RE ALMOST 16.
IT'S TIME YOU THINK ABOUT YOUR FUTURE.
THIS WILL BE THE LAST STONE YOU BRING BACK FROM THE CITY.

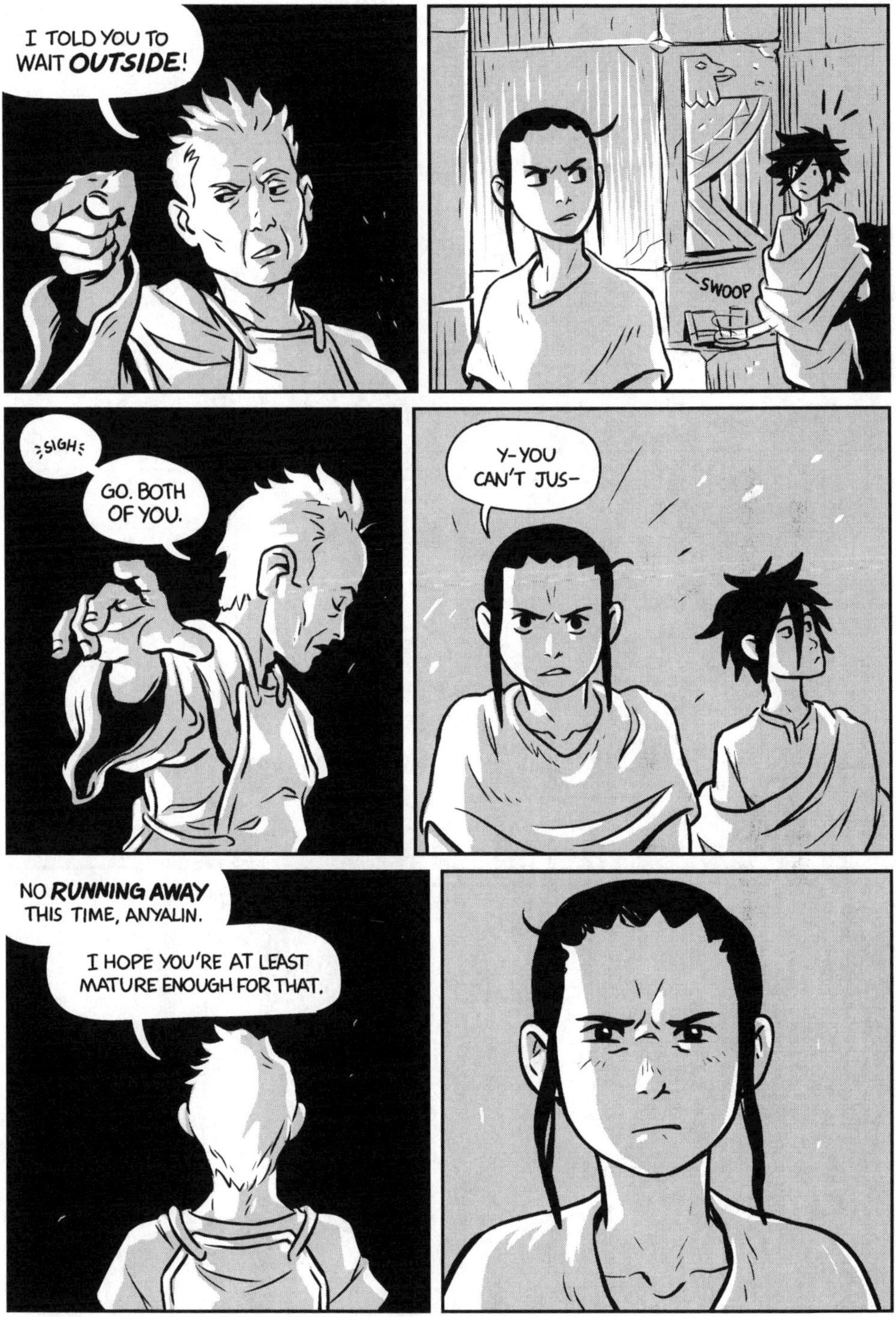
I TOLD YOU TO WAIT OUTSIDE!
SWOOP
SIGH
GO. BOTH OF YOU.
Y-YOU CAN'T JUS-
NO RUNNING AWAY THIS TIME, ANYALIN.
I HOPE YOU'RE AT LEAST MATURE ENOUGH FOR THAT.

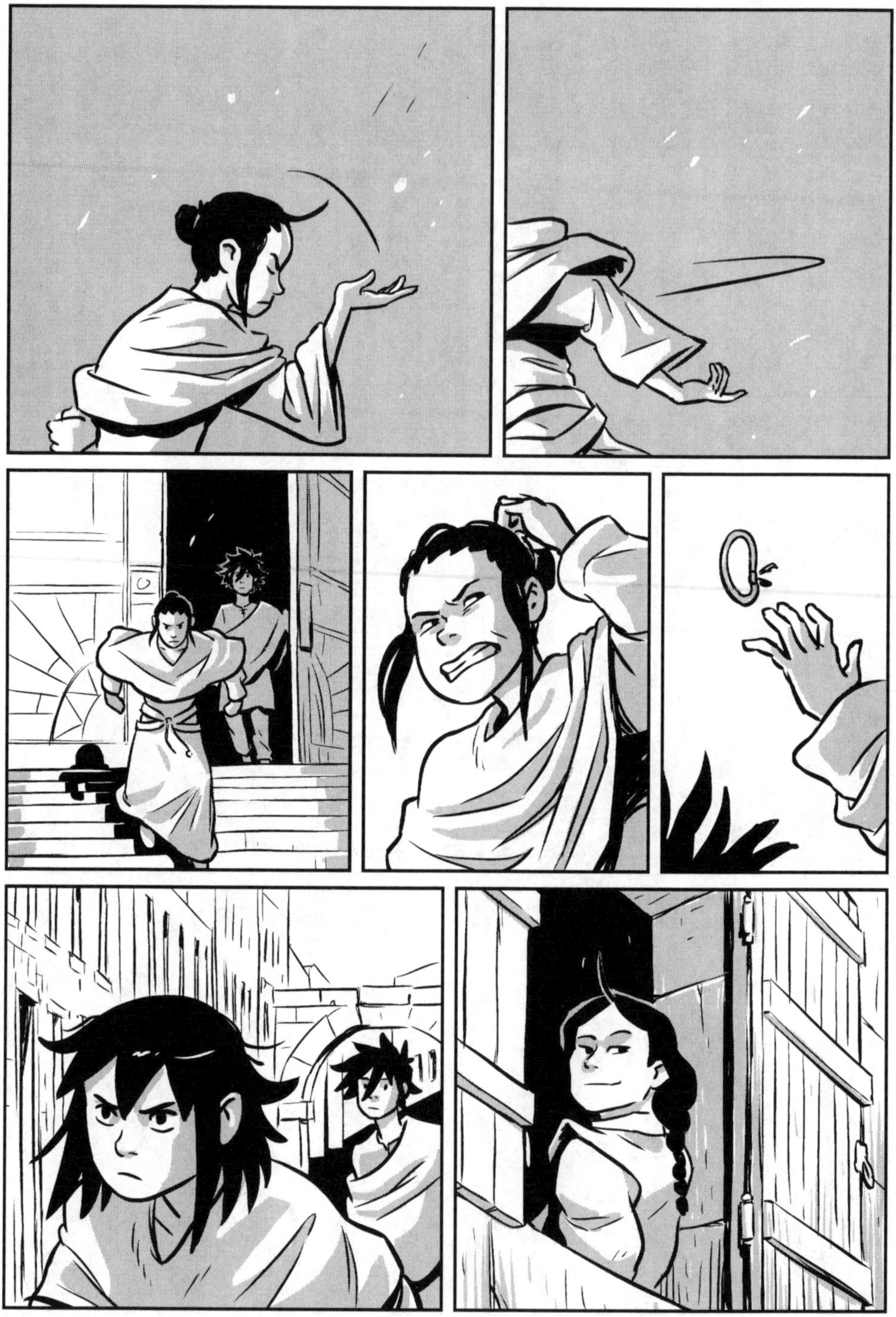

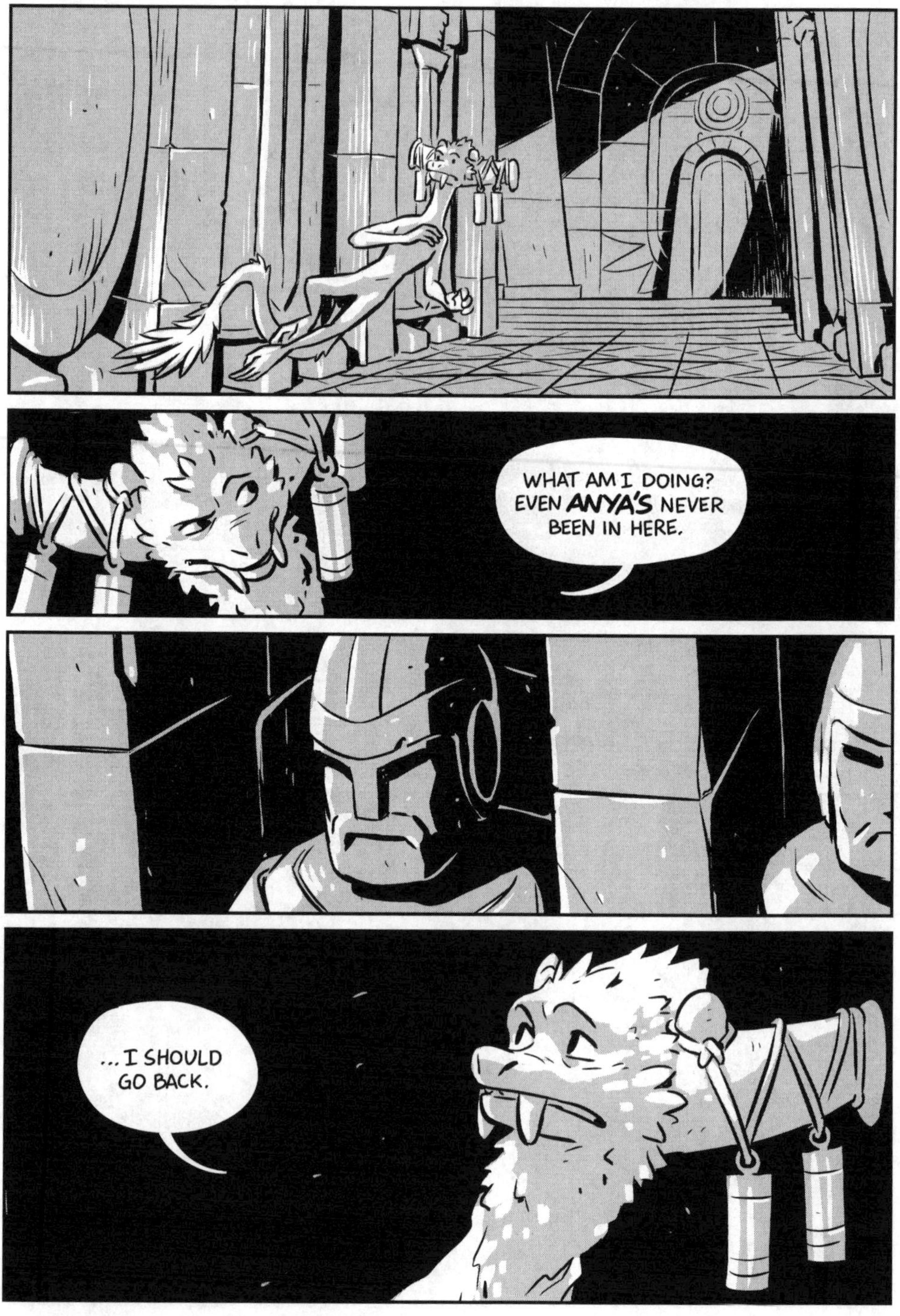
WHAT AM I DOING? EVEN ANYA'S NEVER BEEN IN HERE.
...I SHOULD GO BACK.

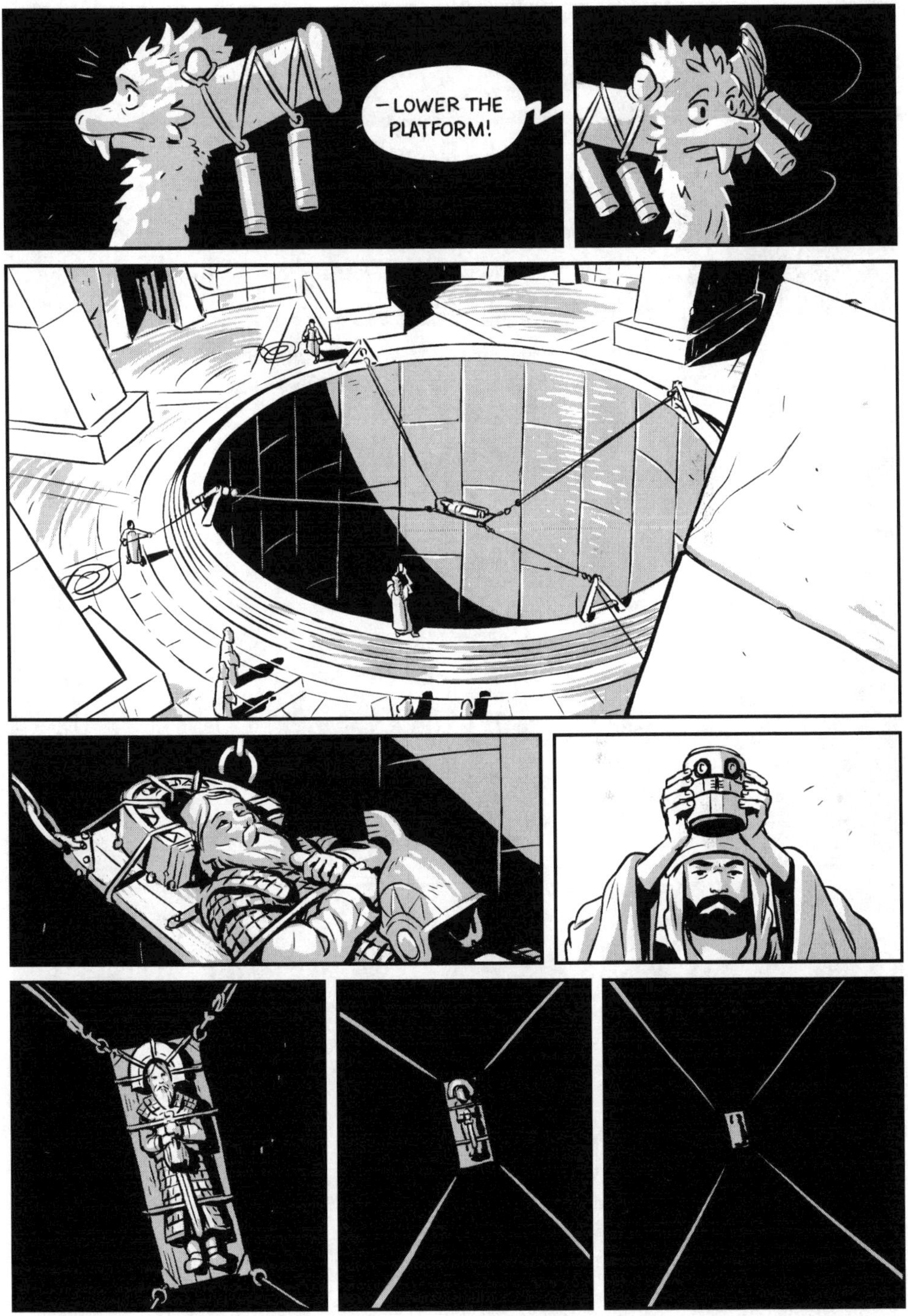
—LOWER THE PLATFORM!

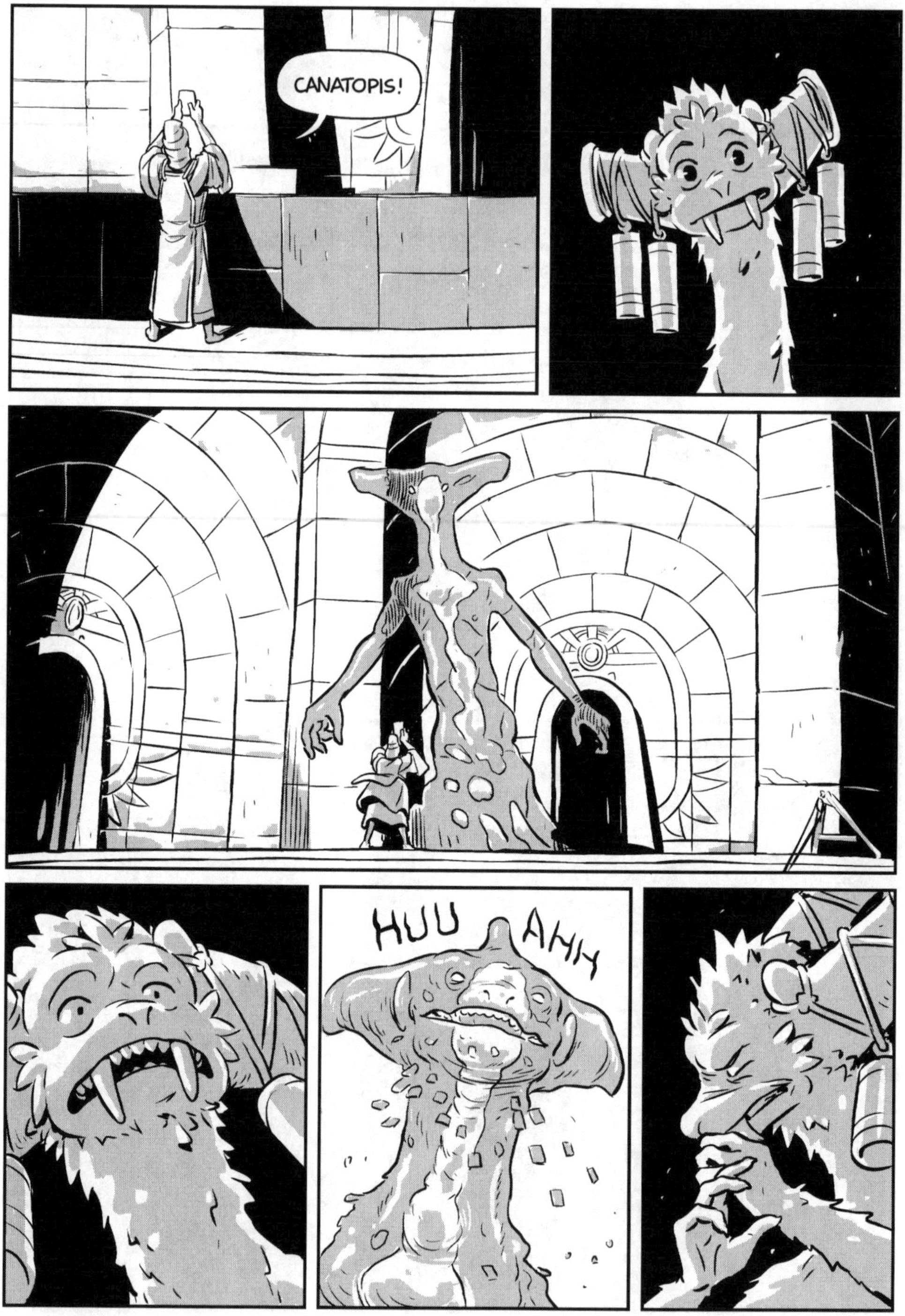
CANATOPIS!
HUU
AHH

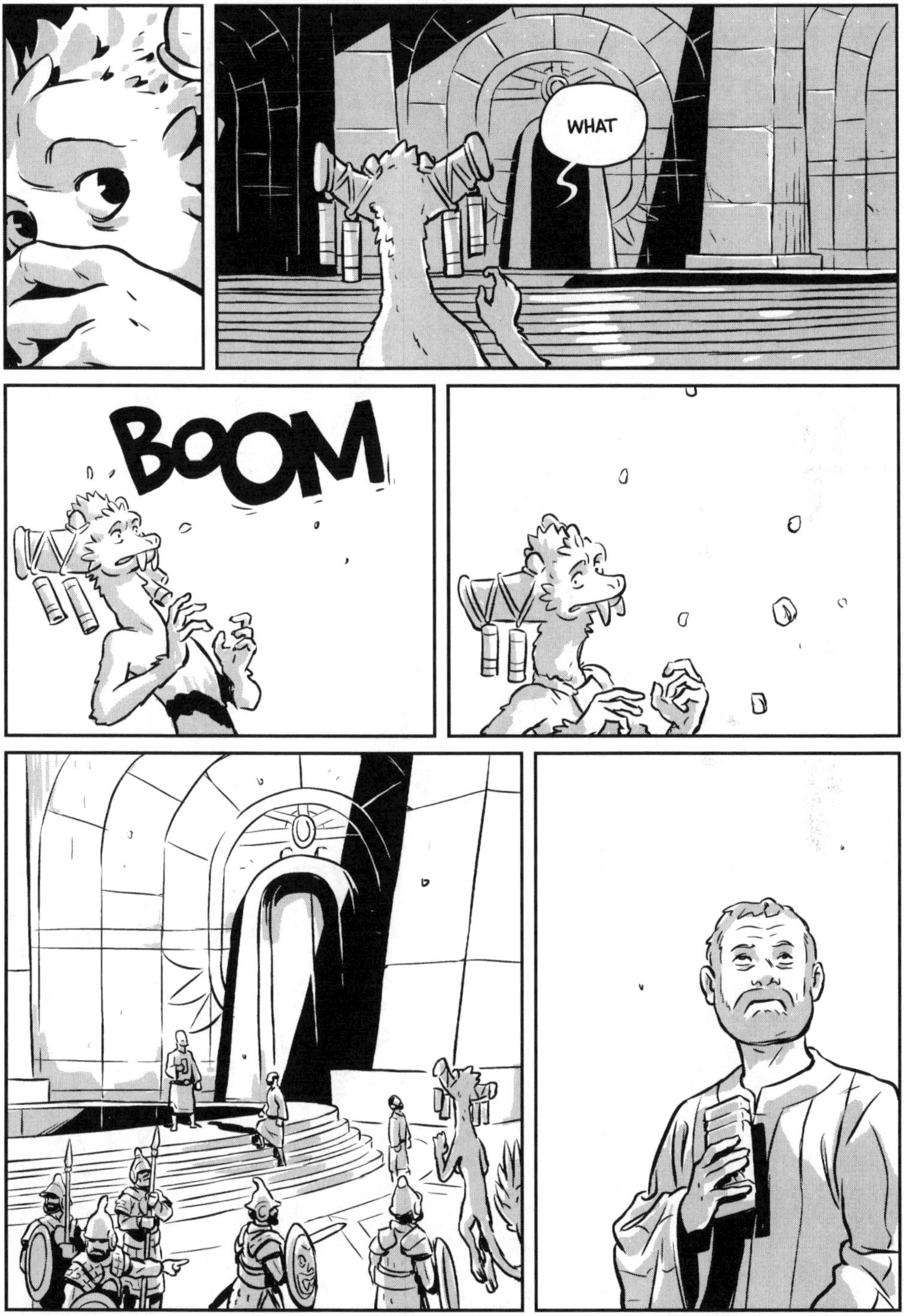
WHAT
BOOM

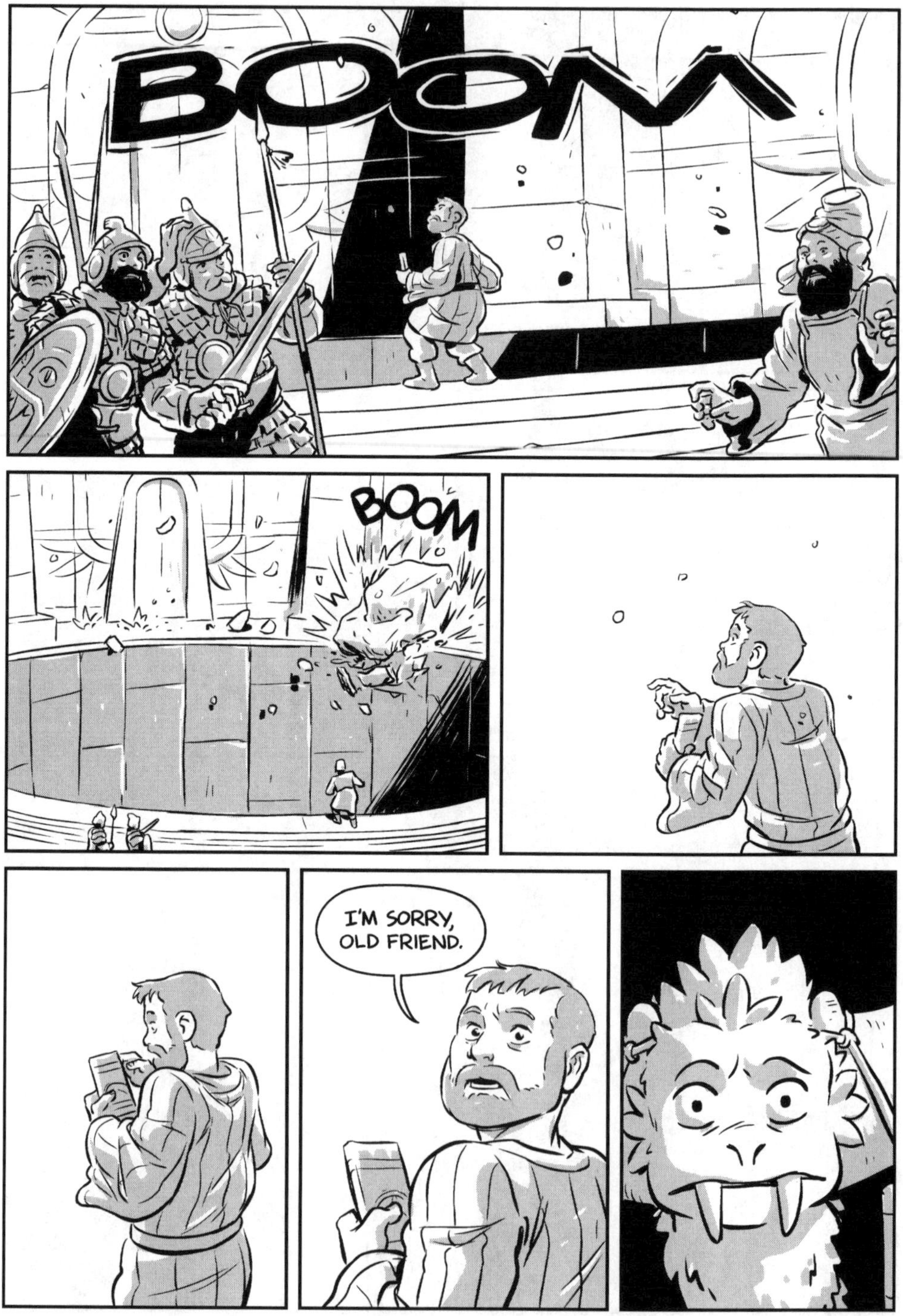
BOOM
BOOM
I'M SORRY, OLD FRIEND.

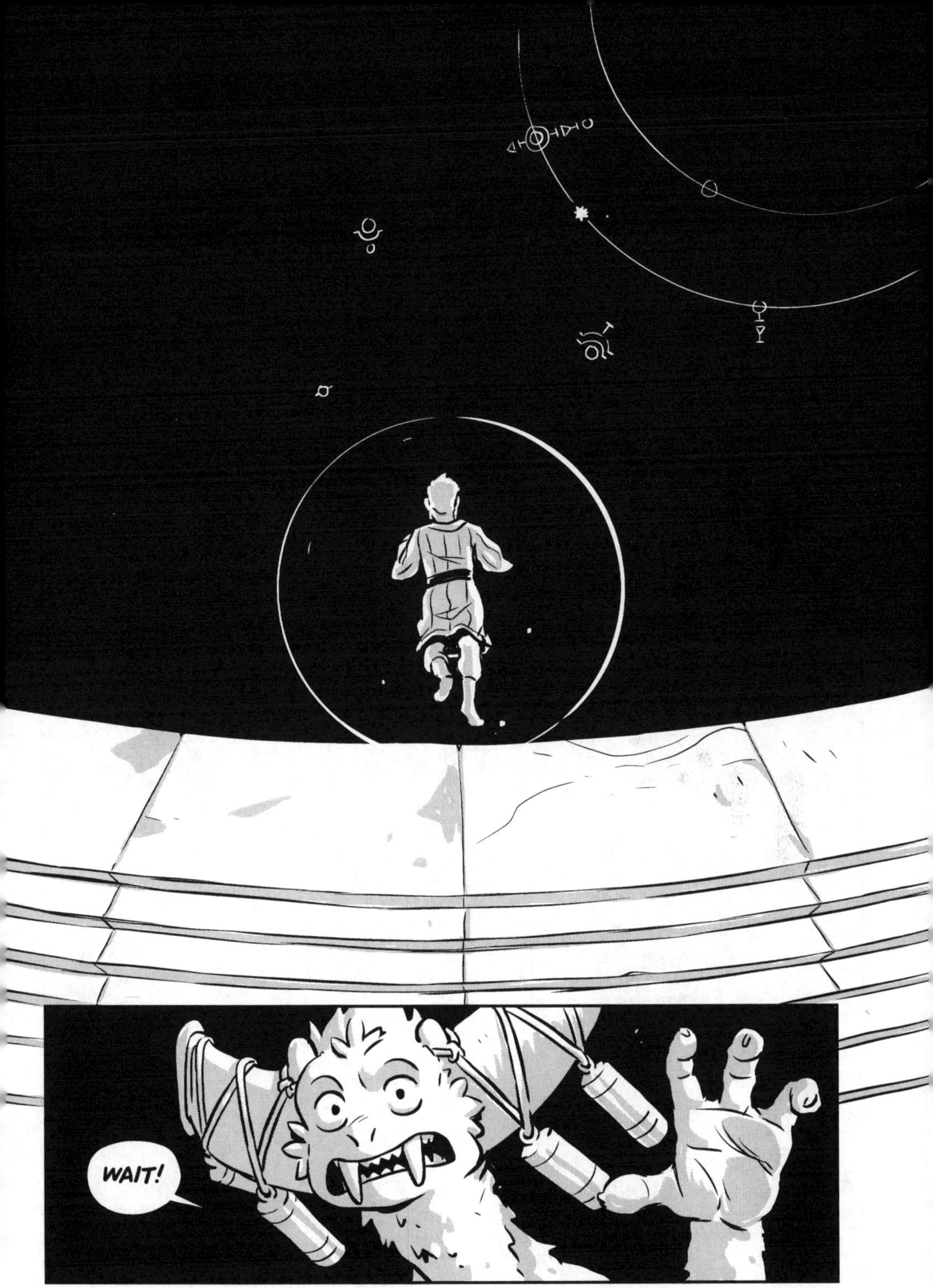
WAIT!

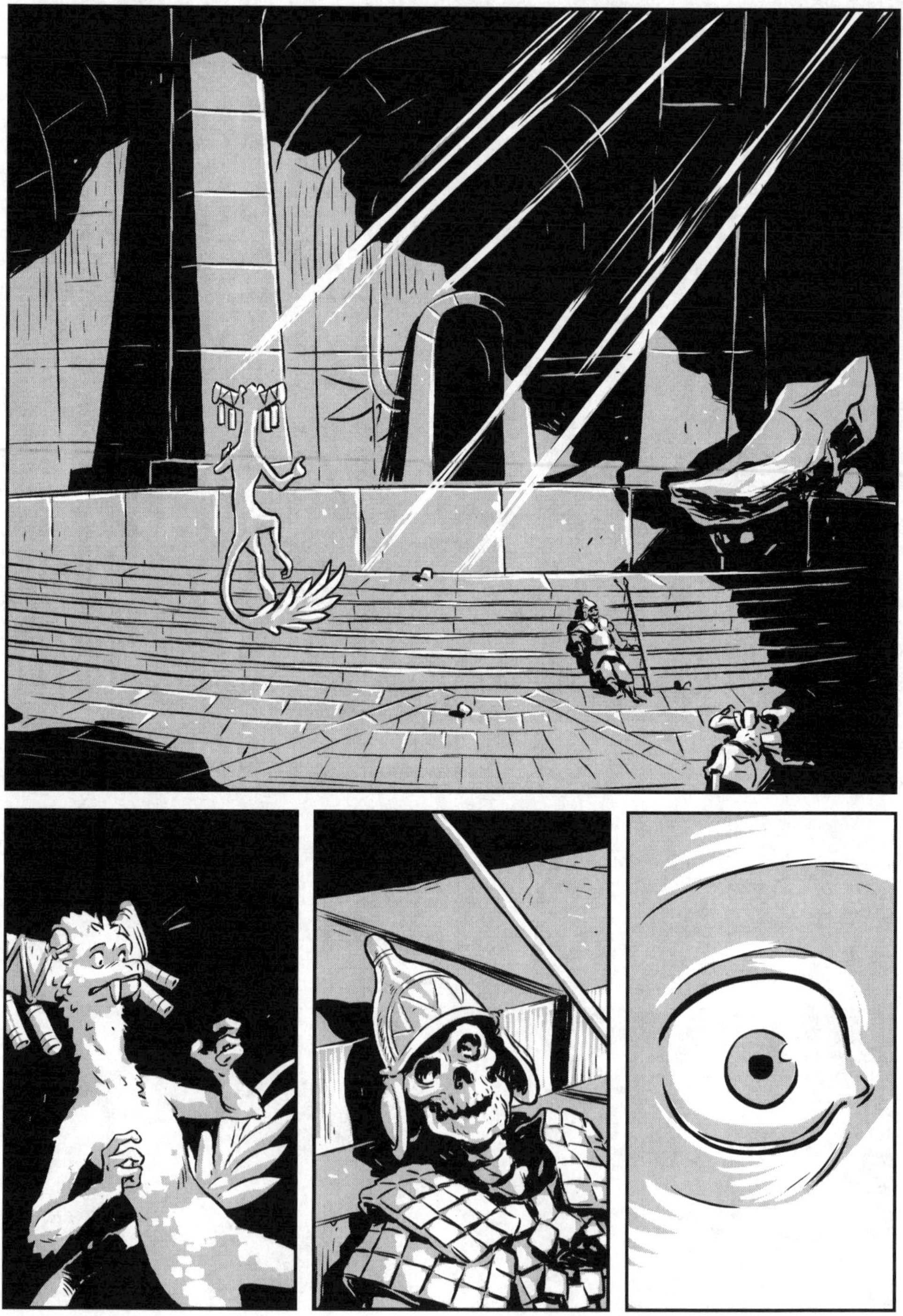

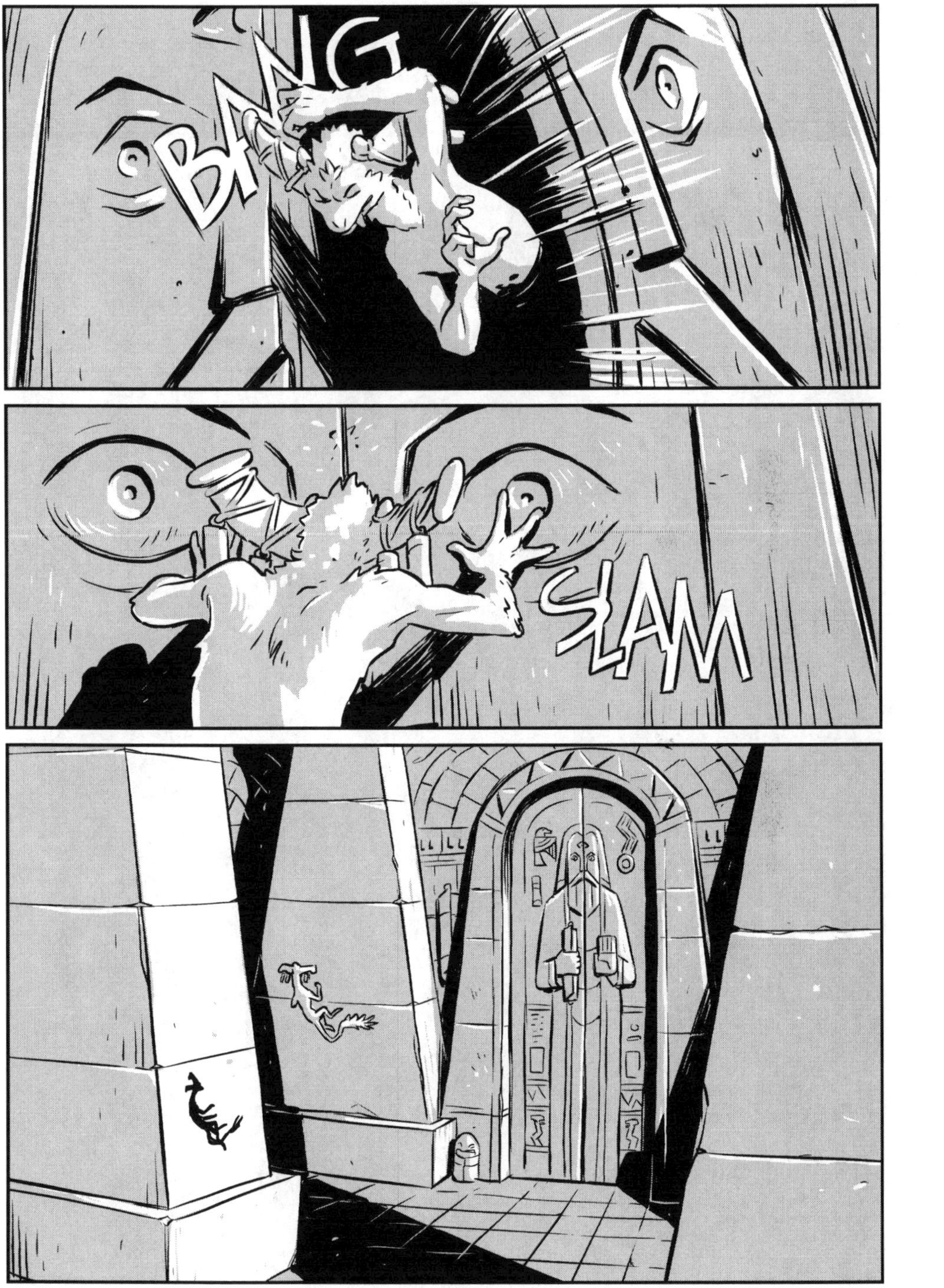
BANG
SLAM

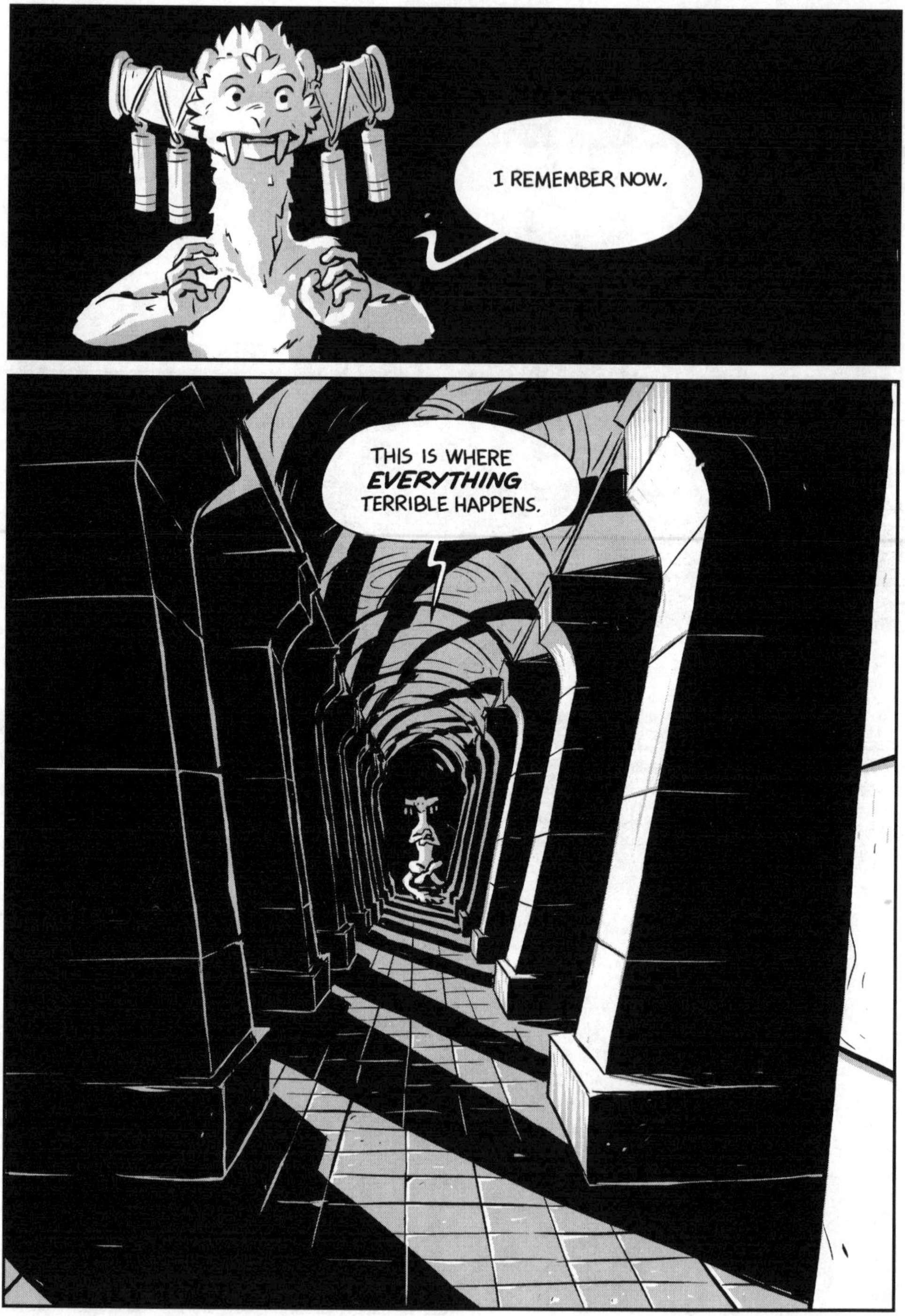
I REMEMBER NOW.
THIS IS WHERE *EVERYTHING* TERRIBLE HAPPENS.

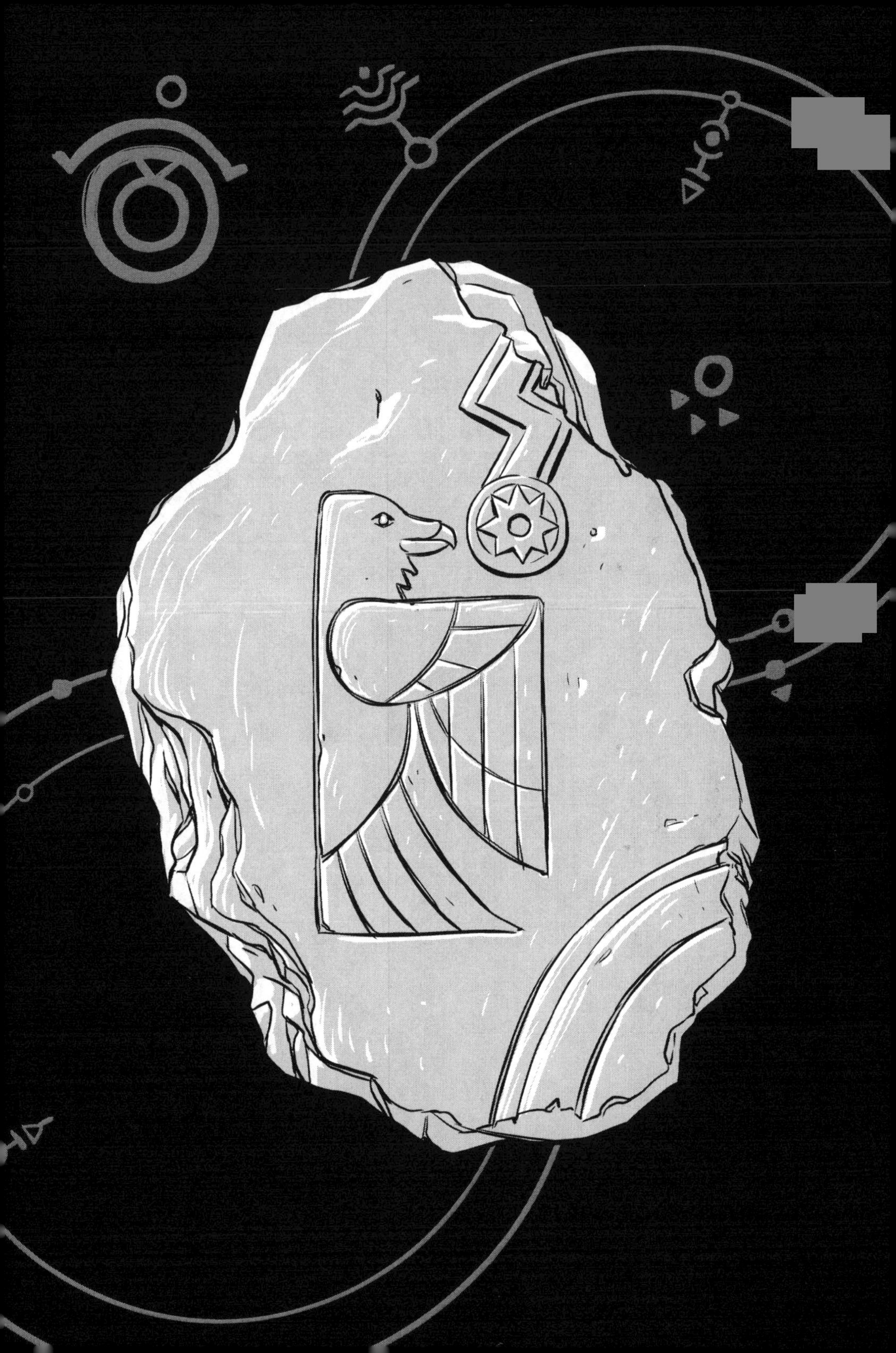

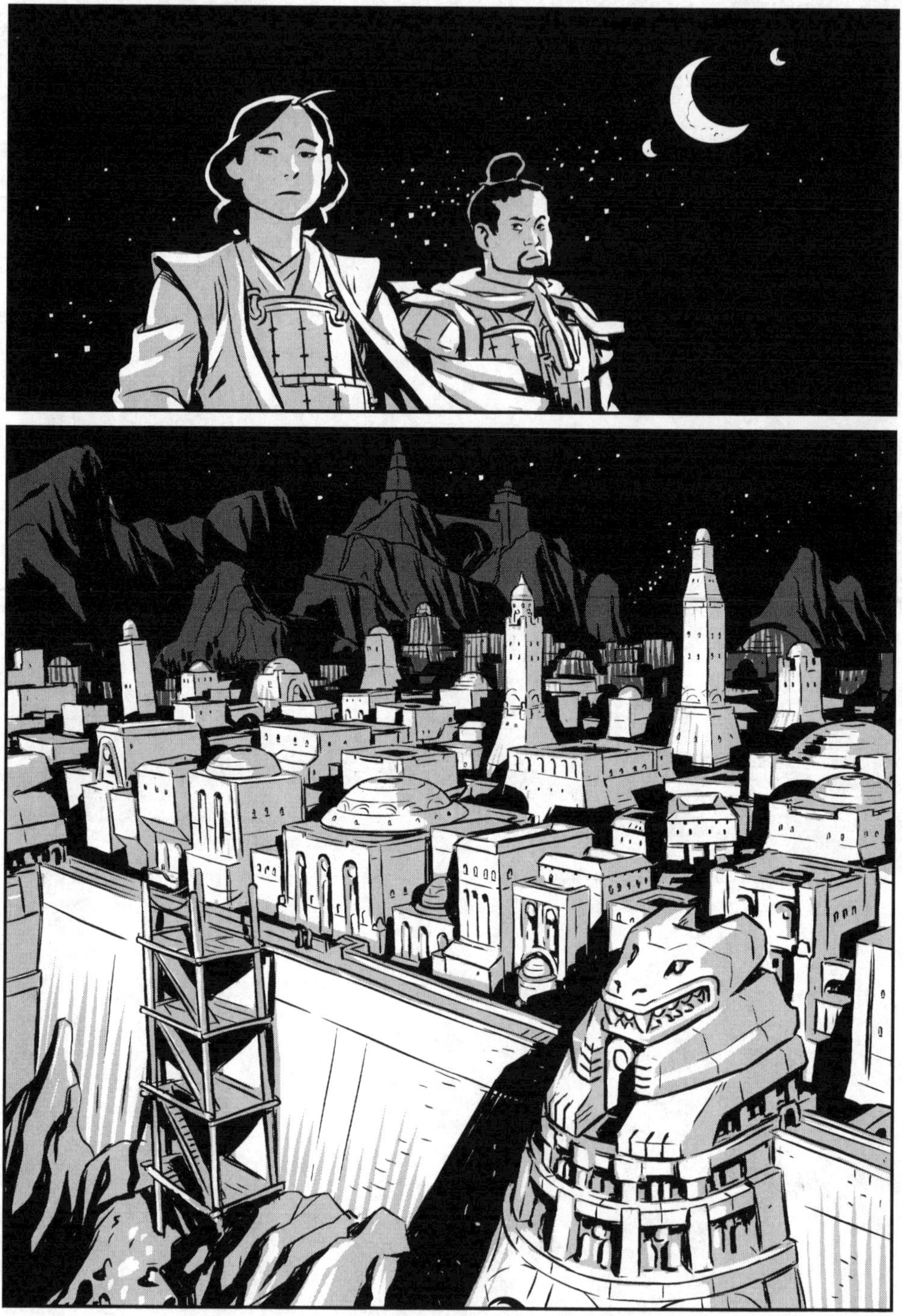

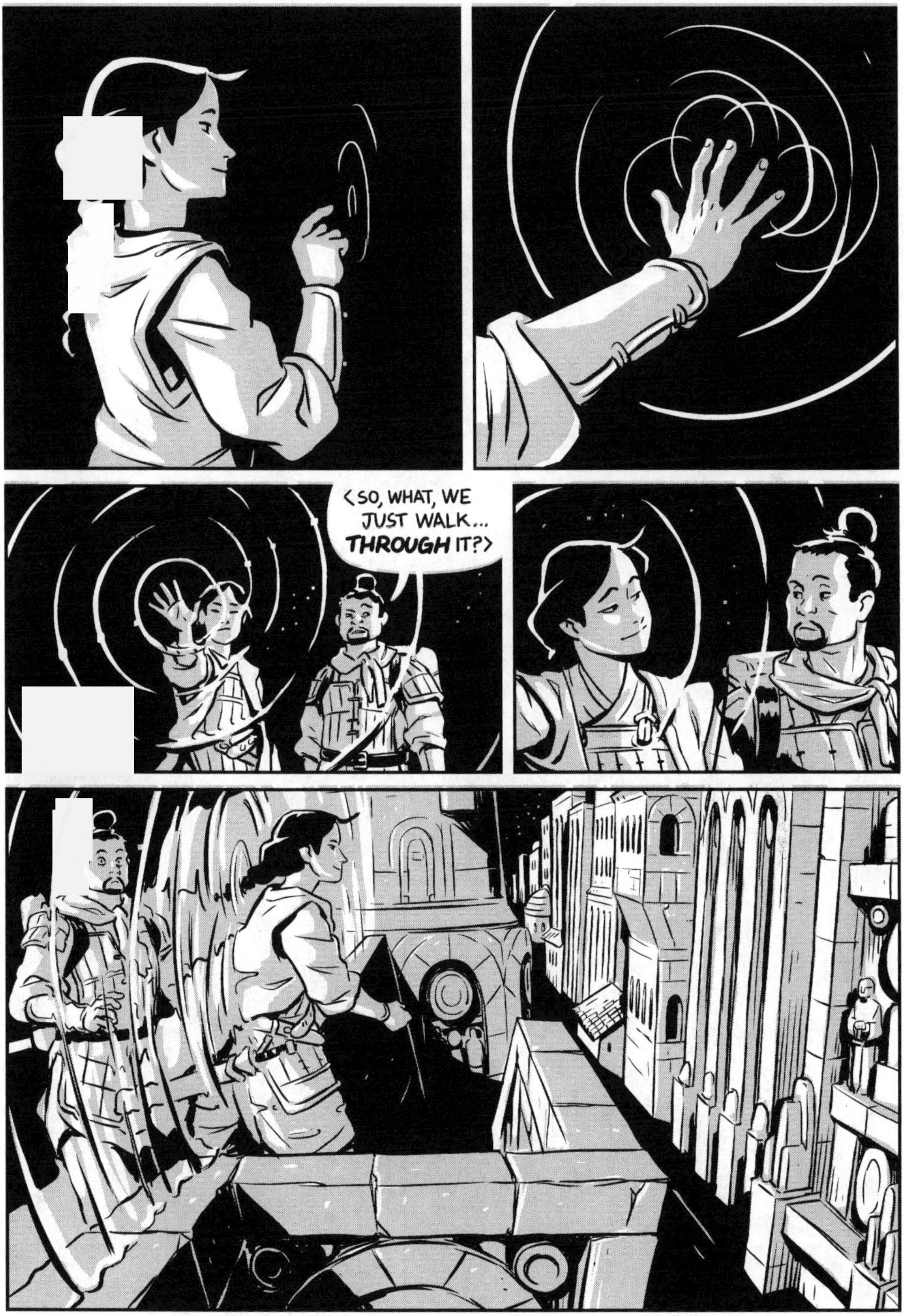
<SO, WHAT, WE JUST WALK... THROUGH IT?>

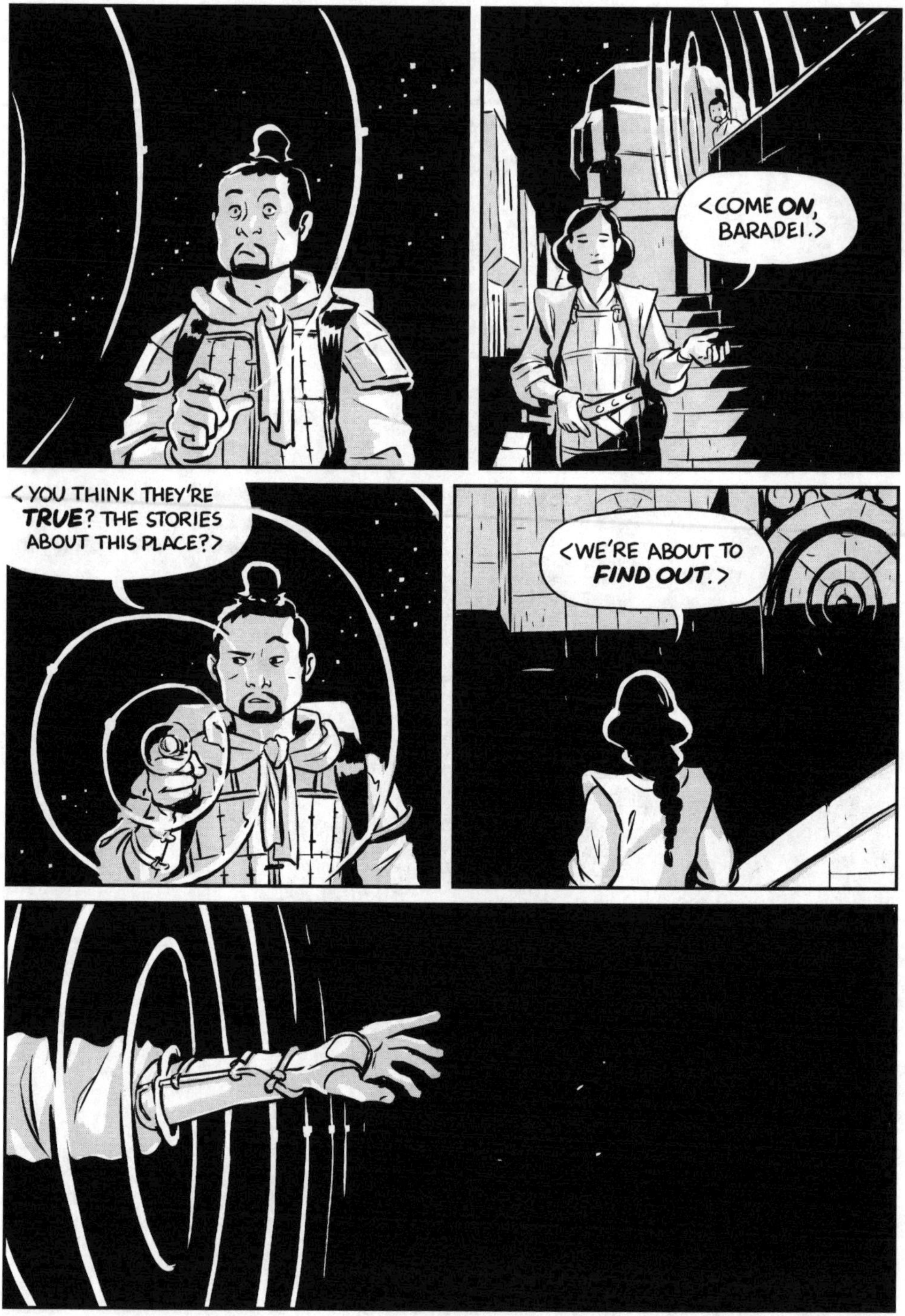
<COME ON, BARADEI.>
<YOU THINK THEY'RE TRUE? THE STORIES ABOUT THIS PLACE?>
<WE'RE ABOUT TO FIND OUT.>

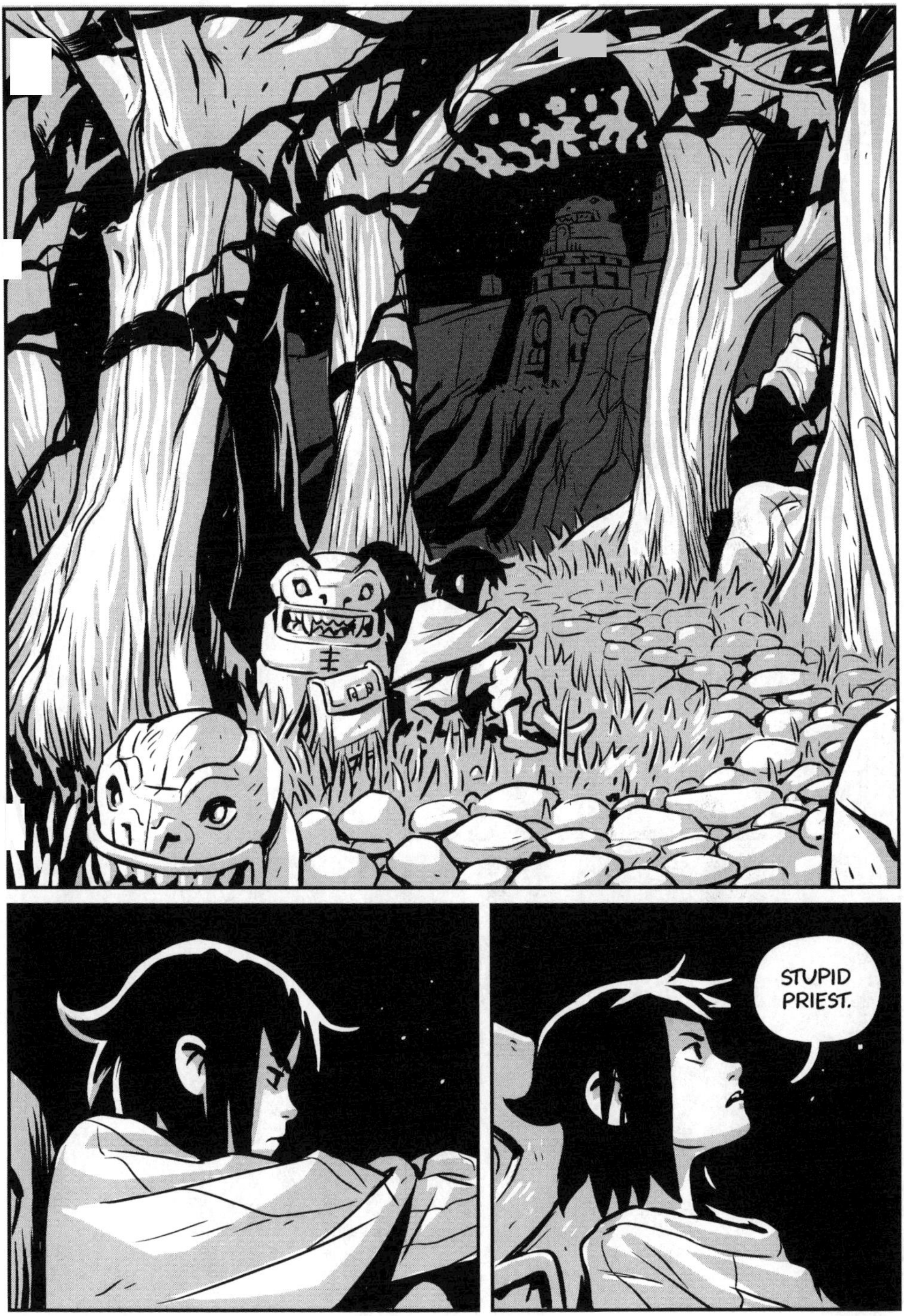
STUPID PRIEST.

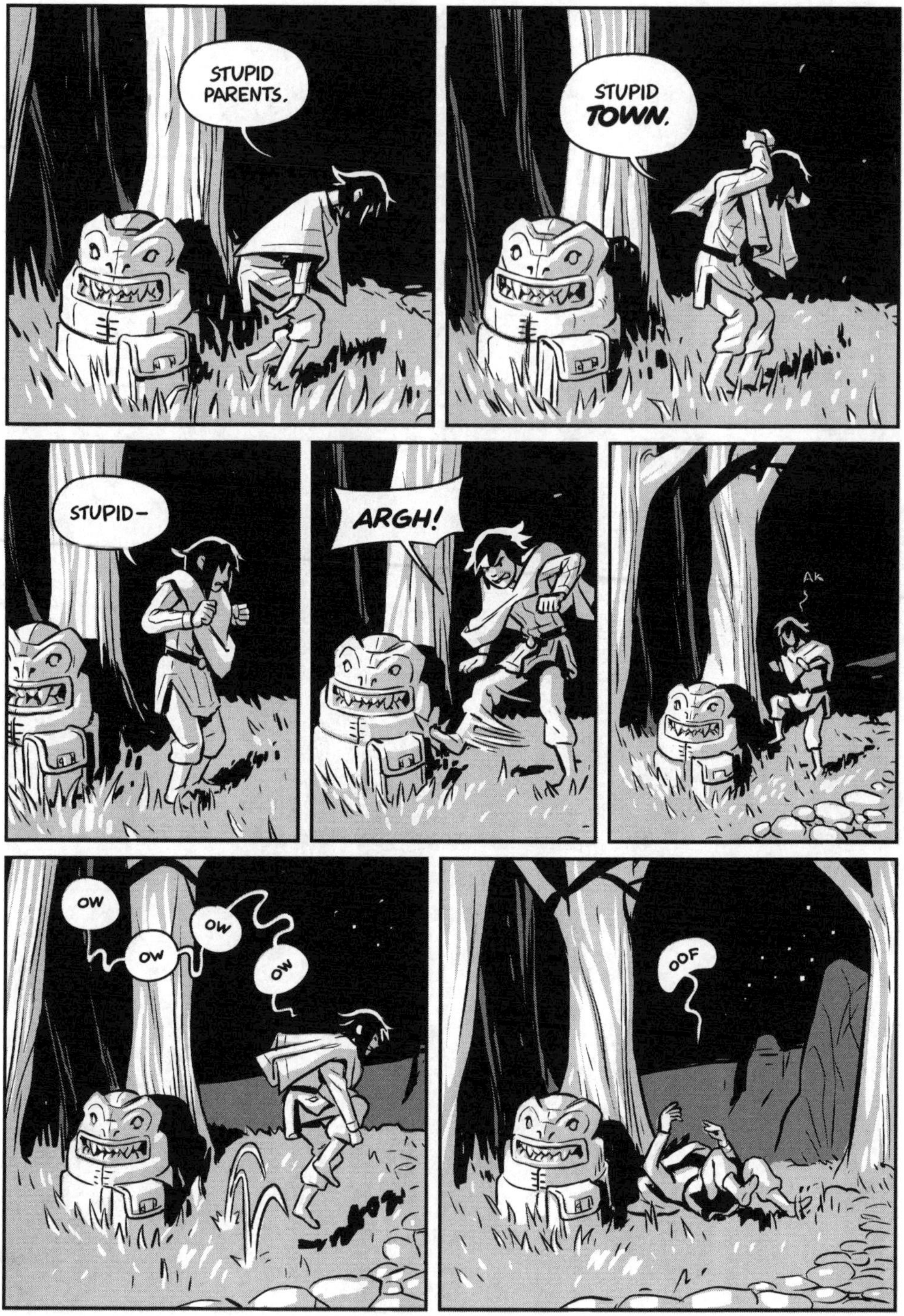
STUPID PARENTS.
STUPID TOWN.
STUPID-
ARGH!
AK
OW
OW
OW
OW
OOF

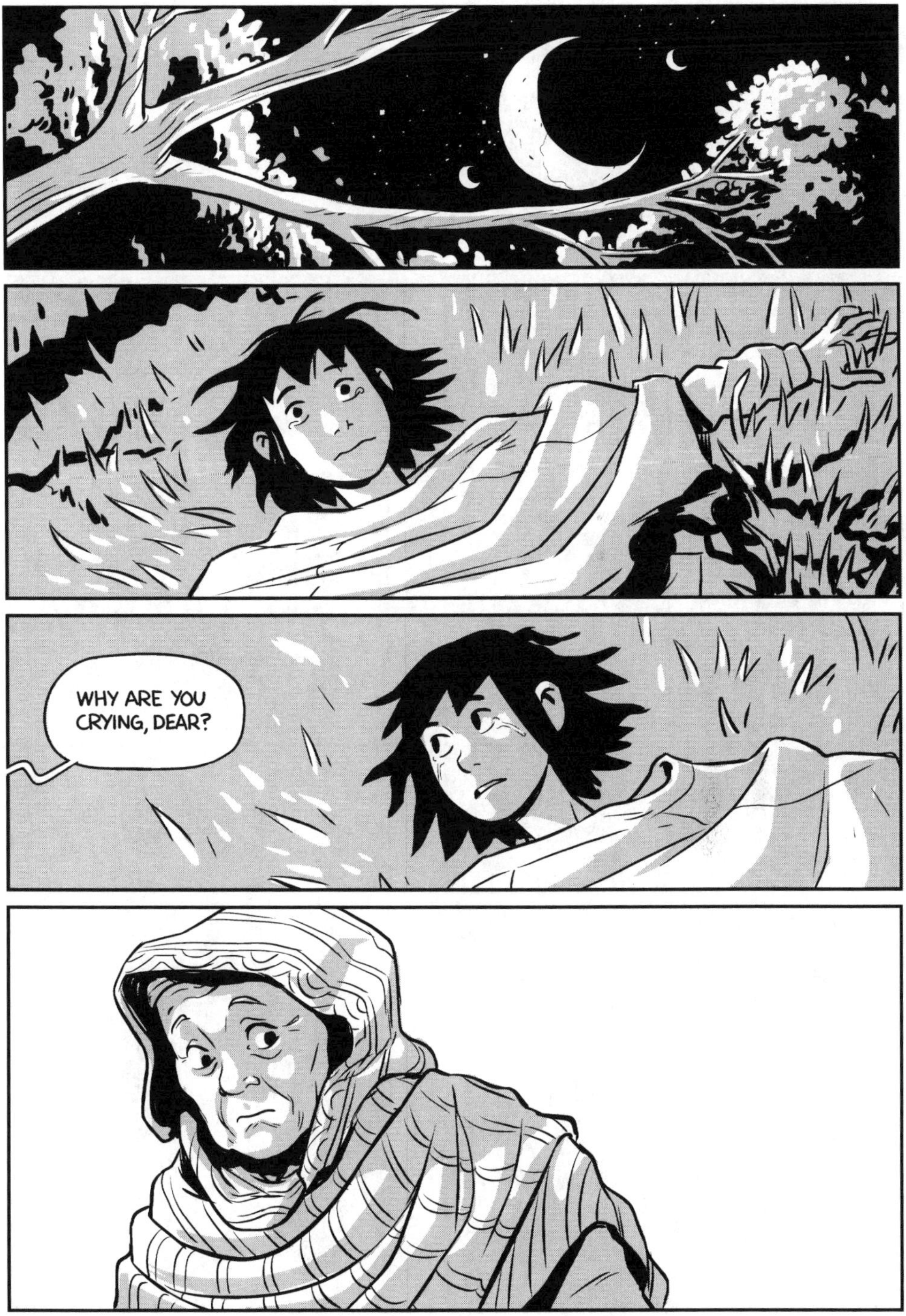
WHY ARE YOU CRYING, DEAR?

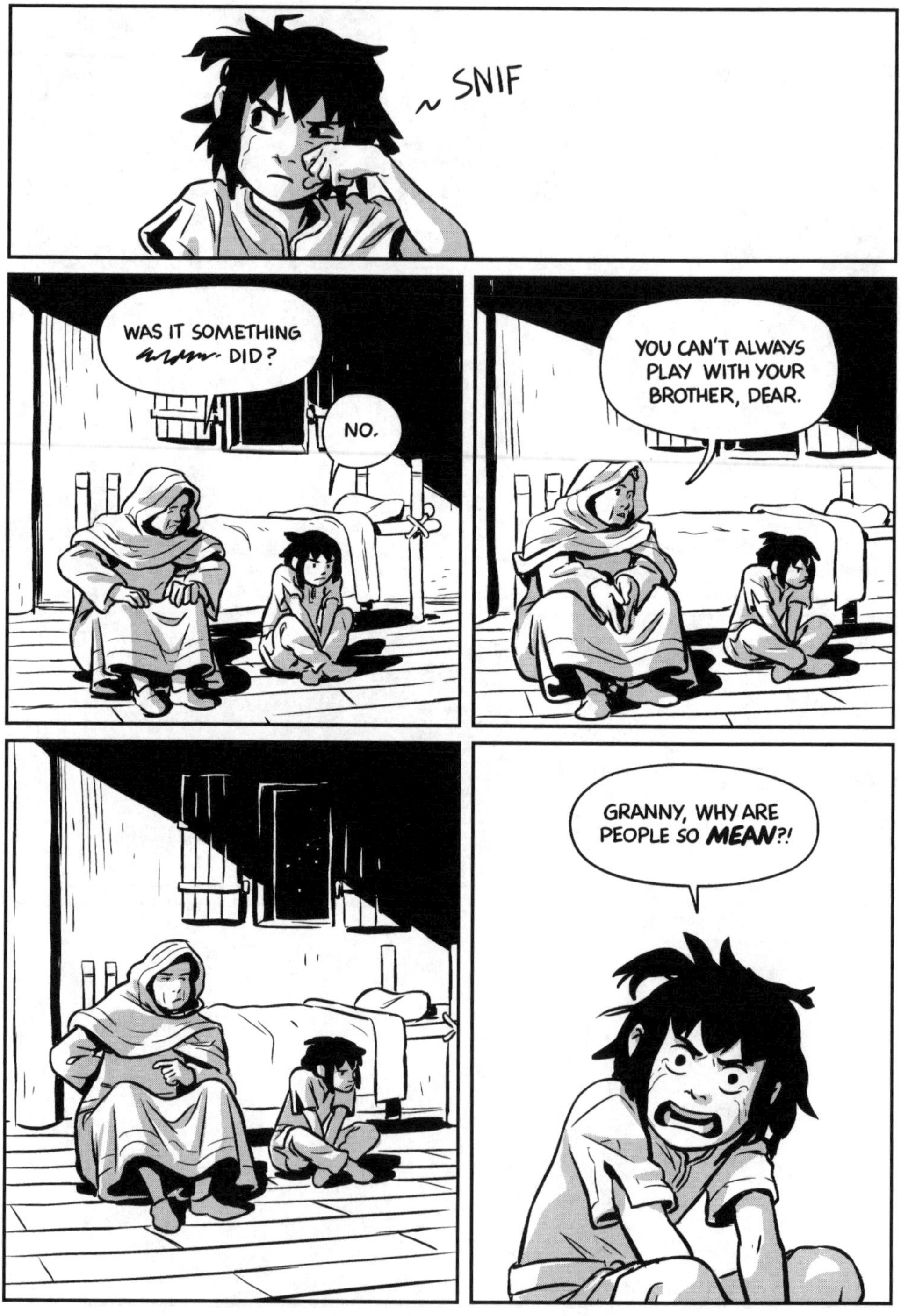
~ SNIF
WAS IT SOMETHING DID?
NO.
YOU CAN'T ALWAYS PLAY WITH YOUR BROTHER, DEAR.
GRANNY, WHY ARE PEOPLE SO MEAN?!

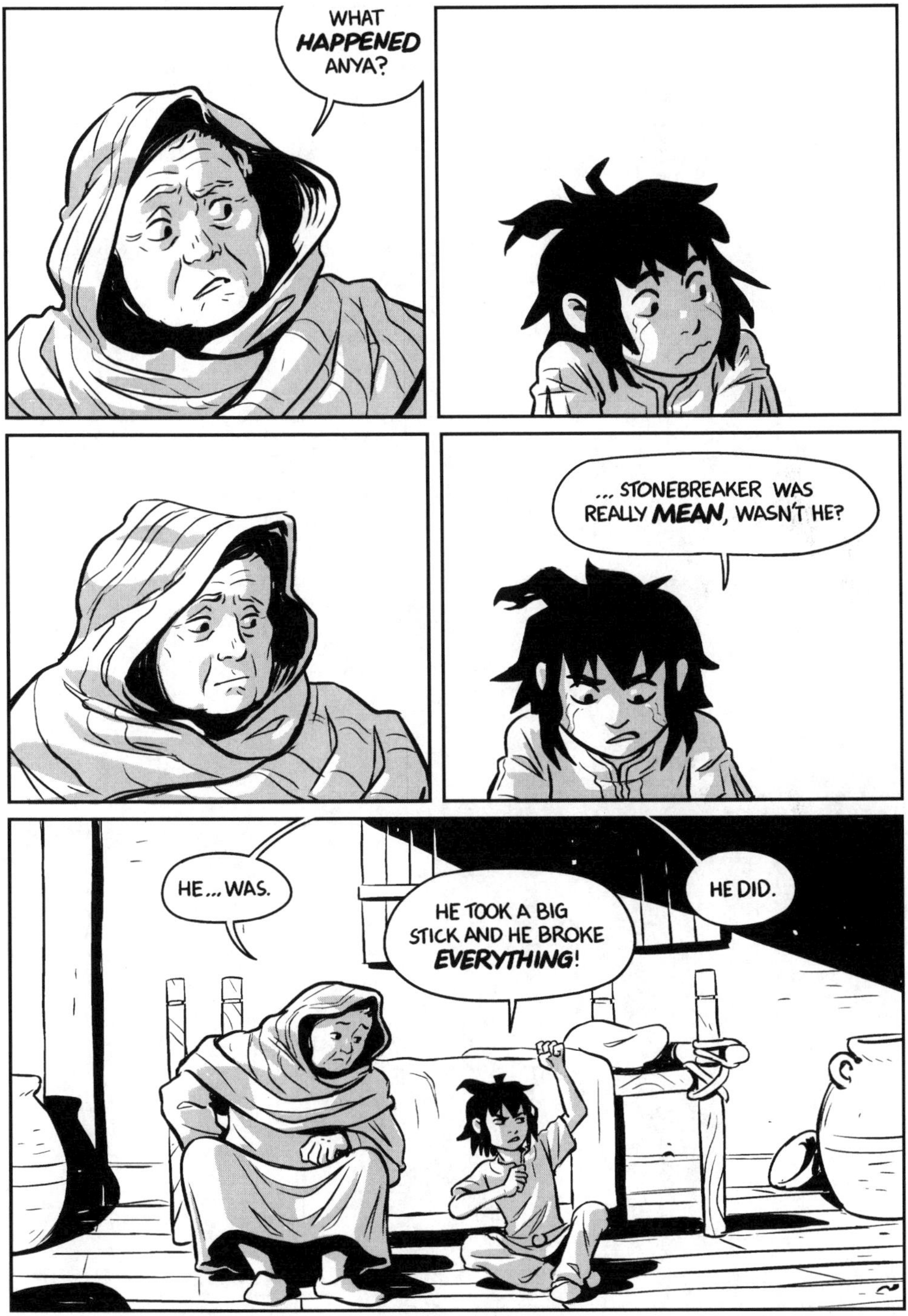

WHAT HAPPENED ANYA?
... STONEBREAKER WAS REALLY MEAN, WASN'T HE?
HE... WAS.
HE TOOK A BIG STICK AND HE BROKE EVERYTHING!
HE DID.

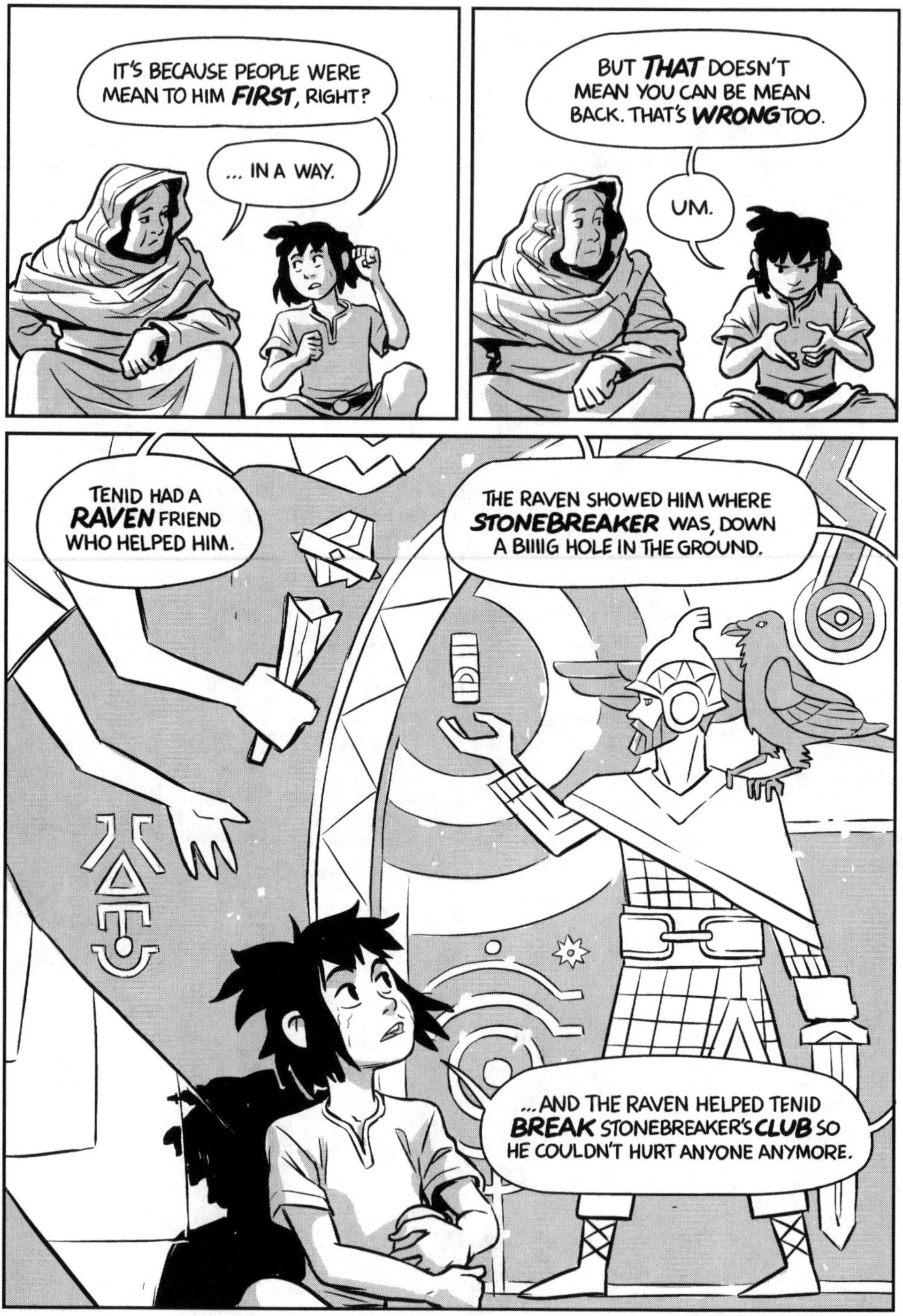
IT'S BECAUSE PEOPLE WERE MEAN TO HIM **FIRST**, RIGHT?
... IN A WAY.
BUT **THAT** DOESN'T MEAN YOU CAN BE MEAN BACK. THAT'S **WRONG** TOO.
UM.
TENID HAD A **RAVEN** FRIEND WHO HELPED HIM.
THE RAVEN SHOWED HIM WHERE **STONEBREAKER** WAS, DOWN A BIIIG HOLE IN THE GROUND.
...AND THE RAVEN HELPED TENID **BREAK** STONEBREAKER'S **CLUB** SO HE COULDN'T HURT ANYONE ANYMORE.

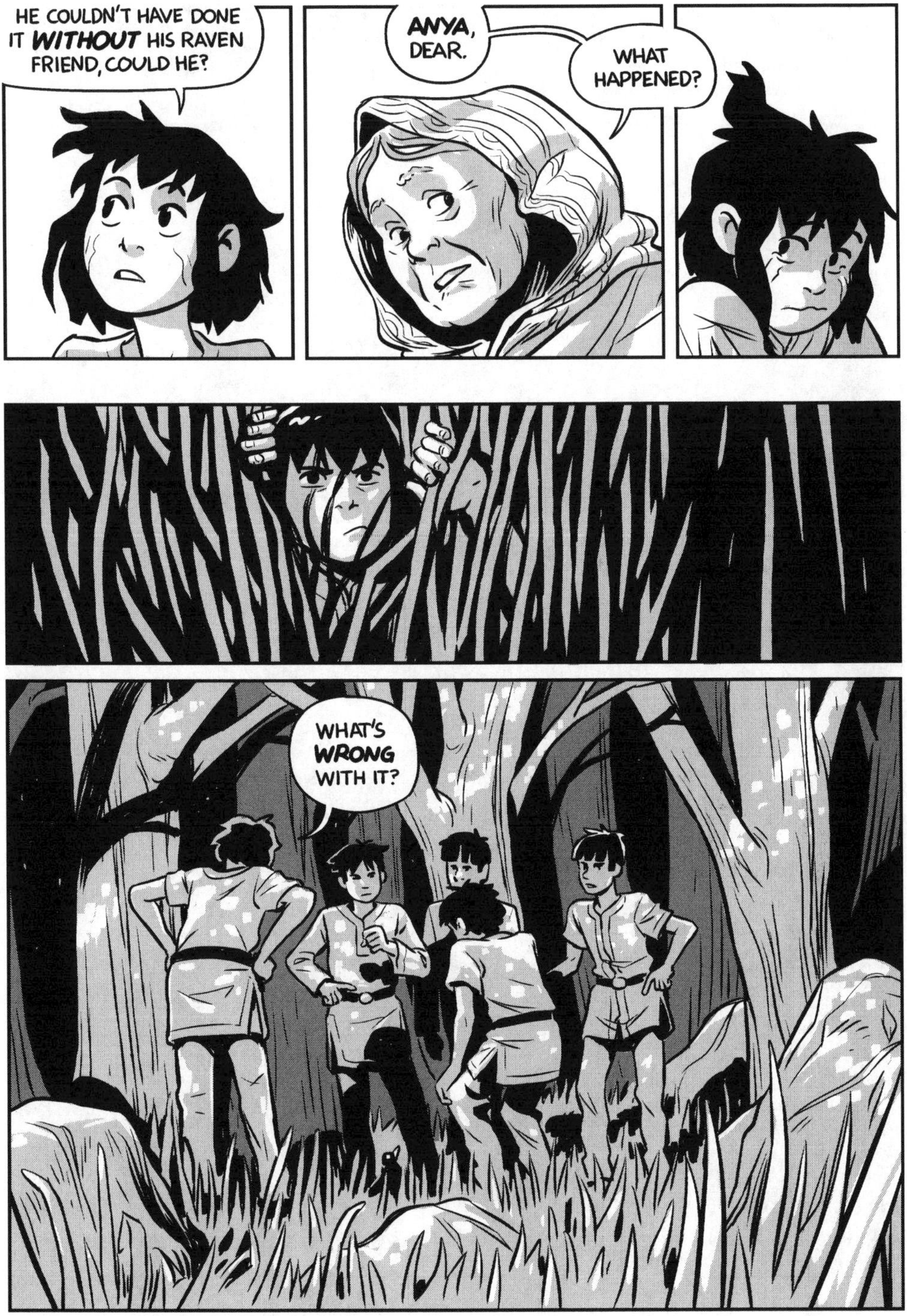
HE COULDN'T HAVE DONE IT WITHOUT HIS RAVEN FRIEND, COULD HE?
ANYA, DEAR.
WHAT HAPPENED?
WHAT'S WRONG WITH IT?

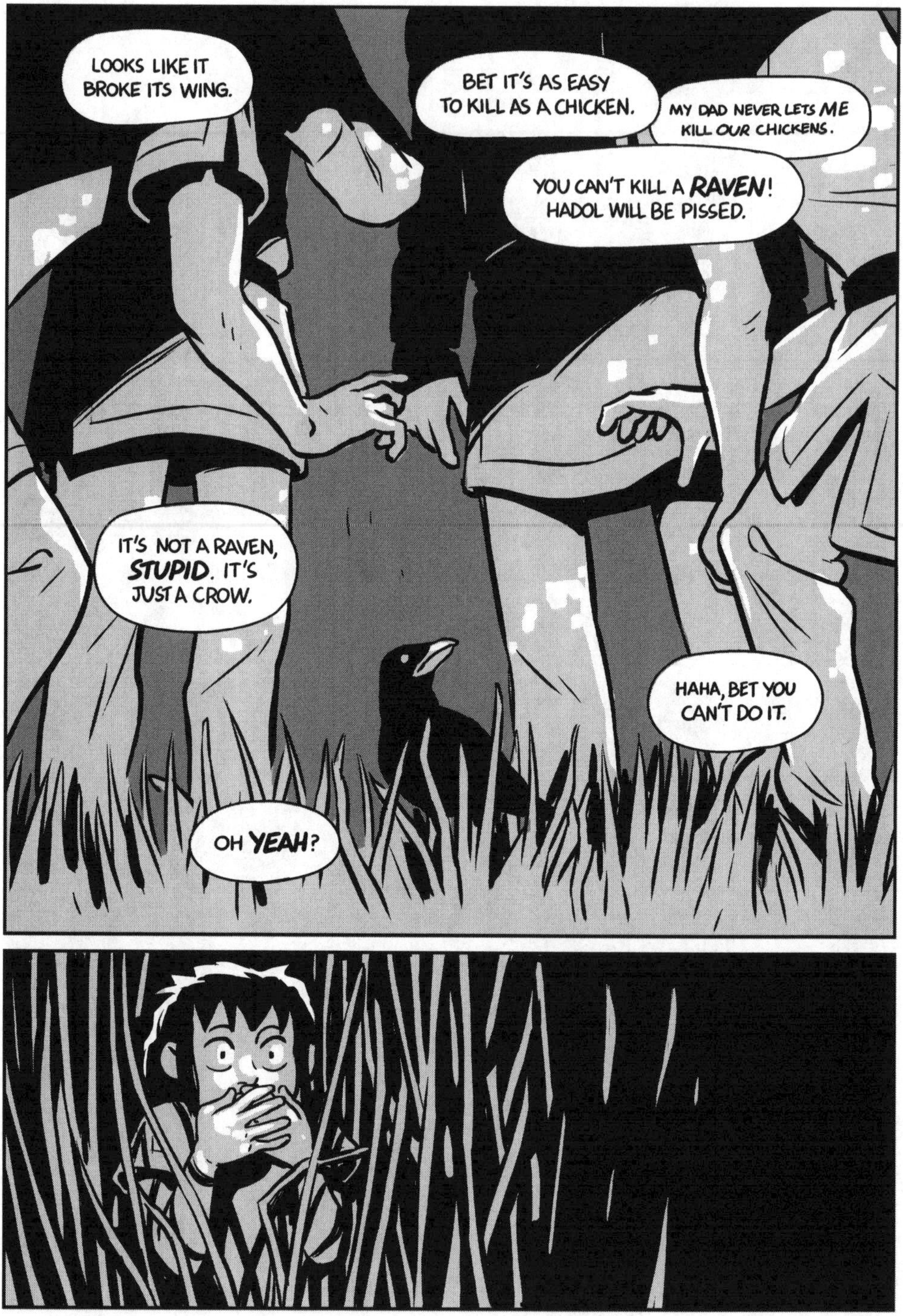
LOOKS LIKE IT BROKE ITS WING.
BET IT'S AS EASY TO KILL AS A CHICKEN.
MY DAD NEVER LETS ME KILL OUR CHICKENS.
YOU CAN'T KILL A RAVEN! HADOL WILL BE PISSED.
IT'S NOT A RAVEN, STUPID. IT'S JUST A CROW.
HAHA, BET YOU CAN'T DO IT.
OH YEAH?

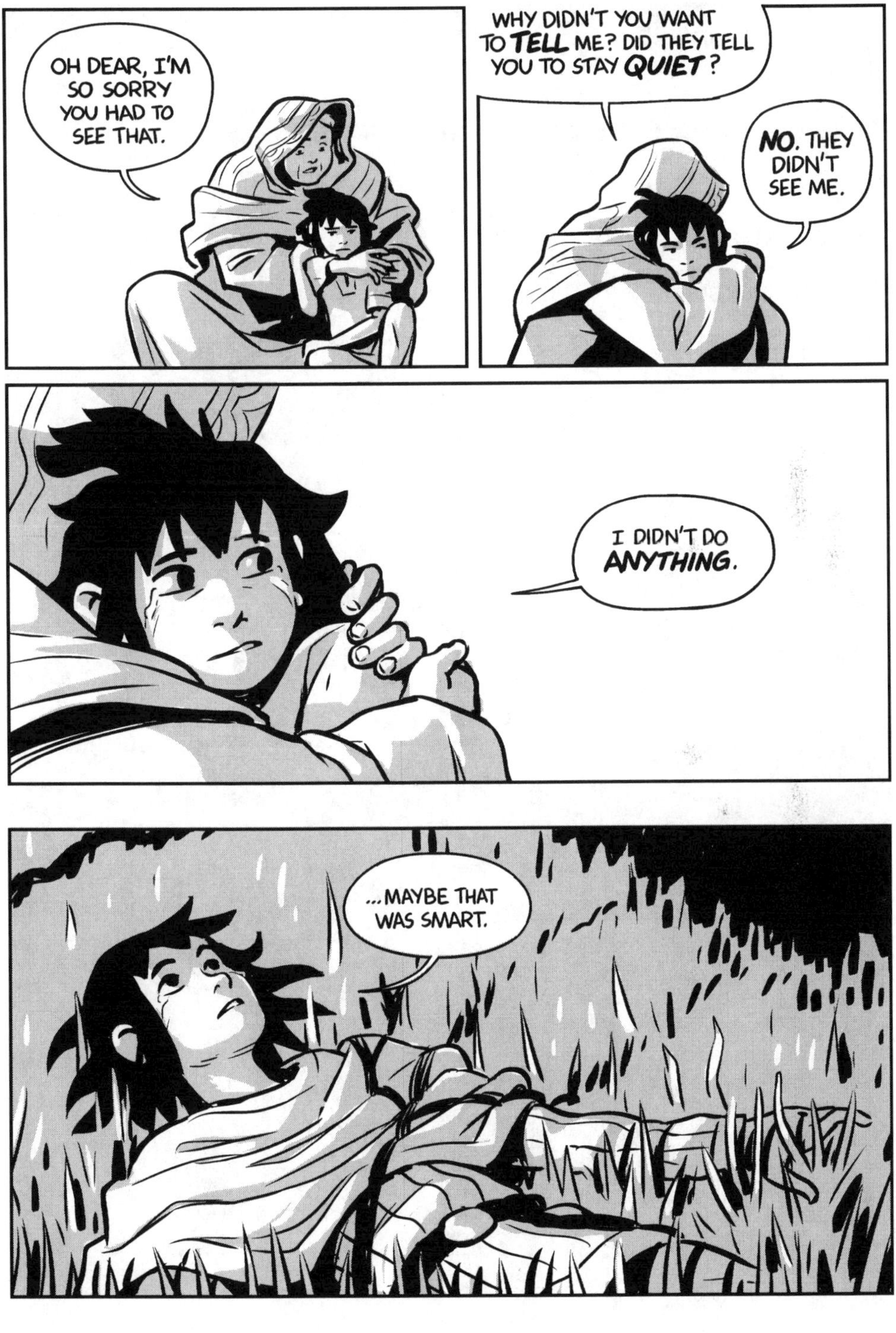
OH DEAR, I'M SO SORRY YOU HAD TO SEE THAT.
WHY DIDN'T YOU WANT TO TELL ME? DID THEY TELL YOU TO STAY QUIET?
NO. THEY DIDN'T SEE ME.
I DIDN'T DO ANYTHING.
...MAYBE THAT WAS SMART.

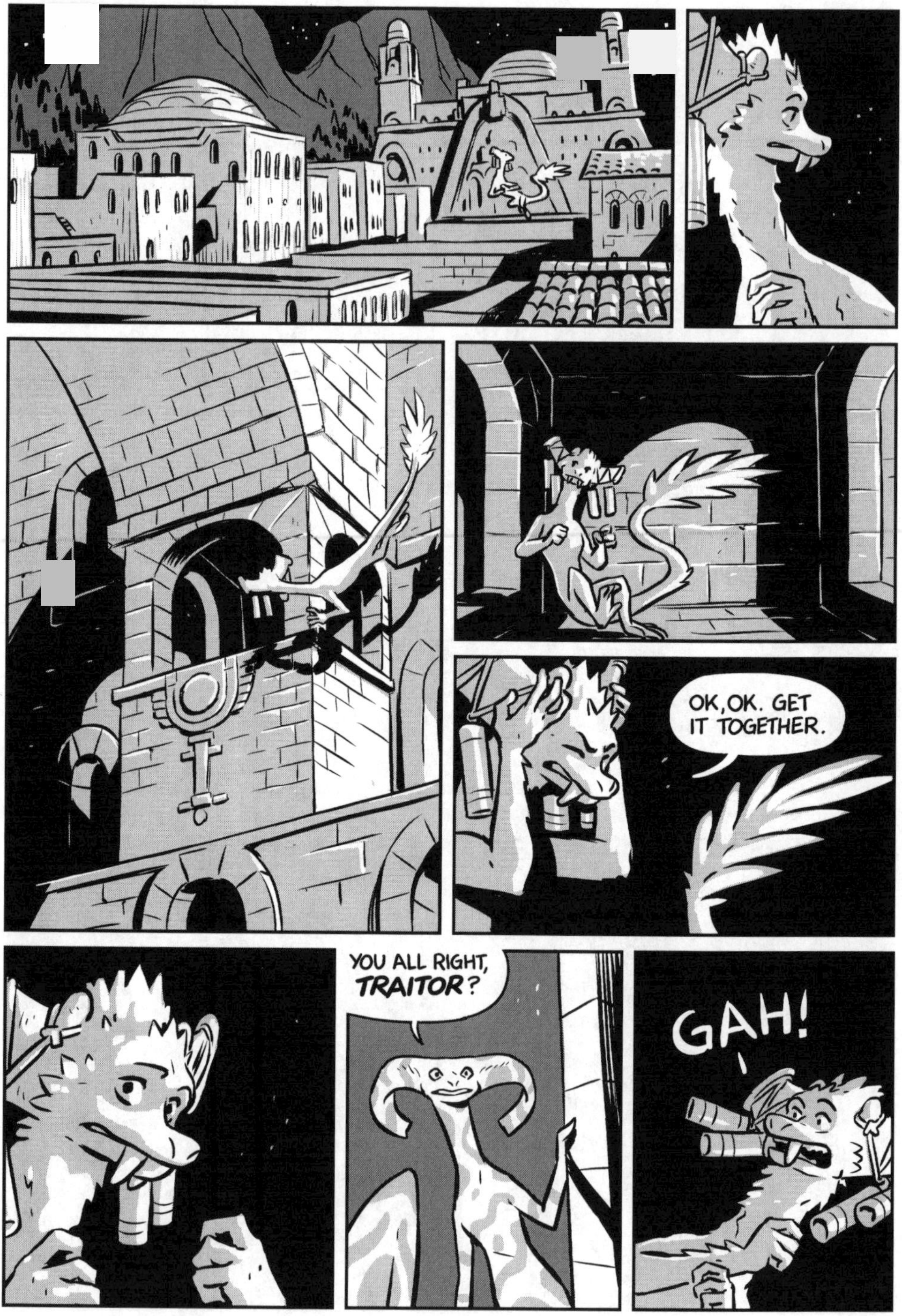

OK, OK. GET IT TOGETHER.
YOU ALL RIGHT, TRAITOR?
GAH!

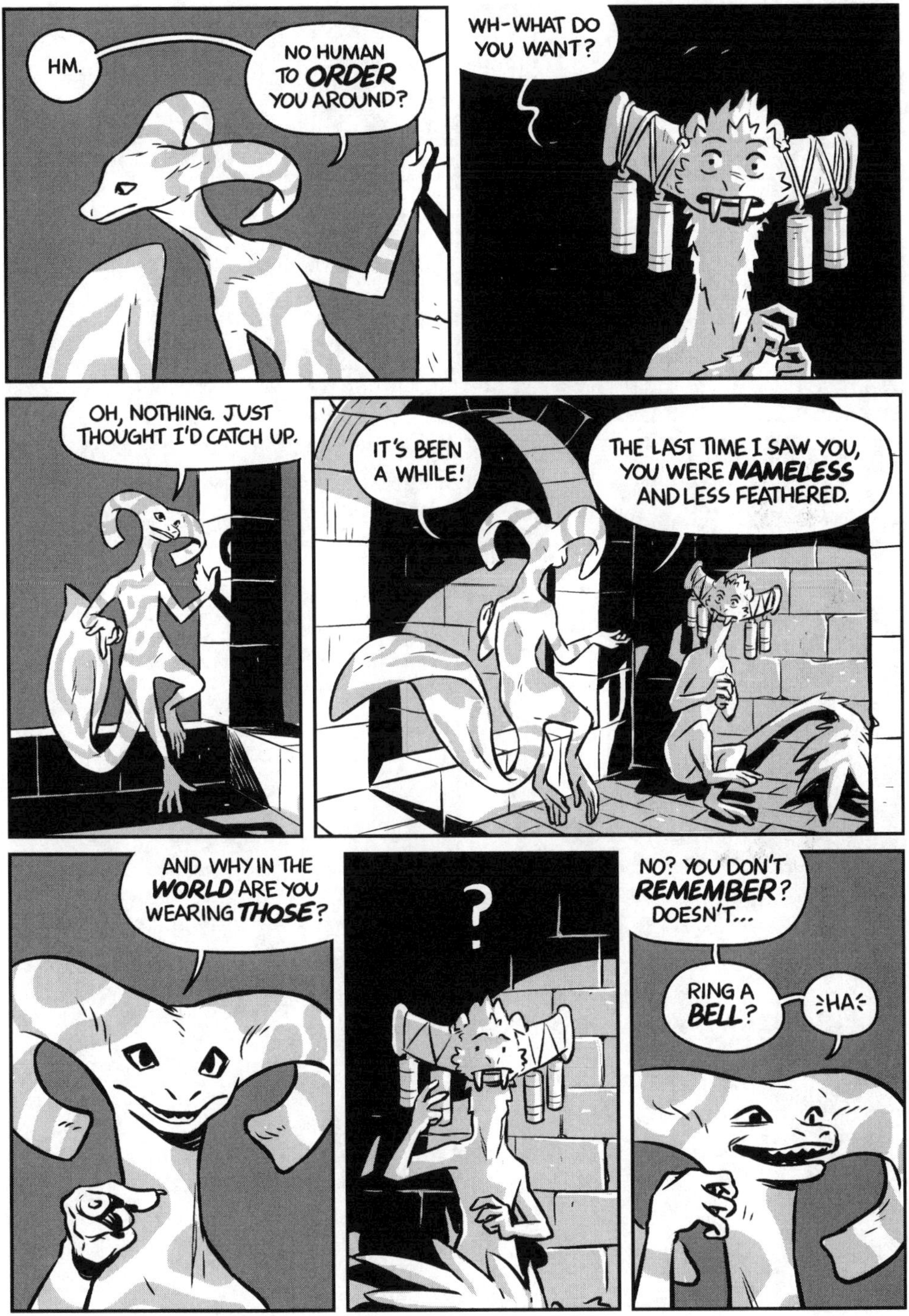
HM.
NO HUMAN TO ORDER YOU AROUND?
WH-WHAT DO YOU WANT?
OH, NOTHING. JUST THOUGHT I'D CATCH UP.
IT'S BEEN A WHILE!
THE LAST TIME I SAW YOU, YOU WERE NAMELESS AND LESS FEATHERED.
AND WHY IN THE WORLD ARE YOU WEARING THOSE?
?
NO? YOU DON'T REMEMBER? DOESN'T...
RING A BELL?
HA

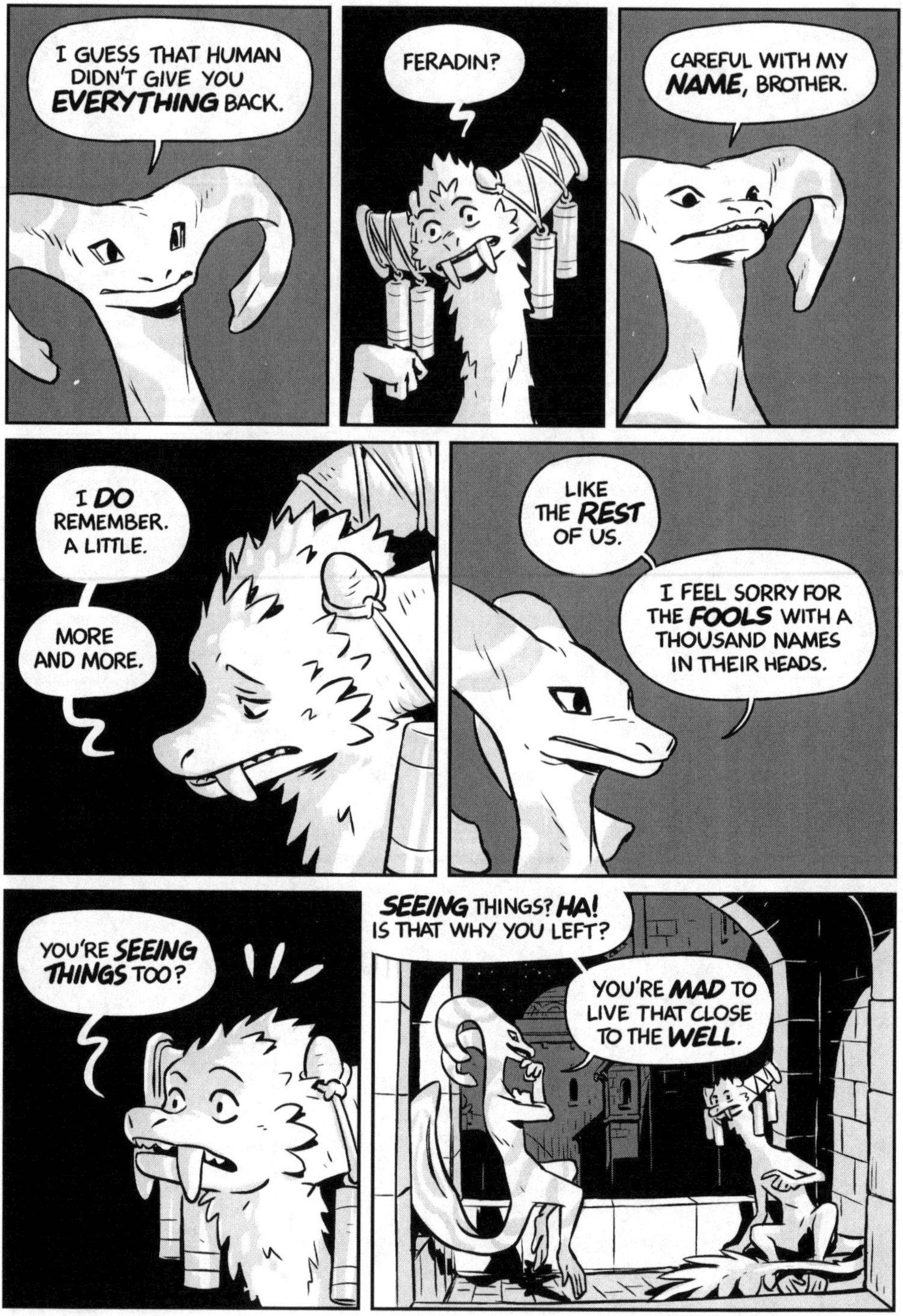
I GUESS THAT HUMAN DIDN'T GIVE YOU EVERYTHING BACK.
FERADIN?
CAREFUL WITH MY NAME, BROTHER.
I DO REMEMBER. A LITTLE.
MORE AND MORE.
LIKE THE REST OF US.
I FEEL SORRY FOR THE FOOLS WITH A THOUSAND NAMES IN THEIR HEADS.
YOU'RE SEEING THINGS TOO?
SEEING THINGS? HA! IS THAT WHY YOU LEFT?
YOU'RE MAD TO LIVE THAT CLOSE TO THE WELL.

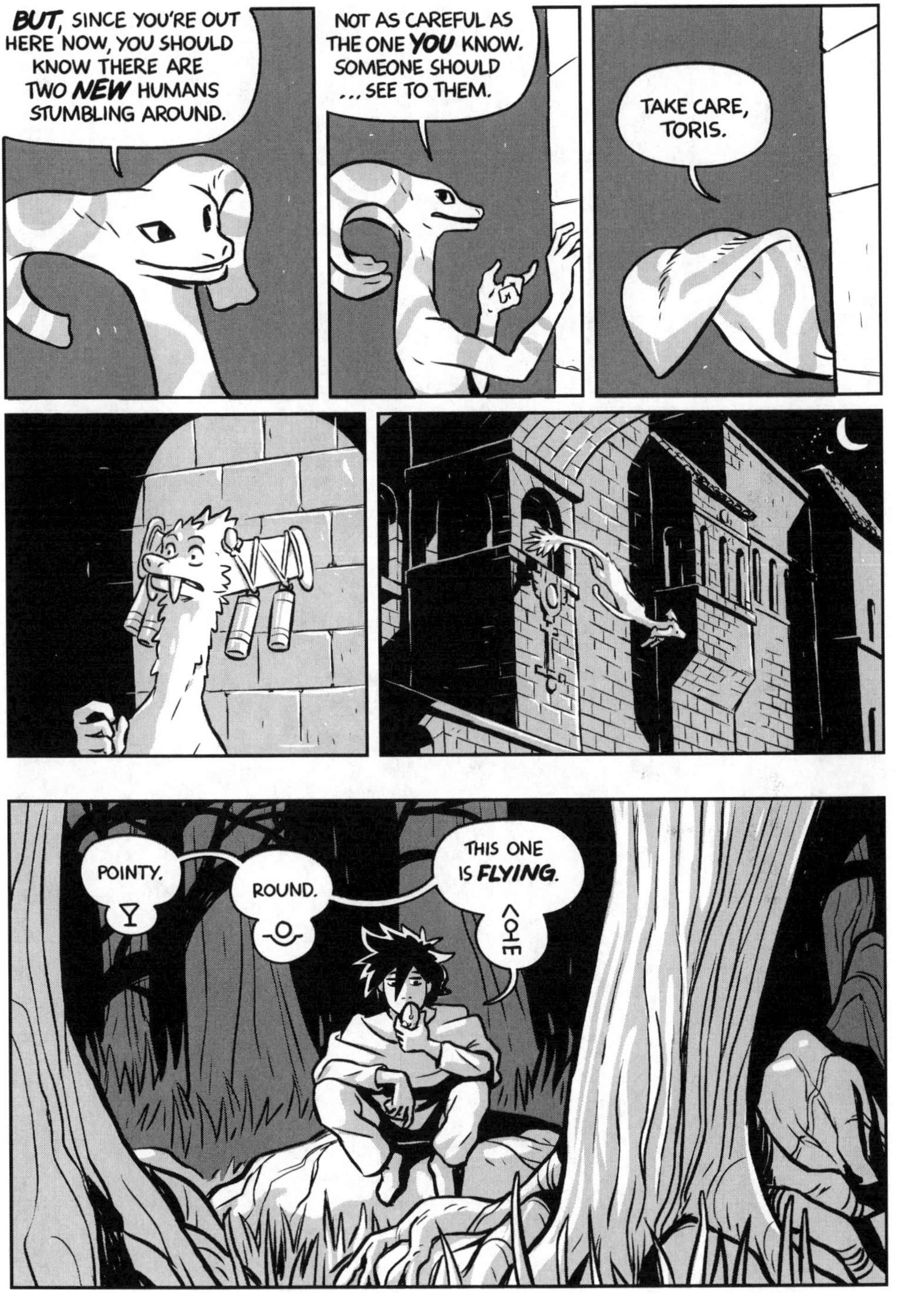
BUT, SINCE YOU'RE OUT HERE NOW, YOU SHOULD KNOW THERE ARE TWO NEW HUMANS STUMBLING AROUND.
NOT AS CAREFUL AS THE ONE YOU KNOW. SOMEONE SHOULD ...SEE TO THEM.
TAKE CARE, TORIS.
POINTY.
ROUND.
THIS ONE IS FLYING.

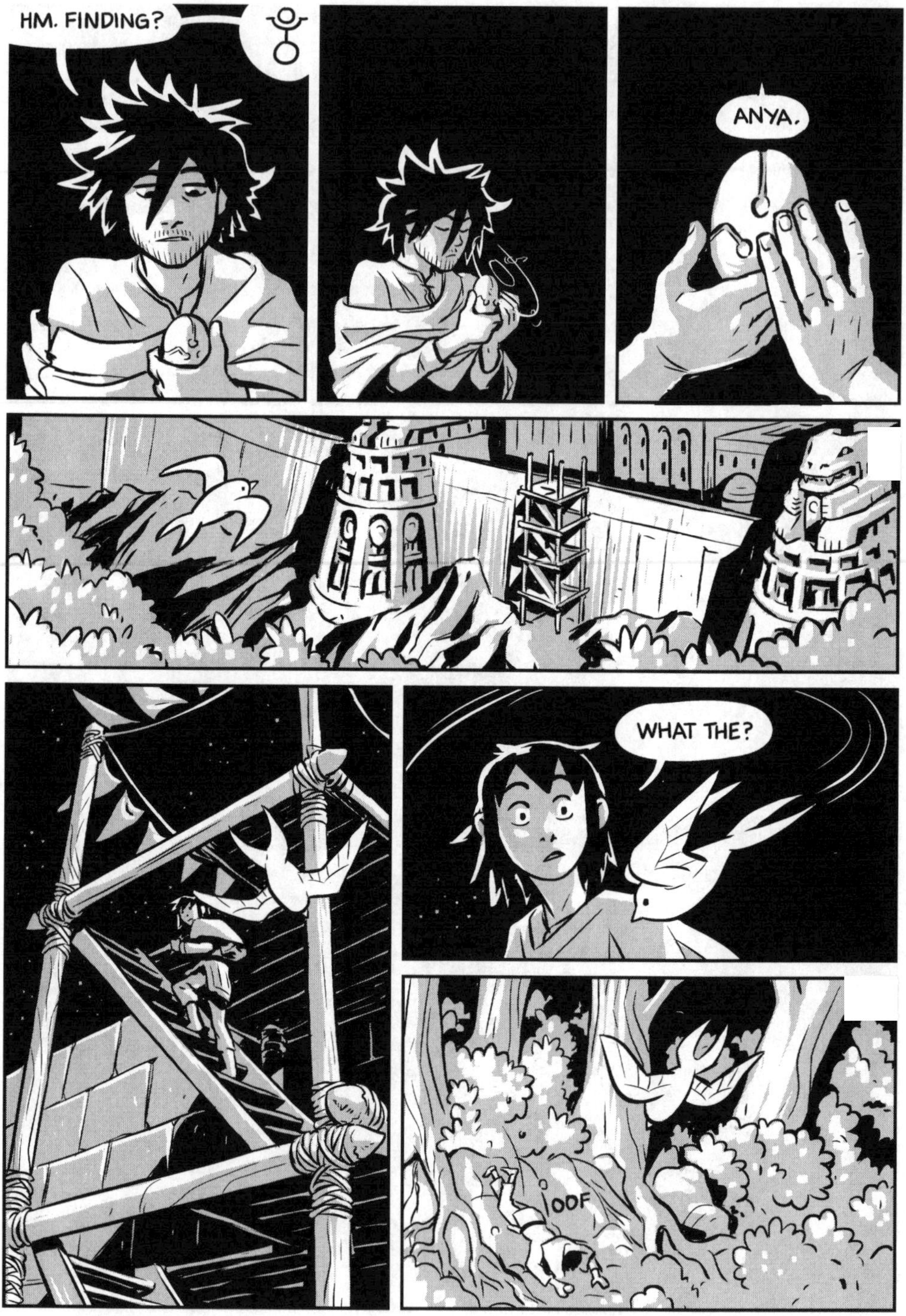
HM. FINDING?
ANYA.
WHAT THE?
OOF

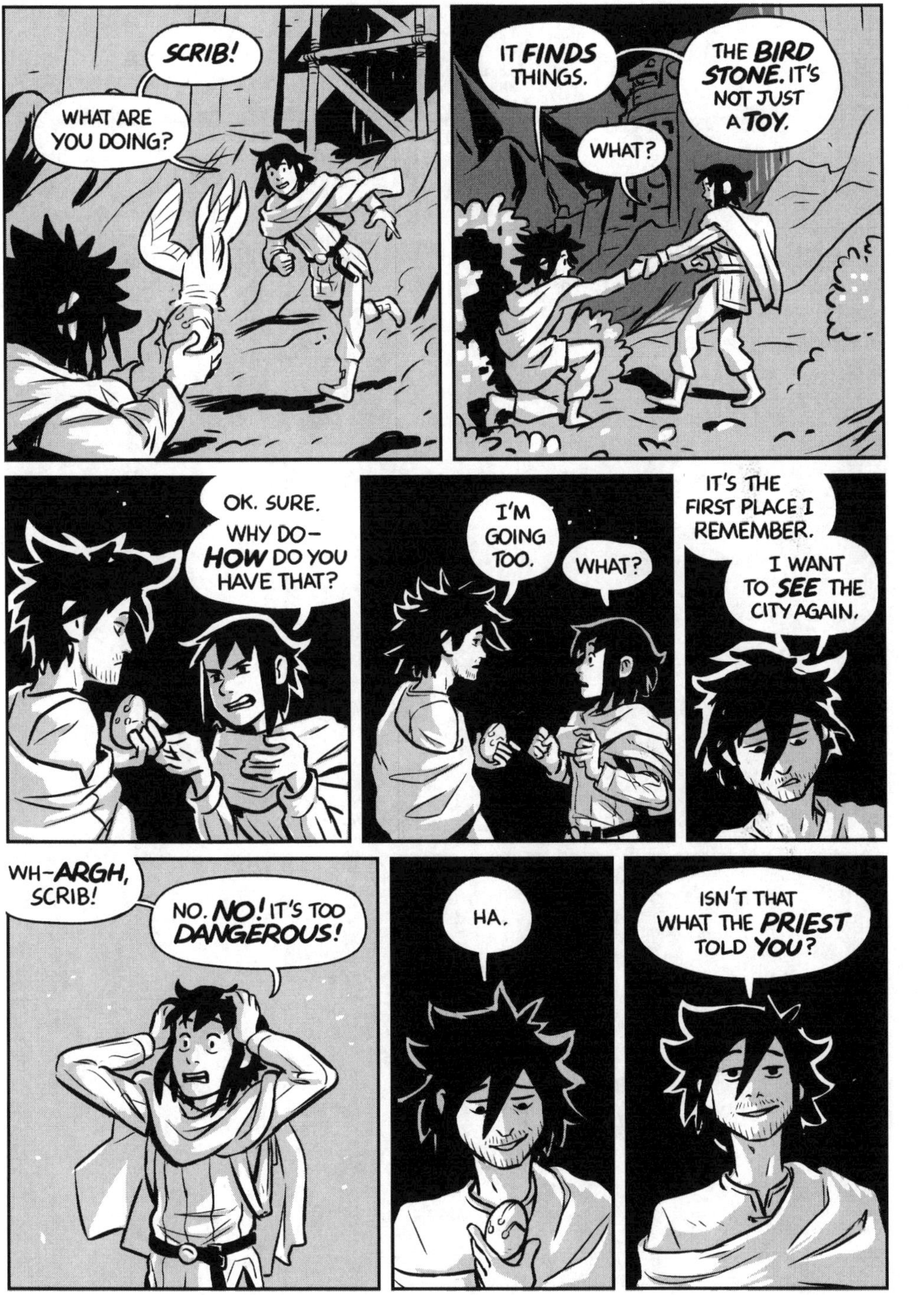
SCRIB!
WHAT ARE YOU DOING?
THE BIRD STONE. IT'S NOT JUST A TOY.
IT FINDS THINGS.
WHAT?
OK. SURE.
WHY DO—HOW DO YOU HAVE THAT?
I'M GOING TOO.
WHAT?
IT'S THE FIRST PLACE I REMEMBER.
I WANT TO SEE THE CITY AGAIN.
WH-ARGH, SCRIB!
NO. NO! IT'S TOO DANGEROUS!
HA.
ISN'T THAT WHAT THE PRIEST TOLD YOU?

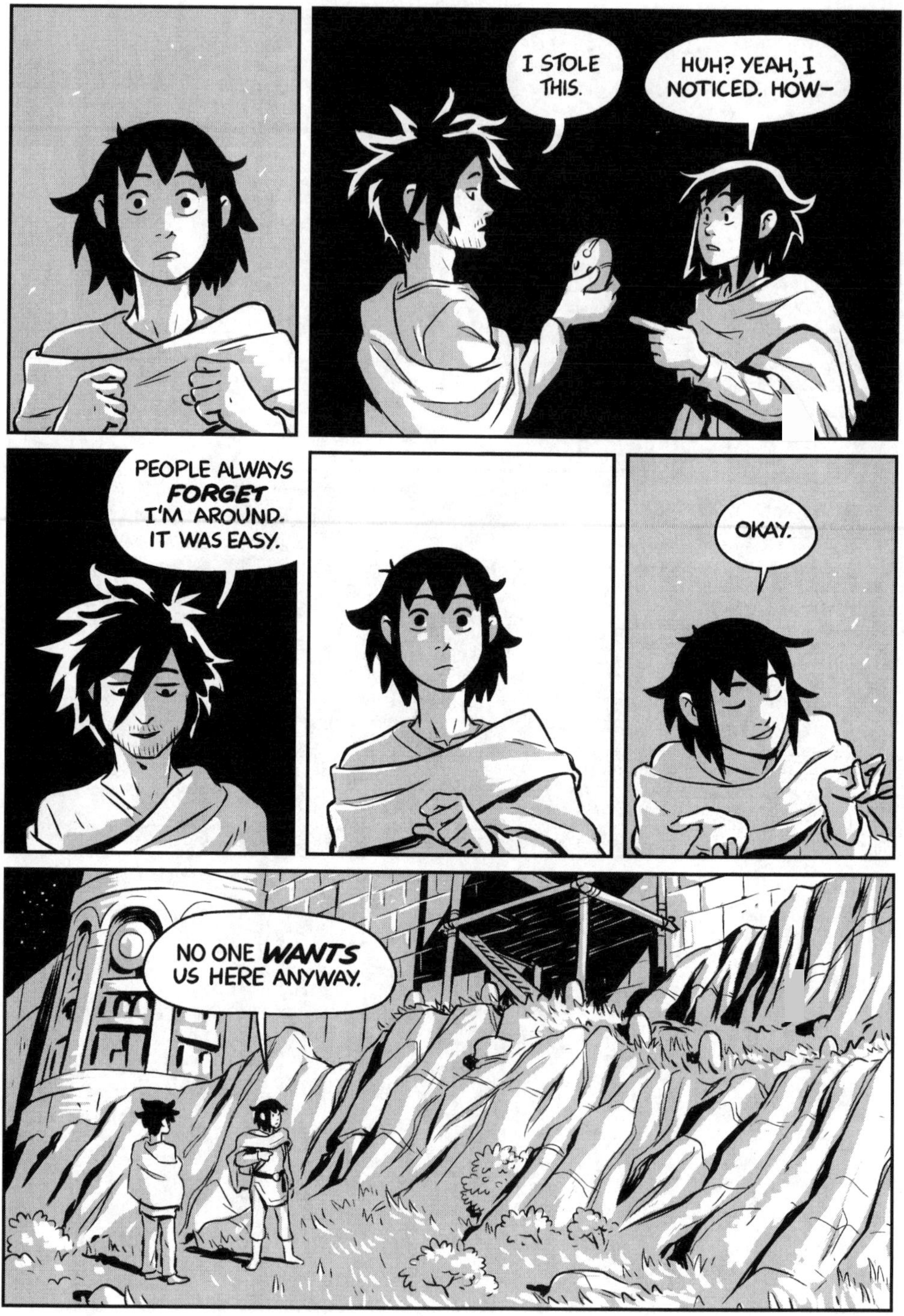
I STOLE THIS.
HUH? YEAH, I NOTICED. HOW–
PEOPLE ALWAYS FORGET I'M AROUND. IT WAS EASY.
OKAY.
NO ONE WANTS US HERE ANYWAY.

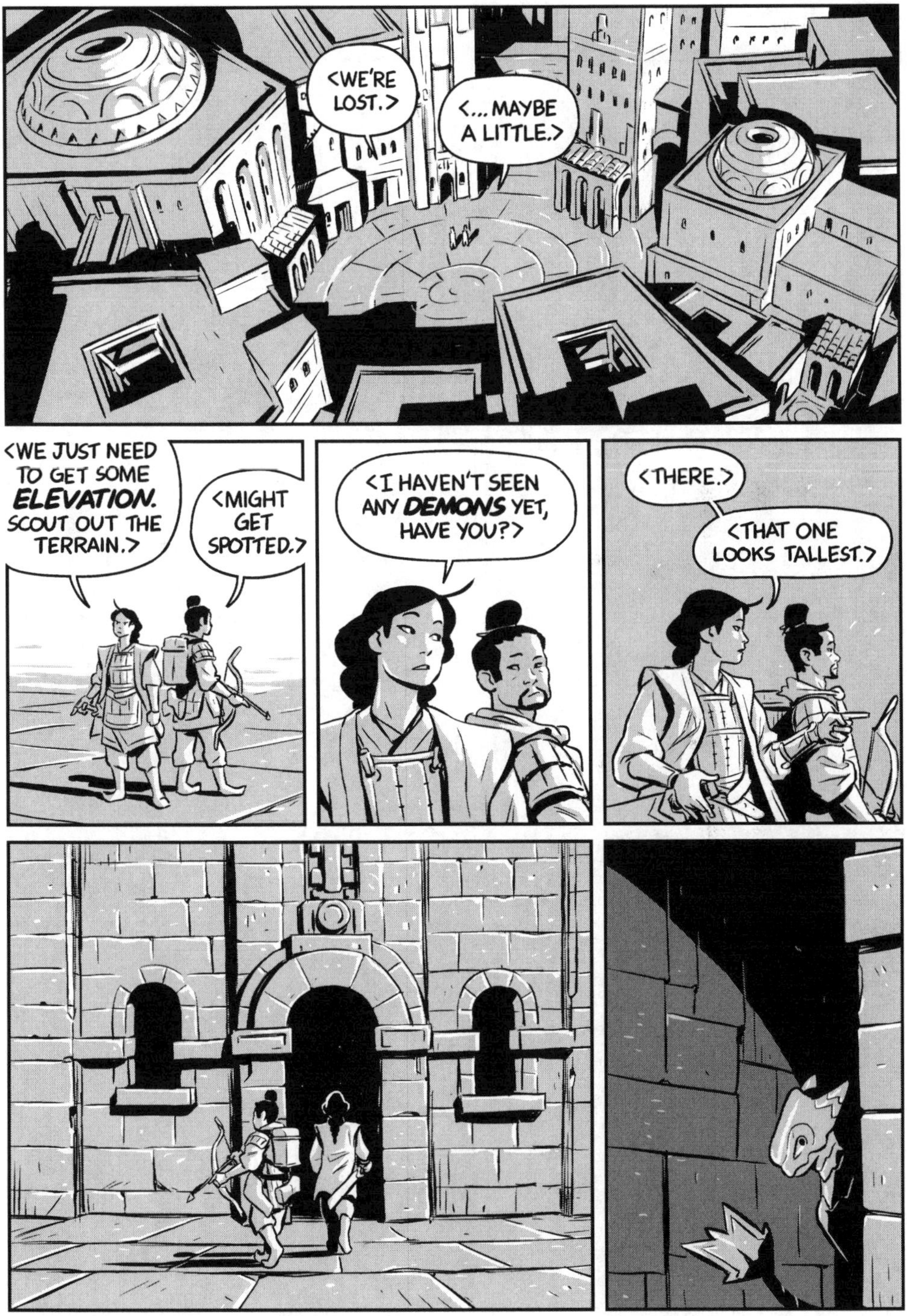

<WE'RE LOST.>
<... MAYBE A LITTLE.>
<WE JUST NEED TO GET SOME ELEVATION. SCOUT OUT THE TERRAIN.>
<MIGHT GET SPOTTED.>
<I HAVEN'T SEEN ANY DEMONS YET, HAVE YOU?>
<THERE.>
<THAT ONE LOOKS TALLEST.>

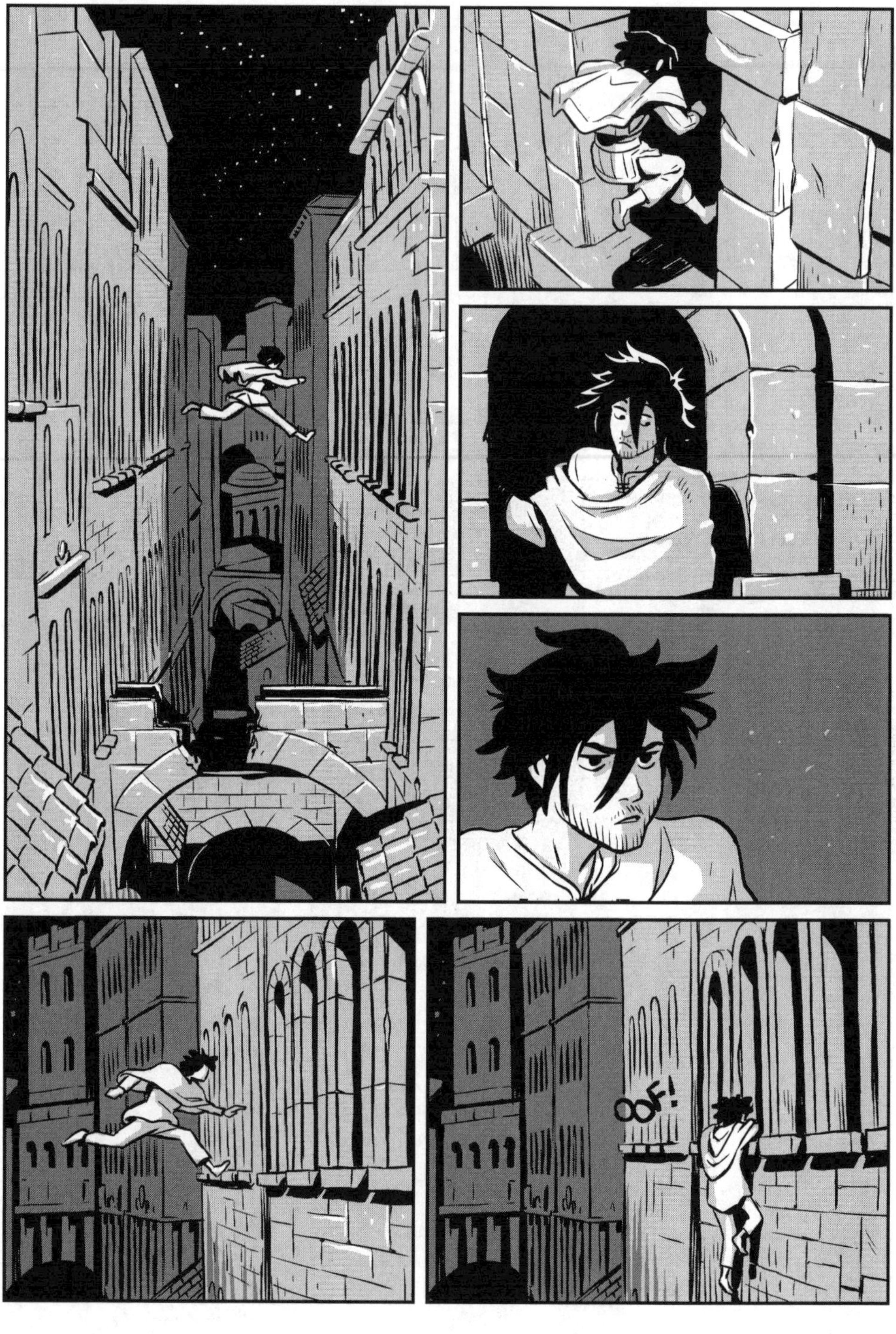
OOF!

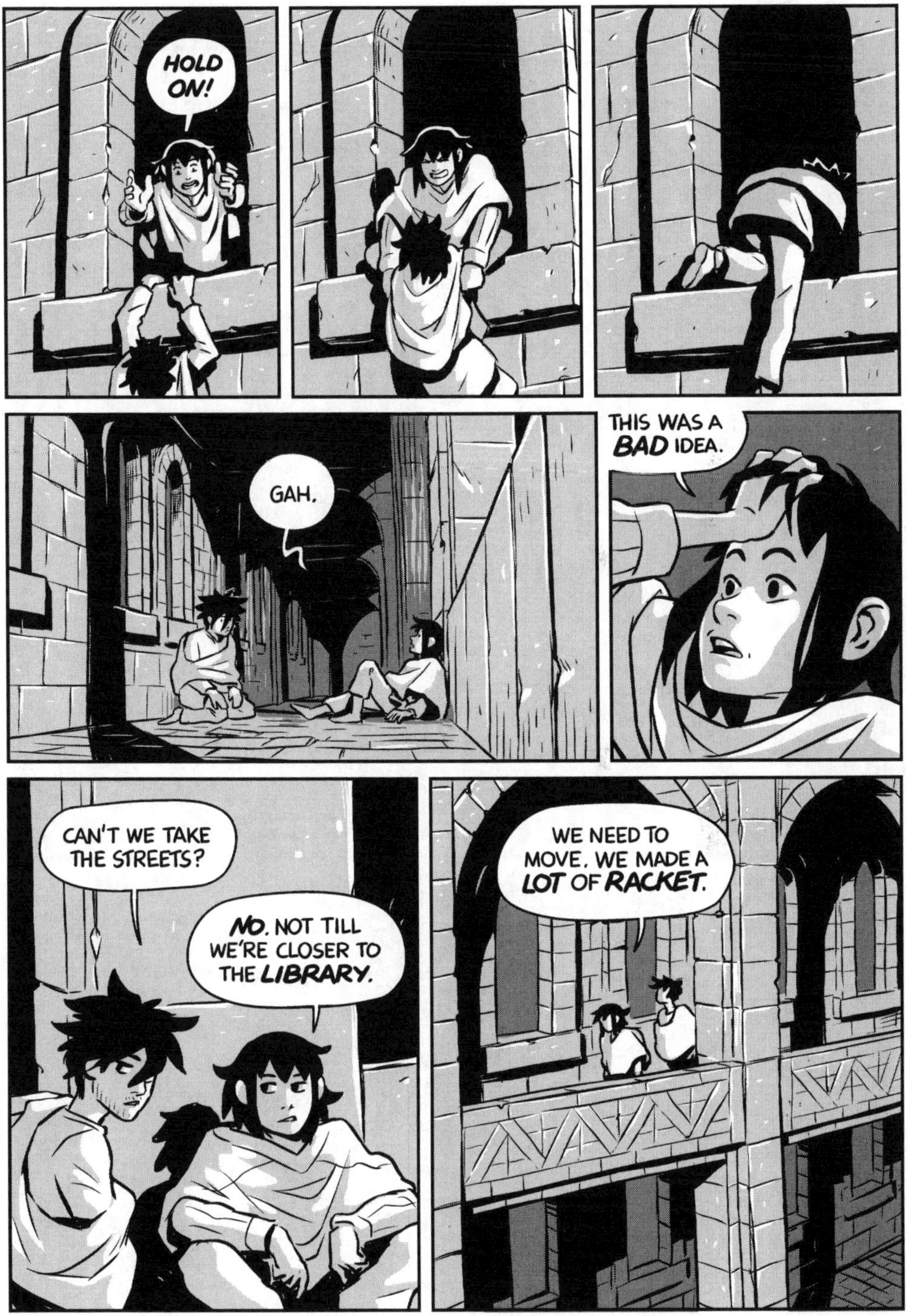
HOLD ON!
GAH.
THIS WAS A BAD IDEA.
CAN'T WE TAKE THE STREETS?
NO. NOT TILL WE'RE CLOSER TO THE LIBRARY.
WE NEED TO MOVE. WE MADE A LOT OF RACKET.

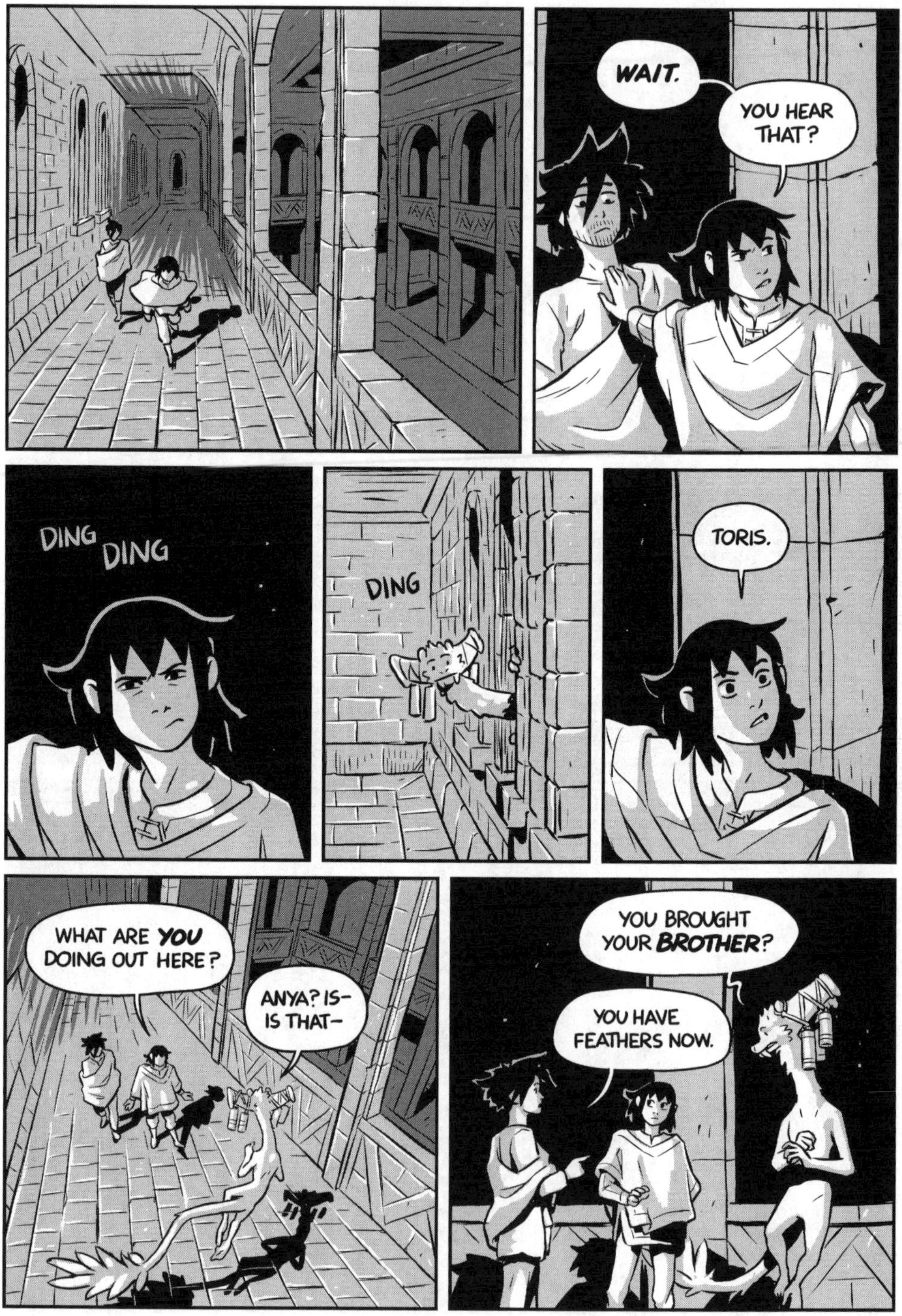
WAIT.
YOU HEAR THAT?
DING DING
DING
TORIS.
WHAT ARE YOU DOING OUT HERE?
ANYA? IS- IS THAT-
YOU BROUGHT YOUR BROTHER?
YOU HAVE FEATHERS NOW.

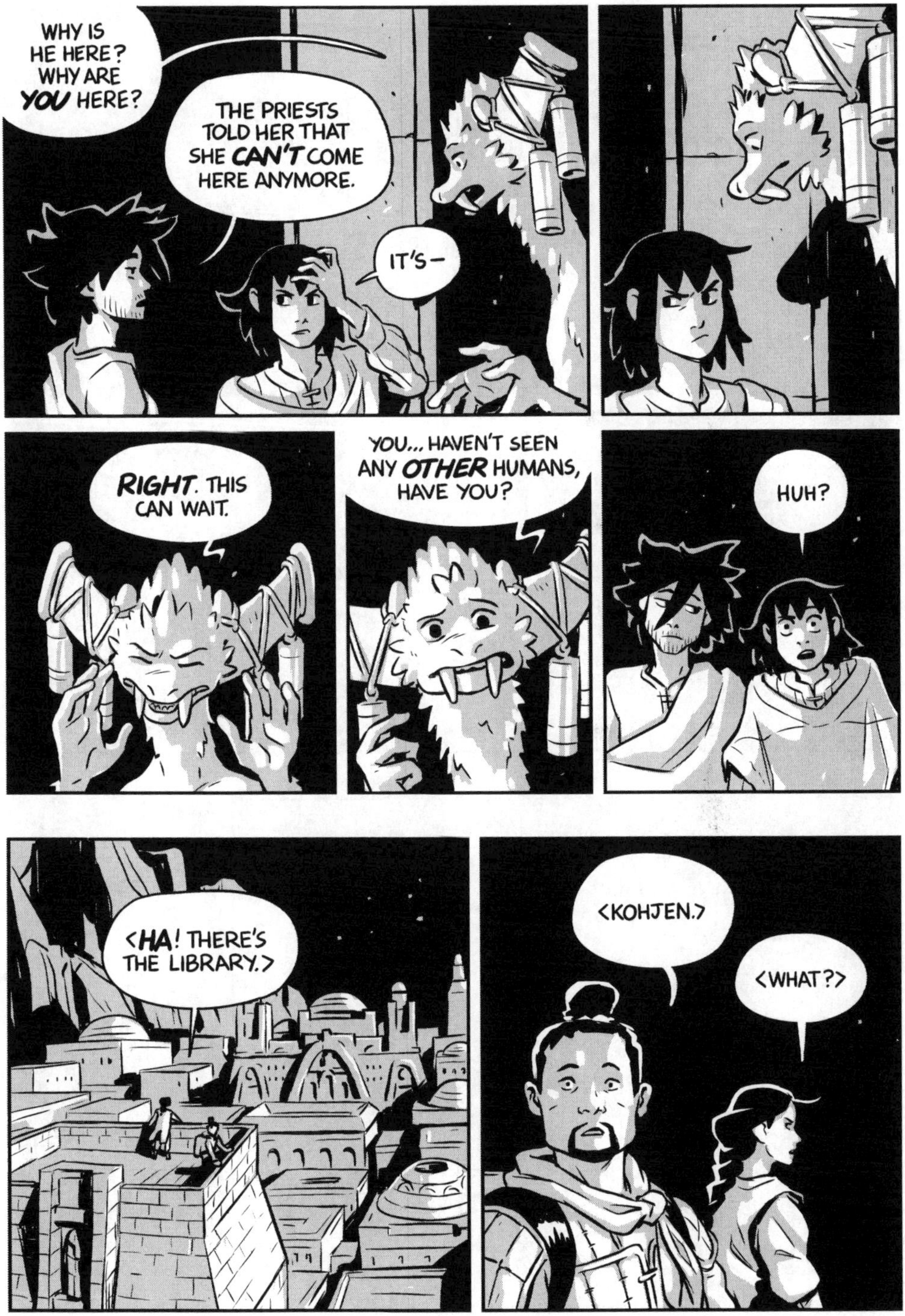
WHY IS HE HERE? WHY ARE *YOU* HERE?
THE PRIESTS TOLD HER THAT SHE *CAN'T* COME HERE ANYMORE.
IT'S—
RIGHT. THIS CAN WAIT.
YOU... HAVEN'T SEEN ANY *OTHER* HUMANS, HAVE YOU?
HUH?
<*HA*! THERE'S THE LIBRARY.>
<KOHJEN.>
<WHAT?>

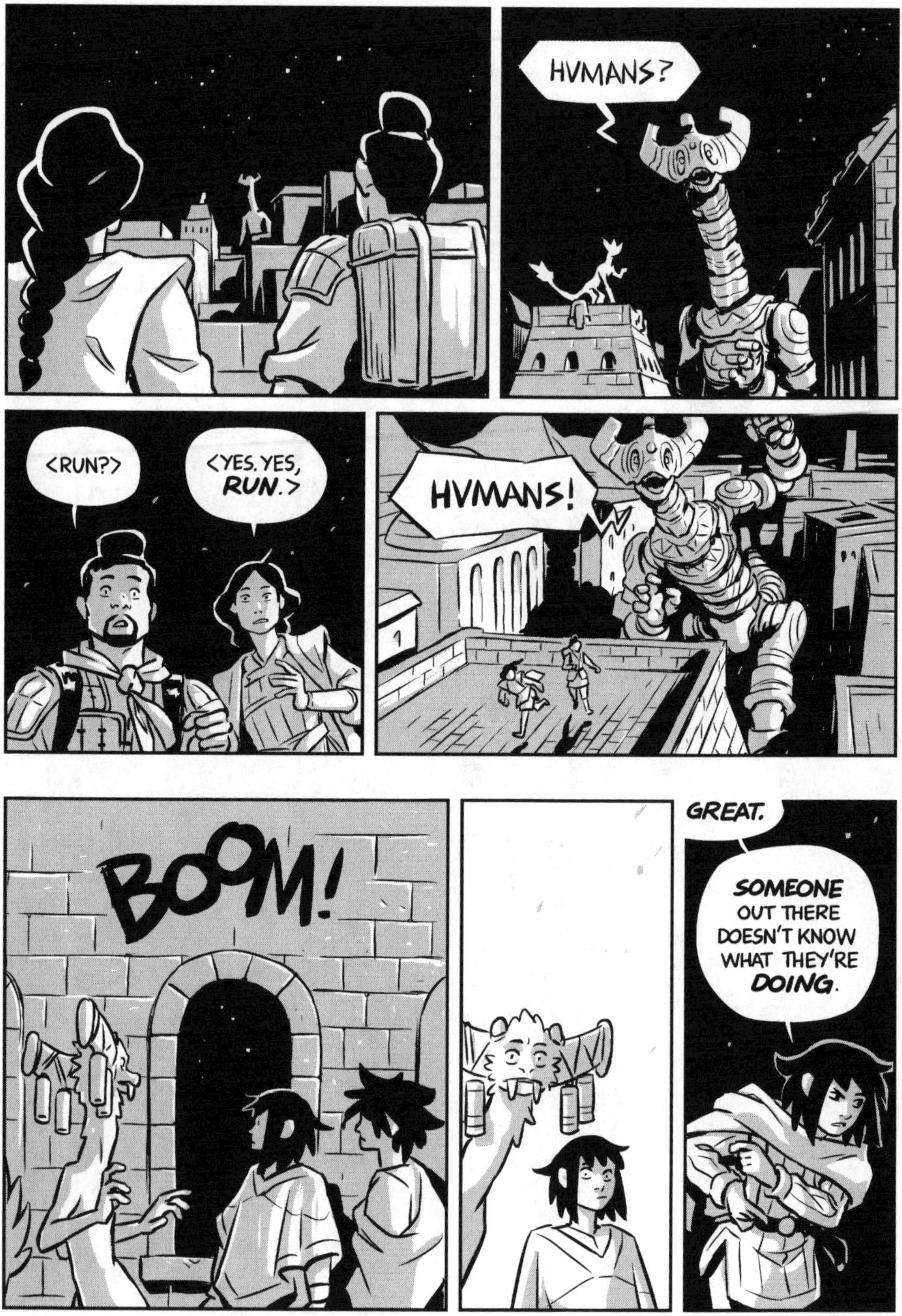
HVMANS?
<RUN?>
<YES. YES, RUN.>
HVMANS!
BOOM!
GREAT.
SOMEONE OUT THERE DOESN'T KNOW WHAT THEY'RE DOING.

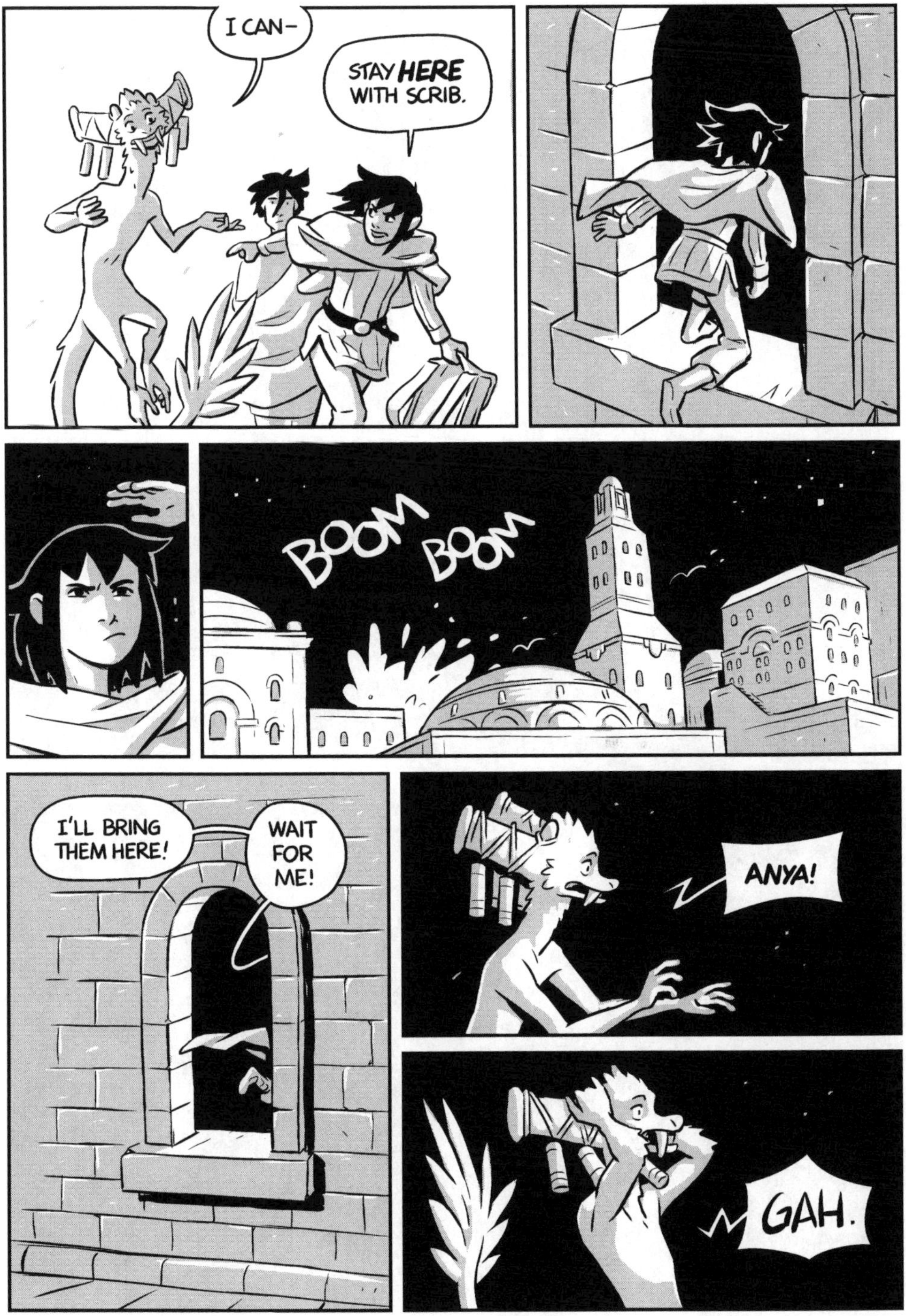
I CAN–
STAY **HERE** WITH SCRIB.
BOOM BOOM
I'LL BRING THEM HERE!
WAIT FOR ME!
ANYA!
GAH.

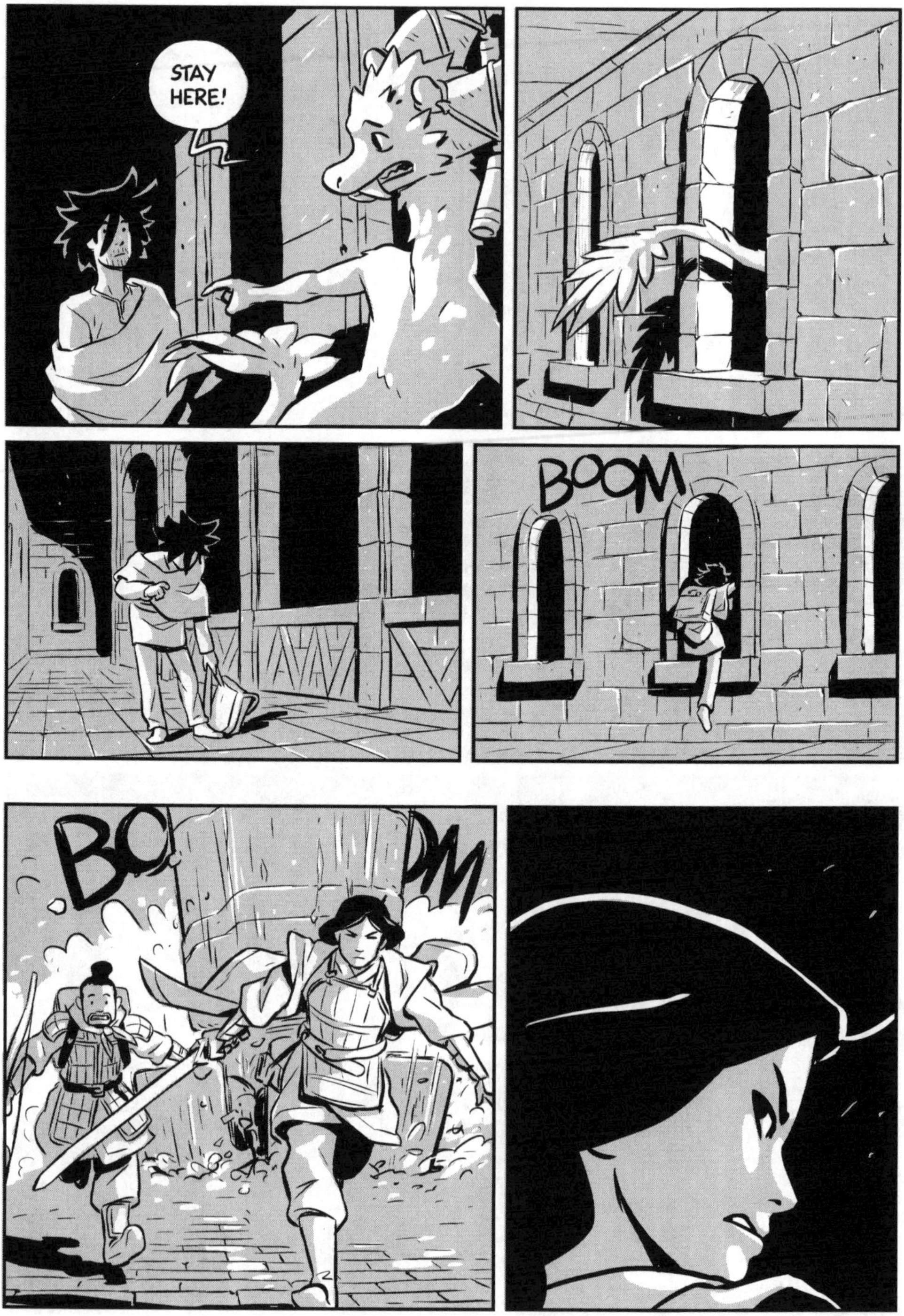
STAY HERE!
BOOM
BOOM

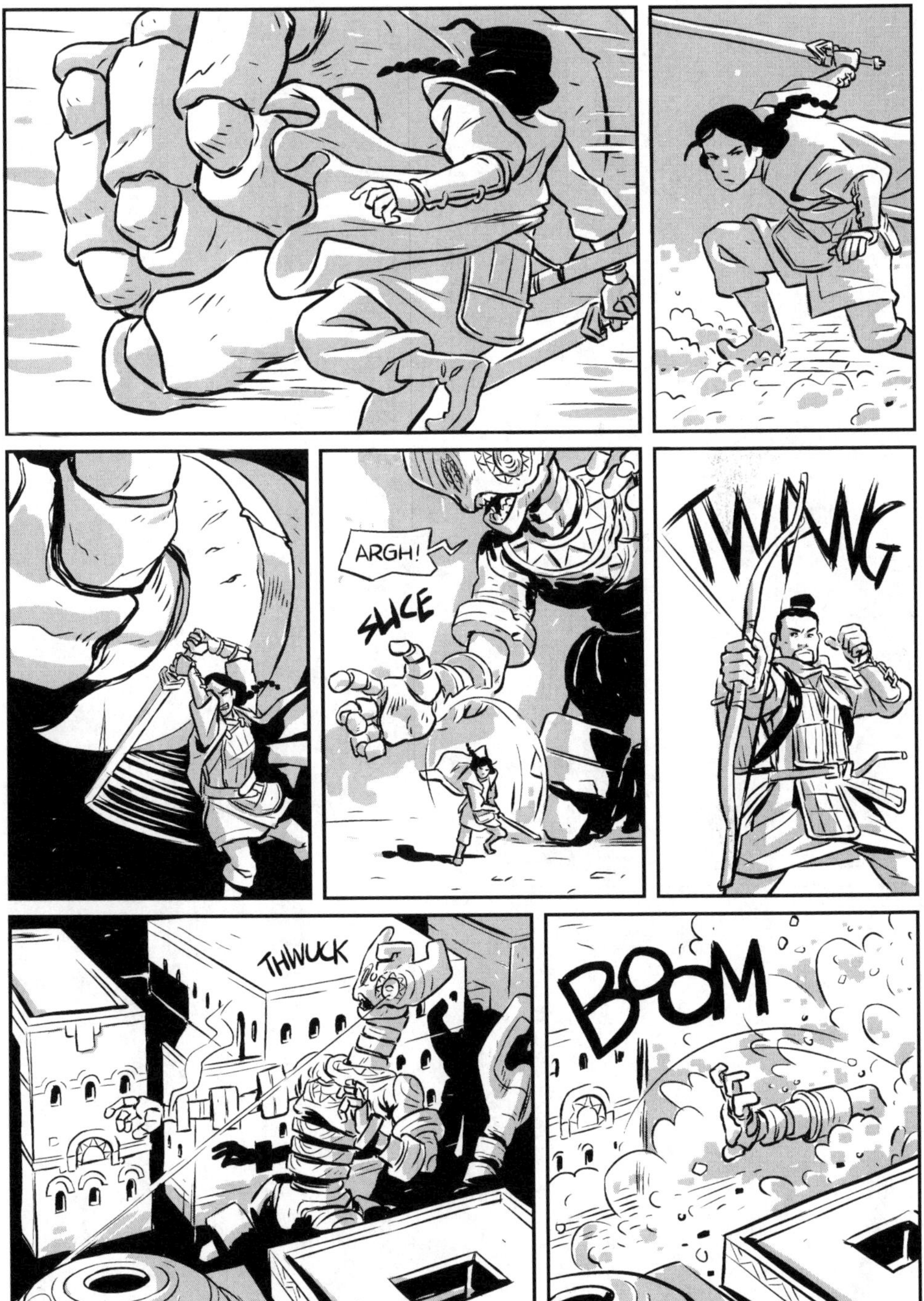
ARGH!
SLICE
TWANG
THWUCK
BOOM

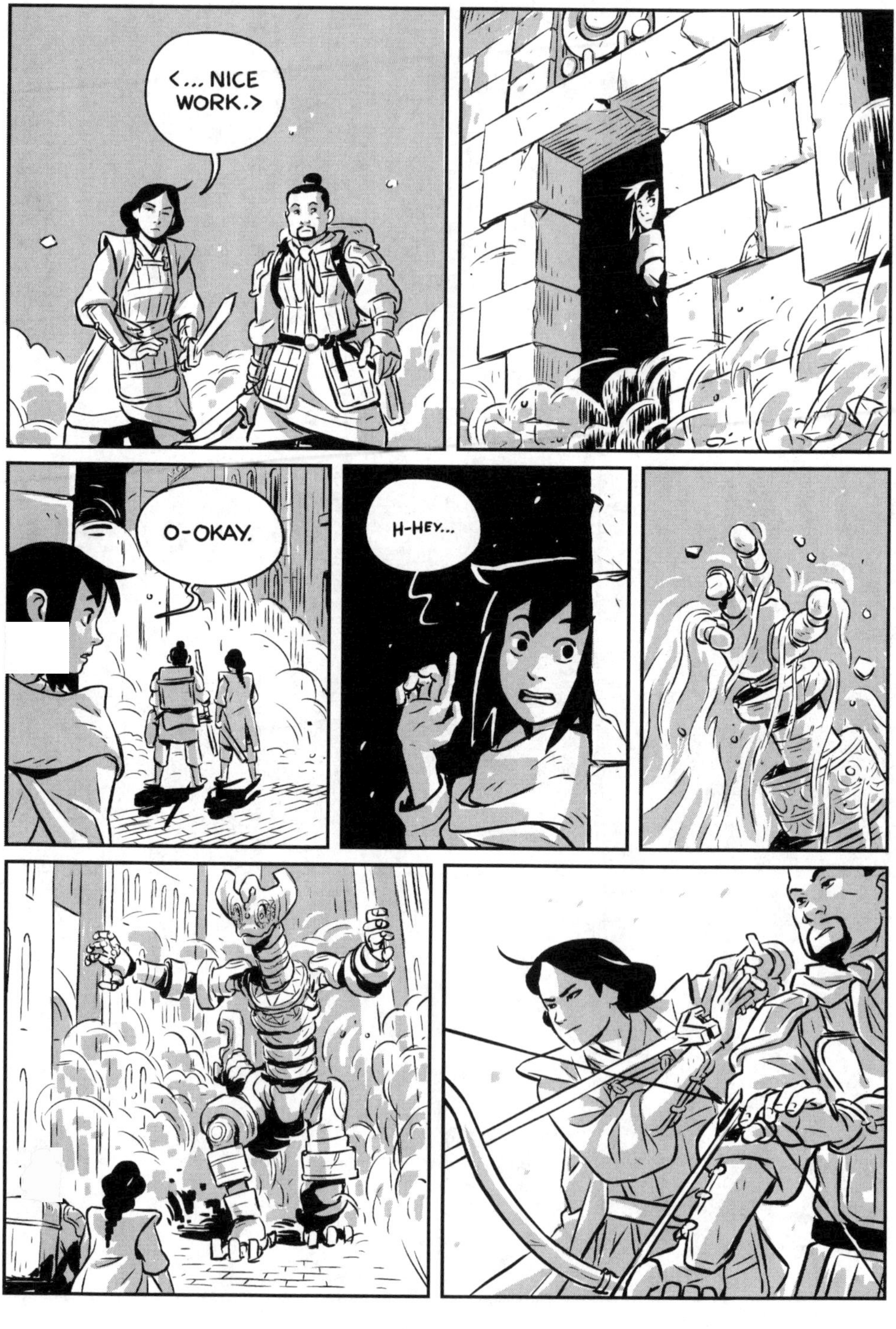
<... NICE WORK.>
O-OKAY.
H-HEY...

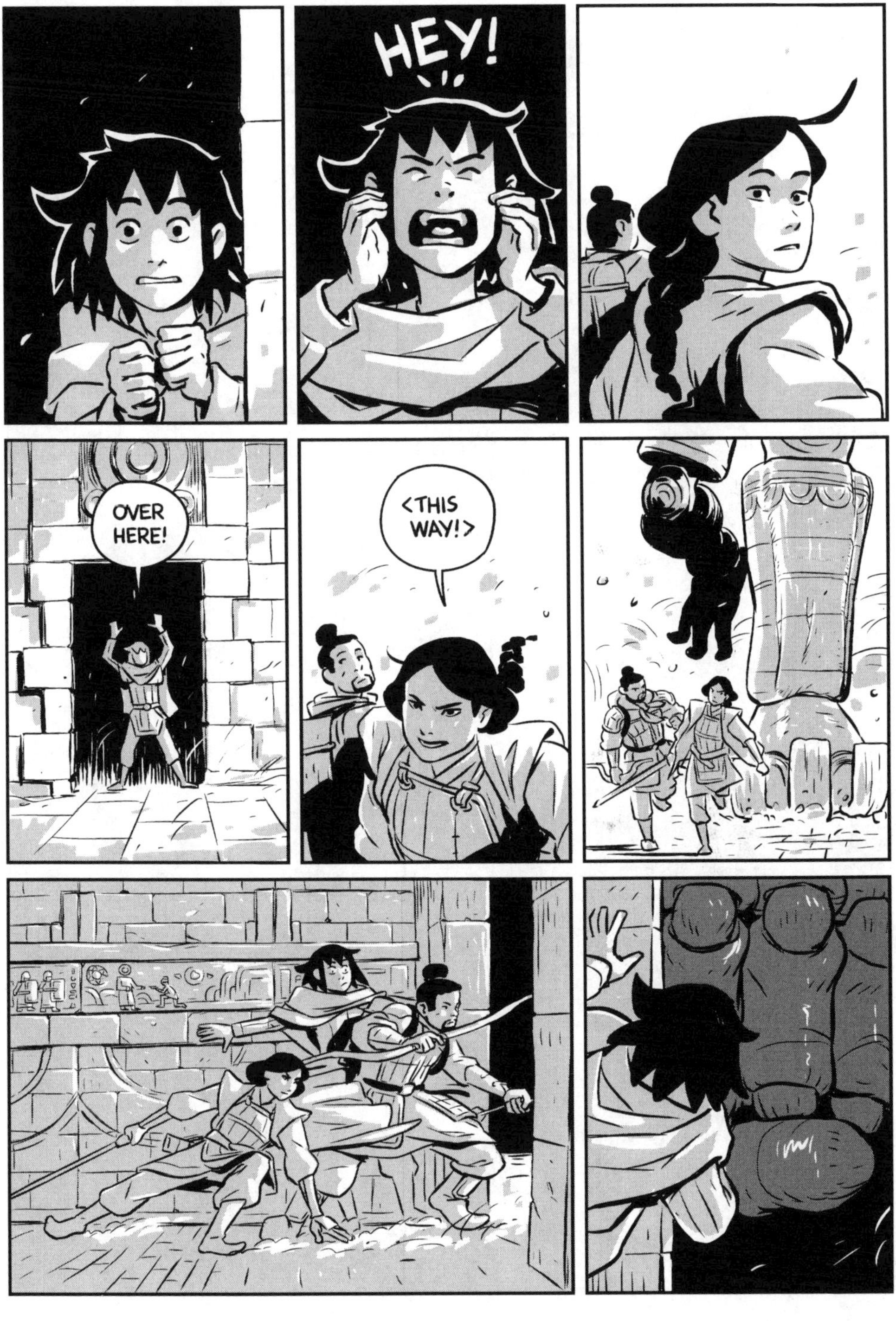
HEY!
OVER HERE!
<THIS WAY!>

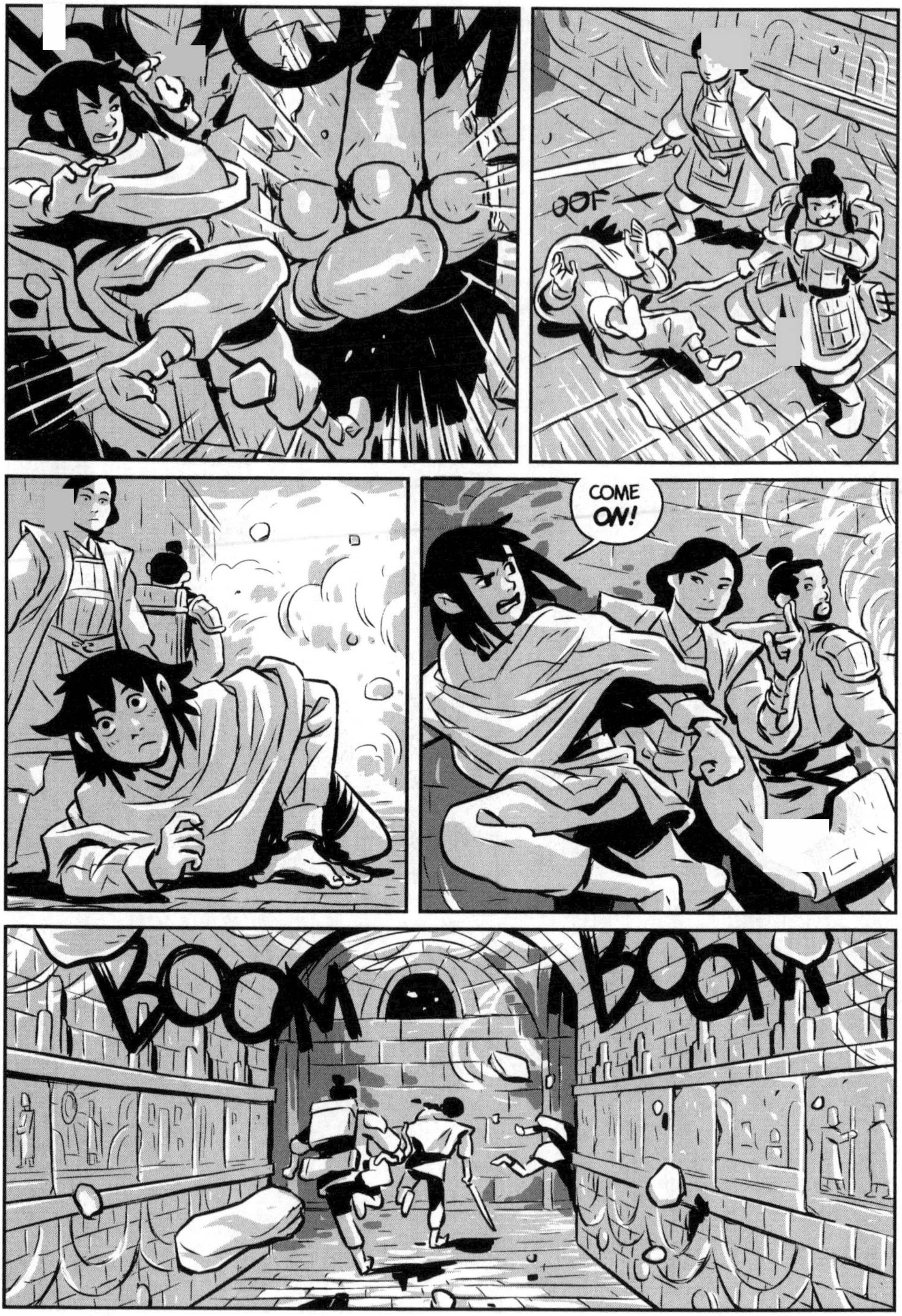
OOF
COME ON!
BOOM
BOOM

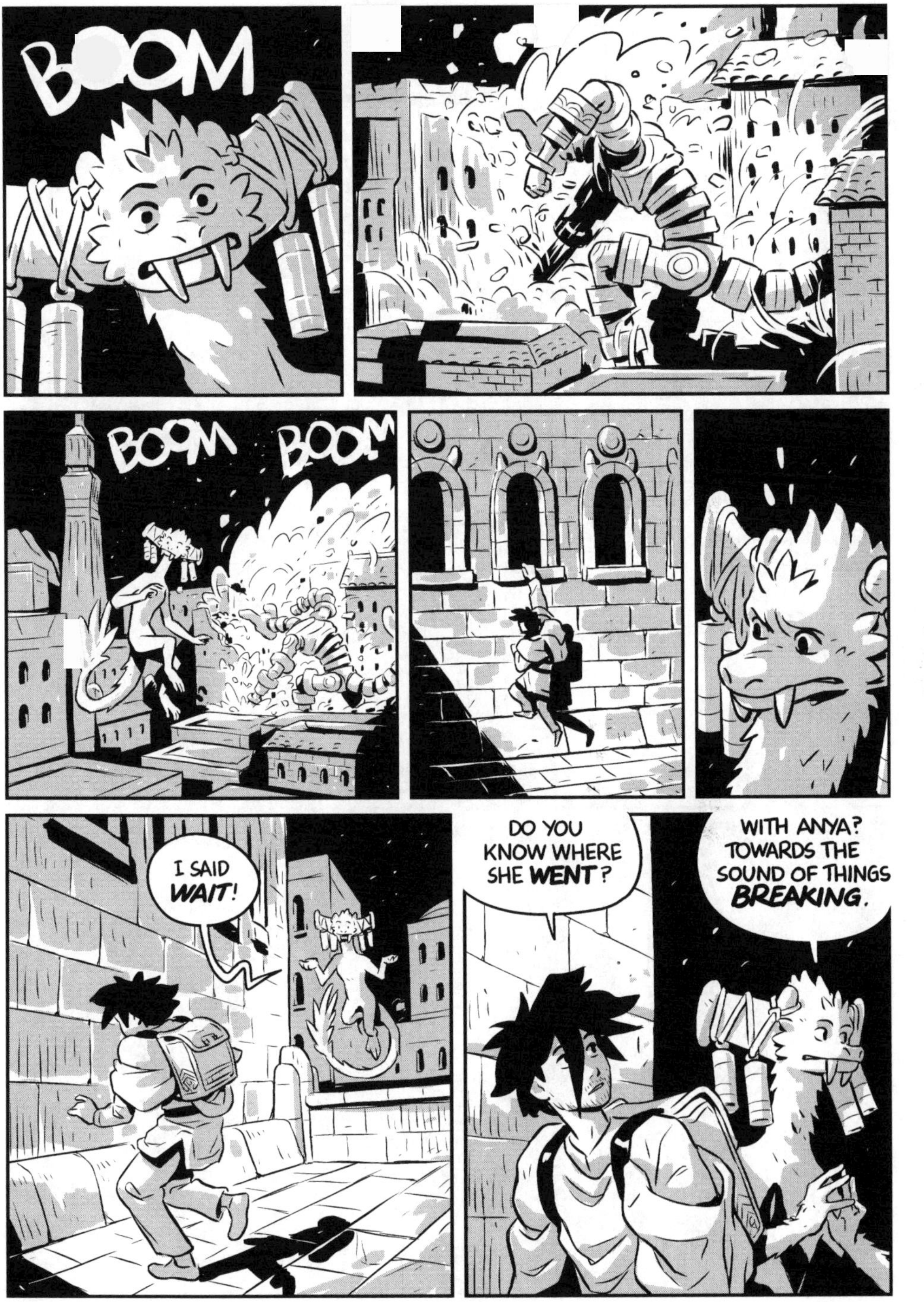

BOOM
BOOM
BOOM
I SAID WAIT!
DO YOU KNOW WHERE SHE WENT?
WITH ANYA? TOWARDS THE SOUND OF THINGS BREAKING.

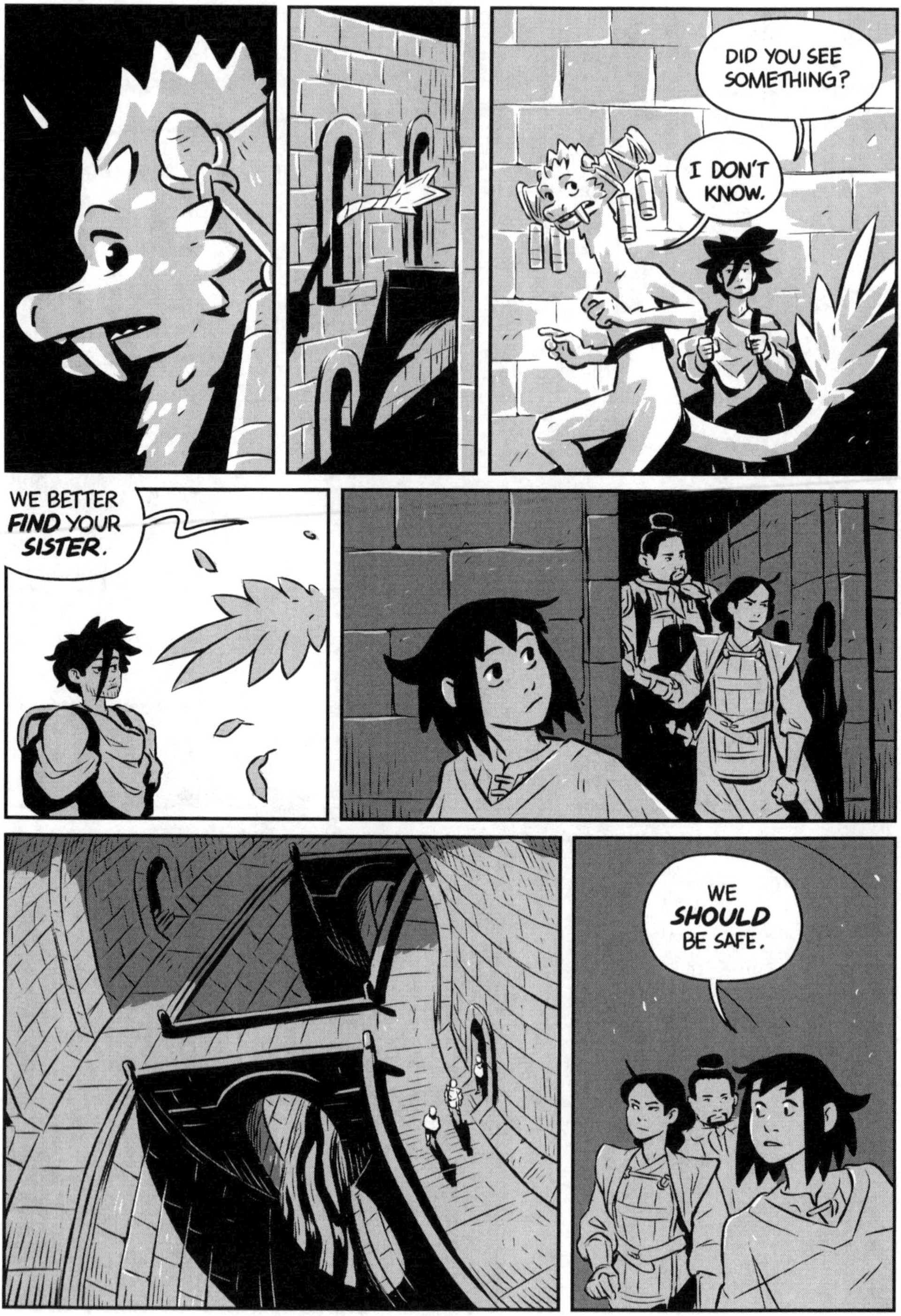
DID YOU SEE SOMETHING?
I DON'T KNOW.
WE BETTER **FIND** YOUR **SISTER**.
WE **SHOULD** BE SAFE.

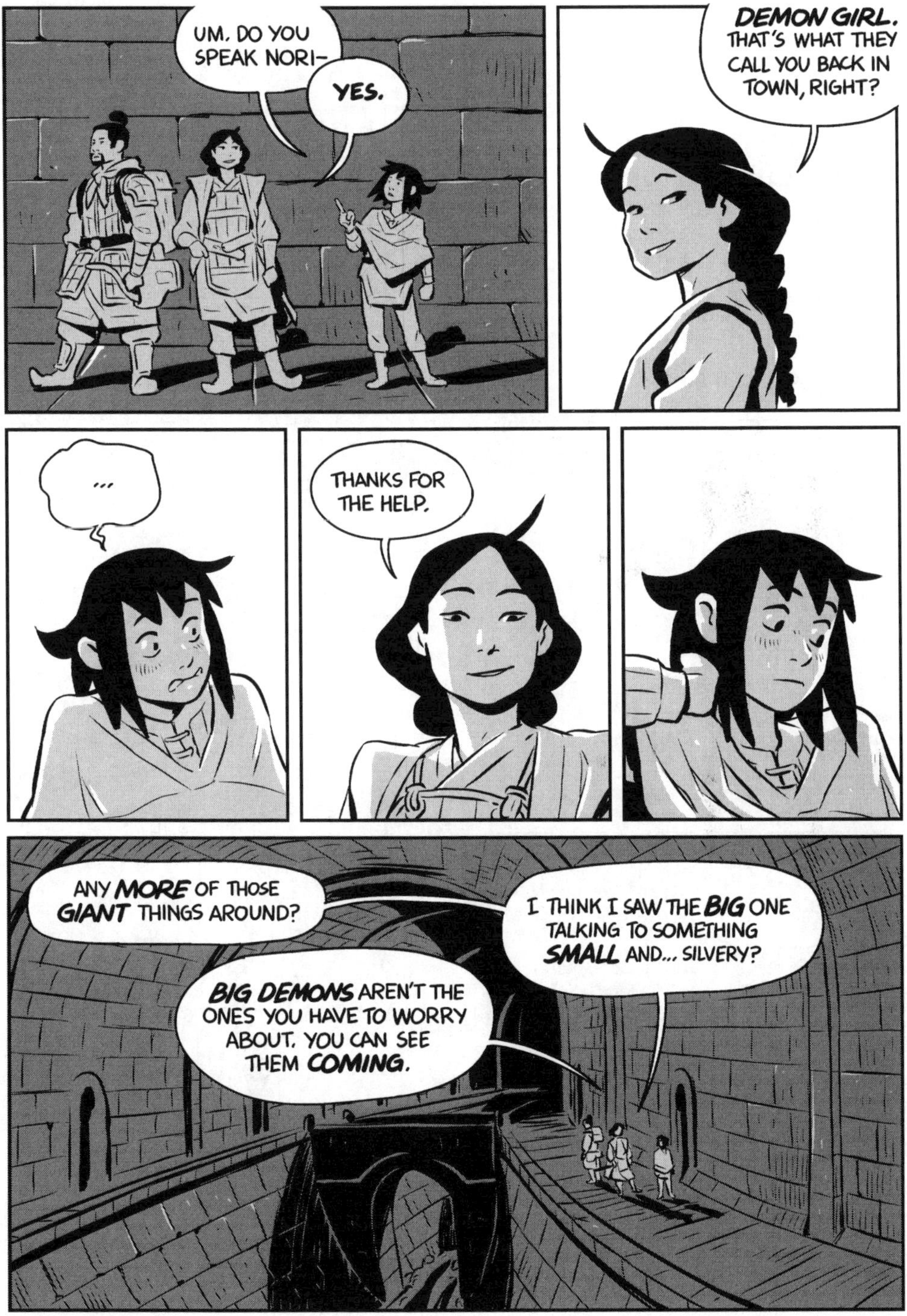
UM. DO YOU SPEAK NORI–
YES.
DEMON GIRL. THAT'S WHAT THEY CALL YOU BACK IN TOWN, RIGHT?
...
THANKS FOR THE HELP.
ANY MORE OF THOSE GIANT THINGS AROUND?
I THINK I SAW THE BIG ONE TALKING TO SOMETHING SMALL AND... SILVERY?
BIG DEMONS AREN'T THE ONES YOU HAVE TO WORRY ABOUT. YOU CAN SEE THEM COMING.

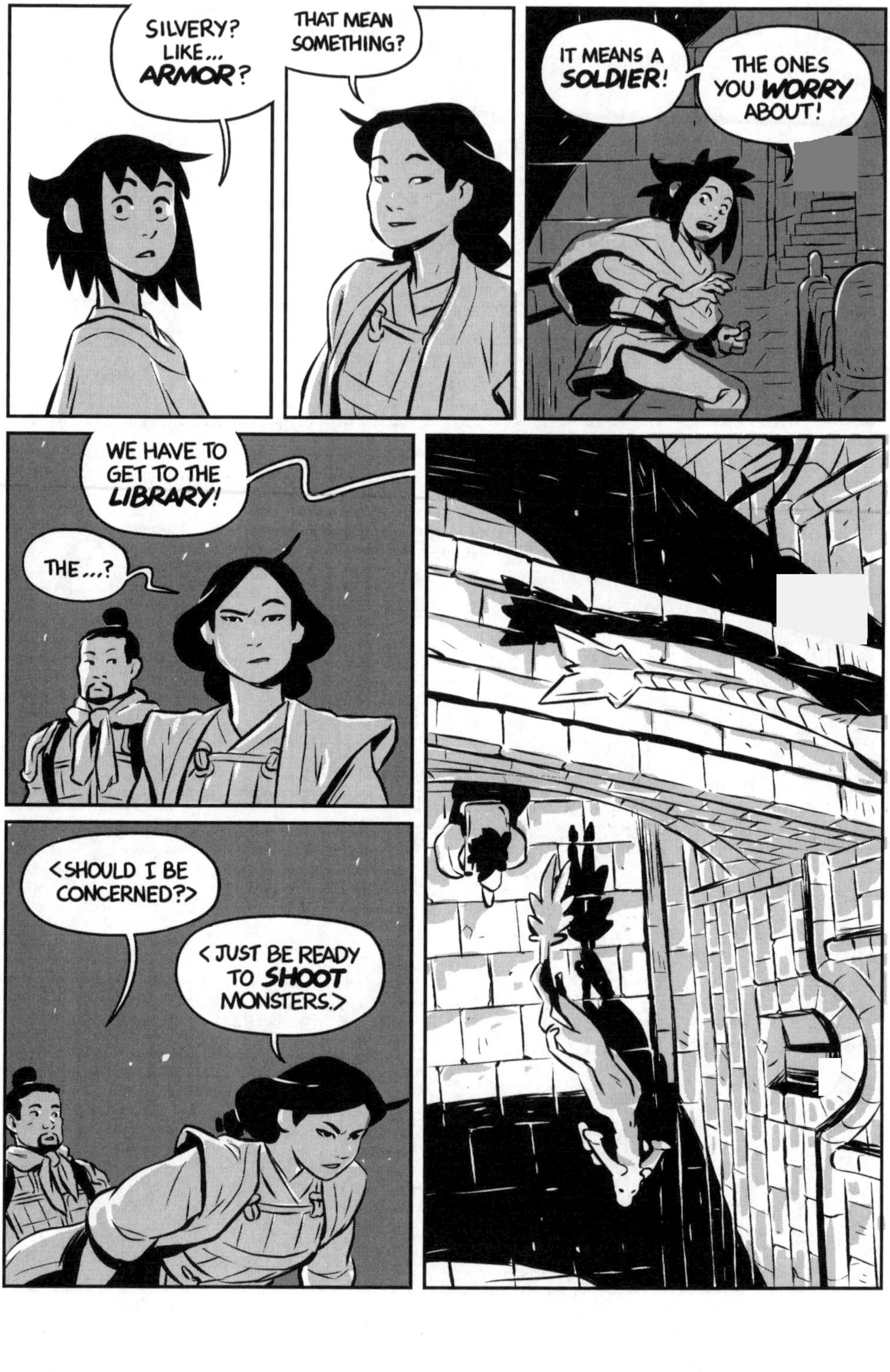
SILVERY? LIKE... ARMOR?
THAT MEAN SOMETHING?
IT MEANS A SOLDIER!
THE ONES YOU WORRY ABOUT!
WE HAVE TO GET TO THE LIBRARY!
THE...?
<SHOULD I BE CONCERNED?>
<JUST BE READY TO SHOOT MONSTERS.>

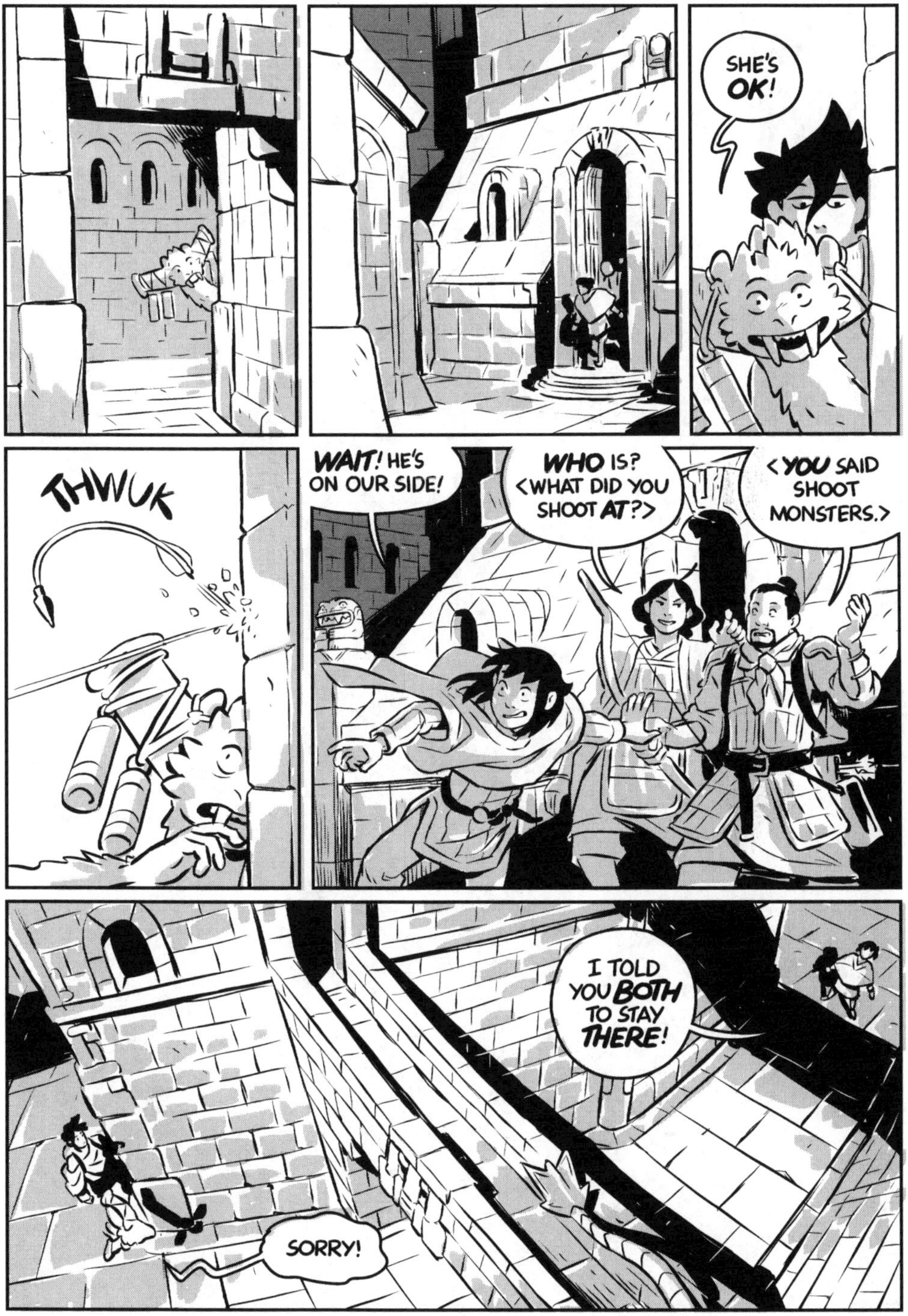
SHE'S OK!
THWUK
WAIT! HE'S ON OUR SIDE!
WHO IS? <WHAT DID YOU SHOOT AT?>
<YOU SAID SHOOT MONSTERS.>
I TOLD YOU BOTH TO STAY THERE!
SORRY!

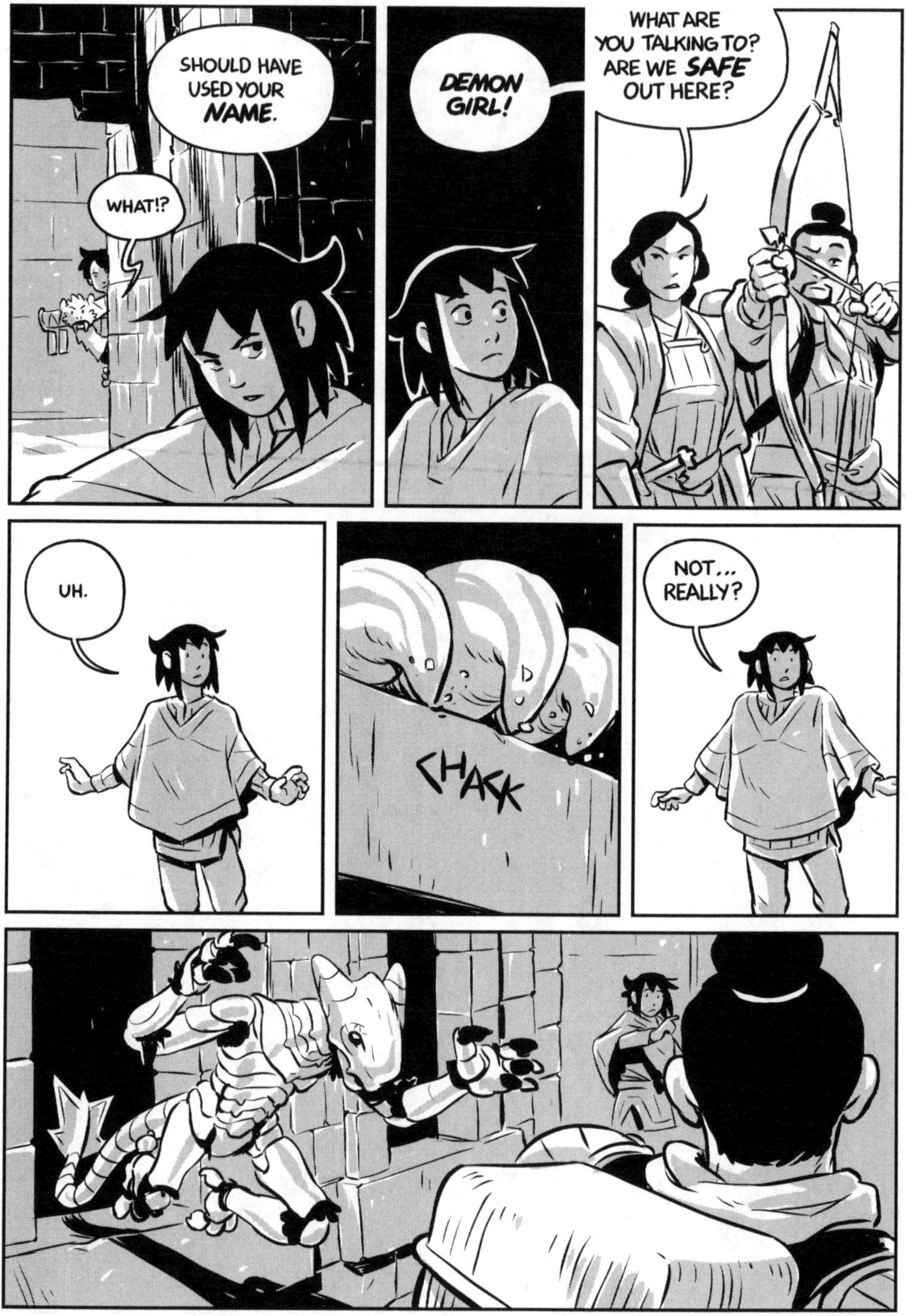

SHOULD HAVE USED YOUR NAME.
WHAT!?
DEMON GIRL!
WHAT ARE YOU TALKING TO? ARE WE SAFE OUT HERE?
UH.
CHACK
NOT... REALLY?

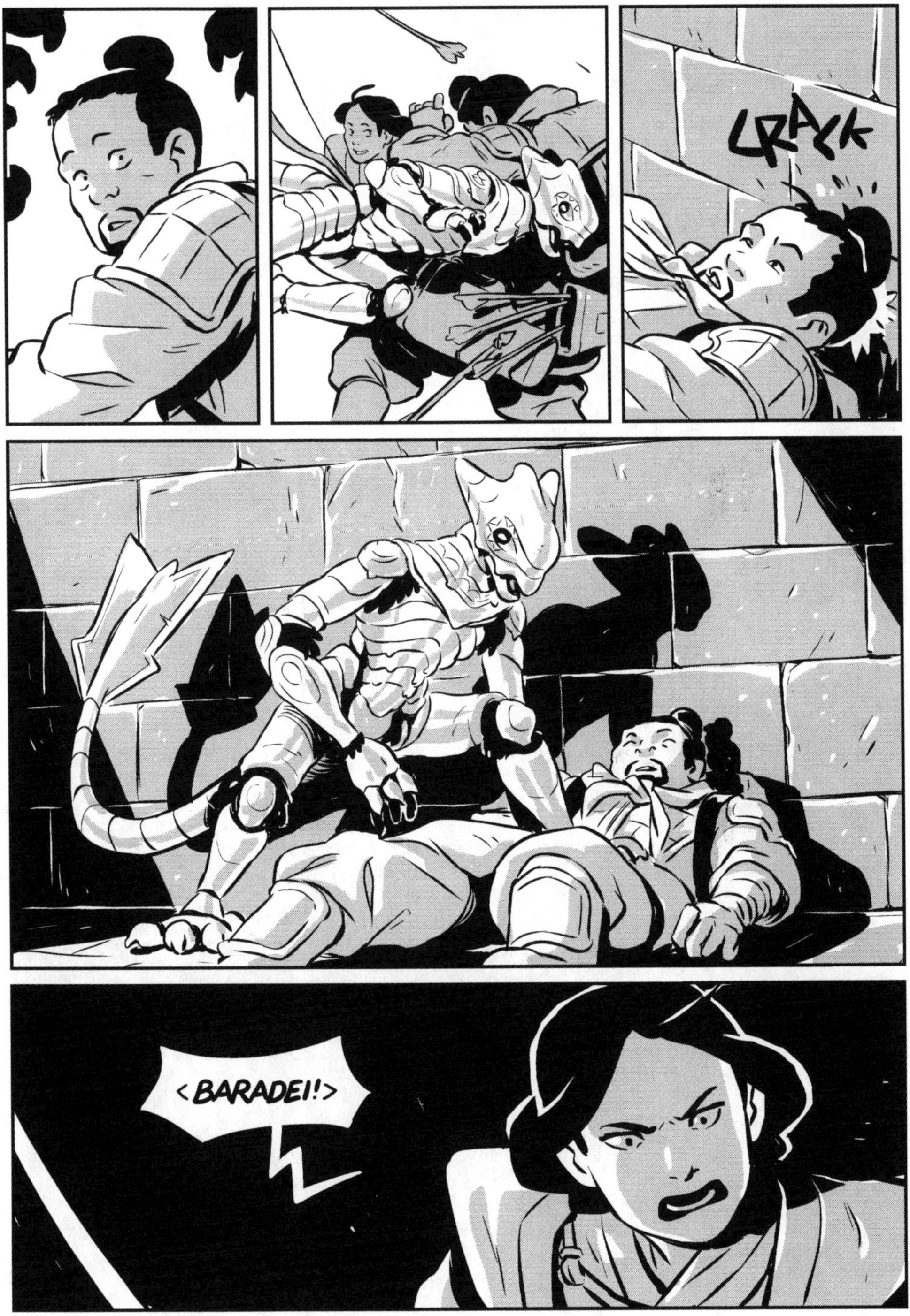
CRACK
<BARADEI!>

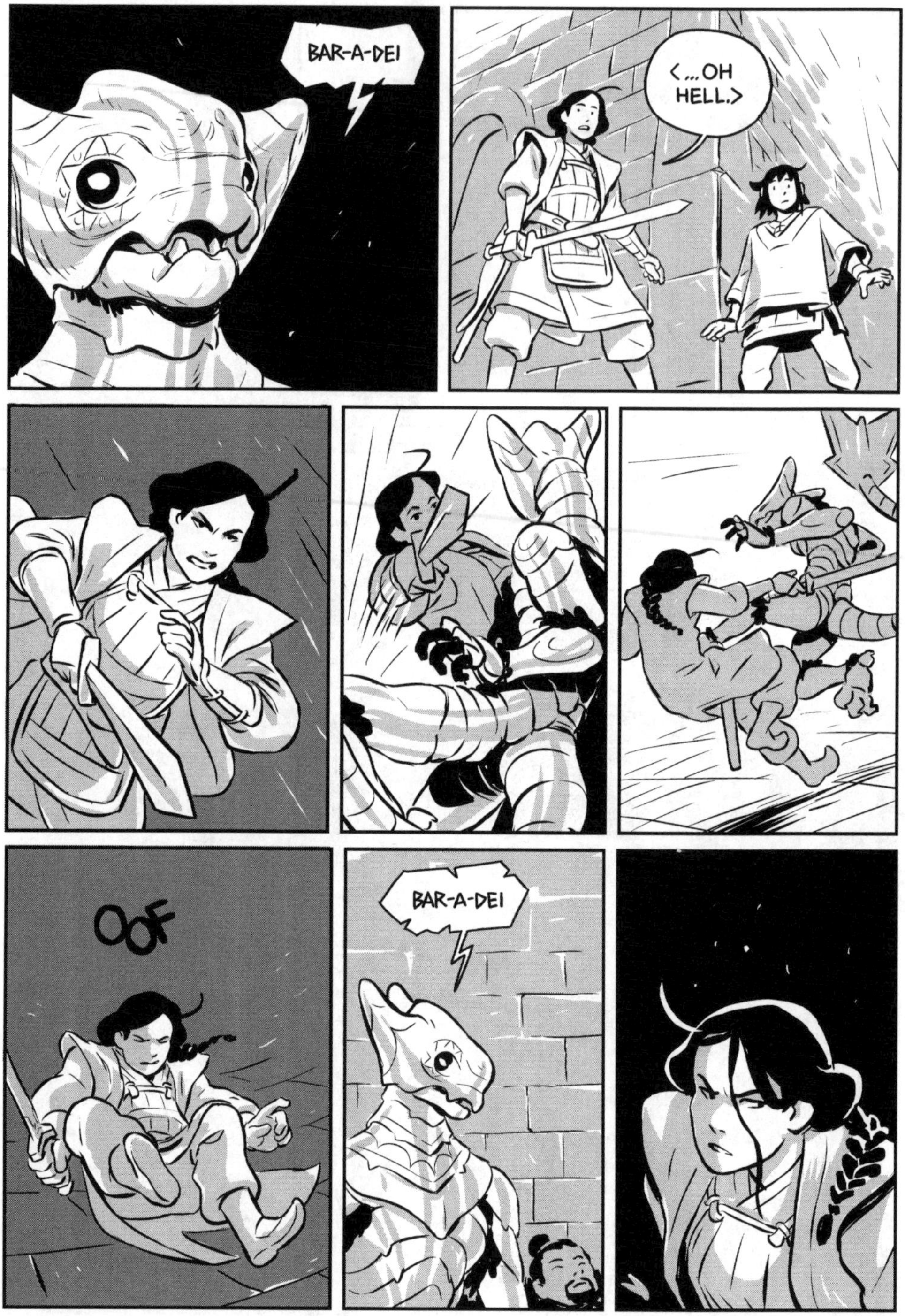
BAR-A-DEI
<...OH HELL.>
OOF
BAR-A-DEI

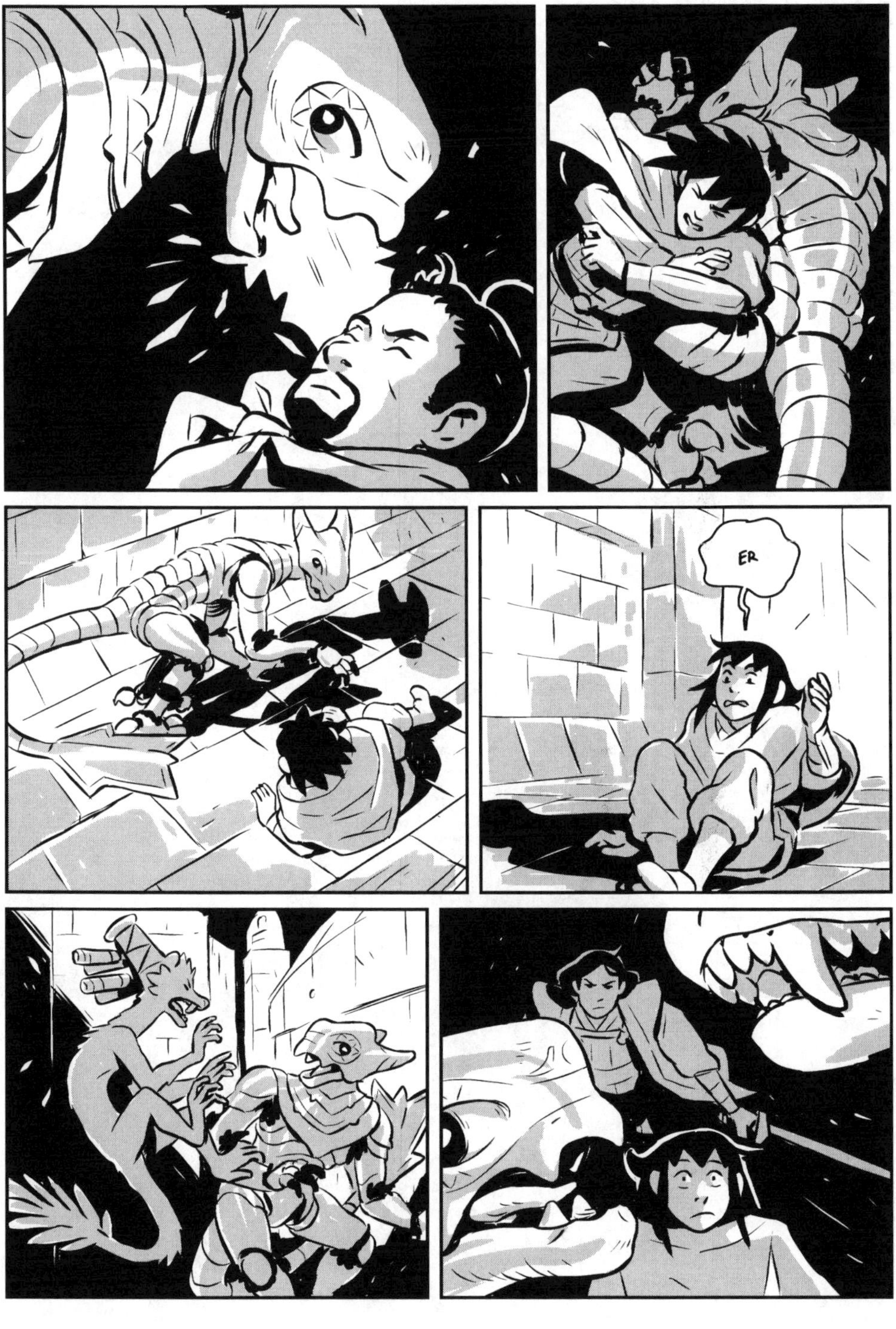
ER

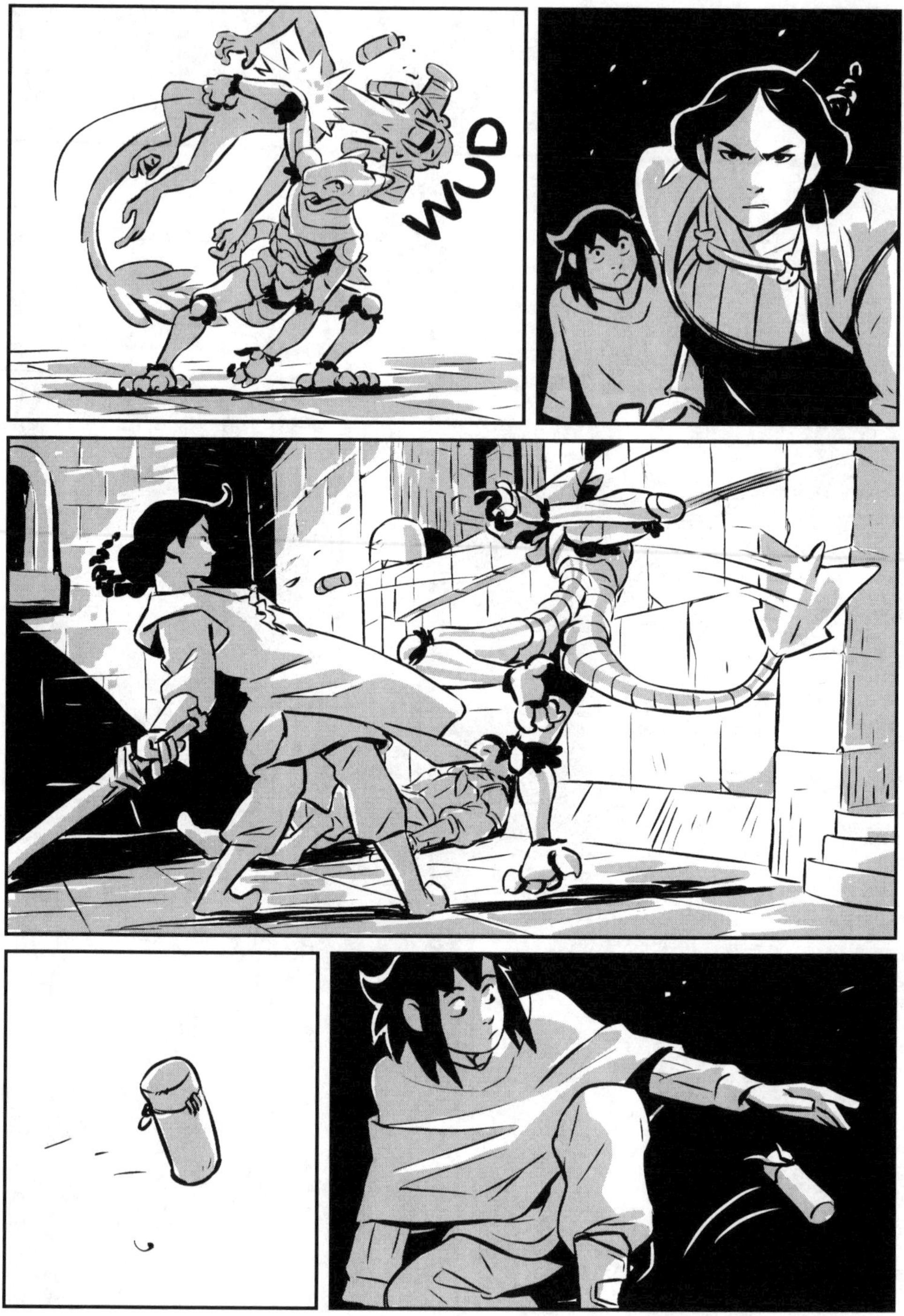
WUD

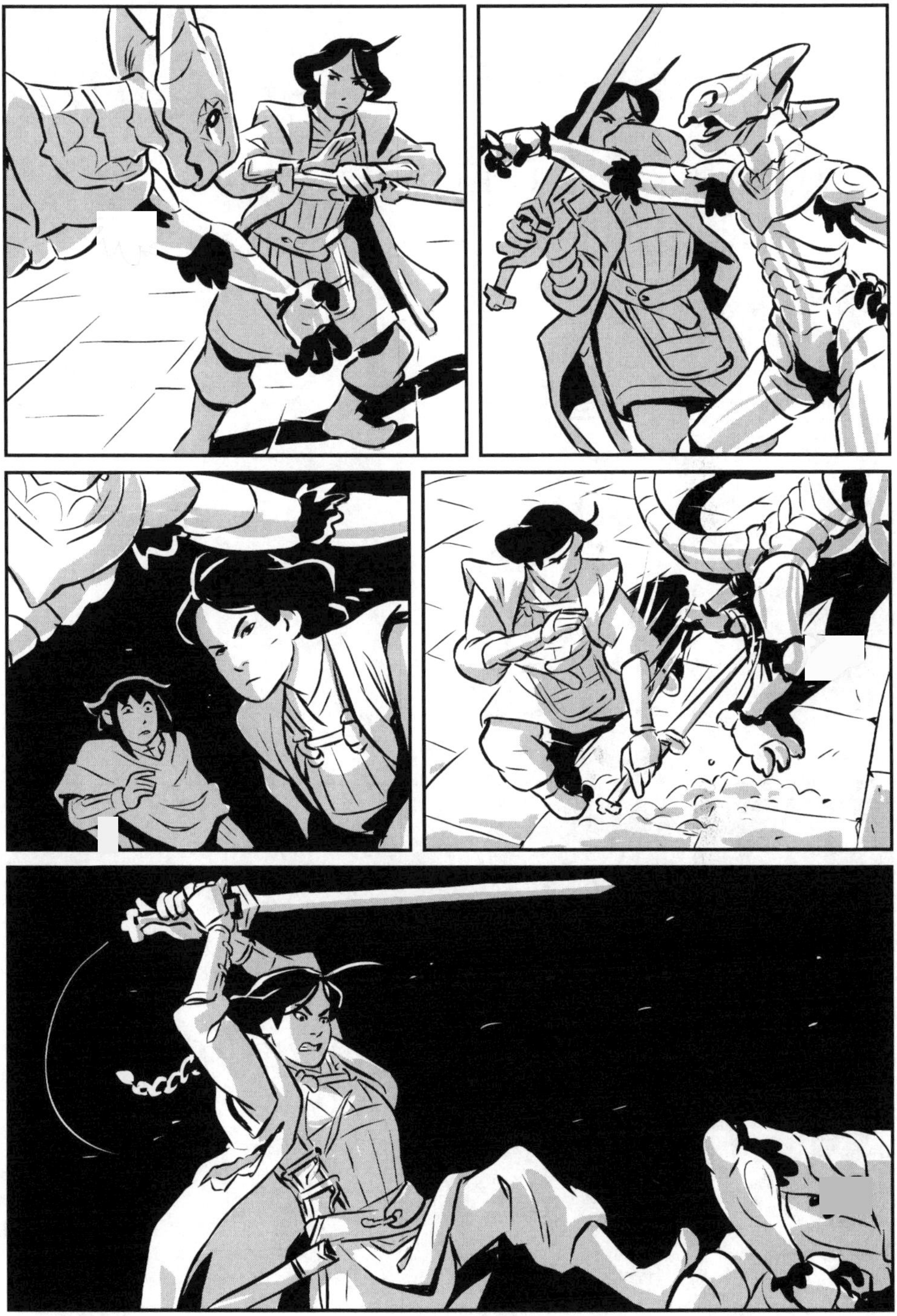

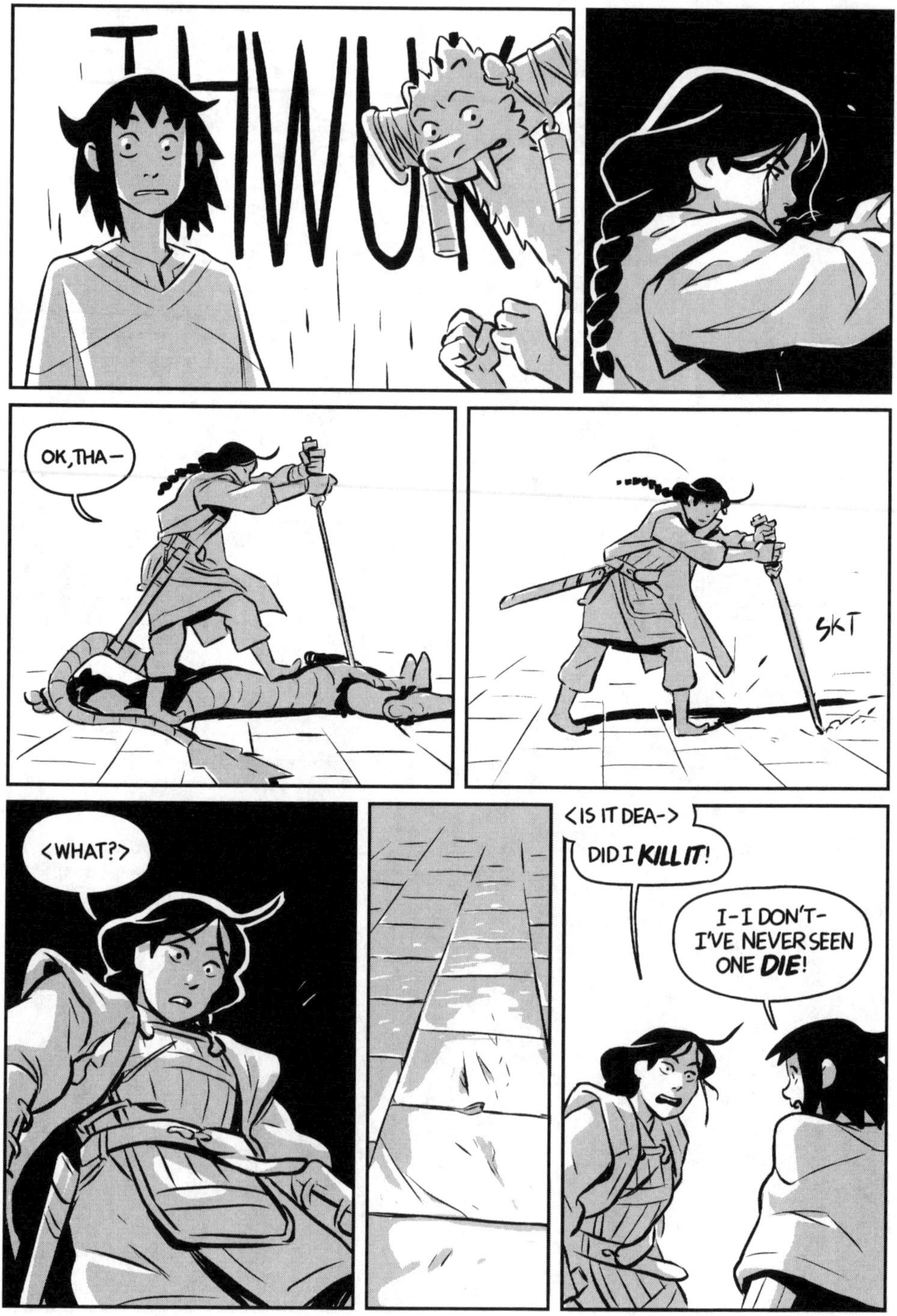
THWUK
OK, THA—
SKT
<WHAT?>
<IS IT DEA->
DID I **KILL IT**!
I-I DON'T-
I'VE NEVER SEEN ONE **DIE**!

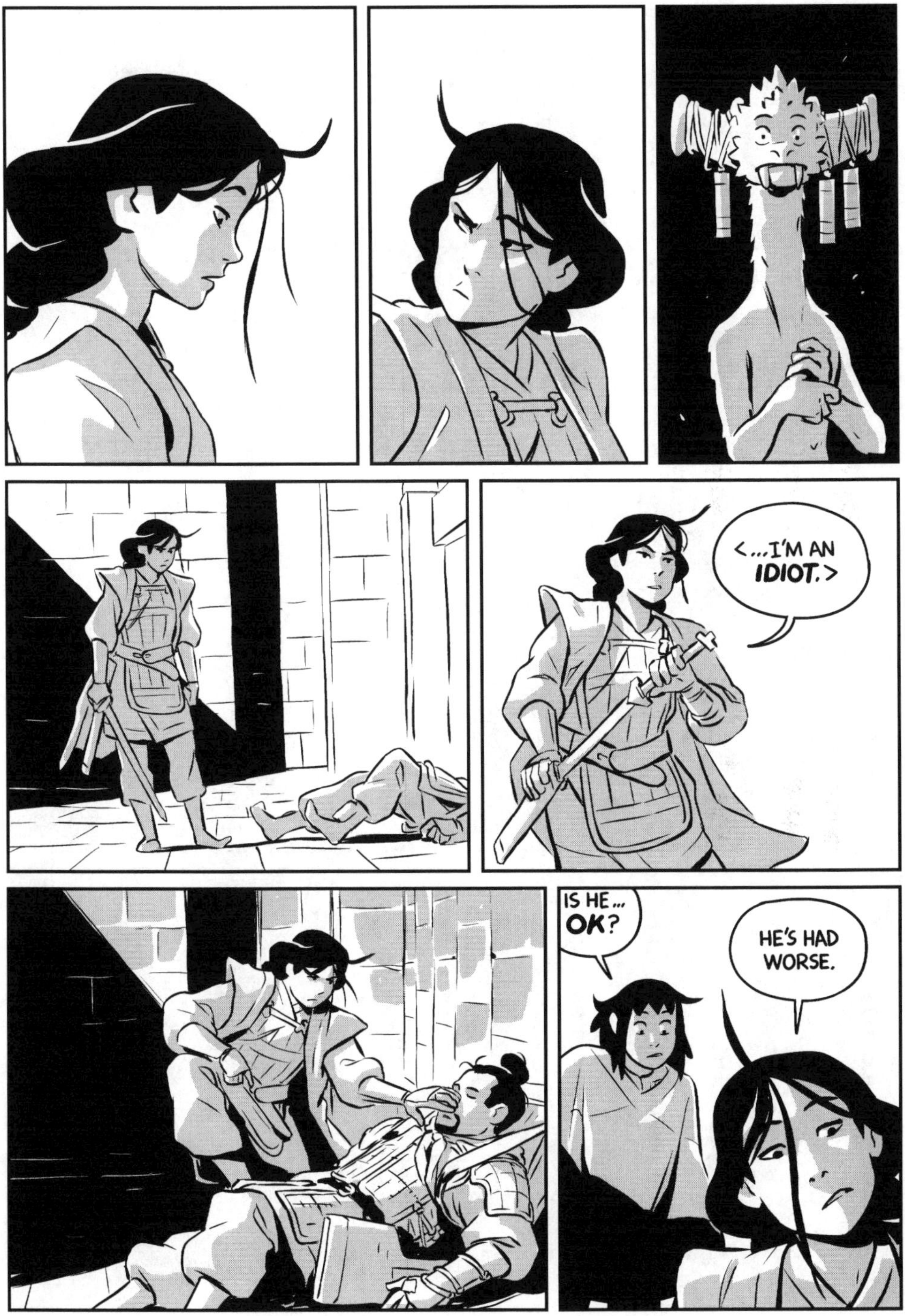

<...I'M AN IDIOT.>
IS HE... OK?
HE'S HAD WORSE.

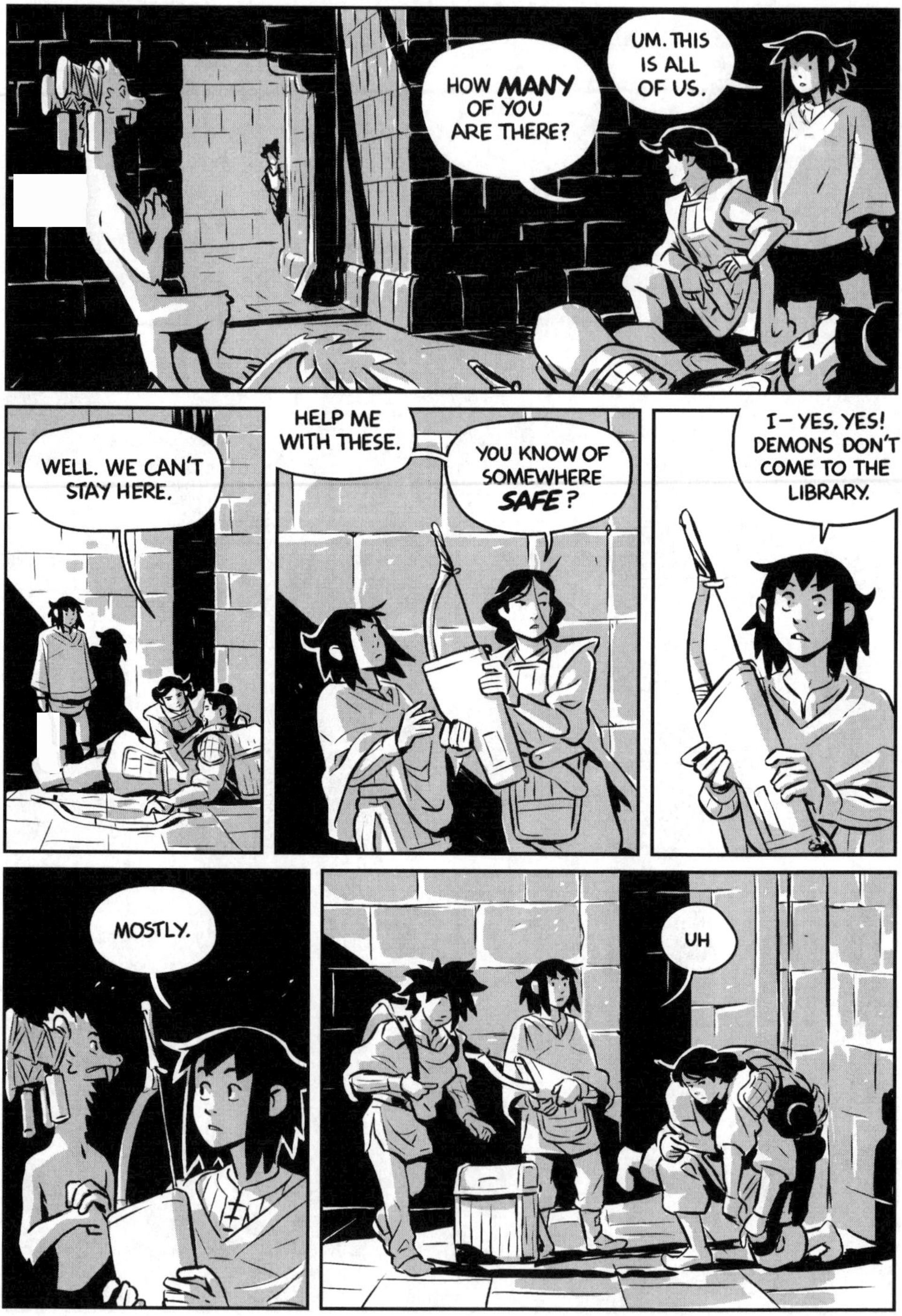
HOW MANY OF YOU ARE THERE?
UM. THIS IS ALL OF US.
WELL. WE CAN'T STAY HERE.
HELP ME WITH THESE.
YOU KNOW OF SOMEWHERE SAFE?
I— YES. YES! DEMONS DON'T COME TO THE LIBRARY.
MOSTLY.
UH

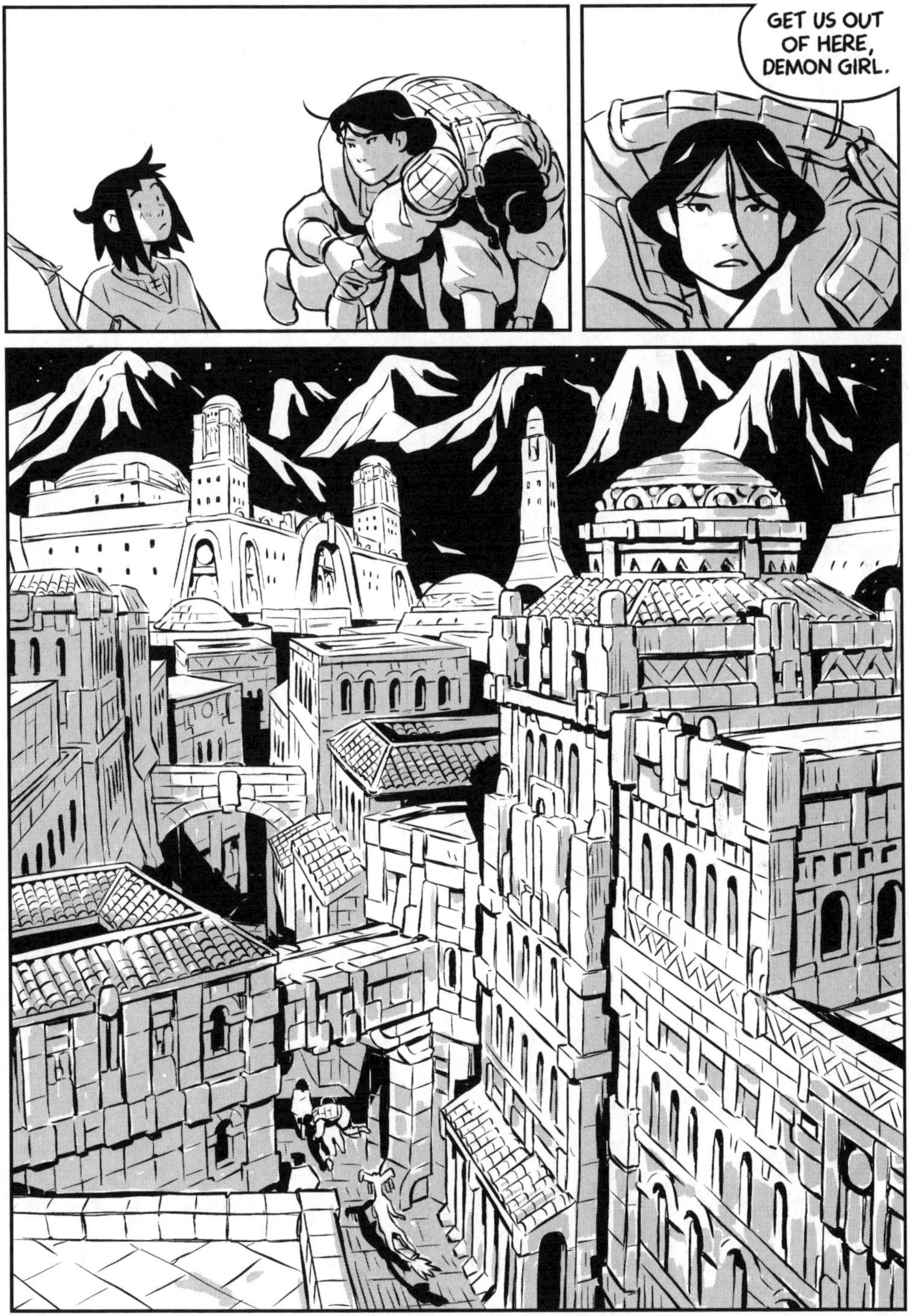
GET US OUT OF HERE, DEMON GIRL.

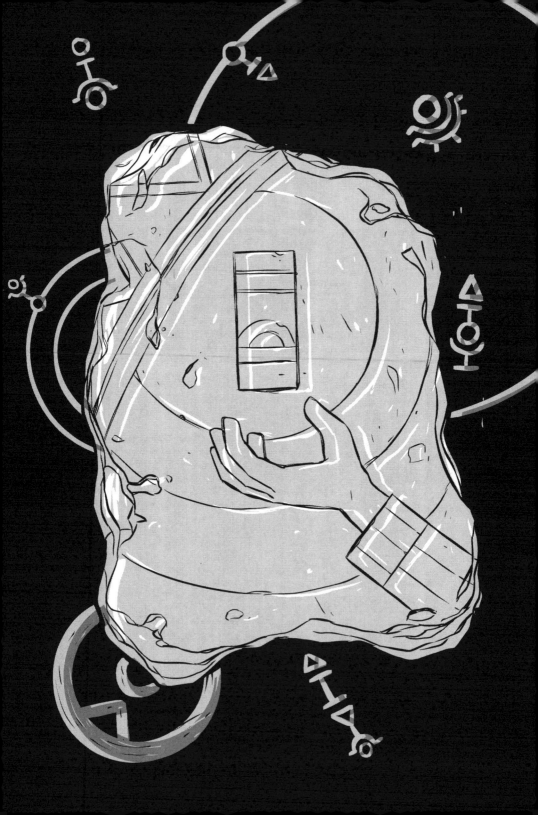

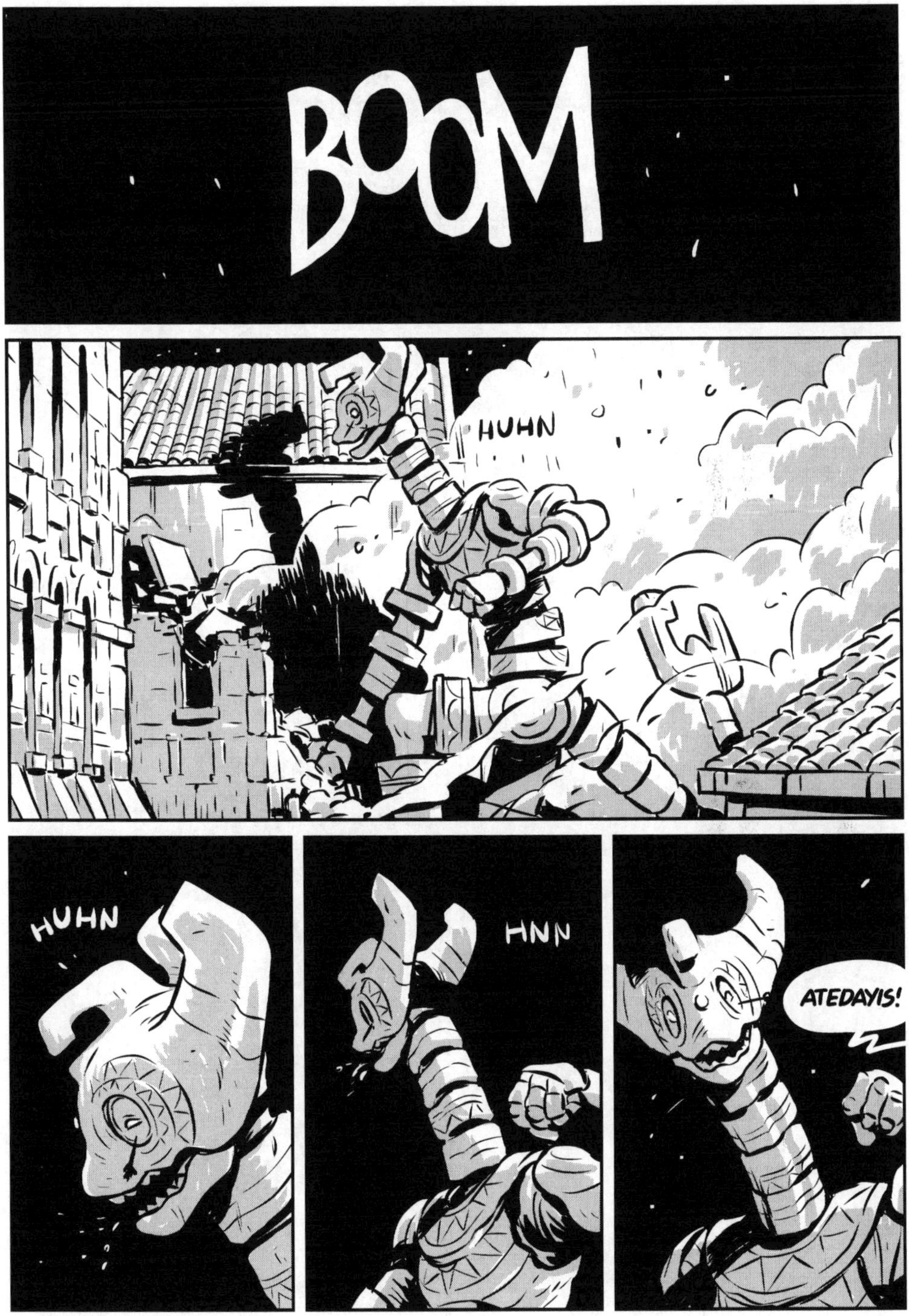
BOOM
HUHN
HUHN
HNN
ATEDAYIS!

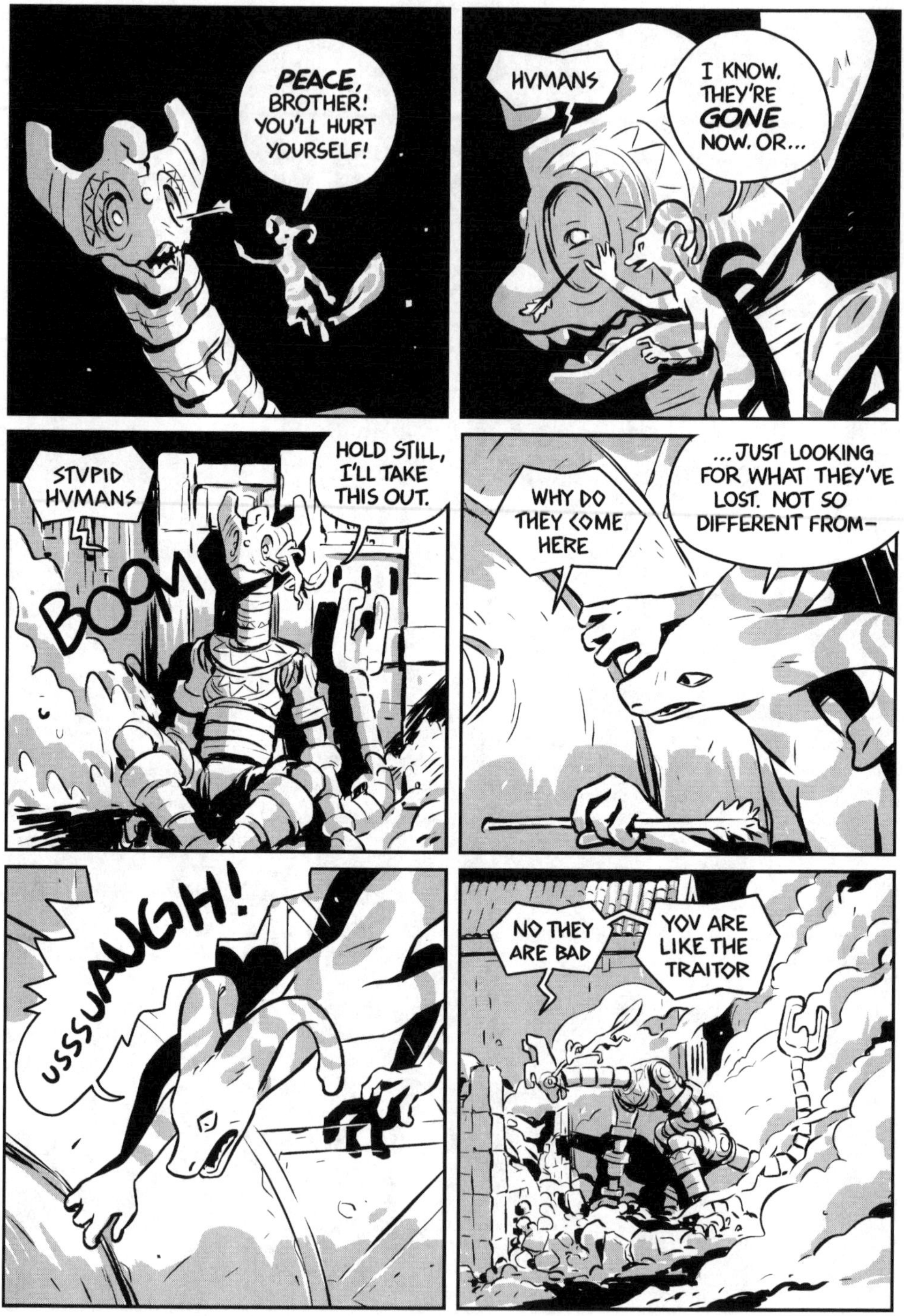
PEACE, BROTHER! YOU'LL HURT YOURSELF!
HVMANS
I KNOW. THEY'RE GONE NOW. OR...
STVPID HVMANS
HOLD STILL, I'LL TAKE THIS OUT.
BOOM
WHY DO THEY COME HERE
...JUST LOOKING FOR WHAT THEY'VE LOST. NOT SO DIFFERENT FROM-
USSSUAUGH!
NO THEY ARE BAD
YOV ARE LIKE THE TRAITOR

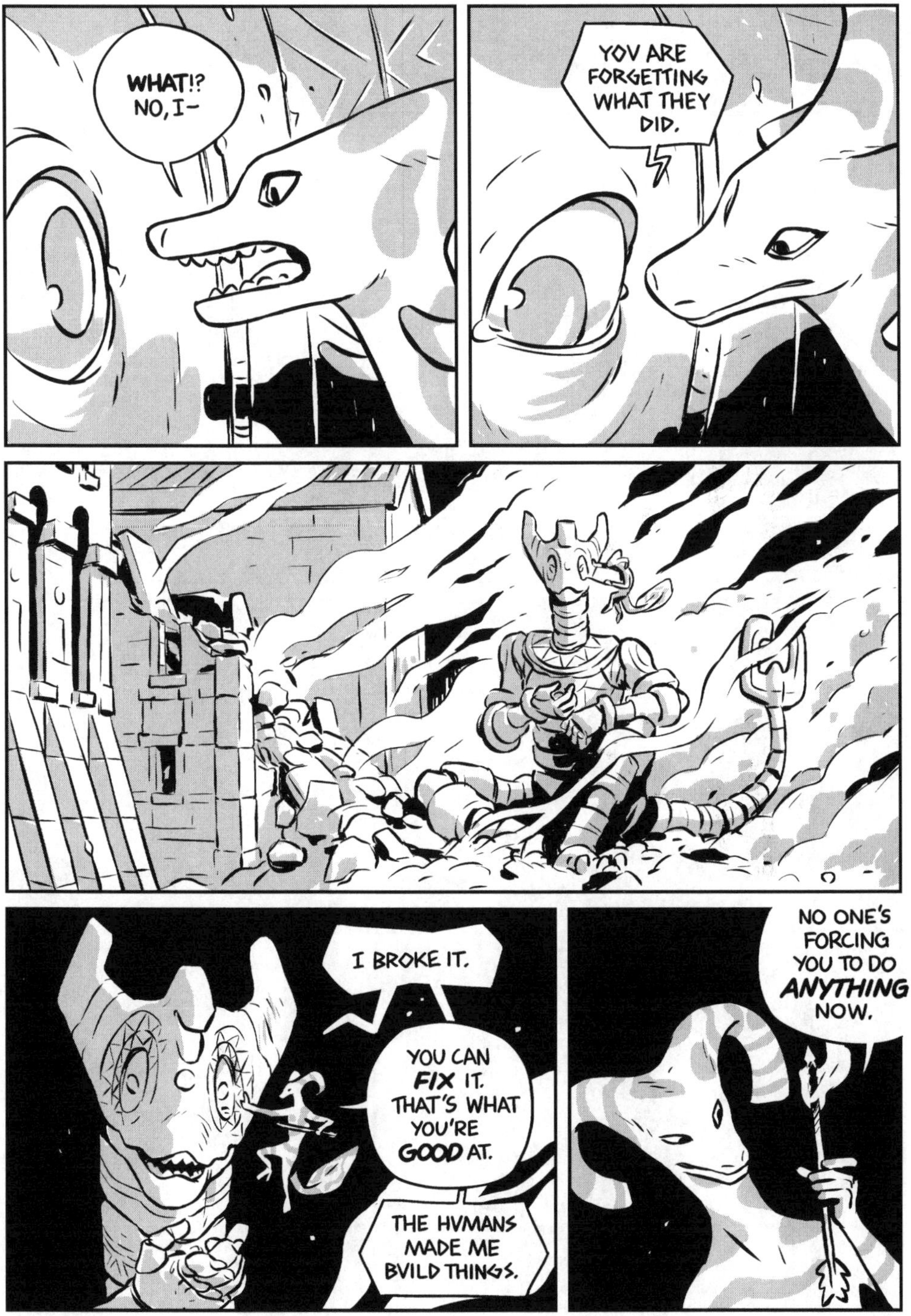
WHAT!? NO, I–
YOV ARE FORGETTING WHAT THEY DID.
I BROKE IT.
YOU CAN ***FIX*** IT. THAT'S WHAT YOU'RE ***GOOD*** AT.
THE HVMANS MADE ME BVILD THINGS.
NO ONE'S FORCING YOU TO DO ***ANYTHING*** NOW.

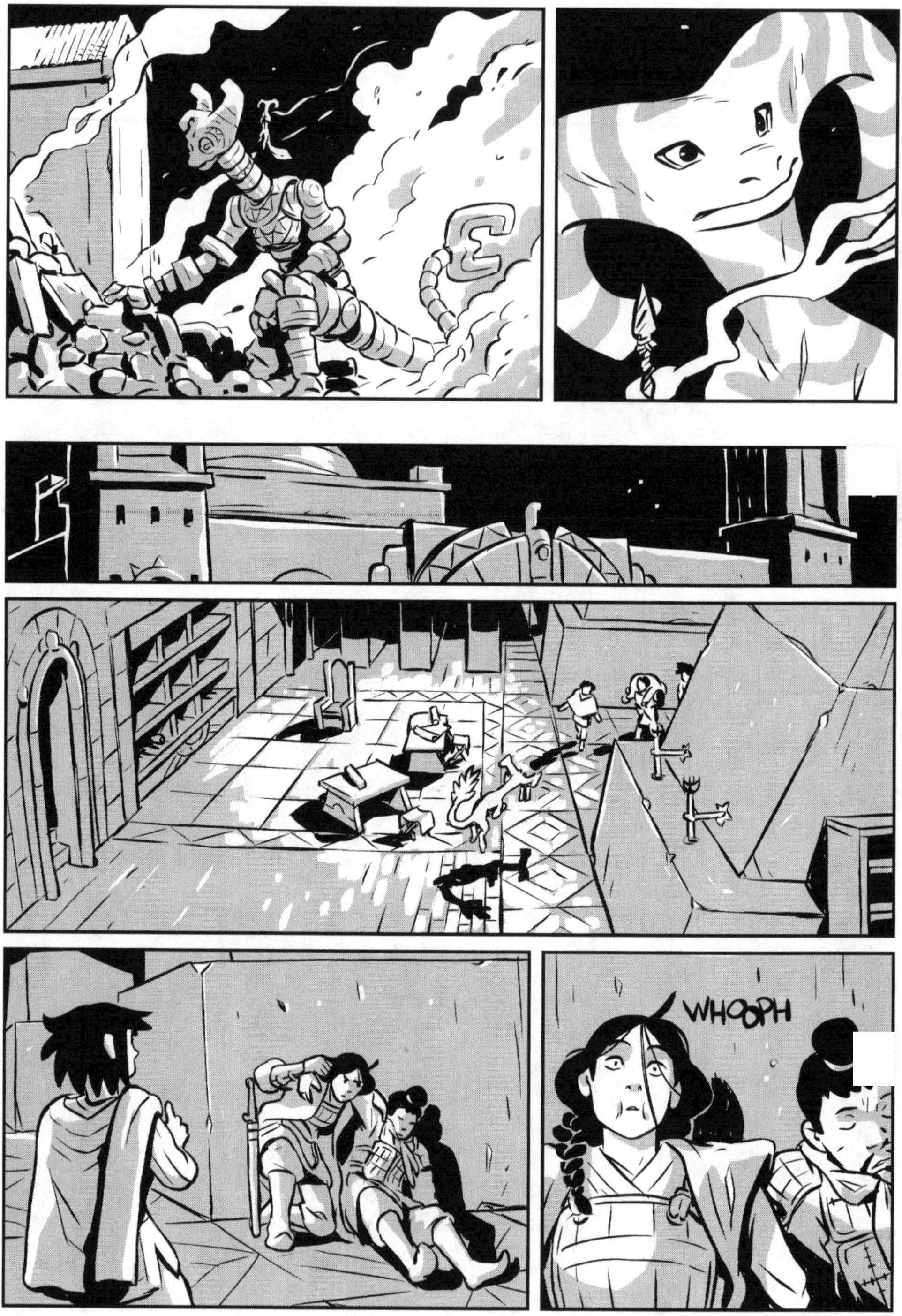
WHOOPH

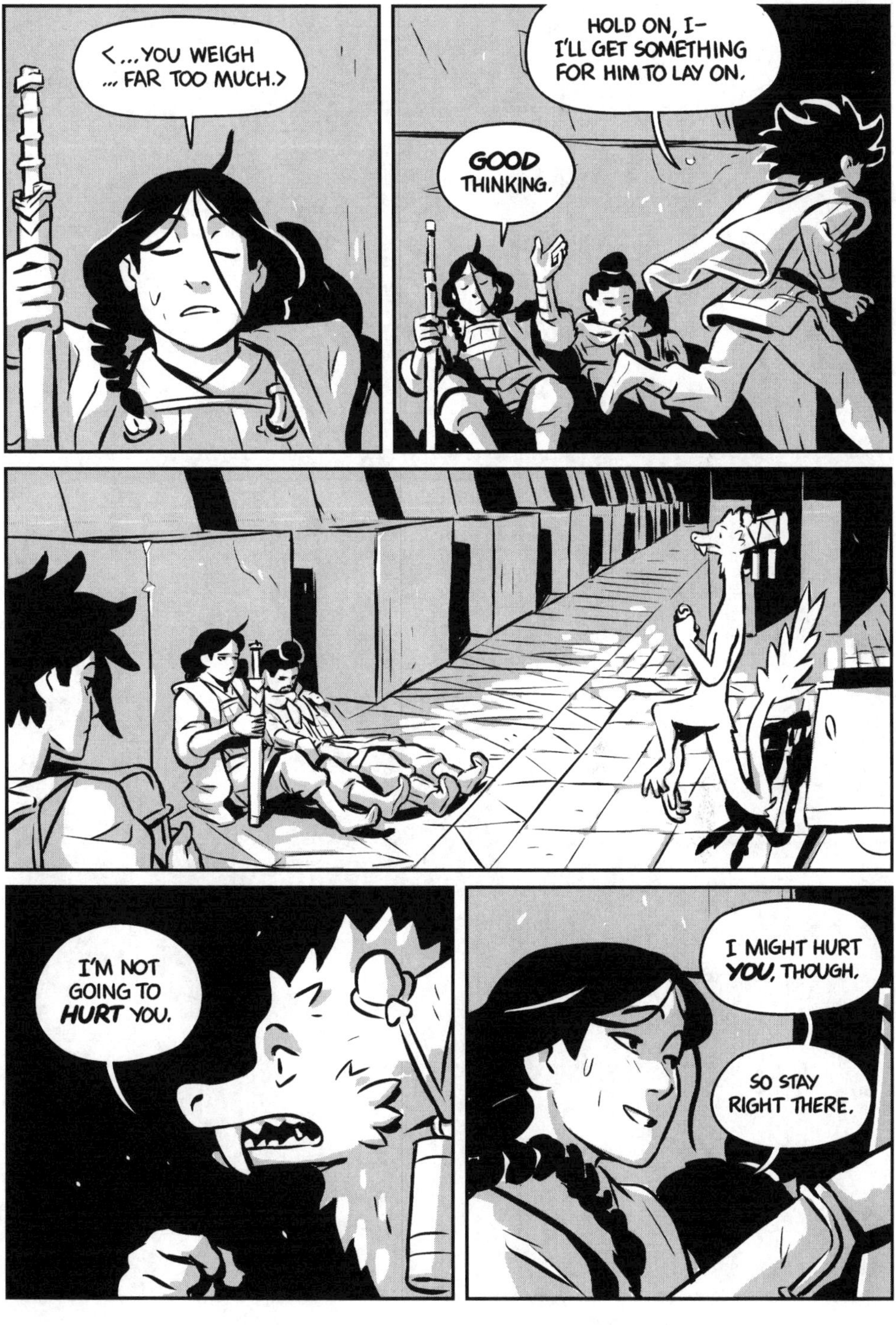
<...YOU WEIGH
... FAR TOO MUCH.>
HOLD ON, I–
I'LL GET SOMETHING FOR HIM TO LAY ON.
GOOD THINKING.
I'M NOT GOING TO HURT YOU.
I MIGHT HURT YOU, THOUGH.
SO STAY RIGHT THERE.

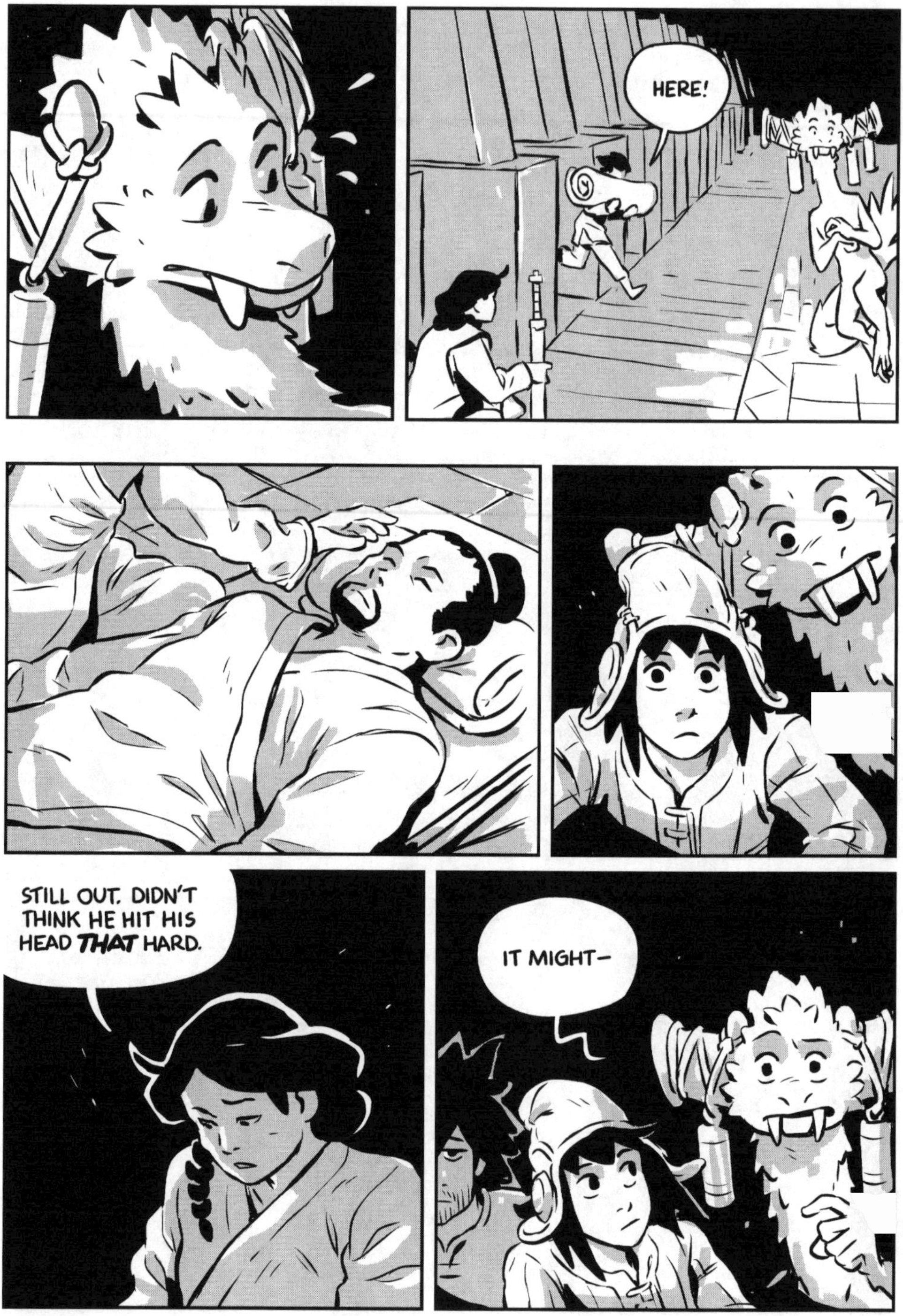
HERE!
STILL OUT. DIDN'T THINK HE HIT HIS HEAD THAT HARD.
IT MIGHT–

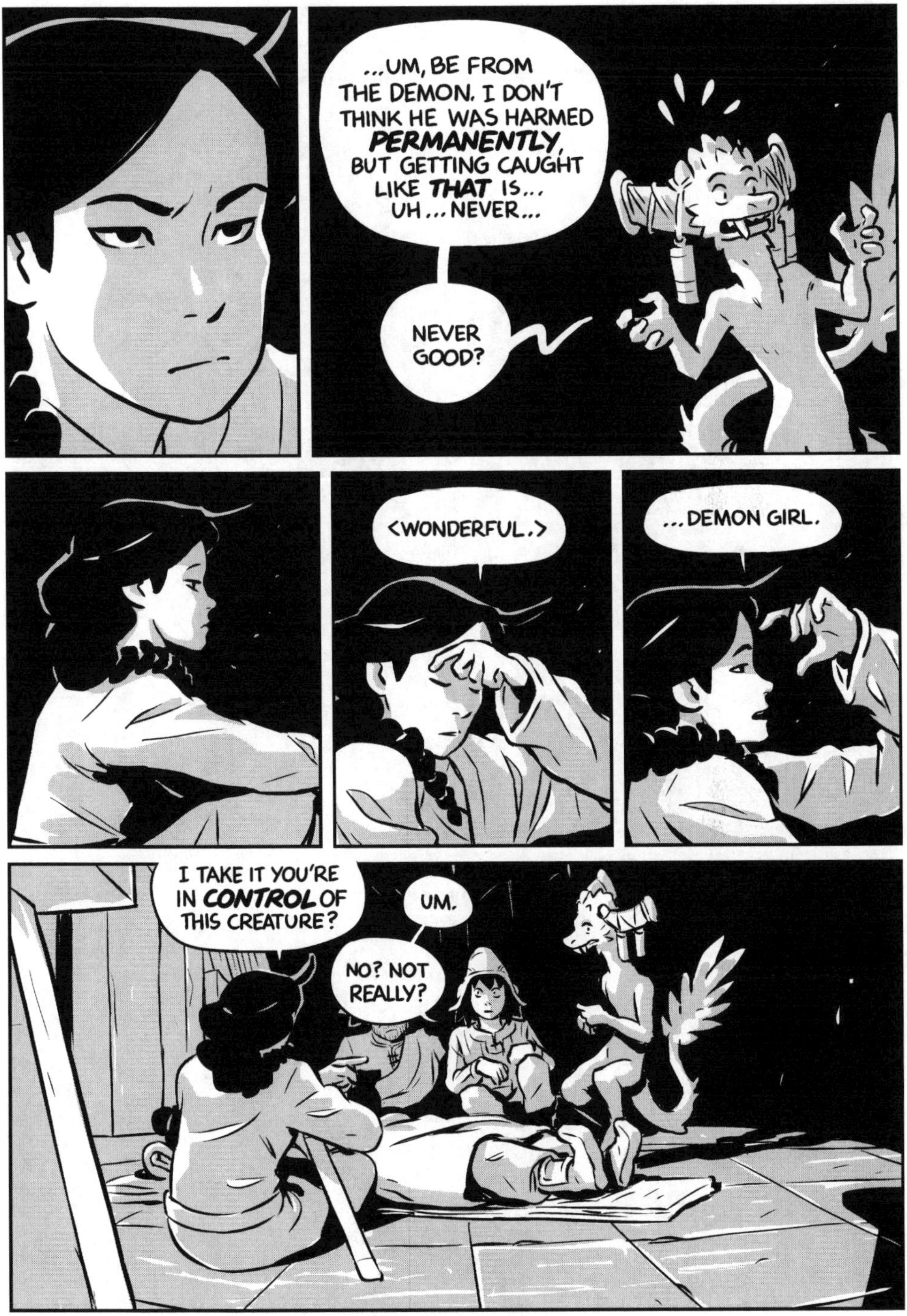
...UM, BE FROM THE DEMON. I DON'T THINK HE WAS HARMED **PERMANENTLY**, BUT GETTING CAUGHT LIKE **THAT** IS... UH... NEVER...
NEVER GOOD?
<WONDERFUL.>
...DEMON GIRL.
I TAKE IT YOU'RE IN **CONTROL** OF THIS CREATURE?
UM.
NO? NOT REALLY?

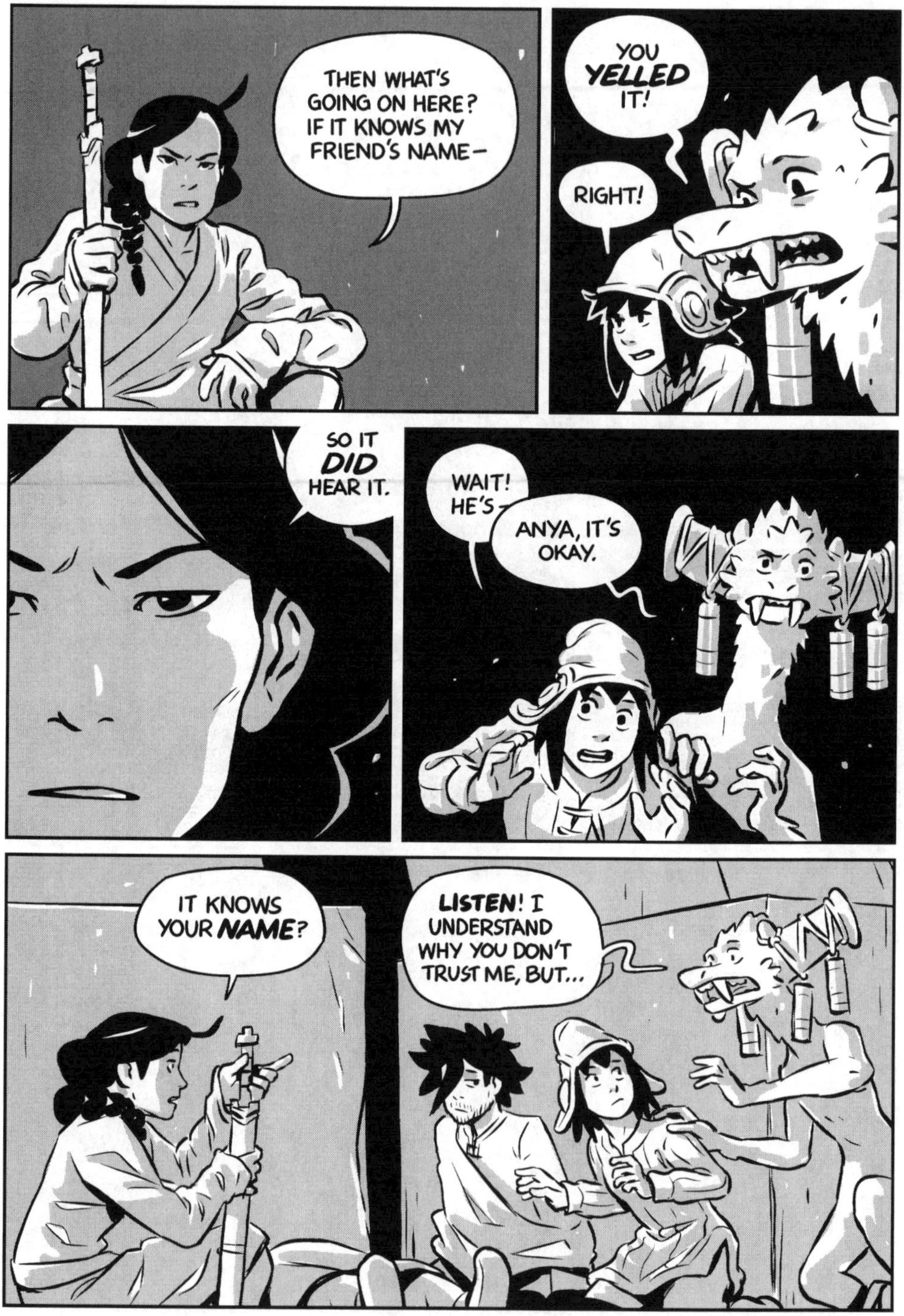
THEN WHAT'S GOING ON HERE? IF IT KNOWS MY FRIEND'S NAME–
YOU **YELLED** IT!
RIGHT!
SO IT **DID** HEAR IT.
WAIT! HE'S–
ANYA, IT'S OKAY.
IT KNOWS YOUR **NAME**?
LISTEN! I UNDERSTAND WHY YOU DON'T TRUST ME, BUT...

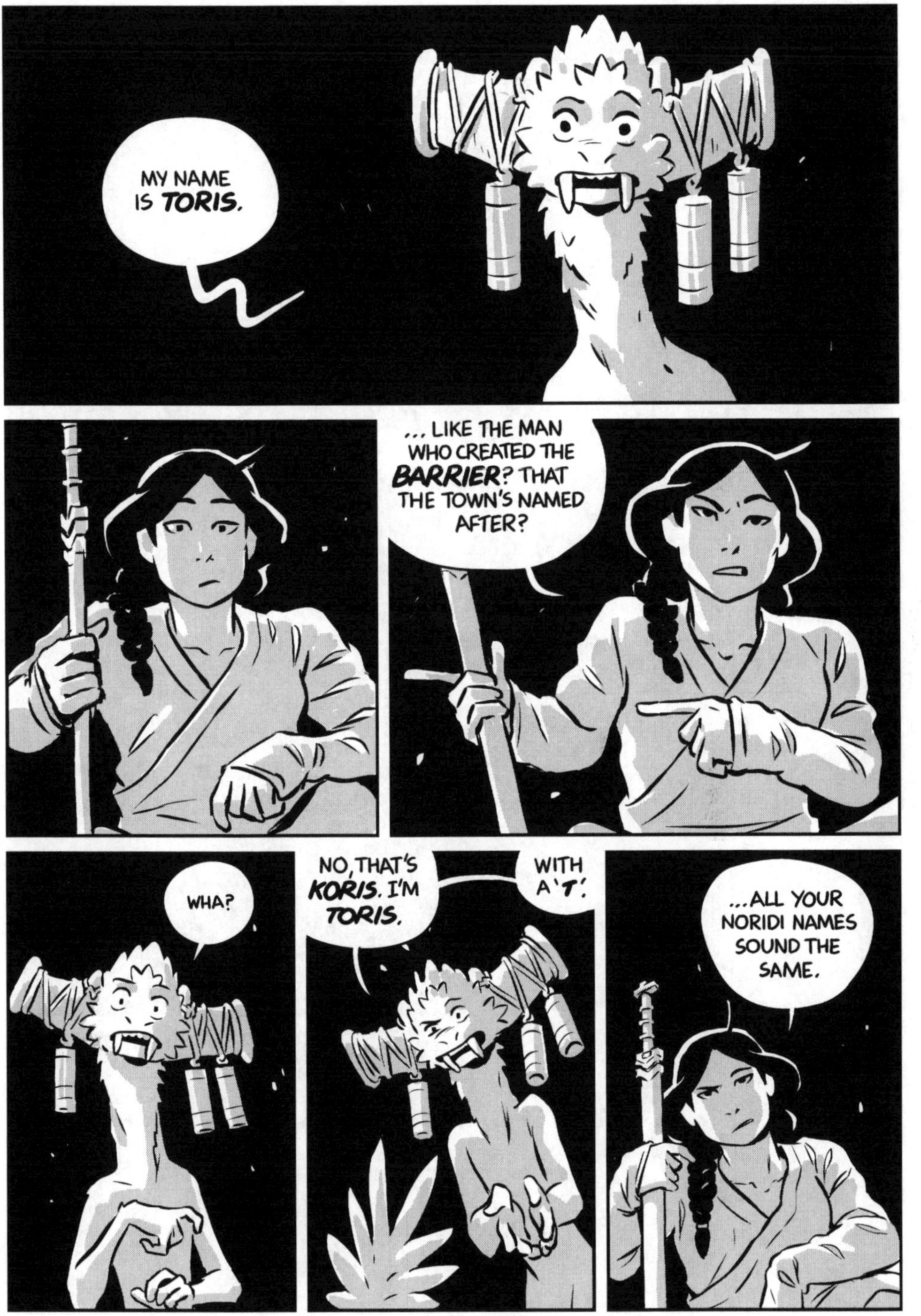
MY NAME IS **TORIS.**
... LIKE THE MAN WHO CREATED THE **BARRIER**? THAT THE TOWN'S NAMED AFTER?
WHA?
NO, THAT'S **KORIS**. I'M **TORIS.**
WITH A '**T**'.
...ALL YOUR NORIDI NAMES SOUND THE SAME.

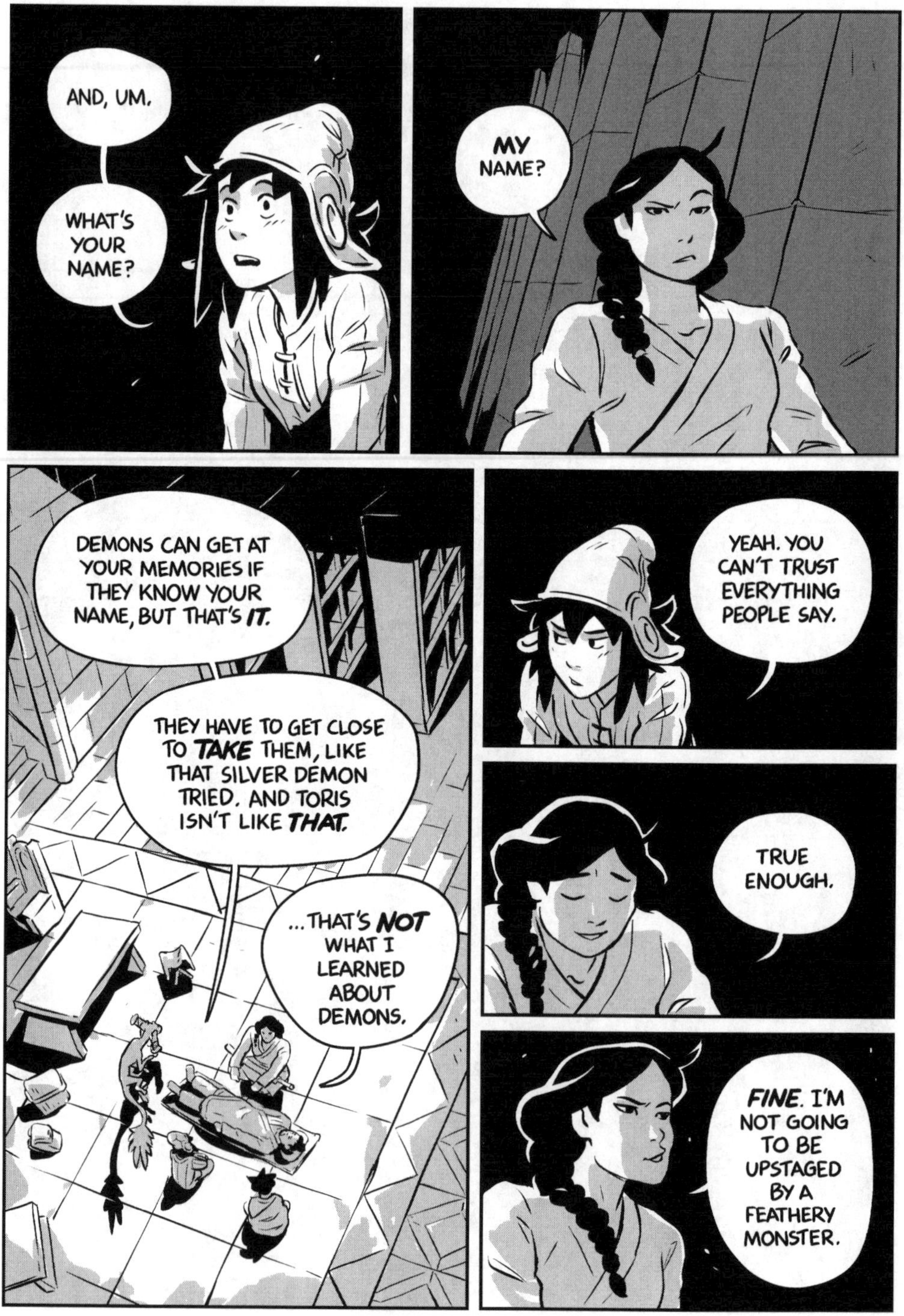
AND, UM.
WHAT'S YOUR NAME?
MY NAME?
DEMONS CAN GET AT YOUR MEMORIES IF THEY KNOW YOUR NAME, BUT THAT'S IT.
THEY HAVE TO GET CLOSE TO TAKE THEM, LIKE THAT SILVER DEMON TRIED. AND TORIS ISN'T LIKE THAT.
...THAT'S NOT WHAT I LEARNED ABOUT DEMONS.
YEAH. YOU CAN'T TRUST EVERYTHING PEOPLE SAY.
TRUE ENOUGH.
FINE. I'M NOT GOING TO BE UPSTAGED BY A FEATHERY MONSTER.

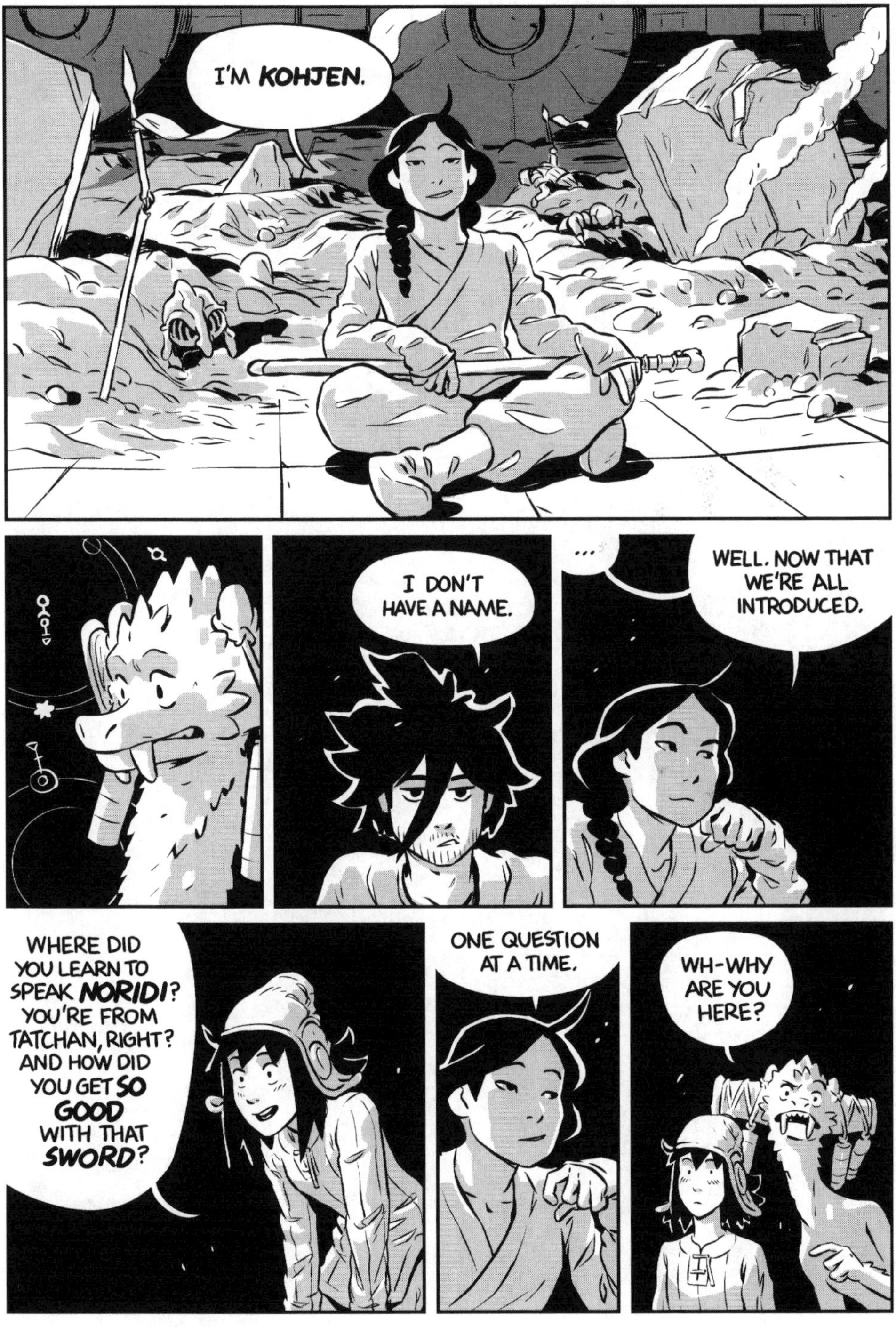
I'M **KOHJEN**.
I DON'T HAVE A NAME.
...
WELL. NOW THAT WE'RE ALL INTRODUCED.
WHERE DID YOU LEARN TO SPEAK **NORIDI**? YOU'RE FROM TATCHAN, RIGHT? AND HOW DID YOU GET **SO GOOD** WITH THAT **SWORD**?
ONE QUESTION AT A TIME.
WH-WHY ARE YOU HERE?

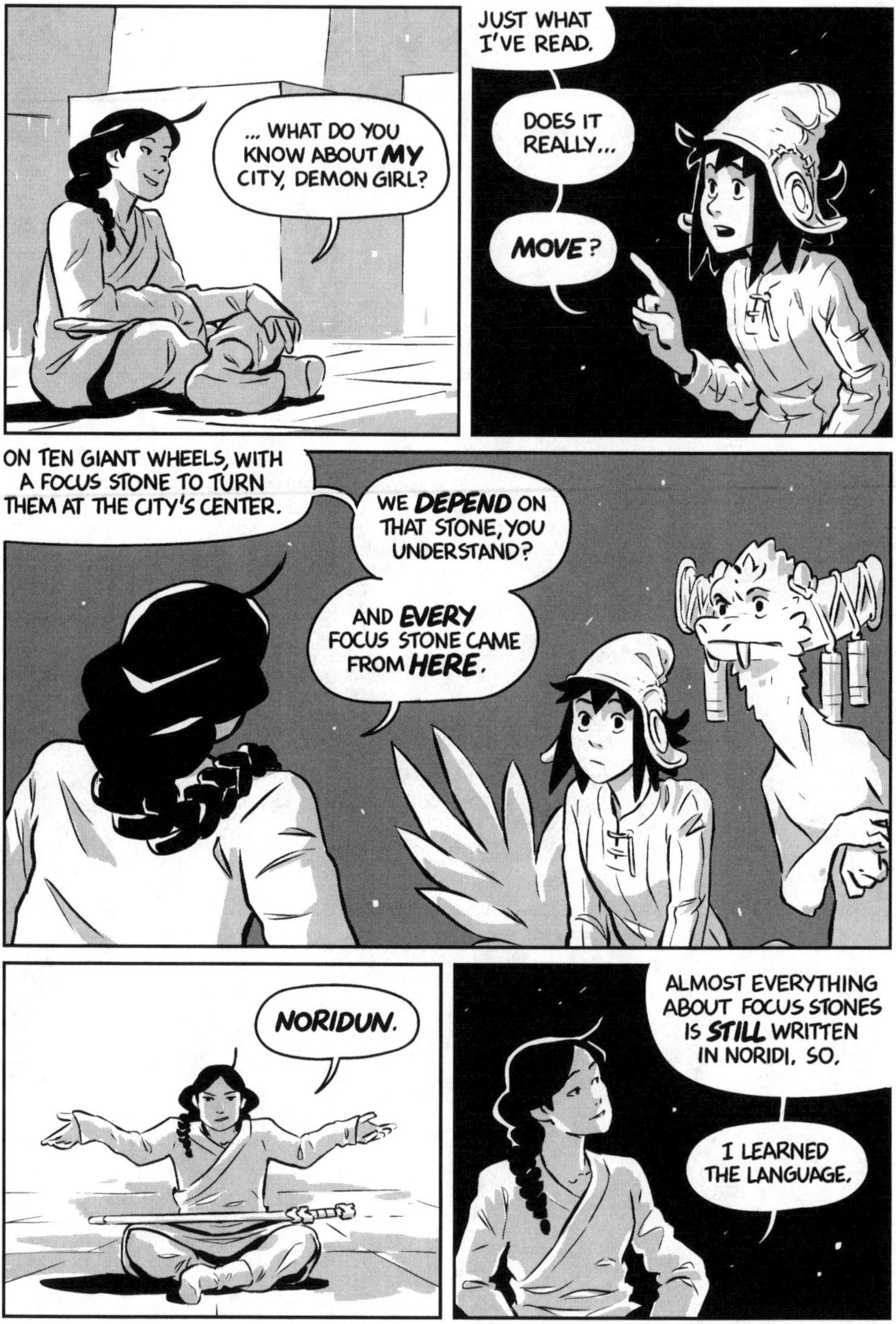
... WHAT DO YOU KNOW ABOUT MY CITY, DEMON GIRL?
JUST WHAT I'VE READ.
DOES IT REALLY...
MOVE?
ON TEN GIANT WHEELS, WITH A FOCUS STONE TO TURN THEM AT THE CITY'S CENTER.
WE DEPEND ON THAT STONE, YOU UNDERSTAND?
AND EVERY FOCUS STONE CAME FROM HERE.
NORIDUN.
ALMOST EVERYTHING ABOUT FOCUS STONES IS STILL WRITTEN IN NORIDI. SO,
I LEARNED THE LANGUAGE.

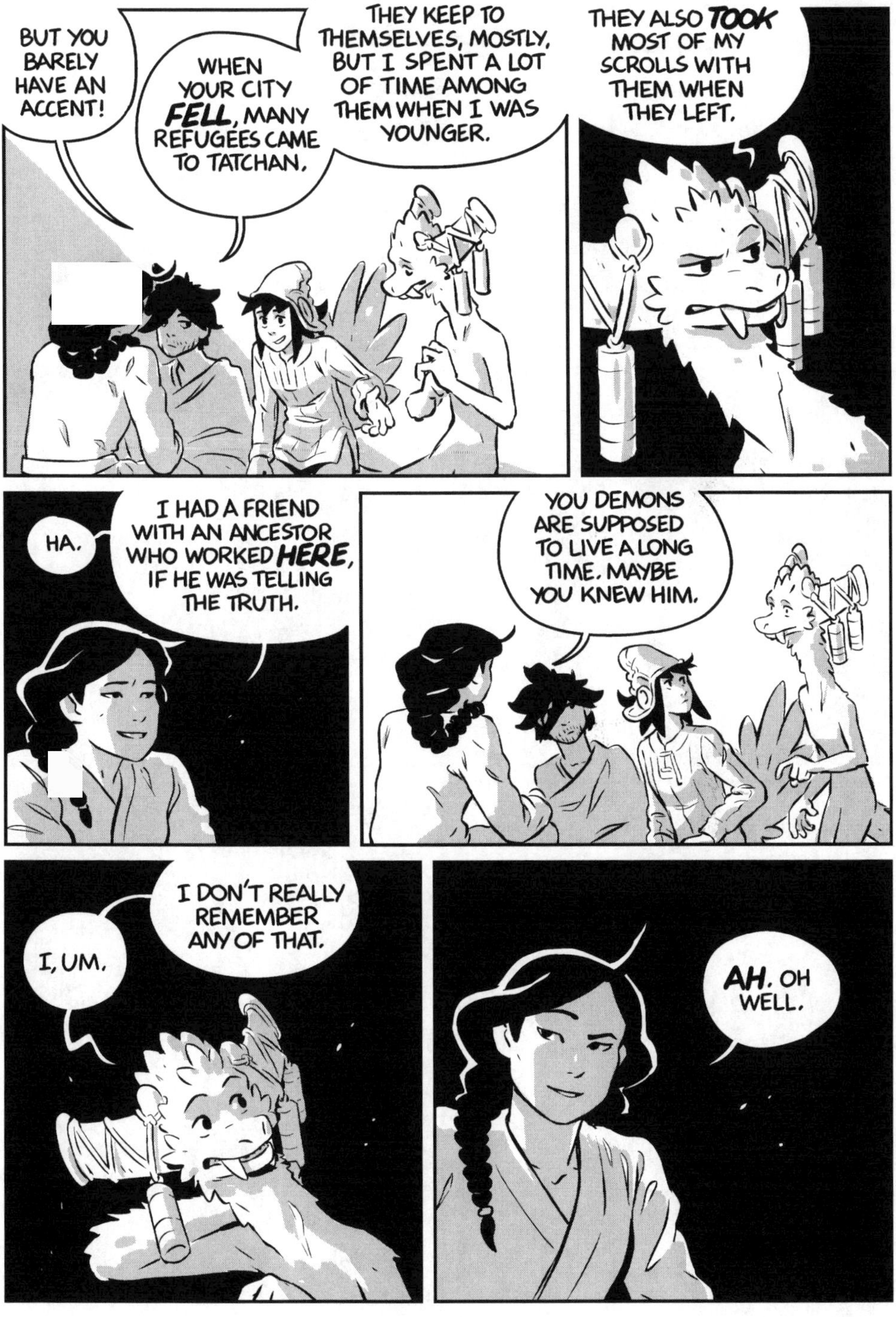
BUT YOU BARELY HAVE AN ACCENT!
WHEN YOUR CITY FELL, MANY REFUGEES CAME TO TATCHAN.
THEY KEEP TO THEMSELVES, MOSTLY, BUT I SPENT A LOT OF TIME AMONG THEM WHEN I WAS YOUNGER.
THEY ALSO TOOK MOST OF MY SCROLLS WITH THEM WHEN THEY LEFT.
HA.
I HAD A FRIEND WITH AN ANCESTOR WHO WORKED HERE, IF HE WAS TELLING THE TRUTH.
YOU DEMONS ARE SUPPOSED TO LIVE A LONG TIME. MAYBE YOU KNEW HIM.
I, UM.
I DON'T REALLY REMEMBER ANY OF THAT.
AH. OH WELL.

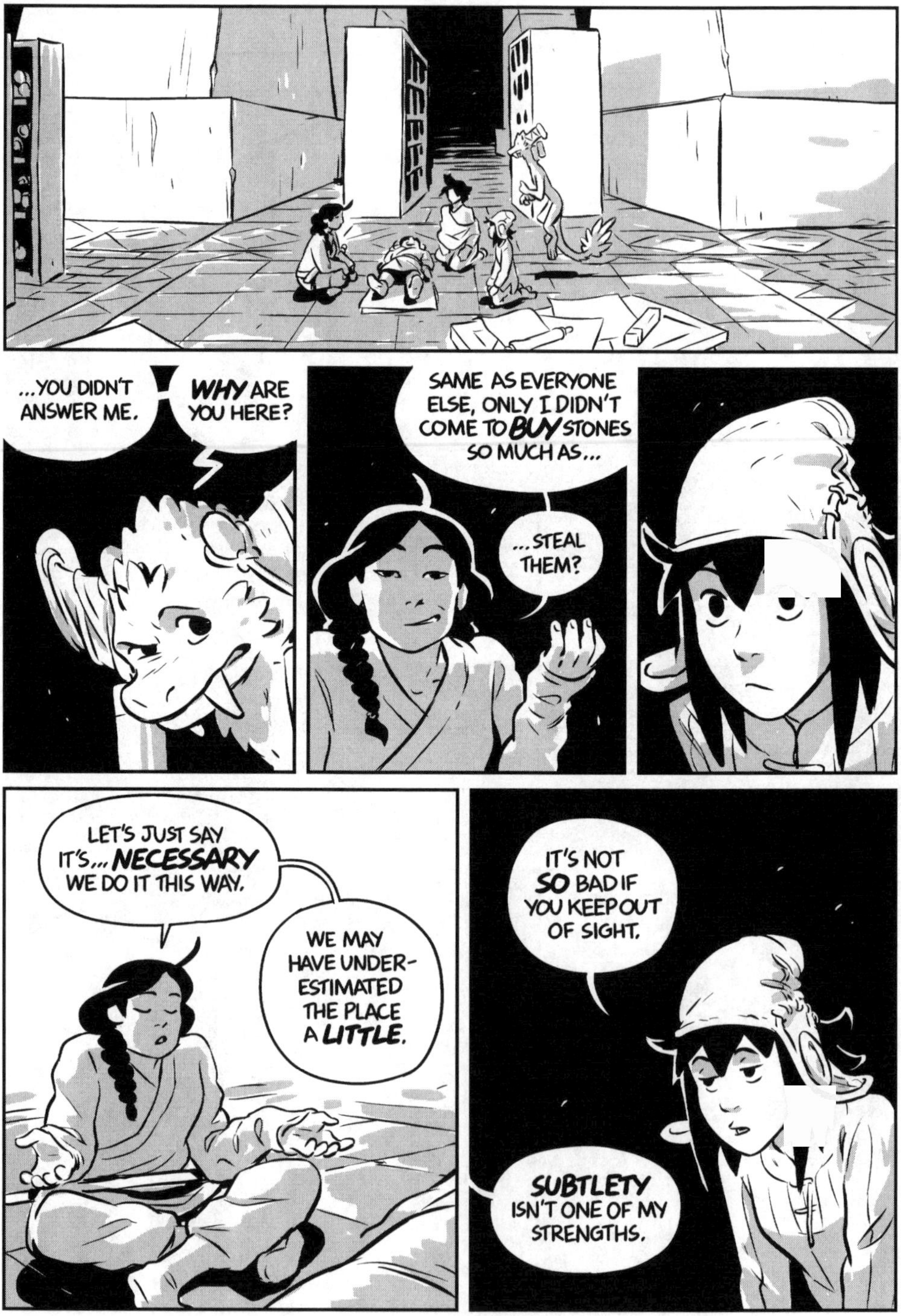
...YOU DIDN'T ANSWER ME.
WHY ARE YOU HERE?
SAME AS EVERYONE ELSE, ONLY I DIDN'T COME TO BUY STONES SO MUCH AS...
...STEAL THEM?
LET'S JUST SAY IT'S... NECESSARY WE DO IT THIS WAY.
WE MAY HAVE UNDER-ESTIMATED THE PLACE A LITTLE.
IT'S NOT SO BAD IF YOU KEEP OUT OF SIGHT.
SUBTLETY ISN'T ONE OF MY STRENGTHS.

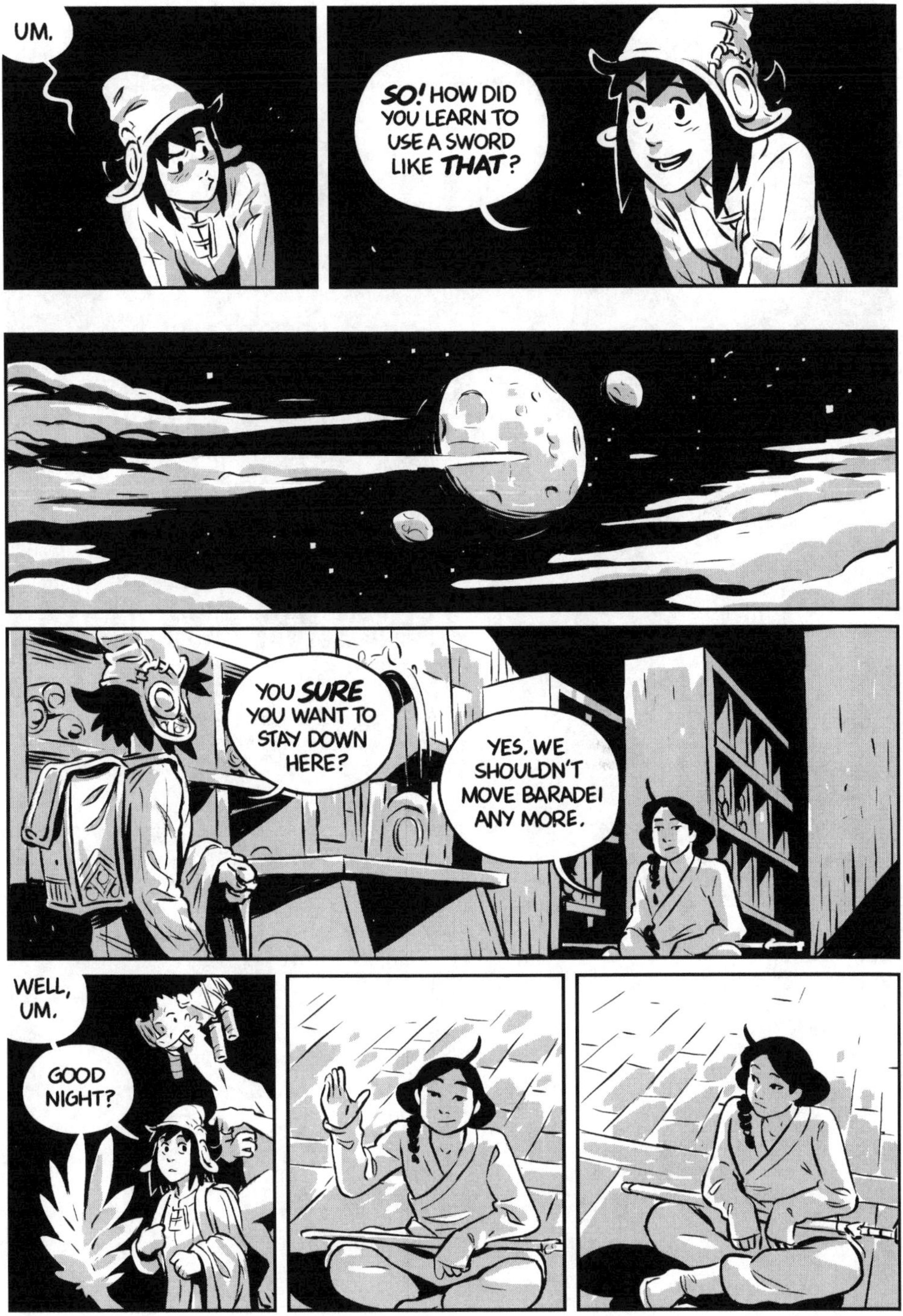
UM.
SO! HOW DID YOU LEARN TO USE A SWORD LIKE THAT?
YOU SURE YOU WANT TO STAY DOWN HERE?
YES. WE SHOULDN'T MOVE BARADEI ANY MORE.
WELL, UM.
GOOD NIGHT?

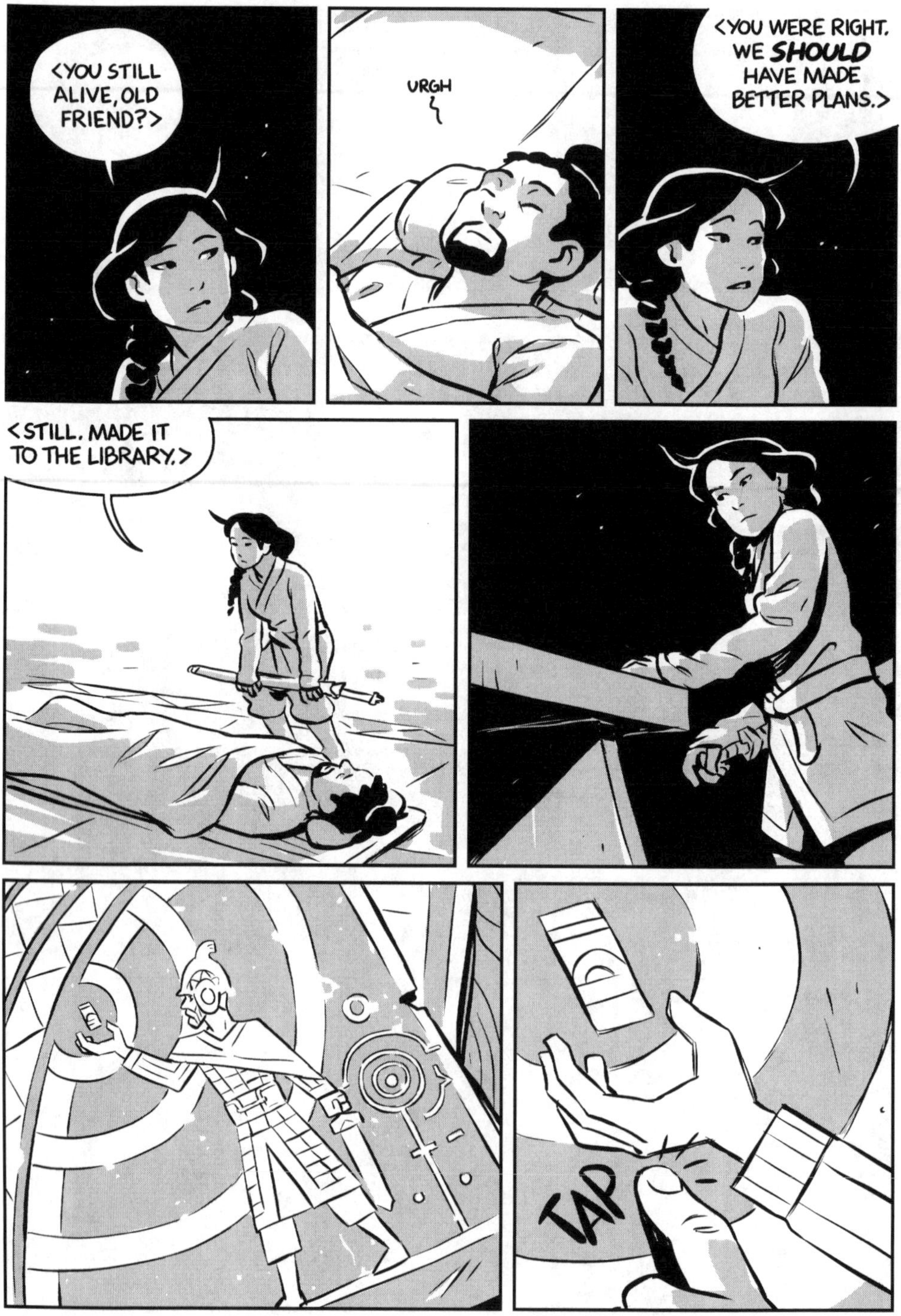

<YOU STILL ALIVE, OLD FRIEND?>
URGH
<YOU WERE RIGHT. WE SHOULD HAVE MADE BETTER PLANS.>
<STILL. MADE IT TO THE LIBRARY.>
TAP

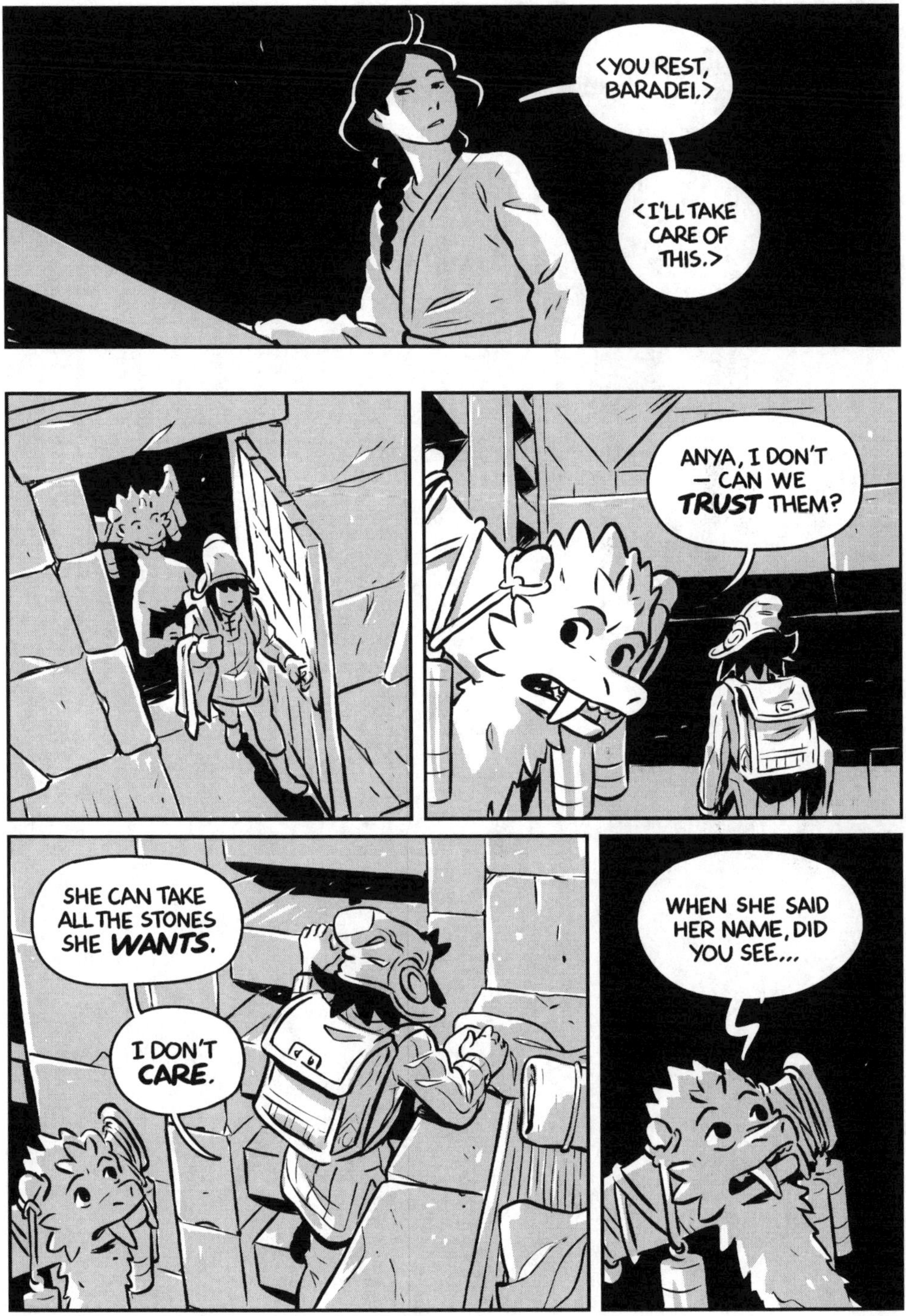

<YOU REST, BARADEI.>
<I'LL TAKE CARE OF THIS.>
ANYA, I DON'T — CAN WE TRUST THEM?
SHE CAN TAKE ALL THE STONES SHE WANTS.
I DON'T CARE.
WHEN SHE SAID HER NAME, DID YOU SEE...

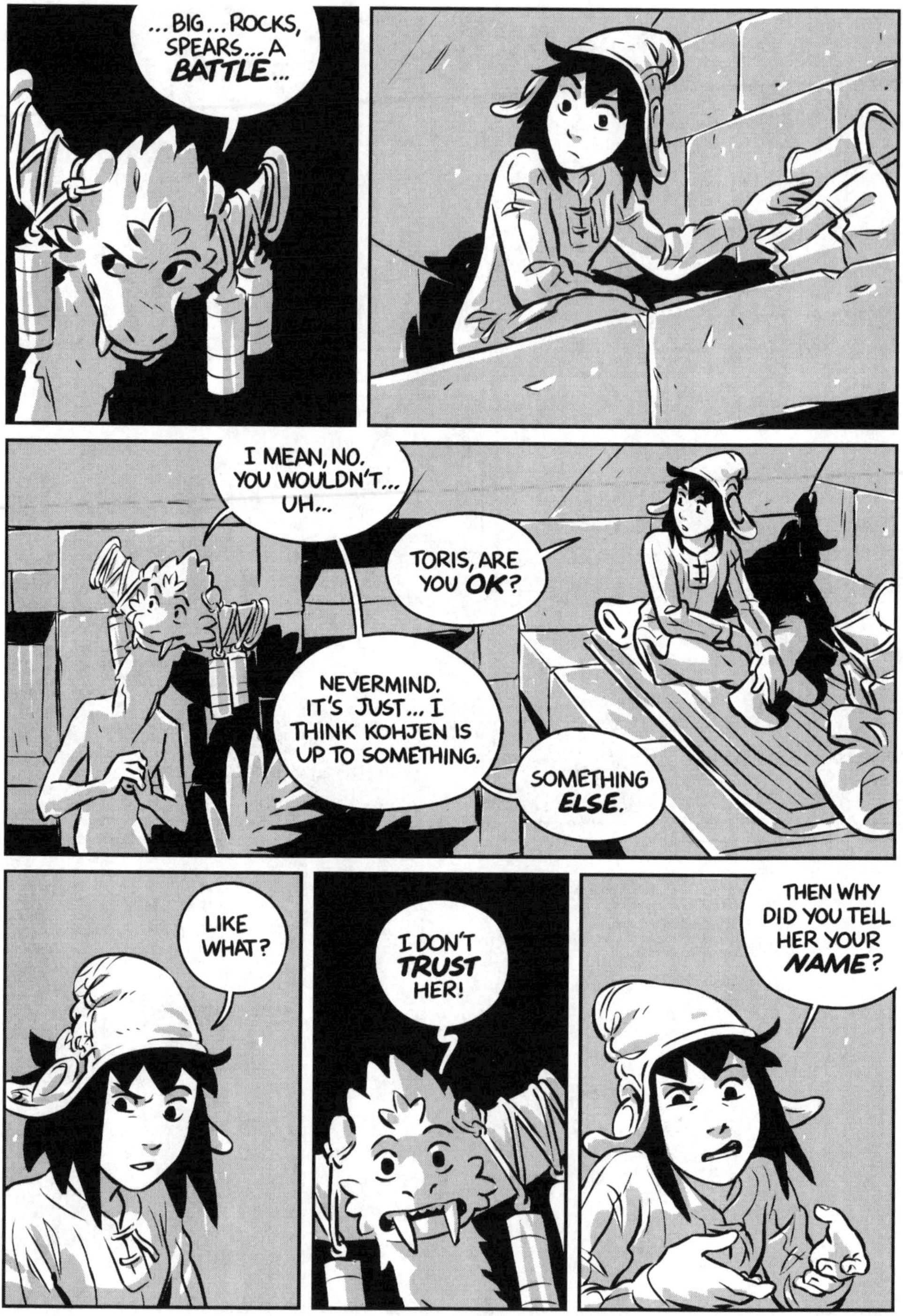
...BIG...ROCKS, SPEARS... A BATTLE...
I MEAN, NO. YOU WOULDN'T... UH...
TORIS, ARE YOU OK?
NEVERMIND. IT'S JUST... I THINK KOHJEN IS UP TO SOMETHING.
SOMETHING ELSE.
LIKE WHAT?
I DON'T TRUST HER!
THEN WHY DID YOU TELL HER YOUR NAME?

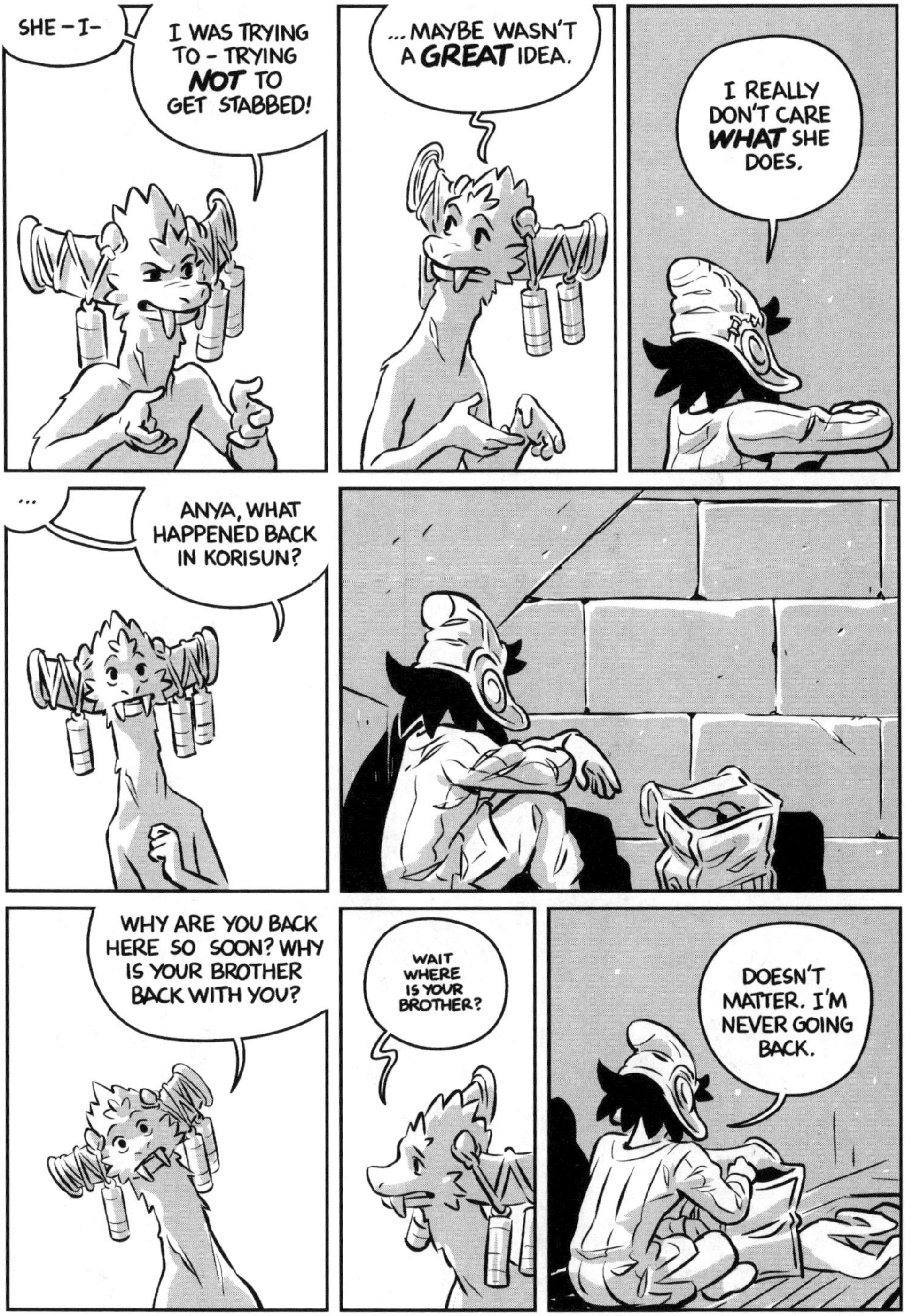
SHE – I–
I WAS TRYING TO – TRYING NOT TO GET STABBED!
...MAYBE WASN'T A GREAT IDEA.
I REALLY DON'T CARE WHAT SHE DOES.
...
ANYA, WHAT HAPPENED BACK IN KORISUN?
WHY ARE YOU BACK HERE SO SOON? WHY IS YOUR BROTHER BACK WITH YOU?
WAIT WHERE IS YOUR BROTHER?
DOESN'T MATTER. I'M NEVER GOING BACK.

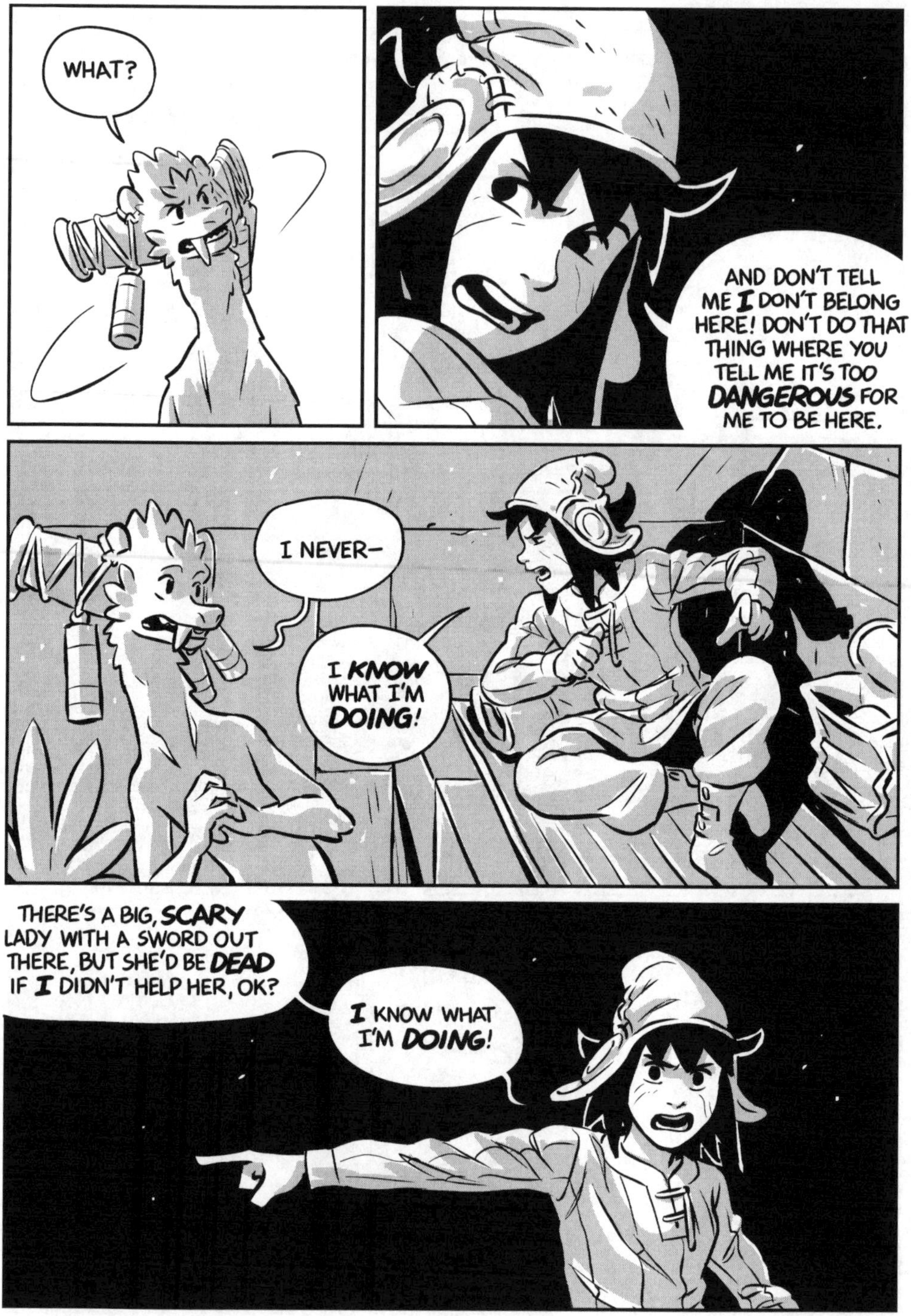
WHAT?
AND DON'T TELL ME I DON'T BELONG HERE! DON'T DO THAT THING WHERE YOU TELL ME IT'S TOO DANGEROUS FOR ME TO BE HERE.
I NEVER–
I KNOW WHAT I'M DOING!
THERE'S A BIG, SCARY LADY WITH A SWORD OUT THERE, BUT SHE'D BE DEAD IF I DIDN'T HELP HER, OK?
I KNOW WHAT I'M DOING!

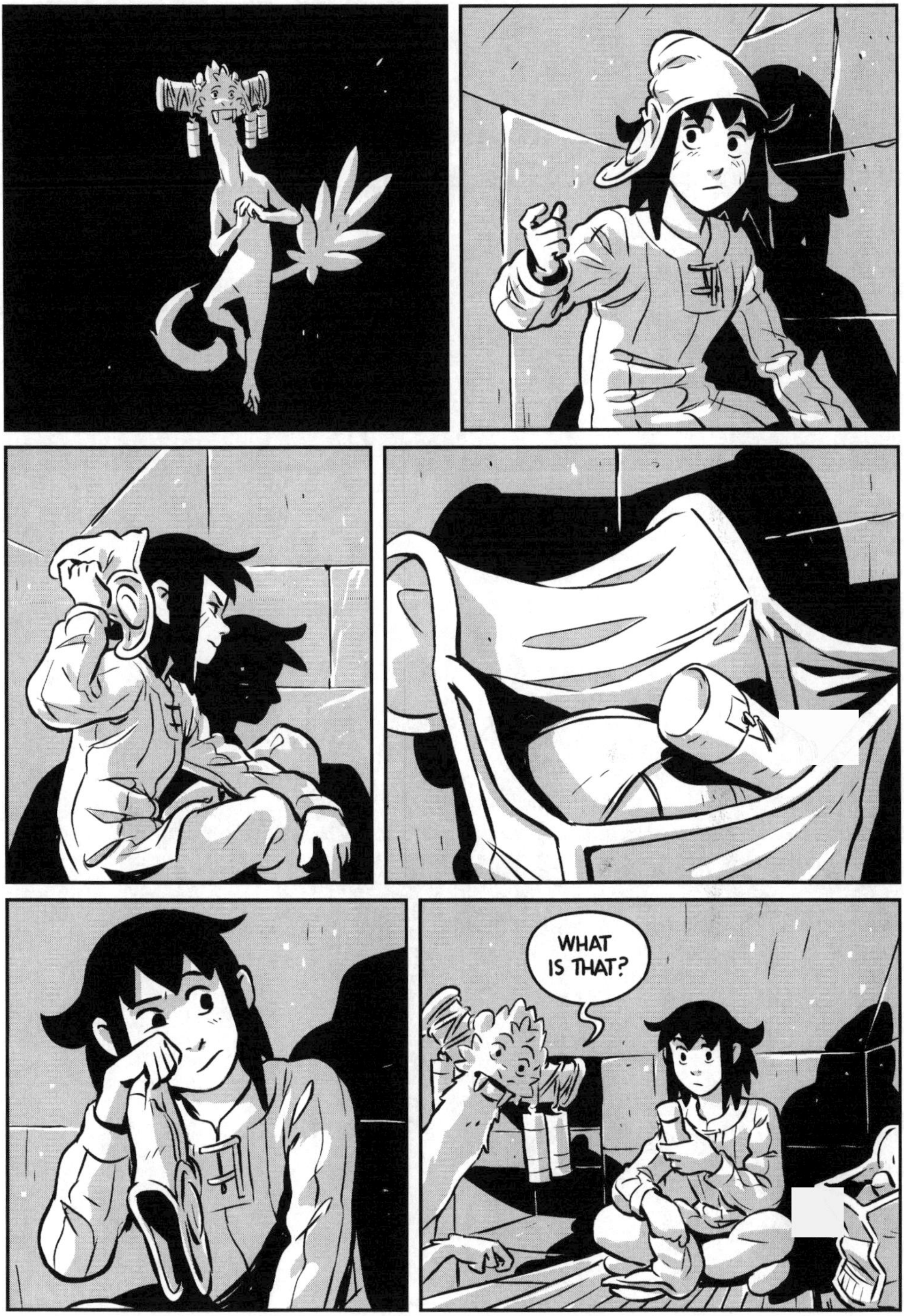
WHAT IS THAT?

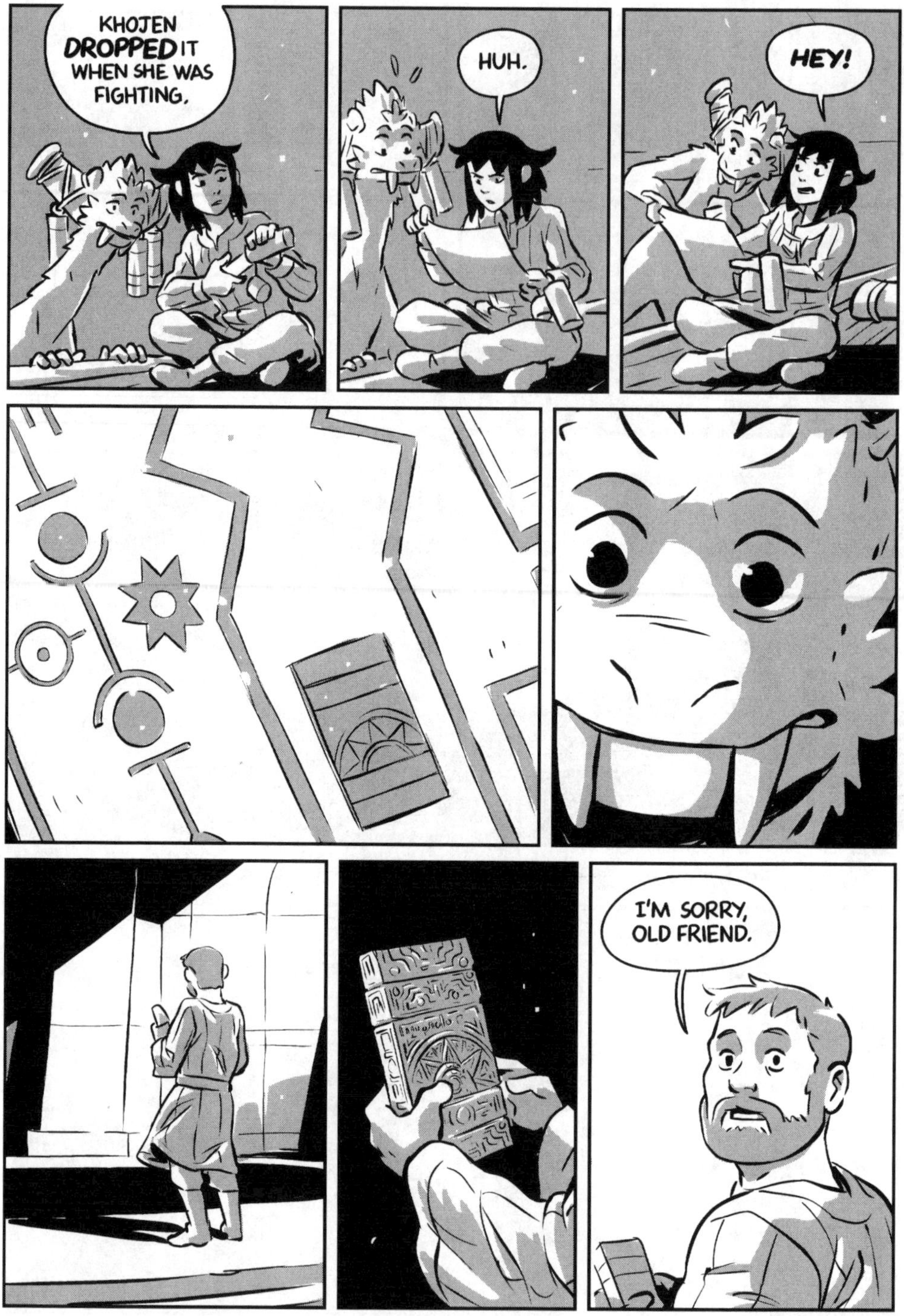
KHOJEN DROPPED IT WHEN SHE WAS FIGHTING.
HUH.
HEY!
I'M SORRY, OLD FRIEND.

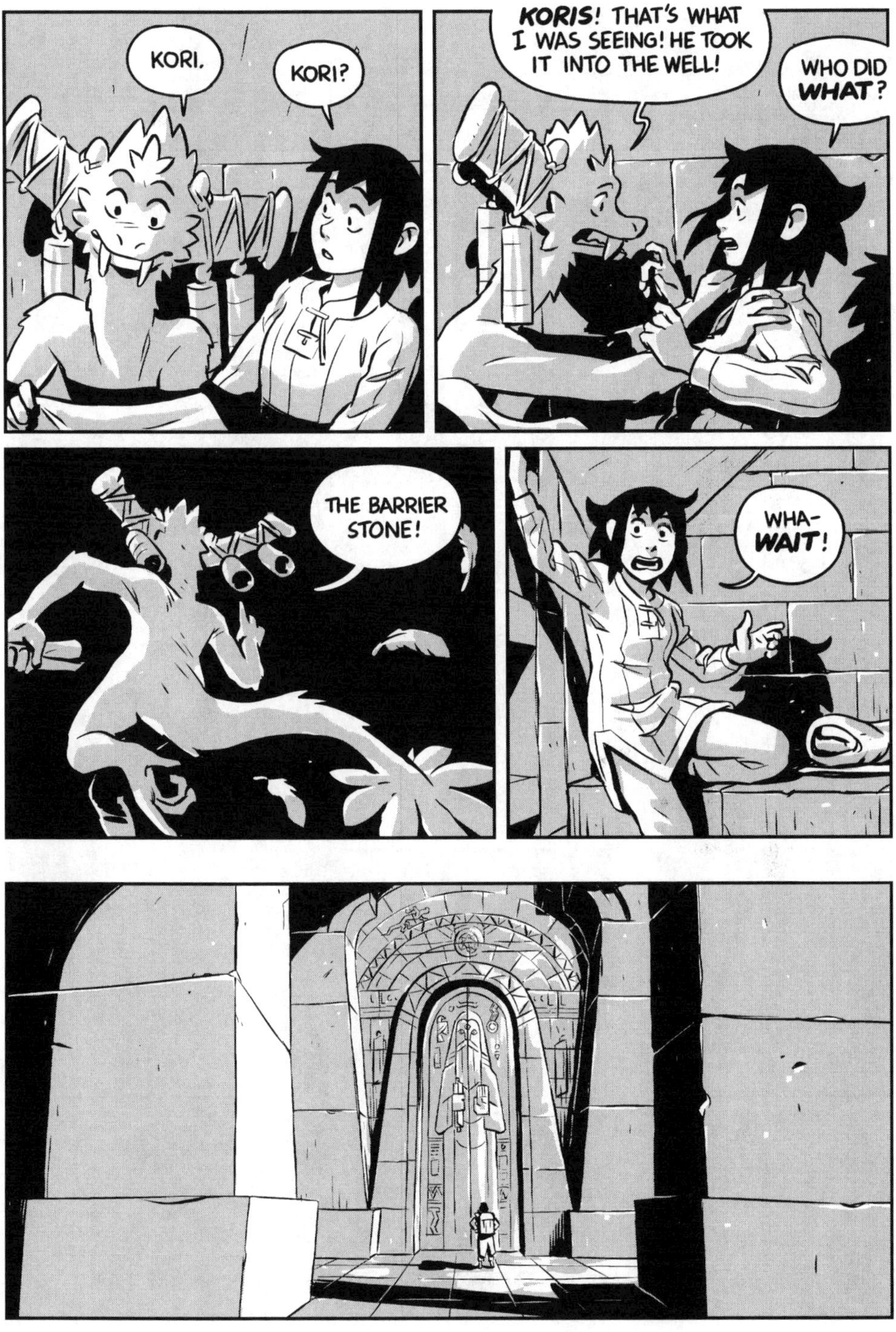

KORI.
KORI?
KORIS! THAT'S WHAT I WAS SEEING! HE TOOK IT INTO THE WELL!
WHO DID WHAT?
THE BARRIER STONE!
WHA- WAIT!

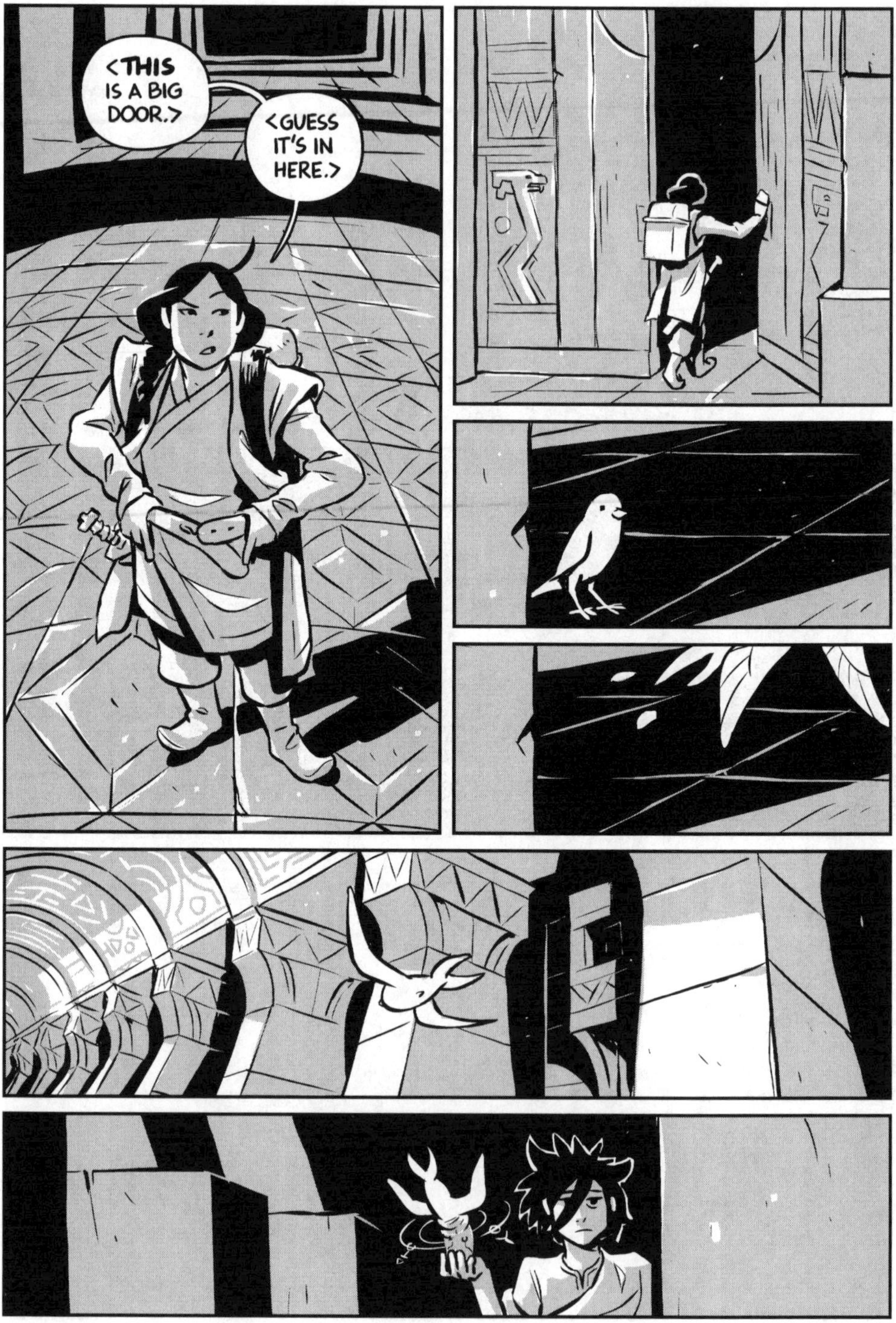
<THIS IS A BIG DOOR.>
<GUESS IT'S IN HERE.>

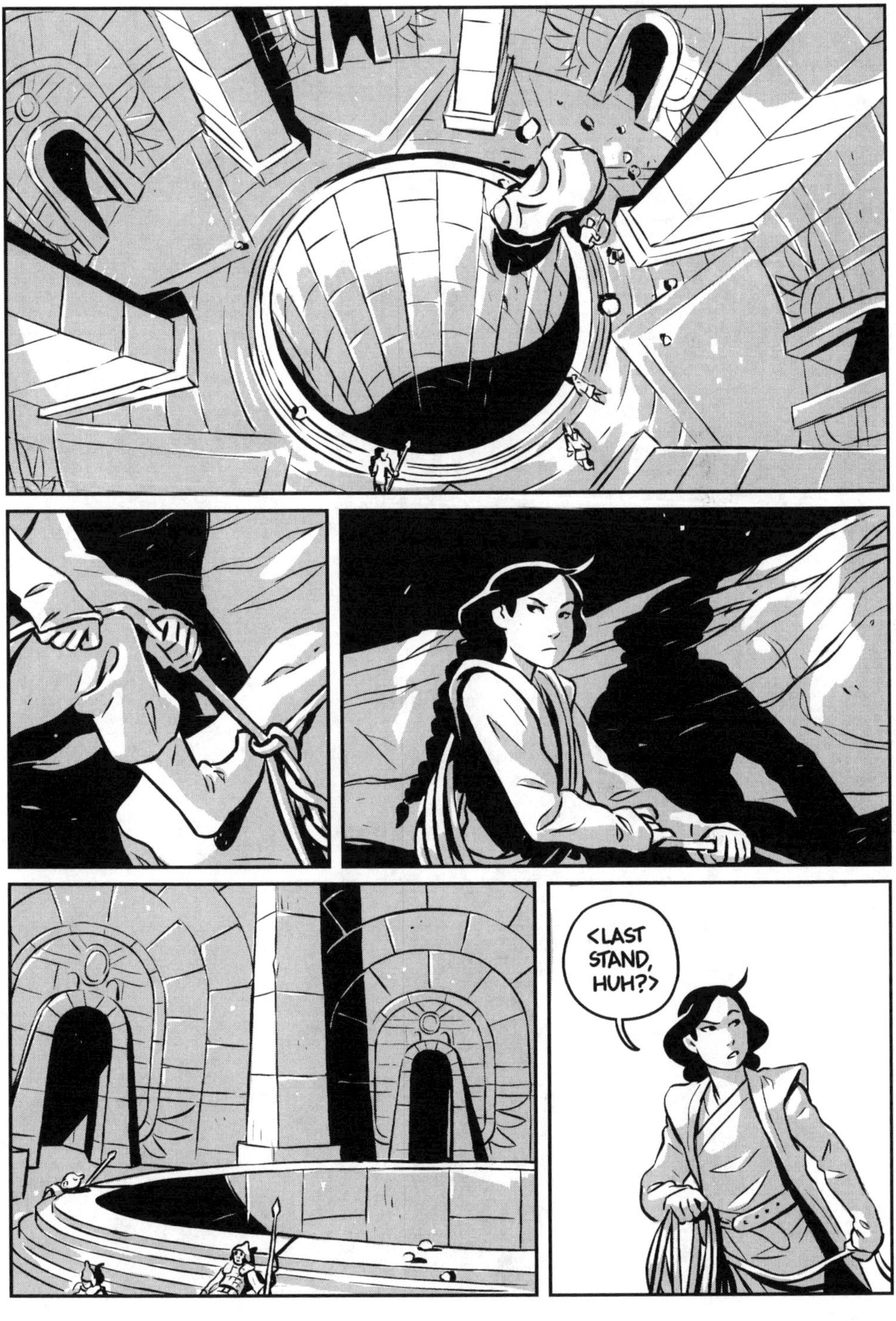
<LAST STAND, HUH?>

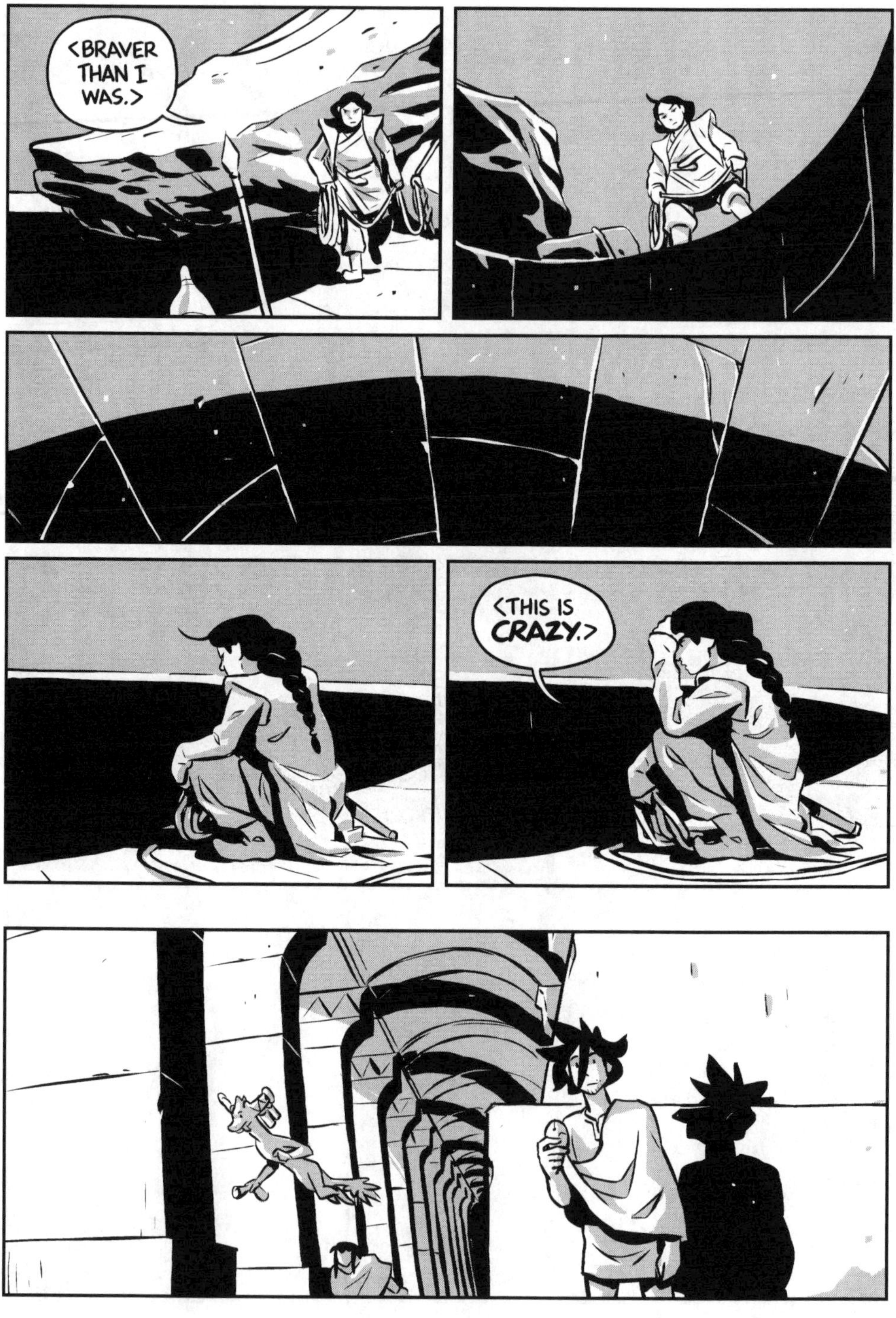

<BRAVER THAN I WAS.>
<THIS IS CRAZY.>

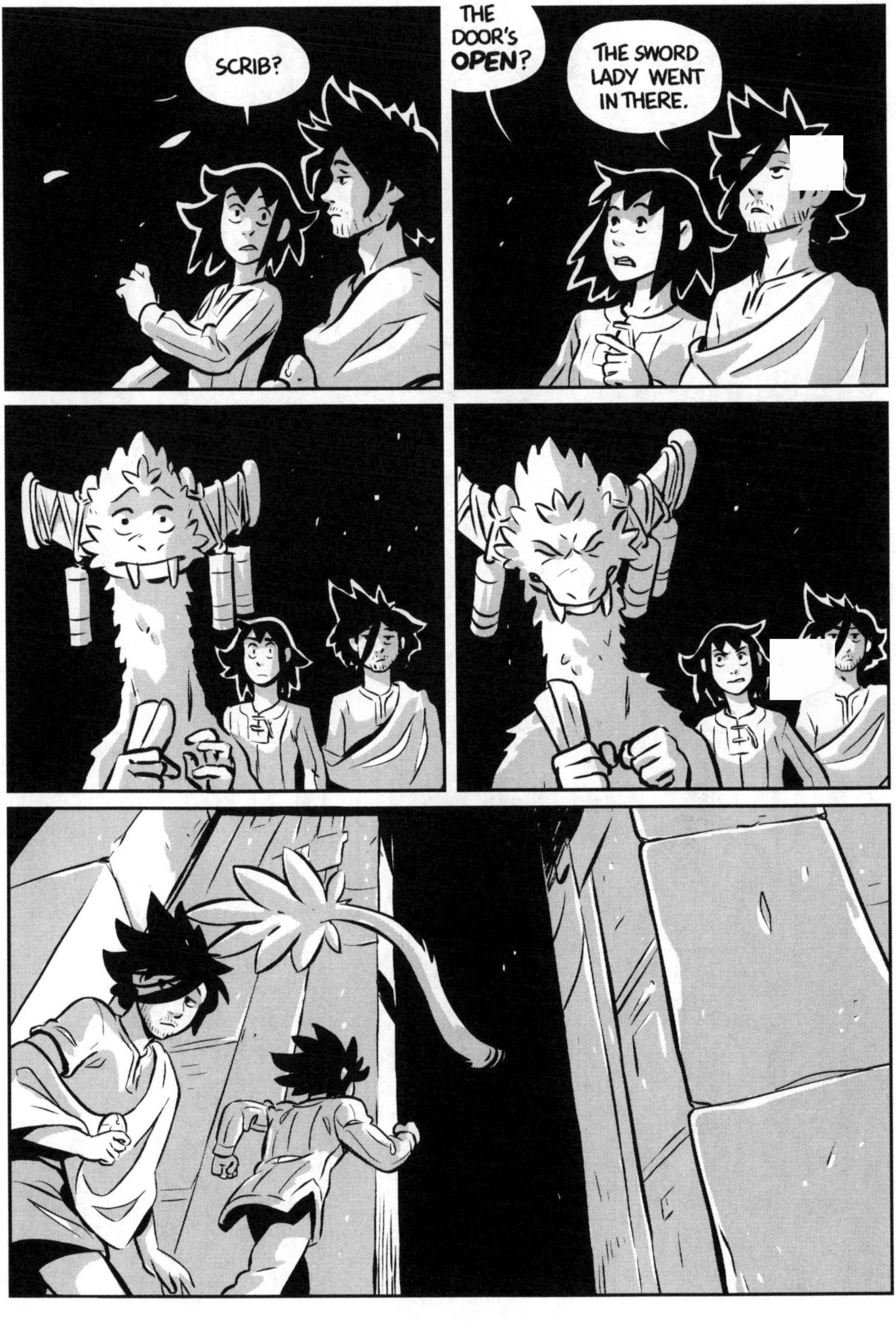
SCRIB?
THE DOOR'S OPEN?
THE SWORD LADY WENT IN THERE.

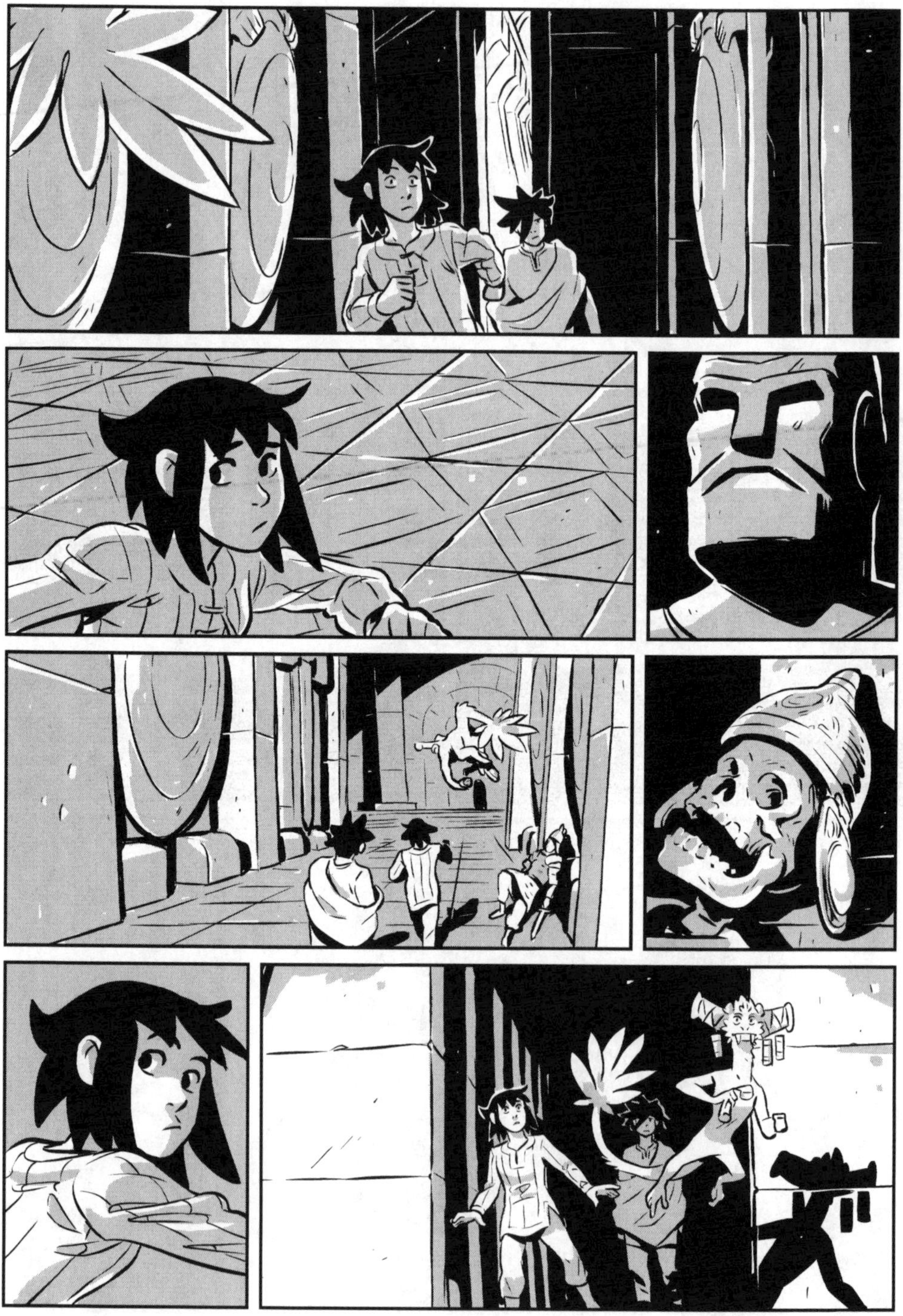

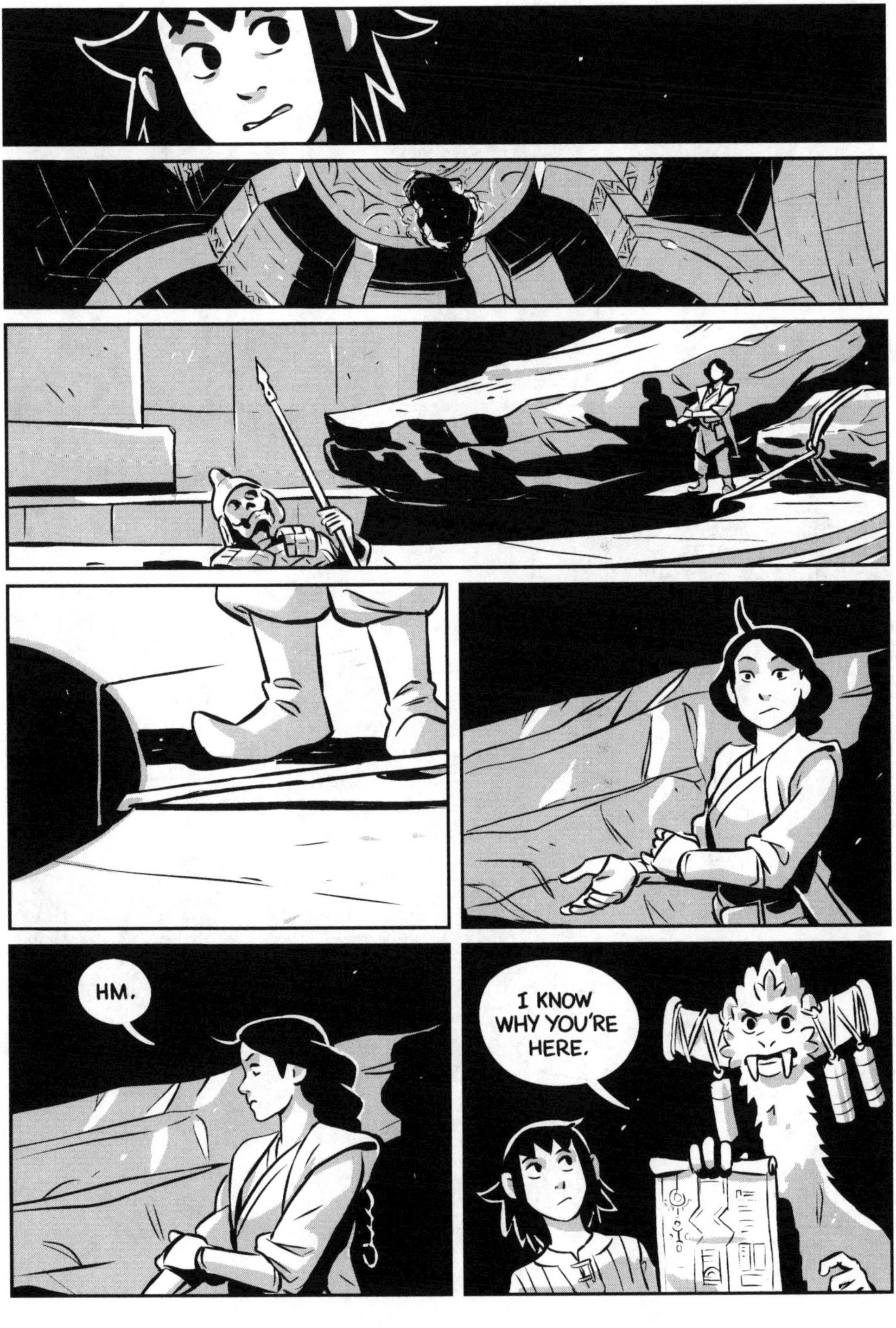
HM.
I KNOW WHY YOU'RE HERE.

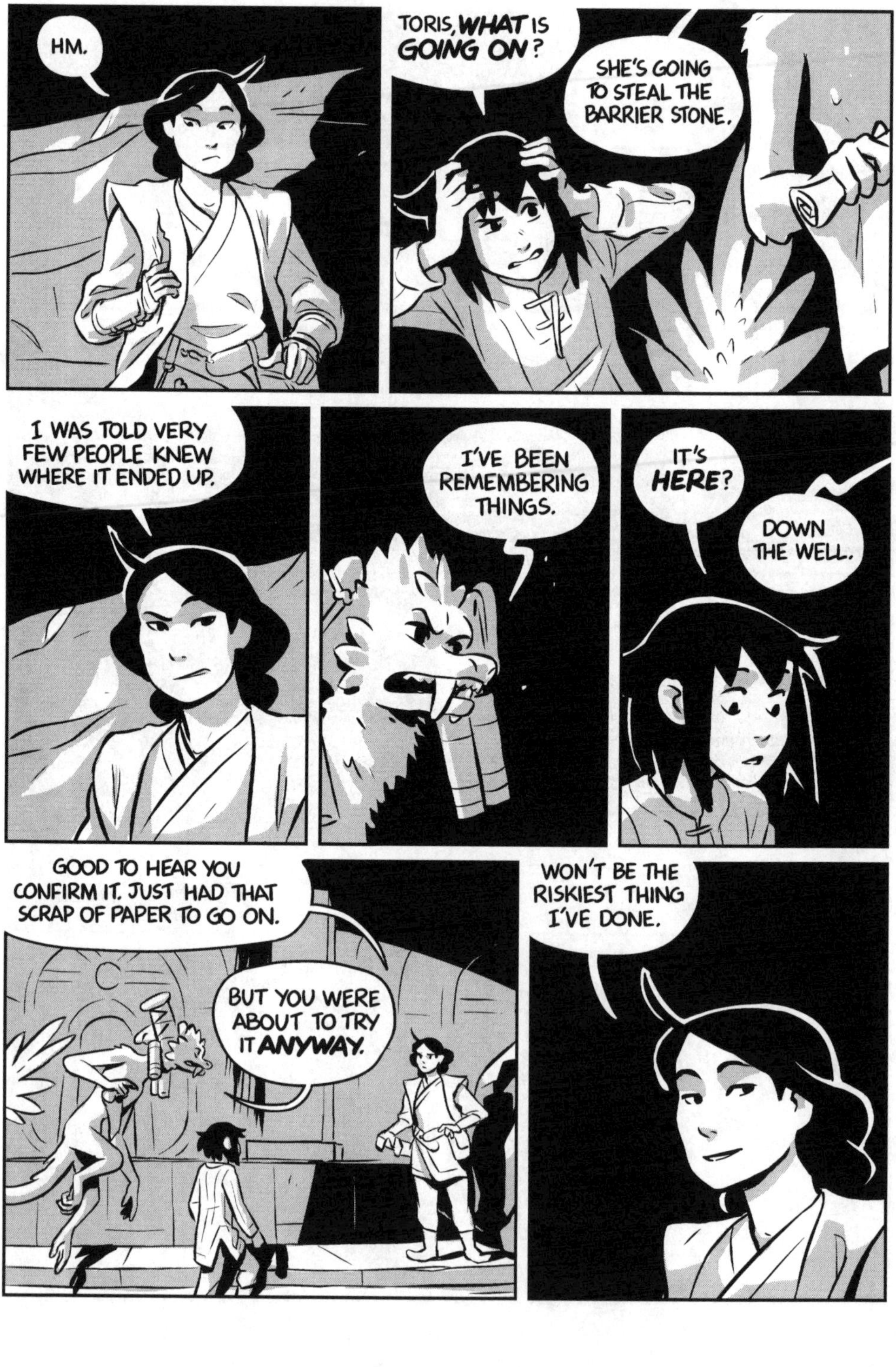
HM.
TORIS, WHAT IS GOING ON?
SHE'S GOING TO STEAL THE BARRIER STONE.
I WAS TOLD VERY FEW PEOPLE KNEW WHERE IT ENDED UP.
I'VE BEEN REMEMBERING THINGS.
IT'S HERE?
DOWN THE WELL.
GOOD TO HEAR YOU CONFIRM IT. JUST HAD THAT SCRAP OF PAPER TO GO ON.
BUT YOU WERE ABOUT TO TRY IT ANYWAY.
WON'T BE THE RISKIEST THING I'VE DONE.

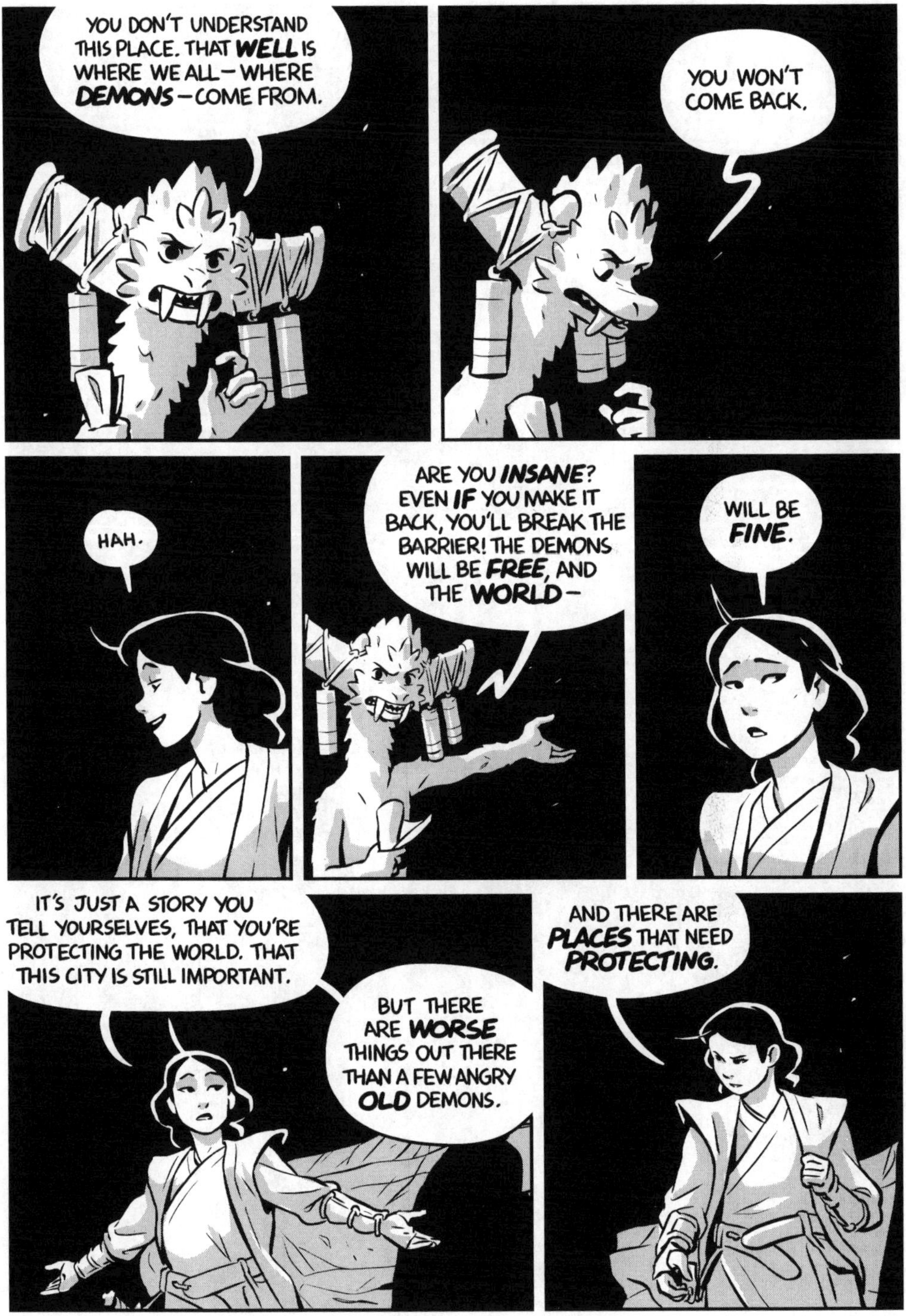

YOU DON'T UNDERSTAND THIS PLACE. THAT WELL IS WHERE WE ALL—WHERE DEMONS—COME FROM.
YOU WON'T COME BACK.
HAH.
ARE YOU INSANE? EVEN IF YOU MAKE IT BACK, YOU'LL BREAK THE BARRIER! THE DEMONS WILL BE FREE, AND THE WORLD—
WILL BE FINE.
IT'S JUST A STORY YOU TELL YOURSELVES, THAT YOU'RE PROTECTING THE WORLD. THAT THIS CITY IS STILL IMPORTANT.
BUT THERE ARE WORSE THINGS OUT THERE THAN A FEW ANGRY OLD DEMONS.
AND THERE ARE PLACES THAT NEED PROTECTING.

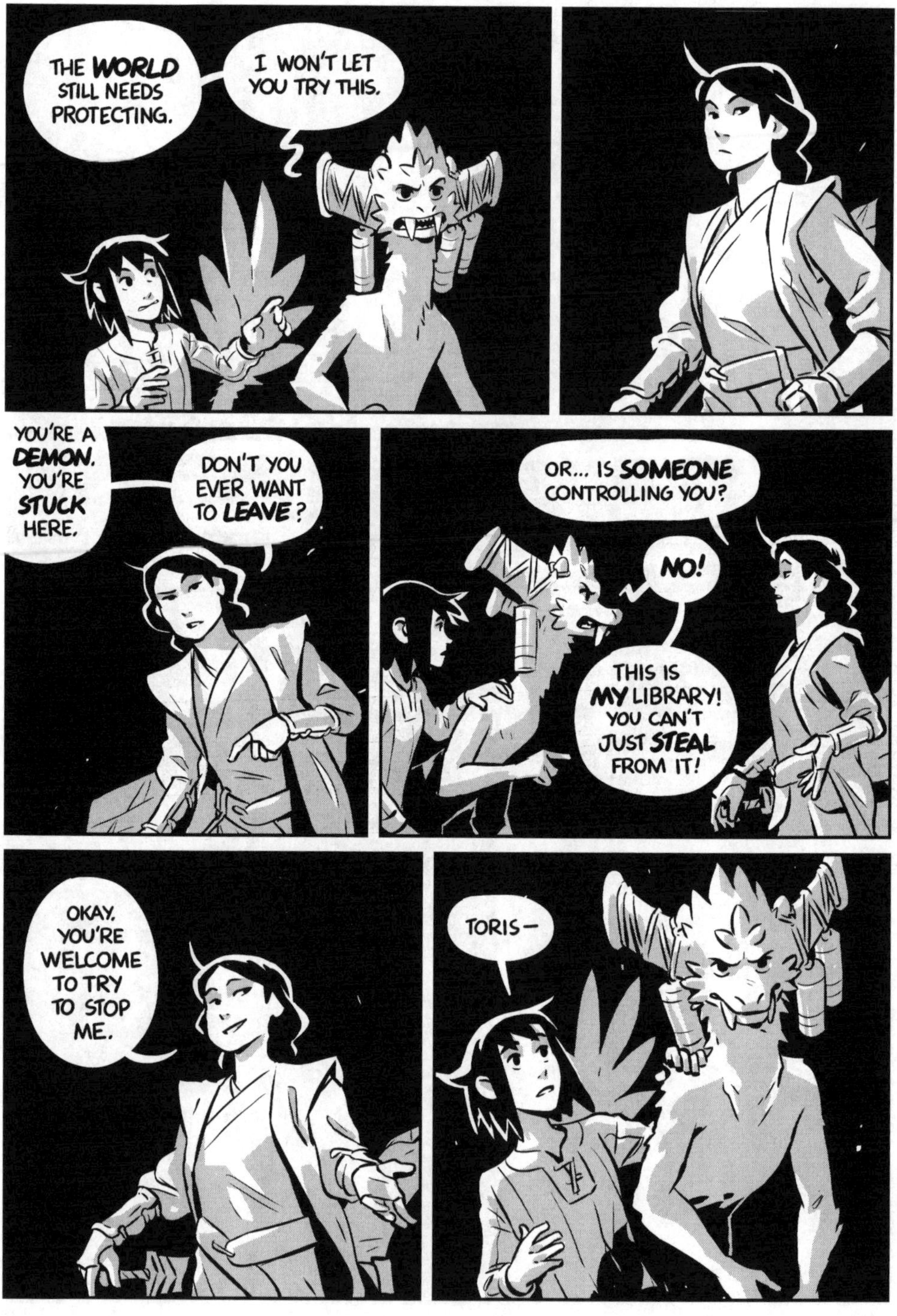
THE WORLD STILL NEEDS PROTECTING.
I WON'T LET YOU TRY THIS.
YOU'RE A DEMON. YOU'RE STUCK HERE.
DON'T YOU EVER WANT TO LEAVE?
OR... IS SOMEONE CONTROLLING YOU?
NO!
THIS IS MY LIBRARY! YOU CAN'T JUST STEAL FROM IT!
OKAY. YOU'RE WELCOME TO TRY TO STOP ME.
TORIS—

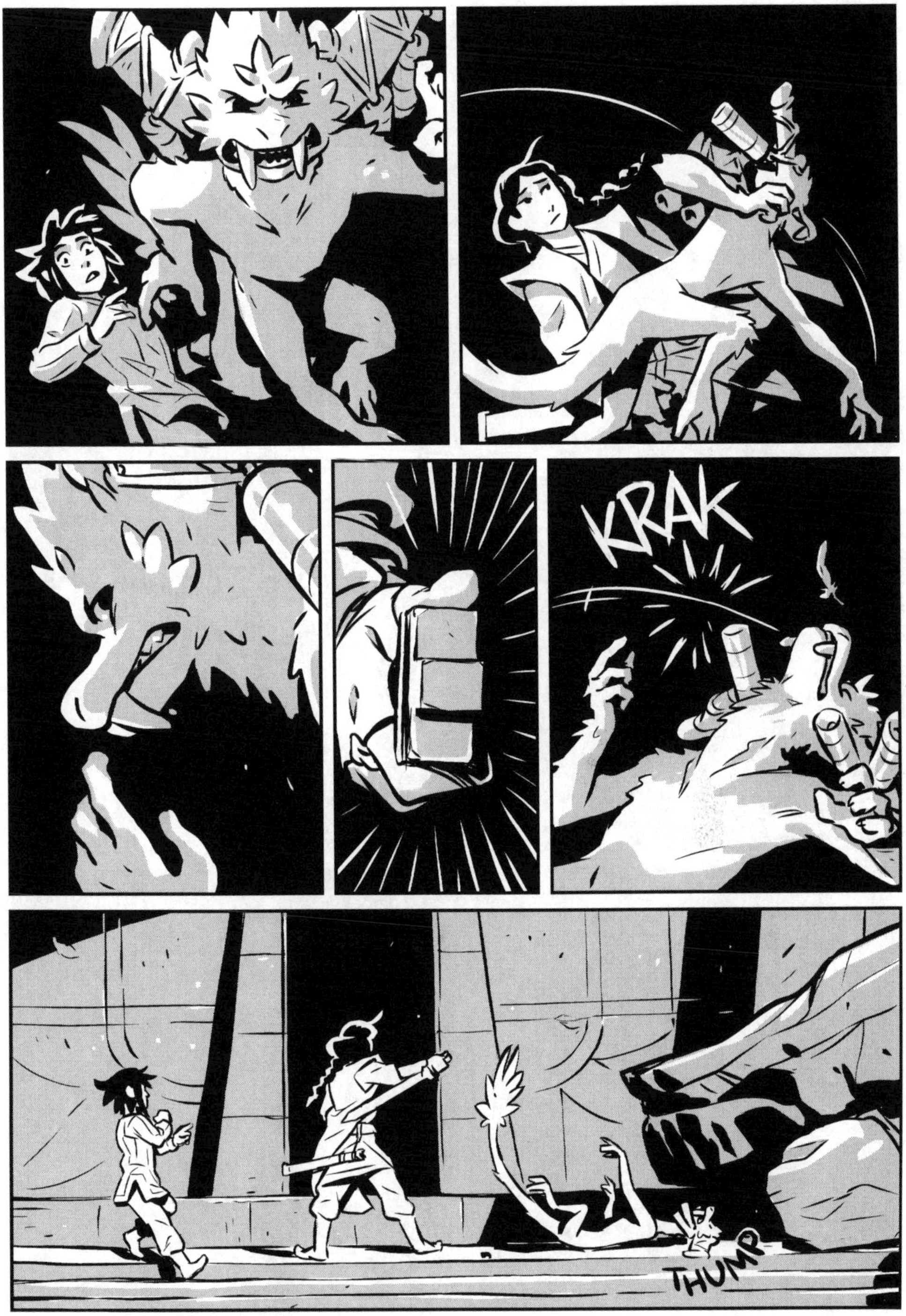
KRAK
THUMP

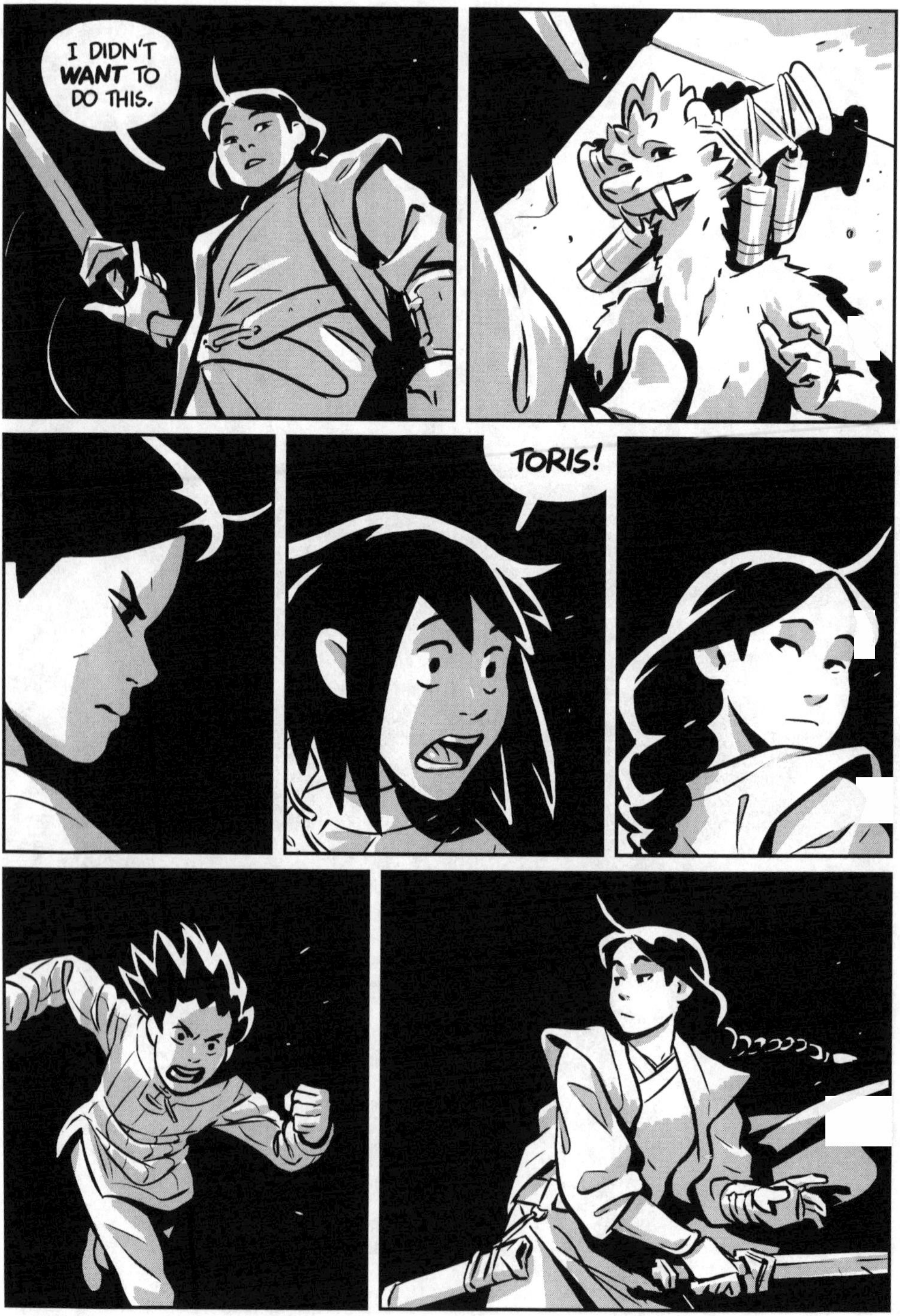
I DIDN'T WANT TO DO THIS.
TORIS!

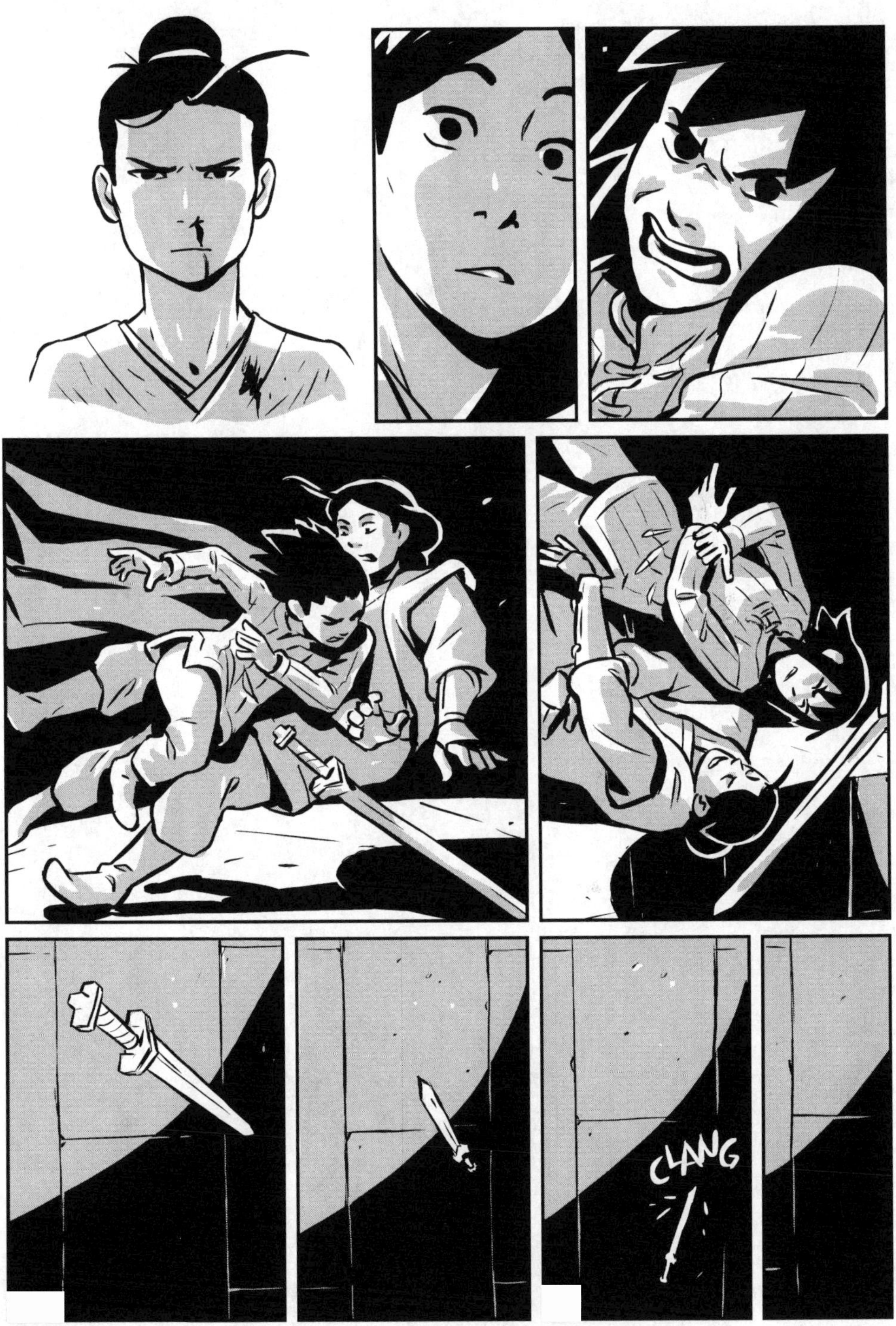
CLANG

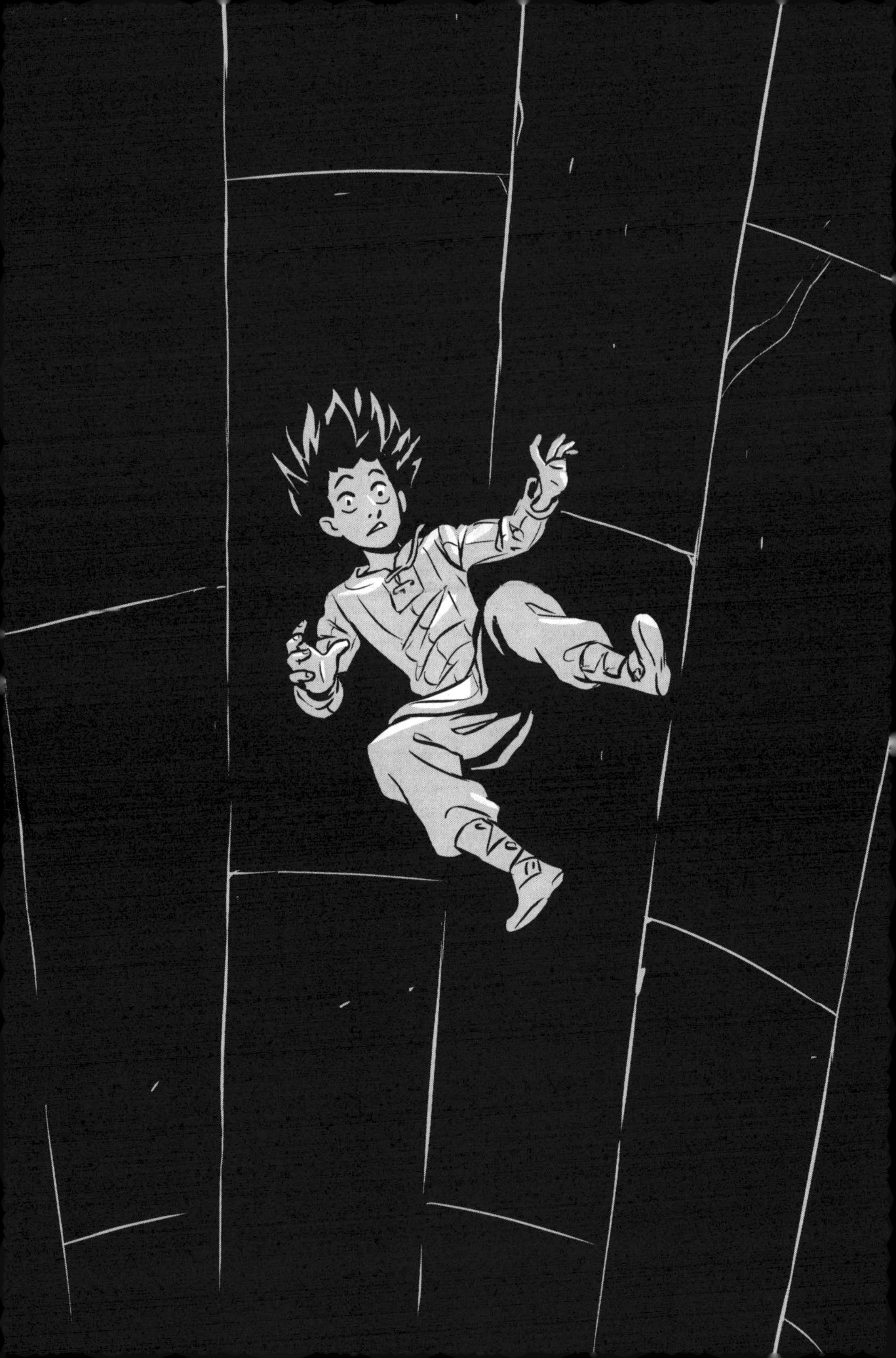

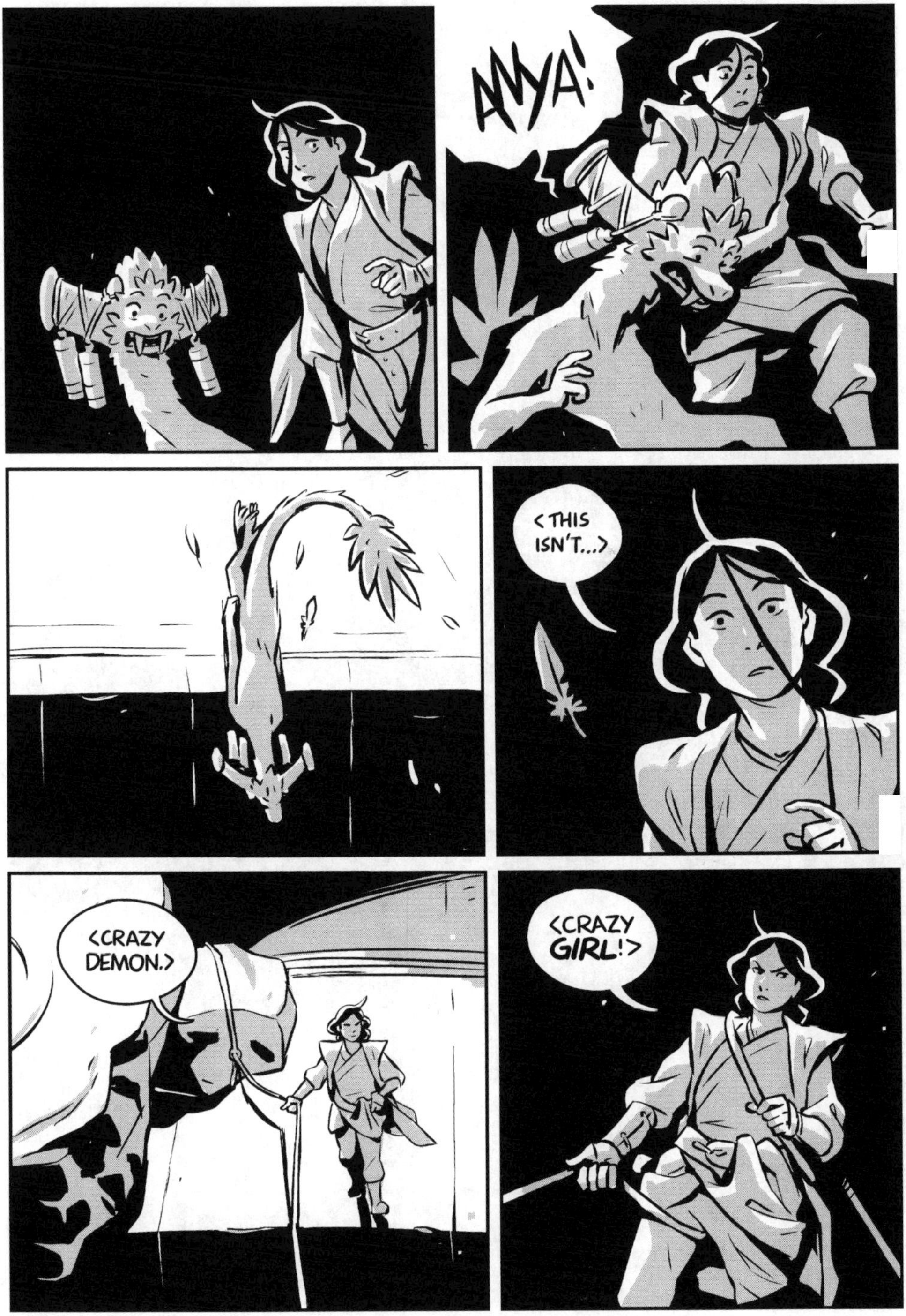
AIYA!
<THIS ISN'T...>
<CRAZY DEMON.>
<CRAZY **GIRL**!>

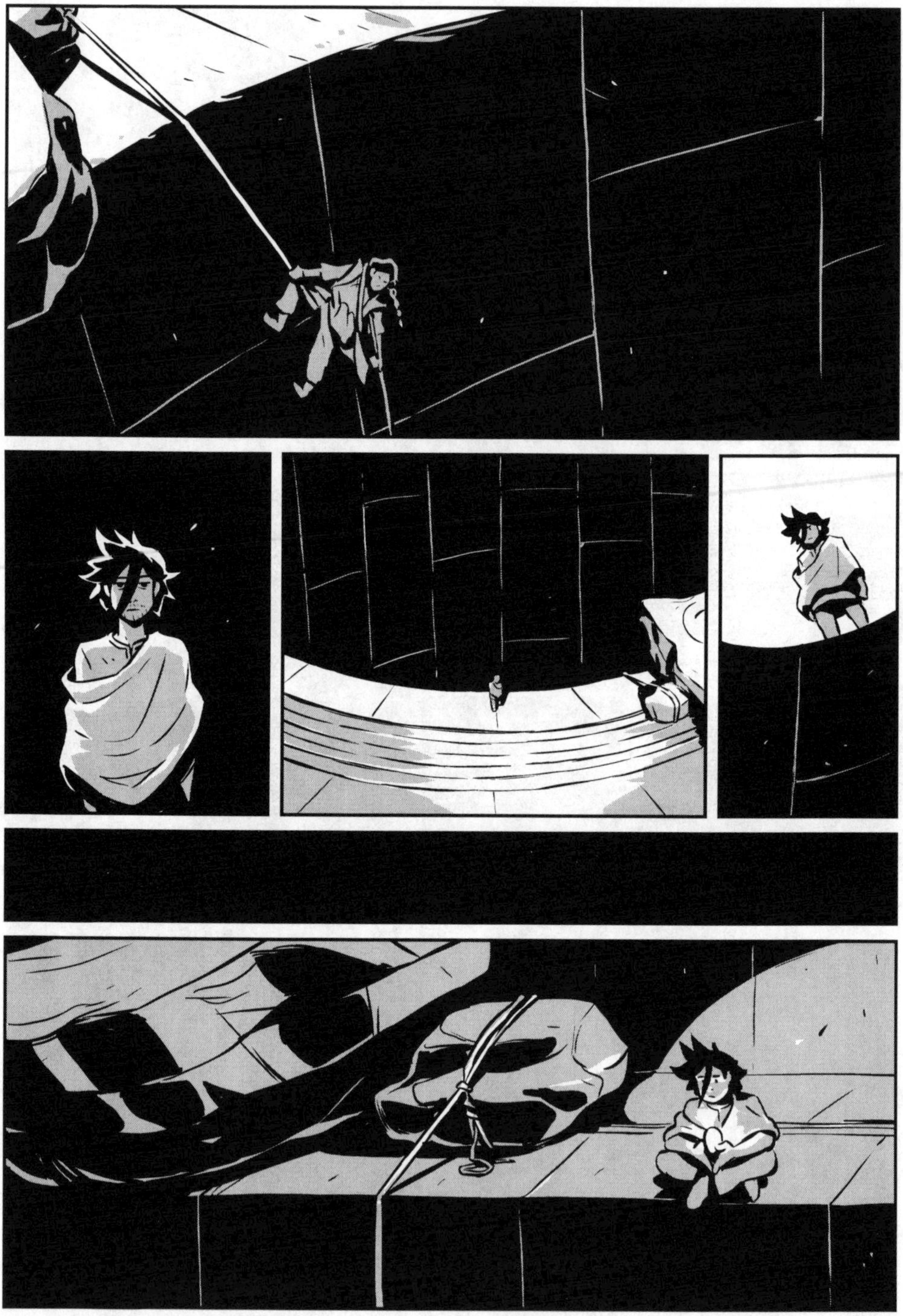

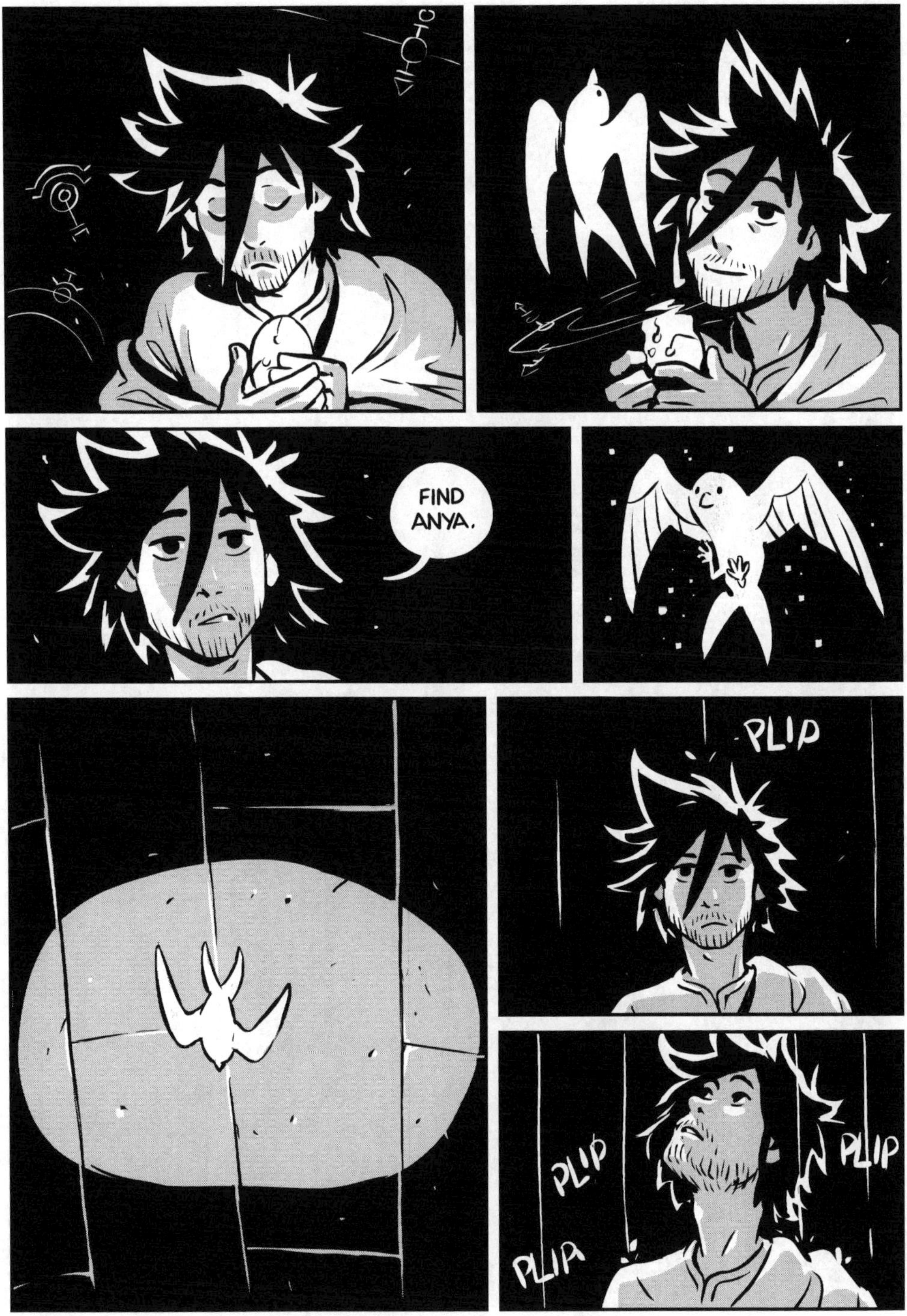
FIND ANYA.
PLIP
PLIP
PLIP
PLIP

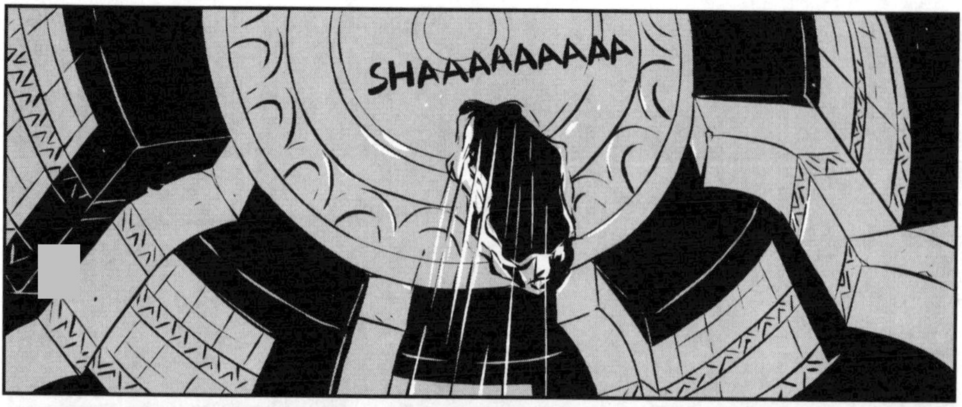
SHAAAAAAAAP

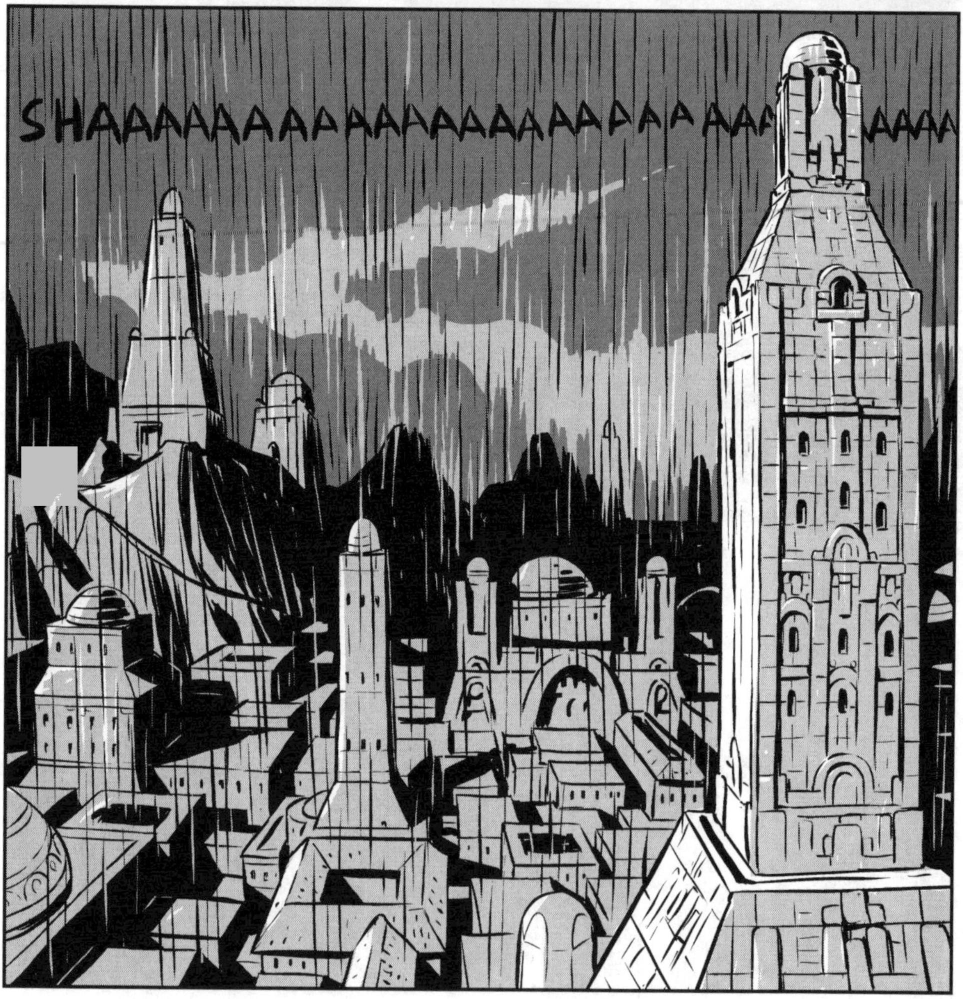
SHAAAAAAAAPAAAAAAAAAAAPAPAAAAAAA